LOTUS

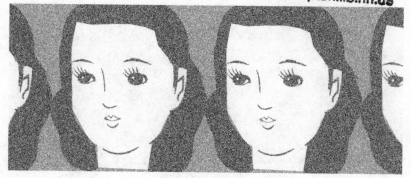

LOTUS

a novel

LIJIA ZHANG

HENRY HOLT AND COMPANY   NEW YORK

Henry Holt and Company
Publishers since 1866
175 Fifth Avenue
New York, New York 10010
www.henryholt.com

Henry Holt® and 🄷® are registered trademarks of Macmillan Publishing Group, LLC.

Library of Congress Cataloging-in-Publication Data
Names: Zhang, Lijia, 1964– author.
Title: Lotus : a novel / Lijia Zhang.
Description: First edition. | New York : Henry Holt and Company, 2017.
Identifiers: LCCN 2016010682 | ISBN 9781627795661 | ISBN 9781627795678 | ISBN 9781250138668
Subjects: LCSH: Prostitutes—Fiction. | Choice (Psychology)—Fiction. | Shenzhen Shi (China)—
    Fiction. | Psychological fiction. | CYAC: Self-actualization (Psychology) in women—Fiction.
Classification: LCC PR9450.9.Z53 L67 2016 | DDC 823/.92—dc23
LC record available at https://lccn.loc.gov/2016010682

Our books may be purchased in bulk for promotional, educational, or business use.
Please contact your local bookseller or the Macmillan Corporate and Premium Sales Department
at (800) 221-7945, extension 5442, or by e-mail at MacmillanSpecialMarkets@macmillan.com.

First Edition 2017

Designed by Kelly S. Too

Printed in the United States of America

1 2 3 4 5 6 7 8 9 10

This is a work of fiction. All of the characters, organizations, and events portrayed in this novel
either are products of the author's imagination or are used fictitiously.

To my beloved maternal grandmother, Yang Huizhen,
who survived her life as a "flower girl" in the 1930s

CONTENTS

1   In Nature, There Are Unexpected Storms, and in Life
Unpredictable Vicissitudes   1

2   Where Water Flows, a Channel Is Formed   7

3   If You Stay Long in a Fish Market, You'll Soon
Get Used to the Stink   20

4   As Buddha Needs Incense, So a Man Needs Self-respect   38

5   Those Who Have the Same Illness Sympathize with Each Other   51

6   The Lotus Root Snaps, but Its Fibers Stay Joined   66

7   Choose a General from Among the Dwarfs   82

8   Her Beauty Outshines the Moon and Puts the
Flowers to Shame   95

9   The Weak Are the Prey of the Strong   109

10   The Benevolent See Benevolence and the Wise See Wisdom   119

11   Standing Under the Eaves, You Have to Lower Your Head   128

12   The Clouds Disperse and the Sun Starts to Shine   137

13   Speeding Back Home with the Swiftness of an Arrow   150

14   A Newborn Calf Isn't Afraid of Tigers   166

15   A Thunderbolt from a Clear Sky   180

16   Heaven Is High and the Emperor Is Far Away   191

17   A Big Tree Affords Good Shade   197

18   Shooting Higher and Higher Like Sesame Flowers   211

19   A Stone Tossed into the Water Raises a Thousand Ripples   219

20   Near to Rivers, We Recognize Fish, Near to Mountains,
     We Recognize the Songs of Birds   229

21   A Single Slip May Become the Regret of a Lifetime   240

22   No Sorrow Is Greater Than the Death of the Heart   251

23   Every River Has Its Source and Every Tree Its Roots   261

24   Don't Let the Opportunity Slip Away   272

25   The Wind Sweeping Through the Tower Heralds a
     Rising Storm in the Mountain   278

26   Fly in the Sky Like the Legendary Birds That Pair Off
     Wing to Wing   288

27   You Can't Wrap Fire in Paper   294

28   You Can't Catch a Fish and a Bear Paw at the Same Time   303

29   Can't See the Forest for the Trees   313

30   Past Experience, If Not Forgotten, Is a Guide for the Future 328

31   The Cart Will Find Its Way Around the Hill
     When It Gets There   338

32   The Tree Craves Calm, but the Wind Does Not Subside   350

33   While the Mountain Remains, We Shan't Lack Firewood   364

Acknowledgments   367

LOTUS

CHAPTER 1

天有不测风云，人有旦夕祸福

In Nature, There Are Unexpected Storms, and in Life Unpredictable Vicissitudes

"*Wei*, you!"

The shout rang out across the peaceful embankment.

Sitting on a wooden bench, Lotus stared at the grayish-yellow sea. There were no ships in sight. The tickling hands of the wind made ripples on the water, and clouds floated in a slate-blue sky like massive cotton flowers. In the vast space between the heavens and the waves, seagulls circled around freely, squealing in glee. Closer to the shore, white egrets and colorfully feathered ducks played among the rocks.

"*Wei*, you!" the shout thundered again.

Startled, she looked up into the broad face of a young policeman. His narrowed eyes glared at her.

Lotus looked around. A young couple, both in suits, were leaning against the seawall at the edge of the promenade, also gazing out to the sea, their heads touching, arms crossed behind their backs. Nearby, a grandma was chasing a little boy who toddled away from her, giggling, his bare bottom wiggling in his split pants. An old man was walking his birds, carrying them in a bamboo cage.

"Me?" Lotus asked.

"Yes, you!" he barked. "Show me your Three Documents."

She glanced up at the policeman. The shining badge on his hat gleamed officiously.

"Don't pretend you didn't hear me. Show me your documents: ID card, resident's permit, and work permit."

Lotus saw stars, as if his words had clubbed her. Biting her lower lip, she searched in her fake leather bag and fished out her resident permit, which she had obtained by sleeping with the district security officer. As for her ID card, knowing its importance, she never carried it with her, in case she lost it.

The policeman snatched the resident permit from her hand. "How about the other documents?"

"I, er . . ." she began, aware of the drumming of her heart. Fingering the jade beads of her bracelet, she took a quick calming breath. "I left them at home."

"Where is your home?"

After a moment's hesitation, she replied: "One hundred ten East Station Road."

The policeman let out a laugh, loud and dry like a wild duck quacking. "East Station Road, indeed! Come off it. Besides, no decent girl would dress up like this in the morning."

Lotus looked down at her sleeveless black fishnet top and short skirt. This morning, she had simply thrown a cardigan over last night's outfit. She buttoned it up.

"What are you doing here? Offering a massage?" he asked with an arch smile.

"Nothing," she said resentfully. "I'm just resting."

He grabbed her wrist. "Come on," he snapped. "Don't sit here like a Buddha."

Lotus instinctively held on to the bench but the officer's iron claw pulled her up. He dragged her toward a pickup truck parked farther up on the embankment.

A crowd started to gather, obviously enjoying the spectacle. Lotus could make out the young lovers, the toddler, his grandmother, and the old man holding his birdcage. Their stares pierced her flesh. She hated them for watching her, and she wished for a crack in the ground she could disappear into.

Out of the corner of her eye, Lotus saw an older policeman, standing by the truck.

"Now, now, silly girl," he chided in a hoarse smoker's voice. "This is no place to hustle. Our provincial governor is coming here for the millennium gala this afternoon. Didn't you know?"

Lotus moved her dry lips, but no words came out. What could she say? Argue that she wasn't trying to hustle or explain that she never read the papers?

"Get into the truck. Squat there, hands on your head," the young policeman ordered as he pushed Lotus into the vehicle.

She stumbled and fell flat on the metal floor. Her tongue caught between her teeth. She tasted blood. The truck was already filled with three young women, most likely working girls, in scanty dresses, their made-up faces spoiled by tears and sweat; an old beggar in a tattered jacket with matted hair; and four oily-haired thugs. They all squatted against the sides of the truck, their hands on the backs of their heads.

Lotus picked herself up, wiping her mouth clean with one hand. A girl, her eyes as red as her body-hugging dress, moved aside to make room for her. Lotus nodded gratefully and leaned heavily against the side of the truck. Fleetingly she toyed with the idea of escaping, but thought better of it. "Please, Guanyin Buddha, bless me," she murmured. "Whatever happens, please don't send me back home! Not like this."

Several policemen were standing around behind the pickup truck. She couldn't see them, but could smell the smoke from their cigarettes and hear their conversations. The older policeman complained about his teenage son spending far too much time playing computer games. Another policeman half complained about and half praised his daughter's obsession with painting.

Lotus had the urge to turn her head to look but didn't dare. How could they stand around and talk about such mundane things while her life was being turned upside down?

Today, the first day of the millennium, ought to have been an auspicious day, she thought bitterly. She hadn't even meant to come here, but after wiring money home from the main post office, she had walked past the dense forest of skyscrapers in the city center and somehow wandered toward the sea, pulled by the faint scent of salt. The view from the embankment delighted her eyes. She found a bench and perched on it, drinking in the unusual luxury of space and quiet.

Even after three years of living in the city, Lotus had never set foot here. Trapped in her massage parlor, day in and day out, she usually forgot that Shenzhen was on the coast.

Lotus had first learned about the city and the sea from watching television at a neighbor's house back in Mulberry Gully, a village up in the mountains, more than a thousand miles north of Shenzhen. Everyone had been so excited when her neighbor Luo Yijun's family brought back a magic box called a *dianshi*—electric screen. The Luos' yard was packed with enthusiastic viewers craning their necks for a better view of the moving pictures on the box. The unceasing stream of visitors bothered the family so much that they locked up the *dianshi* after a week and only took it out for public viewing during festivals. But Luo Yijun, her classmate, would invite Lotus to watch it from time to time. Once, they saw a show about Shenzhen, the city just north of Hong Kong. How glorious it looked! Palm trees, buildings clad in shining mirrors soaring into the sky, colorful neon signs that were dazzling to the eye, and large ships docking on blue water in a busy harbor.

How stupid and naïve she was!

It was a cool January morning, yet everyone in the truck was sweating. No one dared to talk. The shadows of the palm trees cast woven patterns on the truck's metal floor. The crowds on the embankment were dispersing as lunchtime approached.

Lotus saw everything through the eyes of a detached observer. From the back of the truck she could see, on the roadside, a giant poster of Deng Xiaoping, China's top boss, who had introduced the economic reforms. The old man, one of his eyes larger than the other, waved a hand. Beneath the picture, a slogan blazed in red characters: "The policy of reform will not change for a hundred years."

The policy had allowed peasants like herself to come to the city to work and make money. Lotus hadn't needed to wire the money home today. Spring Festival was still five weeks away. As a child, she had lived for the festival, for celebrating the lunar New Year and for the family reunion dinner on New Year's Eve. It was the only day in the year when their dining table was piled with rare delicacies. After dinner, when the moon climbed over the tips of the Chinese scholar trees, she would go out into the yard to set off firecrackers with the boys while the other girls watched from a safe distance, covering their ears to muffle the noise. Holding her breath, she would light the fuse on a string of firecrackers tied to a long bamboo stick. The string would jump to life, cracking and spitting fire and noise, like a miniature dragon. She was never sure if the deafening roar would really drive away evil spirits, as her grandma claimed, but it definitely drove her all the way up to Ninth Heaven.

Usually, the western New Year wasn't such a big deal, but last night, fireworks of all sorts had decorated the Shenzhen sky for hours for the millennium celebration. Lotus's heart was suddenly suffused with a longing for home and a pang of guilt for not being with her family. But she didn't want to go home before she could win back her face in front of her family and prove that her journey into the city had been worthwhile, not the disaster it had proved to be. Her homesickness had prompted a trip to the post office this morning. The five thousand yuan she had sent home—more than her father could make from several years tilling the land—would ensure a fat New Year for them.

A voice from outside the truck interrupted her thoughts.

"Done, guys, we're done. Let's get out of here."

"Okay then," said the older policeman.

Lotus heard the coughing of the truck engine. The broad-faced young policeman jumped on the back of the truck with a colleague and slammed the door shut. The vehicle lurched ahead.

Lotus grabbed tightly on to the edge of the truck. She looked back as the sea grew smaller and smaller.

CHAPTER 2

水到渠成

◆────────────────────────────◆

Where Water Flows, a Channel Is Formed

Bing's cell phone started to vibrate on his desk, as if having a seizure.

"*Wei?*" said Bing, half-expecting the voice of an overly keen salesman.

"Hu Laoshi?"

Lotus! She was the only person in the world who would call him *laoshi*. Despite his repeated protests, she always insisted on addressing him with this respectful term, which originally meant "teacher." Bing didn't even know that she had his cell number. Then he remembered that he had once pushed his name card into her hand when he tried to get permission to photograph her. "Yes, it's me. Are you all right?"

"I've been arrested!"

He shot up out of his chair. "Where are you?"

"Zhangmutou Detention Center."

Bing had heard of the place from other working girls. The mere mention of Zhangmutou turned their faces pale. "Yes, I know the place," he said, pressing the phone closer to his ear.

"Our boss is away. Could you please come as my guarantor, Hu Laoshi?" she pleaded, her voice trembling over the cracked line.

"Absolutely!" Bing understood well how the system worked. When there was no hard evidence, a guarantor, usually a well-respected professional, could help a suspect's case. Lotus might not be in such deep trouble, then. "How did you get arrested?"

Lotus explained briefly. Bing knew that to keep the floating population under control, there were routine police clampdowns on illegal migrants before major festivals. Perhaps Lotus had just been in the wrong place at the wrong time. Or perhaps the young policeman, tempted by the girl's beauty, was simply looking for excuses to coerce a little illicit fun.

"I'll come right away!" he promised.

"Hu Binbing?" A bespectacled policeman in his mid-thirties called out Bing's name. Sitting behind his desk in the front hall of Zhangmutou Detention Center, he studied Bing's blue plastic journalist card while he chewed a toothpick, his pudgy face puffed with casual indifference.

"Yes, that's me," Bing replied, offering a pack of Grand China cigarettes, the most expensive brand he could find that morning.

The policeman took one out of the pack and placed it behind his ear for future enjoyment, then continued to gaze at the journalist card. It had been issued by the *Special Economic Zone Herald*, a local newspaper Bing had been stringing for, shooting the opening of another toy factory or some new high-tech product. Upon receiving Lotus's call, he had unearthed it from one of his dusty drawers. To act as her guarantor, he needed an official identity. Stating that he was a freelance photographer, which was the way he now saw himself, wouldn't have worked.

Standing in front of the policeman, Bing combed back his thick hair and shifted uncomfortably in his suit. He rarely wore one these days, but he had figured it might increase the level of respect from the police officers. Behind the policeman, two officers were questioning several suspects, young men clad in dirty vests and shorts. Farther back toward a guarded entrance, policewomen were conducting general checkups on new arrivals.

In slow motion, the policeman handed back the card to Bing. He spat out his toothpick and asked: "So, how do you know this woman Luo Xiangzhu?"

"We are neighbors," Bing said, trying to keep his composure. "She is a law-abiding citizen. Why has she been arrested, may I ask?"

The policeman didn't answer but stared at Bing, his eyes narrowing behind his glasses. A moment later, his face relaxed and he said with a weary wave of his hand: "Okay, I'll take your word for it." He pressed an intercom and shouted: "Bring in Luo Xiangzhu."

Within a few minutes, Lotus, in a black outfit, appeared through the iron entrance, trailing behind a gray-uniformed man. She walked hunched over, her arms closely folded around her chest. When she saw Bing, her pretty face, the shape of a sunflower seed, flooded with relief. She glanced at the policeman, who was now smoking his cigarette. His face had switched back into casual indifference. Turning toward Bing, Lotus clasped her hands in front of her in a gesture of gratitude and bowed deeply. "Hu Laoshi!" That was all she managed to say. Biting her lip, she was clearly embarrassed.

"Are you all right, Lotus?"

"I'm okay," she said as she pulled one side of her mouth into a smile. "Really."

There were no apparent injuries, though she looked tired and pale. Her hair was confused and her almond-shaped eyes were anxious. She looked pitiful, yet appealing as ever.

Bing forced himself to focus on the policeman. "Can we, er . . ." He cleared his throat. "Excuse me, Officer: can we leave now?"

There was a long pause. Then the policeman flicked his cigarette butt into a bin and pushed the guarantor letter toward him. "Sign the paper first."

———————

Outside, the gray day looked sickly, the thick dough of dark clouds billowing and swelling in a low sky. A west wind was buffeting the earth. Apart from several "ground rats"—motorized rickshaws, parked a safe distance away from the entrance of the detention center—there was little traffic, and few people or houses in sight.

Breathing the brisk air with Lotus freshly liberated by his side, Bing had a sense of elation he hadn't experienced in years. In some ways, he felt he was reliving a glorious moment in his youth. He cupped his hands to light a cigarette, took a drag, and let out a long plume of smoke.

Lotus glanced up at the high-security wall laced with barbed wire and started to march toward the rickshaws without waiting for him, her hair flying in the wind.

He followed her, puffing on his cigarette.

"What did you say to them, Hu Laoshi?" she asked, in a voice breathy with appreciation. "To convince them to let me go like this?"

Bing raised his chin and said: "Maybe they didn't want to mess around with a journalist."

Slowing her pace, she said: "Thank Buddha that you came to rescue me. I wasn't sure you'd bother."

"I regard you as a friend," Bing said, pushing up his glasses. But the term was a bit of a stretch. So far, his efforts to befriend Lotus had been met with subtle resistance.

Lotus hugged herself against a gust of strong wind.

Bing tossed his cigarette. It flashed in an arc before landing on the dirt road. From his backpack, he took out a pale pink jacket. "You must be cold. I borrowed this from Mimi."

Lotus put on the jacket. It was too big. She rolled up the sleeves and fingered the floral decoration pinned to the chest—the sort of tacky girlish thing that Mimi, her friend and a fellow worker, loved.

"You are a very good man."

Her voice, regaining its usual softness, warmed his bones. "No big deal," he said.

When they reached the ground-rat stand, Lotus turned to face Bing. "I don't get you, Hu Laoshi."

"What?"

"Why do you take such an interest in us mere *ji*?" It was the first time Bing had heard her use the term *ji*—"chickens," a degrading homonym for the word "prostitutes."

"I told you, I am working on a photo documentary about working girls." Bing realized as the words left his mouth that it didn't sound convincing to Lotus. There was a pregnant pause. "Well you see, *ji* is such a blurred and dirty word in many people's minds. I'd like my pictures to give you, all of you working girls, a human face, to show you as ordinary women."

Lotus's striking eyes held his. "Is the project very important to you?"

"Extremely important." Bing knew that it wasn't the right moment to lobby his case, but he couldn't let such an opportunity slip by. "Also, I am aiming to get the pictures published in a magazine for professional photographers, not the sort that you can buy from a common newsstand."

"I see."

Bing helped her to climb into the tin box of a ground rat. "Sorry, I would have kept the taxi if I had known it wouldn't take me long at the detention center."

"This is okay." Lotus settled on the hard seat.

He sat down beside her. The ground rat delivered an almighty fart, which startled them both, then charged ahead along the muddy path. By the time they reached the paved road, Lotus, half buried in the pink jacket, had fallen asleep, her head bobbing against the window and occasionally onto Bing's shoulder.

In the cramped space, his thigh touched hers. He tried to shift away. Her skirt rolled up, revealing more of her legs, which were slim and well-shaped. He noticed several scars on her knees, worming on her wheat-colored skin like pale caterpillars.

He never tired of looking at Lotus's face. She wasn't the showy sort who lured people into turning their heads in the street, but rather the sort that could endure scrutiny: the longer Bing looked at her, at those symmetric features as delicate as the finest embroidery, the more beautiful she seemed.

Lotus had caught his attention as soon as Mimi, his next-door neighbor, had introduced them about six months ago. The twenty-three-year-old appeared rather different from the other girls: quiet, reserved, and somewhat aloof. He wasn't sure whether her aloofness was calculated to attract clients or merely her way of salvaging some dignity for herself. When Bing had asked to photograph her, wearing his lips thin to explain the significance of his photo documentary on prostitution, she shook her head in resolute refusal. It was as if she had slammed a door in his face. However, she seemed to like to ask him questions on a wide range of subjects: about hygiene, about Buddhism, and about life in general. But she rarely talked about herself.

Now squeezed beside Lotus, Bing thought about how little he knew this girl. He made sure that his hands stayed on his lap. He was a professional photographer, a decent man with his own firm moral grounding and clear conscience, yet he found himself stealing glances toward her again and again.

Lotus's semi-naked form came into view and Bing's heart started to beat like a drum on an ancient battlefield.

As he rocked the tray back and forth to keep the paper submerged in solution, the girl's face and one bare breast swayed beneath the liquid. They had only just completed the photo session hours ago, but Bing was eager to see the results. Bing had been half expecting such an invitation ever since he rescued her from the detention center three months ago. She probably had been hesitating or had been waiting for the right moment.

There was something magical in watching an image emerge on photographic paper. He rocked more gently, soaking the paper evenly. He bent down closer to the tray, squinting behind his glasses. The red glow from the overhead safelight wasn't enough, so he grabbed a portable safelight from a nearby table and ran the beam up and down the print.

Bing dried the sweat off his face with the towel slung around his neck. Using a pair of tongs, he carefully pulled the print out, dipped it into the stop bath and then the fixer. He turned on the fluorescent lamp.

"That's it, *tamade*!"

Under the bright light, Bing examined his print with the satisfaction of a jewel collector studying a newly acquired gem.

This gem lay on a bed, half covered by a white sheet printed with flowers and random Roman letters. Behind her, a white mosquito net hung limply against the wall. Her hair was spread across a floral-patterned pillow, which had one corner split open. Must be a new tear, Bing decided, because Lotus was a very tidy girl. Maybe one of her more enthusiastic clients had used the pillow as a prop. Her slightly slanted eyes gazed out, not toward the camera, but somewhere more distant. Her tilted face shone in the moonlight seeping in through a window, highlighting the exhaustion and sadness on those delicate contours. Her left breast was partially hidden under her forearm, while the other one swelled alluringly. The nipple was large on her slender body. It reminded him of a knotted button.

Bing had taken this photo with his Nikon in her room behind the Moonflower Massage Parlor. Lotus had issued the invitation as soon as Moon, the owner of the parlor, had left Shenzhen for a home visit. Bing had already gotten Moon's permission to photograph her charges, but he could sense that Lotus didn't want her boss to know about the photo session. Knowing Moon, she'd insist on overseeing everything. Though remaining guarded, Lotus had become markedly warmer toward him and permitted general exterior shots: waiting for clients outside the parlor; writing letters home in the small yard in back of the parlor; hunching over a stool and playing mah-jongg with her friends in the quiet hours of the early afternoon.

That evening, Lotus had instructed him to wait in the yard until the light in her room came on; then he could enter through the back door, which she would leave unlocked for him. He knew that Lotus's allowing his camera into her bedroom had been her way of repaying a debt of gratitude for her rescue.

Lotus's room smelled of a mixture of talcum powder, incense, and sweat. A double bed took up most of the space, plus a cupboard that stood against the wall. On it was a white porcelain statue of Guanyin, the Goddess of Mercy, and a small three-legged copper pot filled with incense ashes. A portrait of the same deity looked down from the wall. If I were a client, thought Bing, I wouldn't want to drop my trousers down here, in front of a Guanyin shrine.

It was the first time that Bing had ever been to a working girl's bedroom. Well, several times, he had visited the chaos of Mimi's apartment. But Mimi, living next door, had never been very mysterious for him. He was surprised and saddened by the shabbiness of Lotus's place. The Moonflower was one of the more expensive establishments on East Station Road, a generally low-class red-light district that the locals called the "chicken coop."

As he worked in the darkroom, Bing's thoughts turned to a nineteenth-century poem describing the poet's love affair with a silk-clad courtesan in a pavilion. He recalled the poem's description of their night, one accompanied by "a harp melody" and "the perfume of flowers."

The difference between the gloried world of the poem and Lotus's reality was like that between heaven and earth. Throughout the imperial dynasties, intellectual men with money had frequently sought the company of courtesans who were trained in the arts of poetry, calligraphy, and music. Since these men's marriages were arranged, and respectable women were traditionally confined to their houses, courtesans were the only women who could provide elegant company, amusement, and even romance.

There were no more courtesans nowadays. Commercialization and modernity had eaten away China's romantic edge, thought Bing.

After he pulled each print from the tray, he hung it up on a line. One of the last photos showed Lotus, in a silk nightdress, using a terry cloth to wipe down the bamboo bed mat that Shenzhen locals used in the summer instead of sheets. Her loose hair was slightly blurred. Bing had requested that Lotus do whatever she usually did after serving a client. The wet cloth rubbing vigorously against the uneven bamboo made an unnerving sound. Lotus always seemed so calm, even passive. But at that moment, she struck him as being an angry woman, taking her frustration out on the bamboo mat.

For the final print, Bing held back the exposure on Lotus's face. Her skin was so light, so soft, a perfect contrast to the dark background. In her sad eyes, he noticed, for the first time, a hint of defiance.

Pleased with his night's work, Bing stepped out of the darkroom he had built on the side of his living quarters, and into the yard. He loved the shady open space, as it eased the claustrophobic feeling of his cramped room.

A breeze was combing through the sleeping city. Bing greedily drank in the cool dawn air. It was the very end of March, and the temperature was still pleasant. Before long, subtropical heat would engulf the Pearl River Delta and last for the rest of the year.

Up in the western sky, the moon hung like a silver sickle. Gazing at it, Bing wondered what this sickle could harvest. Success? Or perhaps loneliness? He heaved a sigh.

He slumped on a battered wicker chair by a plastic table under the leafy Dragon Eye tree and lit a cigarette, a cheap, locally produced Good Days brand. He chuckled to himself. "Good days," here in the slum where even the devil wouldn't lay eggs?

It had been exactly seven years ago that he had ventured down to Shenzhen from Beijing. As a northerner, he found it hard to cope with the oppressively sultry climate in southern China. Yet he had stayed on. The first five years, he was a businessman living in a very comfortable apartment. Since then, he had been working as a freelance photographer, camping out in various slums populated by working girls. He lived among them, made friends with them, captured their stories on paper, and recorded their daily lives on camera. Rubbing shoulders with these women had massaged his bruised self-esteem.

Ten months ago, clad in a multi-pocketed photographer's vest, Bing had first moved his things to Miaocun, or Temple Village, named after a nearby temple. It was only a long slingshot away from East Station Road. He rented a room in one of the few remaining traditional houses. Years of neglect in the heat and humidity had caused parts of the building to rot. Once large, with elaborate architecture, the house was now sectioned off into three small residences. A migrant couple who sold fried dough at the train station squeezed into the middle room, while Mimi and her boyfriend occupied the other end. Beside Mimi's room crouched a rough building with a communal kitchen and a squat-down toilet. This extension counterbalanced Bing's dark room on the opposite side of the structure, as if they were two weights on a scale.

In Miaocun, the thought of sex stalked him far more frequently than when he had been married. Every night had been torture as he lay in bed, alone, breathing in the sexually charged air. To calm his mind and curb his desire, he ate vegetarian dishes and drank bitter tea. At bedtime, he read Tagore's *The Crescent Moon*. All these efforts, however, proved to be as futile as trying to catch water with a bamboo basket. After all, he was thirty-nine, a man in his prime, with a tiger's energy.

At first, the girls in the neighborhood had showered Bing with all sorts of invitations, offering him haircuts, foot massages, facials, or anything else he wanted. However, Bing was determined to continue his project on the same professional footing he had had in other red-light districts. When he proved too unresponsive, the girls all started to call him "the monk." He came to feel a certain pride about this title: it was a testament to his professionalism as well as his willpower.

As the day broke over Miaocun, roosters crowed one after another. As someone originally from a village, Bing found the sound endearing. He extinguished the cigarette under his flip-flop, rose, looked up once again at the crescent moon, and finally returned to his room.

The next morning, Bing shaved under the light of a naked bulb in the communal kitchen, looking into the cracked mirror that hung on the grease-blackened wall. Despite his short sleep, his soul was filled with a sense of exhilaration. Lightly bearded, he often went for weeks without shaving. This morning, he had suddenly had the urge to clear away what was there, in a symbolic gesture of making a fresh start in the new year of the Golden Dragon. It was an auspicious year, when significant events were supposed to take place. In a minute, his razor had smoothed his chin once more. He patted his face and brushed his hair back with his fingers. Despite his sparse beard, he did boast a mane of jet-black hair, which he kept long, cultivating an image of a bohemian artist. Mei wouldn't have allowed his current hairstyle if they had still been married.

Without his black-framed glasses, Bing's eyes seemed to protrude slightly. As he examined his roundish face in the mirror, he remembered his ex-mother-in-law's reaction to her daughter's marriage to him. "A fresh flower wastes away on a cowpat," she had said. Bing admitted that he hadn't been the most dashing-looking man in his youth. Though taller than average, he was rather thin, with slightly drooping shoulders. And in time, he knew, his ex-wife had secretly come to agree with her mother's assessment, not so much because of his looks as because of his lack of accomplishments. Mei used to complain bitterly, *"Meichuxi"*—no prospects, no achievements—after her repeated efforts to push him to success had ended in failure. Bing felt insulted, but pretended that he didn't care. Now, in his middle age, his body had filled out and he felt more comfortable with his more sturdy, sophisticated appearance. And one day soon his ex-wife would realize how she had underestimated him.

Chuxi had first gloriously entered Bing's consciousness after he was accepted by Tsinghua University. It was his father's alma mater, and one of the two best universities in the country. Everywhere he went, people congratulated him for becoming the first university student their county in Jilin, in the northeast of China, had ever produced: *"Chuxi!"* they cried, their northern accents lending the phrase a weight and sense of satisfaction. Upon hearing the news, his mother, who had never showed him much physical affection, patted his head. "My child," she murmured. *"Chuxi* finally."

His mother wasn't the easiest woman in the world to please. Neither was his ex-wife, Bing thought, as he headed out to the village square to buy his breakfast.

A magnificent banyan tree stood at the entrance to the village, its dark brown tendrils hanging in the wind like the strands of a woman's hair. In its shade, a new class of landlords who made a living from collecting rent fought a daily mah-jongg battle.

"Morning, photographer, have you eaten?" the mah-jongg players greeted Bing as he approached.

"Morning, morning," he replied with a wave of a hand. "I am just about to get something to eat." At first, Bing's camera had aroused suspicious stares. Now they were used to the sight of him and his gear.

He bought some *baozi,* stuffed buns, from a cheap eatery sandwiched between the public bathhouse and a convenience store. He ate them as he walked home.

Back in his room, Bing made himself a large jar of strong green tea. Then he sat down and started to comb through piles of contact sheets, searching for the images that most powerfully conveyed an insight into the lives of the working girls. Although his photos had already appeared in newspapers and magazines, his goal was to publish his photo documentary in the bimonthly magazine *Photography,* the best of its kind in China. And there was no better place than Shenzhen, known as China's "capital of sins," to pursue his project.

He often envisioned his favorite photos splashed across the glossy pages, his name, Hu Binbing, perched on top in large black print. His father had named him Binbing, meaning "Refined Soldier." In his youth, his father had dreamed of joining the revolutionary army, but as the son of a landlord, he had the wrong family background.

Prostitution was a controversial topic, Bing was conscious of that. In the West, photographers had started to take photos of prostitutes as soon as the medium had been invented. In China, however, since prostitution was fully illegal, one simply didn't see pictures of *ji* anywhere. It was as if the country's estimated ten million working girls didn't exist. Bing was determined to change that, which was why he was willing to put up with the harsh living conditions.

The walls of his room were crumbling in places, revealing the yellow plaster underneath, like diseased skin. In an attempt to cover them, he had pinned up his own black-and-white photos of Shenzhen. Among them hung a color picture of his daughter, hermetically protected by a golden frame. In it, Hu Li—a name that combined her parents' surnames—was beaming, her lovely round face as bright and uncomplicated as spring sunlight. Eight years old at the time, the girl had been so self-conscious about her missing front teeth that she had refused to smile for the camera until her father said something so funny that she burst out laughing. Two years after that photo was taken, her parents had divorced. How much of a shadow that event had cast over her life, Bing had no way of knowing. The court had given her mother full custody.

While in Beijing visiting his little girl last summer, he had plucked up the courage to visit *Photography* magazine. A bald-headed editor received him warmly. Though he found the subject matter fascinating, he pointed out that Bing's treatment was too simplistic. The editor urged him to get closer to the prostitutes' lives.

"Closer?" Bing said to himself in the empty room, again feasting his eyes on the beautifully delineated gray-black tones of Lotus. "You can't get closer than this."

CHAPTER 3

鲍鱼之薰，久而不闻其臭

If You Stay Long in a Fish Market, You'll Soon Get Used to the Stink

Standing outside the Moonflower Massage Parlor with three other girls, Lotus flashed her red smile at every passing man. She leaned against the glass front of the parlor, one leg bent like a crane's. Luring in the clients with sweet and oily words consumed a surprising amount of energy.

The sun had just rolled down behind the western hills, burning a red trail in the sky. The high-rises in the city center blocked the sea breeze. Without wind, the soup of stale air thickened, filled with the smell of fuel, shampoo, cheap perfume, roast duck, and fried noodles.

In the twilight, the girls lined up along the street looked more colorful than usual. They leaned against buildings or against each other. The luckier ones sat down on white plastic chairs, chatting like magpies, cracking melon seeds between their teeth. The parlors and salons were sandwiched between grocery stores, restaurants, and drugstores. The buildings were all one-story structures encased in white ceramic tiles and fitted with glass fronts. Behind the windows, silk or velvet curtains obscured the view inside, where pink lamps glowed.

"Oh, I'm so tired!" complained Mimi, leaning on Lotus. Her thick eyeliner was layered black and heavy around her big round eyes, making her look like a panda. Messy black curls exploded from her head, in sharp contrast to her bleached blond bangs.

"You are always tired," said Lotus crisply.

"I am." Mimi lit another cigarette, sucked on it desperately, and then stretched into a long yawn, exposing her bushy underarms—two tiny overgrown plots. When she pulled her tiny black shirt down, her robust breasts threatened to spill out over the top.

On the other side of the door was Xia, an older *ji,* and a teenager named Little Jade. Xia, as thin as a stick, was studying herself in a hand mirror. She had permed hair, styled like the old Shanghai film stars', with a tease of a curl on her powdered forehead. She wore a tight black dress that showed her bony back and she smelled of honeysuckle toilet water, which she used as a perfume as well as a balm to soothe her mosquito bites.

Xia eyed Mimi and smirked. "It must be tiring to carry a pair of such heavy tits all the time."

Mimi jiggled her chest. "I'd rather carry something than nothing."

Lotus glanced at Mimi's unusually large breasts with an amused smile. They were like two freshly risen bread buns. Her proud assets had won Mimi the nickname *boba*—queen of waves—among her regulars.

Mimi was the first friend Lotus had made as a *ji.* She was four years younger but more experienced in the game. Mimi had grown up in a broken family, in a town a few hours' bus ride north of Shenzhen. She had an indulgent mother, a cleaner, and a violent father, who made a living selling roast duck. When she was ten, her mother finally gathered enough courage to leave her abusive husband. Since the mother initiated the divorce, and the father had more financial means, the court gave child custody to Mimi's father. With the mother out of the house, the violence only intensified. One night, after yet another severe beating, the fourteen-year-old ran away from home, taking with her only her makeup kit, and came to live on the streets of Shenzhen. To feed herself, she started selling the only marketable commodity she owned.

Mimi elbowed Lotus. "Oh, I almost forgot. The monk wants you to go over tomorrow, at noon."

"After you're done, Lotus, tell him to come to see me," Xia chipped in.

"Writing another letter for you, I suppose?" Lotus said, her voice as sharp as a sour plum.

"Not a letter this time. On the train back, I heard about some kind of medicine for my Baobao. I want to ask the photographer about it." Xia's twelve-year-old son, Baobao, or Little Treasure, was allergic to copper. Even tiny amounts in a handful of peanuts would poison him and he depended on expensive medication to live. Xia had got into the trade to pay for his medical care. Sympathetic as she was, Lotus didn't particularly like the way the woman constantly brought up Baobao, like a little girl inviting people to see her skinned knees. Lotus could just imagine Xia's long train ride home to Anhui, in eastern China, going on about her "treasure" and his illness to anyone within earshot.

"Okay then," Lotus mumbled.

Xia snapped her mirror shut. "Is he really a monk? Mimi, have you seen any women going to his room?"

"Never!" Mimi replied with a shake of her head.

"Is that man all right? I mean, is his cock just for peeing?" An explosion of laughter escaped Xia's bright red lips.

"What are you trying to say, Xia?" asked Mimi. She took a deep drag on her cigarette and exhaled. The thick cloud of smoke forced her to narrow one of her eyes.

Xia wrinkled her nose, her foot drumming against the ground. "That photographer is a weirdo."

"Shut your big mouth, Xia!" Lotus snapped. "How can a peasant like you understand a cultured man like him?"

Lotus was becoming fond of Bing. In the beginning, she had been intrigued by the mild-mannered gentleman willingly living in a slum. He seemed educated and capable, and she couldn't figure out why he didn't have a proper job making big money. He was a freelance photographer, an artist of some sort. He looked like one, with his longish hair. She couldn't help liking him; he was so polite, respectful, and kind. Yet she hadn't trusted him or understood what he wanted from her. Before long, she grew used to him, and also realized that he was a fount of useful knowledge. For example, it was Bing who had warned her that men could carry sexually transmitted diseases without showing any sign of it. Before that, she had followed her boss Moon's rule: if a client was willing to pay double for not using a condom, then go ahead and fuck, as long as his equipment looked clean.

Lotus had kept a friendly distance from Bing until her arrest. At the detention center, when she was allowed to make one call, she dialed his cell phone and he turned up like a flying arrow. She felt she had found a protector, a man with influence. She thought of the old saying: "If you want to climb high, you'd better go for the tall branches."

Now Xia's unkind words about Bing displeased her. Lotus turned her back pointedly.

"Calm your tits!" Xia said crossly as she tapped Lotus on the back. "You must admit that he's a bit unusual, actually a bit strange. Nice guy, though."

Lotus didn't turn around.

Little Jade passed around a paper bag full of sunflower seeds. "Don't argue, sisters. Eat, eat," she said in a high-pitched whine. Little Jade was Mongolian, with high cheekbones and brown narrow eyes. A neat bob framed her goose-egg-shaped face. She was always nibbling something but never committing to a proper meal. Lotus heard that the teenager had been kidnapped and sold into prostitution and somehow ended up at Moonflower.

The girls helped themselves to the sunflower seeds. Lipstick-stained husks snowed down on the pavement.

After a few minutes, Xia began again. "This guy last night had the smallest cock in the world. Look, look, smaller than my little pinkie!" she said, curling her smallest finger and cackling.

Give me a break, Lotus thought to herself. Don't we have enough sex stuff to deal with? She darted a sharp look at Xia. The old hag's wrinkled face was so dark it looked like it had been pickled in soy sauce, and her chest was as flat as a paved road. You wouldn't imagine that clients would return and specifically ask for her, for both "small jobs" and "big jobs," but they did. Lotus had to admit that Xia tried the hardest of them all. She would even work during her period, simply stuffing some cotton pads inside herself. She cheerfully chatted with her clients and flattered them constantly. Xia was secretive about her age, but judging by the fact that her eldest daughter had just married, Lotus suspected that this mother of three had turned forty a few years ago.

"Guess what?" Xia continued. "Mr. Pinkie-Cock actually managed to keep going for such a long time that I had to charge him overtime! Ha!" All the girls burst out laughing.

Lotus made a loud sucking sound and shot out a wad of spittle on the road. In the city, she felt her chest was so filled with filth that she often had the urge to cough and spit.

She shifted her legs. The parlor opened at noon every day. Around this quiet time, she and the others usually took turns cooking. After lunch, they would take a nap in the massage room, keeping their own rooms in the back free for any odd customers who might roll in. The girls would lounge around, playing mah-jongg or watching episodes of *Princess Huan Zhu,* a hugely popular soap opera about a love child of an emperor. Though growing up in poverty, she becomes a *gege,* a princess, and then marries a handsome prince. She wears a massive red silk flower perched on top of her piled-up hair, and she has round lively eyes that must be connected to a fountain, as tears spring to them over the smallest emotions. Watching her in the drab, dark parlor, the girls couldn't help but cry with her. Wiping away their tears, they would slide the next DVD of the series into the player.

Every day at four p.m., as instructed by Moon, the girls all had to stand outside on display, dressed up, painted, and ready for sale.

Lotus's thoughts turned to the last letter from Shadan, her seventeen-year-old brother. In his last letter, he had thanked her for the money she had sent home. Like a sparrow longing for spring, she always hoped for letters from home, especially letters of gratitude. Shadan, her brother's nickname, meant "Stupid Egg," and her own was Chouchou, "Ugly, Ugly." Their superstitious grandma Nai had given them unattractive nicknames in the hopes that the evil spirits would leave them alone. An exceptionally smart boy, Shadan described in vivid detail the reunion dinner on the eve of the lunar New Year: smoked ham, cured fish, and hot pig's-head soup, cooked for a whole day with pig's blood, prickly ash, and five fragrant spices.

Lotus often imagined future scenes of celebrating this festival with her family. She would wear a bright red woolen coat, its sleeves and collar trimmed with fluffy fur, and everyone would be smiling at her. That day will come, she told herself.

As the evening deepened, the street became livelier. Three-wheeled vehicles and motorbikes rattled by, stirring up dust on the narrow worn-out road. Peddlers, selling ice lollies, pineapples on sticks, and meals in boxes, shouted to passersby. In the distance, a train rumbled along toward the nearby East Station, where slow trains stopped en route to neighboring provinces. Every day, trains brought in more migrant workers from the poor interior. Most of them would end up at construction sites or in factories.

Singsong invitations floated up from the girls on the street. "Big brother, massage? Cheap, cheap."

"Come here, we have pretty, big-titted, juicy girls, and the best massage in town!" The word "massage" always came out in three long caressing syllables—*ma sha ji.*

Lotus spotted two tall men in their thirties dressed in suits and ties strutting along the street. No wonder the girls were calling out so loudly: they were a better catch than the usual small fry.

Pulling down the padded bra that forever rode up her flat chest, Xia leaped out into the road and seized the men by their wrists. "Come, come, big brothers, this way. Good service, any service for you."

The thinner and taller of the two men, who looked like a scarecrow, shoved her away with a chuckle. "Big brothers? Do you think you are younger than us? Ha!"

Xia's heavily made-up face hardly changed color as she followed the men. "Brothers, haven't you heard the saying: 'Older ginger is hotter!'"

Three years' experience in the trade had taught Lotus that half-hearted clients were more difficult to please. They could even turn violent, venting their anger on *ji* for their own moments of weakness. So she stayed where she was and parted her legs wider. Her hands went inside her bra to pull her breasts toward the middle to show more cleavage through her V-necked dress, white georgette as sheer as a cicada's wing. She watched the men intently.

Scarecrow's friend stopped to study the red-lettered signboard. "Moonflower. Yes, yes. This is it!" he spoke in standard Mandarin, and his handsome face lit up. A robust man with an athletic build, he had film-star looks marred by a squint eye. He examined the girls and pointed at Lotus and Mimi. "Are you two free tonight? We need some girls at our banquet."

Moonflower had a reputation on this stretch of street, thanks to its enterprising and well-connected owner and attractive girls, even though the prices were higher than most. "The four of us work as a team," Lotus said, smiling sweetly. She could feel Funny Eye's gaze on her face but she stayed cool, ready to back down if he insisted.

"But this one is only a child!" said Scarecrow, lifting his chin in Little Jade's direction.

"I'm seventeen," said Little Jade, brushing back her bob. Wearing a white blouse, a short black skirt, and knee-length white socks, Little Jade looked like a Japanese schoolgirl. It was their boss's idea: you had to play the game either as a slut or a virgin.

Lotus gestured at Little Jade to wipe her face, and the girl complied, brushing off the sunflower husk from the corner of her mouth. She knew that the girl was actually little more than fifteen. Poor thing.

Funny Eye nudged his friend. "Come on," he whispered. "I heard boss Jiang is particularly fond of spring chickens." He waved his long arm expansively. "All right, all of you, then. Come with me."

———

Lotus had forgotten all about being tired. She was now excited and alert as she and the other girls entertained four businessmen in a smoke-clouded private dining room inside a five-star hotel. She giggled when she felt it was the right time to do so and nodded as the men talked.

This time, the occasion was the birthday of boss Jiang, a man well into his sixties. Clad in a traditional silk jacket, his well-nourished body filled the seat directly opposite the door, reserved for the guest of honor. In Shenzhen, everyone called everyone "boss." Jiang looked like a big one.

Funny Eye, the host, had placed himself opposite Jiang. From the beginning, Lotus had figured he would be a better bet than the mean-spirited Scarecrow. During the walk from the parlor to his car, instead of trying to touch him, she had engaged him with her eyes. Moon had taught her the trick of holding a man's gaze, counting to five, casting down the eyes as if shy, then looking up at him again and batting her lashes. Sure enough, after boss Jiang had taken Little Jade as his pick, Funny Eye asked Lotus to sit next to him.

Xia was nestling beside a sturdy man in his fifties, cracking water-melon seeds for him and popping them coyly into his small wet mouth. He was casually dressed in a navy polo shirt, but a gold watch shone from his wrist. Lotus guessed that he was Jiang's deputy.

After enough small talk, the men started to complain about their frustration with China's banking system and discussed how the situation would be improved if China joined some international trade organization. Lotus's thoughts drifted and she began to survey the spacious room. Golden-colored silk brocade decorated the walls, with matching curtains. An oil painting of a blond woman hung on one wall. Up-market restaurants often tried to create some sense of foreignness to show they were sophisticated.

Dishes crowded the moving glass top of their round table—the lobsters were still covered in dry ice and an expensive fish she had forgotten the name of had hardly been touched. The first time she had attended a banquet, the luxurious surroundings and the huge selection of food had overwhelmed her. She hadn't known what to do with her hands, or how to eat some of the shellfish. Nowadays she was coping better at banquets.

Lotus loved food. When she was a child, good food was as scarce as a phoenix feather. One summer evening when she was six, her mother, Ma, having just given birth to her brother, pressed a hard-boiled egg, still warm, into her hand. The egg, a rare luxury, was intended for Ma to eat in order to regain her strength after childbirth. Lotus brought it to the open-air cinema. Though the cinema consisted of a sheet strung between two trees in the village square, it was an occasional summer treat. While she watched the movie—she still remembered the title, *Guerrillas on the Railway,* a popular revolutionary film—she chewed on her egg, taking tiny bites to ensure it lasted till the movie's victorious end. That was one of the happiest days of her childhood.

The egg had somehow eased her resentment toward her baby brother. When Shadan had arrived a few days earlier, Lotus wasn't happy at all. There had been such a fuss over the boy that the little girl felt ignored. The family had taken advantage of a recently relaxed policy that allowed rural couples to have a second child if the firstborn was a girl. And they did get a boy. Their grandma Nai could hardly stop laughing, claiming that the baby's very loud wail, upon his entering the world, was a sign of the great life he would lead. Dispirited, Lotus would spend hours at her auntie's house to play with her dear cousin Little Red, only one year younger. Whenever she was at home, Ma would call her over to her bedside, chatting with her and telling her that one child was too lonely and two could take care of each other. Ma would sometimes share goodies with her, such as a bowl of the precious dark bone chicken soup, and occasionally eggs. One day, Ma allowed Lotus to hold her brother. He looked like an adorable fat baby from Chinese New Year paintings, with large black eyes and chubby legs. She began to like him. The boy grew and learned to sit up and to crawl, and before long he followed her everywhere.

It was their mother's death that had really bonded the siblings. When Lotus was twelve, their mother died from spinal cancer. Those last weeks were so painful for them all, but what Lotus was most struck by was her mother's distress at leaving her little son. She reassured Ma over and over that she would take care of him.

One month after the funeral, when Nai was out in the field, the siblings found their father lying on the floor of his room, in a pool of his own vomit. His wife's death and a debt of close to ten thousand yuan from her medical bills had crushed him. "Is Ba going to die, too?" Shadan kept asking as Lotus cleaned up their father. "Don't worry. I am here," she assured him, her heart suffocating with a longing for their mother. She began to feel the full weight of the promise she had made to Ma. On that day, her childhood ended.

"Seal's treasure on hot plate." A young waitress in a blue cotton uniform interrupted Lotus's thoughts and announced the arrival of a sizzling dish. Lotus knew what the treasure was—the animal's penis. It was supposed to enhance a man's performance in bed. And of all the animals, seal and rhinoceros "treasures" were the most expensive and sought after. "This man must be loaded," she thought and threw a flirtatious look at Funny Eye.

He had removed his jacket to reveal his crisp pale pink shirt, which showed off his trim body. He rose and scooped a large spoonful of treasure onto Boss Jiang's plate. "Eat, eat, Boss Jiang. It's good for you."

Boss Jiang released a nasal laugh. "I manage all right without it!"

The others roared with him.

Funny Eye smiled a lopsided smile. "Why not 'add one more flower to your bouquet'?"

"*Meinu,*" he said, turning toward Lotus. The clients always called her Beauty to her face but *ji* behind her back. "Care to try some?" he asked, holding out a spoon.

Lotus was usually able to eat anything. Now quite full, she had a sudden feeling of revulsion. She stared at the reproductive organ.

As Lotus hesitated, Funny Eye grabbed her left hand, stroked it, and started to squeeze it harder and harder until she thought it was going to break.

She refrained from screaming. Red-faced, she looked up at him.

Funny Eye smiled at her charmingly. "Be a good girl and try a piece," he said unhurriedly.

Lotus realized that everyone was watching her. She forced a smile and took the spoon from him. She picked a piece of darkish meat and put it into her mouth. It tasted like bacon, but not quite as disgusting as she had anticipated.

"Good girl!" Funny Eye cried. He leaned over and pinched her cheek.

Pinching cheeks or groping bottoms: Lotus had learned to tolerate these things. As she rubbed her hand under the table, she scolded herself. "Silly girl! You don't have many opportunities to entertain rich men. Don't screw up this one." She had been perhaps a little too relaxed with this client, partly because he had been unusually polite and attentive. Yet why had he squeezed her hand like that?

The waitress, with sweat beading on her smooth forehead, was now replacing their dirty plates with clean ones. Lotus knew that the girl must be working long hours for a meager salary and her home was probably a dark basement somewhere, shared with a dozen other girls. About a few months into the trade, an encounter with a violent customer had made Lotus reconsider her profession. As soon as the bruises on her face faded, she managed to find a job, waiting tables at a mid-range restaurant. But after the relative freedom and easy pace of life as a *ji*, she found it too hard to cope with working for sixteen hours a day at the restaurant and, at night, sleeping right in the restaurant on a bed made of chairs. At the end of the month, when the restaurant owner handed her a slim envelope, containing her monthly salary that was barely enough to buy a train ticket home, she walked out the door.

Lotus looked at one dish and then another, thinking to herself: "After all, what other job can allow me to make such good money, to eat so well, and at such fancy places?"

"Come on, guys! Full glasses!" shouted Scarecrow, tapping his glass lightly on the rim of the table.

The girls refilled the men's glasses with *baijiu,* a strong white liquor that burned one's throat like fire. The businessmen clanked their glasses in a toast and drained them noisily. Xia drank heartily with them, her cheeks as red as a monkey's bottom. That woman was a bit too fond of her drinks, thought Lotus. What she knew and their boss didn't was that Xia sometimes sipped *baijiu* during working hours. She never threw up, but when she grew tipsy she became sad and whimpering. None of the other girls liked to drink. In toasts, they brought their glasses to their lips, but no more. If a client complained, they would sip a little and then spit it out later into a tissue. To refuse outright could have consequences. Once Little Jade, fresh in the trade then, did so. Her drunken client then poured a whole bottle of the stuff over her face. The poor girl lost both face and pay.

The dark red synthetic carpet in the room reeked of *baijiu*. After Ma's death, Lotus's father had taken up drinking. He drank a cheaper brand of *baijiu* than what was on the table tonight, packaged in a palm-sized clear bottle. The pungent smell always haunted their house like a ghost. When he got drunk, he would sometimes turn violent.

After the waitresses had brought in the fruit plates, signaling the end of the dinner, they left the businessmen and their companions to themselves.

Funny Eye's hand traveled up Lotus's bare arm. "How about a song?" he asked, pointing at the karaoke machine on the far side of the room.

Lotus smiled apologetically. "I can't sing, really," she said, eyeing Xia. "But Sister Xia sings very well."

Lotus knew that Xia was grateful that she had insisted on bringing along everyone. She calculated that the gesture would give her some extra clout. Xia, being the oldest and longest-serving girl in the Moon-flower, often behaved like a self-styled leader, while Lotus, being the most successful at the game, ought, in her own opinion, to have been more highly regarded.

"Okay-la." Xia jumped up, like a dolphin leaping out of water. "I'll sing, if only to win a laugh from you gentlemen!"

Xia glided over and picked up the microphone, sending a crackling noise over the speaker system. She blew into the microphone, and with pouted lips, winked at her audience.

"Farewell, my darling," Xia sang with emotion, her voice magically transformed from the rough gravel of a woman with seven years on the street to the tones of a love-struck young girl. She swung her bony hips, her face animated and her lively eyes flirting with one man and then another, as if each were her parting lover. "Please don't pick the wildflower on the roadside, no matter how tempting. Remember, alone at home, I am waiting, my darling."

When Xia finished, everyone cheered. She bowed, her face radiant, and returned to her seat.

Funny Eye packed some tobacco into a carved wooden pipe. In the countryside, plenty of old men smoked pipes, but Lotus had never seen a city man use one. She watched as he lit it, sucked in, and blew out a plume of smoke. It smelled sweet.

The rest of the men were also smoking, chatting cheerfully.

"How was your trip to Thailand over the New Year, Boss Jiang? Did you see the 'human monsters'?" asked Scarecrow.

"You bet I did." A smile spread across Jiang's doughy face.

"What are 'human monsters'?" Mimi mumbled with her mouth full. She was the only one who was still munching. Lotus, sitting on the other side, had tried to gesture for her friend to stop, but Mimi didn't seem to take any notice.

"A 'human monster' has got a man's dick and a woman's tits," Boss Jiang said, one of his wrinkled hands creeping up to Little Jade's chest, as if no one knew where breasts grew.

"Impossible!" Little Jade's slit eyes widened.

Jiang laughed his nasal laugh. "Possible. With plastic surgery, of course."

"Some can even shake their tits up and down!" claimed Xia's man, hacking his smoker's laugh, thick and coarse like an old engine.

The others joined in laughter that threatened to lift up the roof. Xia's laugh was the loudest.

Funny Eye stood up, raising his glass, and said: "Gentlemen, it's such an honor to celebrate Boss Jiang's birthday together this evening. Chairman Mao once said: 'Political power comes from the barrel of a gun.' I would say: 'A man's prowess comes from this gun, too.'" He winked, and toasted the old man. "Boss Jiang, may you fire your gun until you're one hundred years old!"

In the hotel lobby, Lotus half hid herself behind a marble column while Funny Eye was checking in at the reception. The other men had taken their girls to different vehicles and disappeared into the rainy night. At the last minute, Funny Eye had decided to stay here since he didn't want the rain to ruin his Italian shoes.

Lotus felt out of place in the luxurious setting. An enormous crystal chandelier looked down on her, its hanging bits and pieces reminding her of an octopus brandishing shining tentacles. From the corner of her eye, Lotus saw there were several receptionists at the front desk. She wondered if they suspected what she was, with her see-through dress.

At the coffee shop in one corner of the lobby, three fashionably dressed young women were drinking wine and talking loudly, sprinkling their conversation with English phrases. Lotus watched the girls. They seemed to be about her age, sophisticated and carefree. "Little bitches!" she murmured to herself. Where did they get their money? Parents? Lovers? They were obviously very well educated. I was a top student, too, Lotus thought with bitterness. If only she hadn't been taken out of school so early; if only she wasn't a country girl. She darted another look at the trio. The girl sitting closest to her was clad in a simple but elegant black dress, with an emerald-green pashmina draped over her shoulders. A rather large leather bag, decorated with a green silk scarf, sat next to her pointed leather shoes. The bag looked real.

Lotus clutched her own bag, a knockoff of some famous foreign brand she had bought for fifty yuan at the Big Red Gate wholesale market. She looked down at her leather sandals and noticed that the right heel was a little torn. She shifted it behind her left foot.

Funny Eye soon returned with a room card in his hand and led her by the arm up to their room on the thirtieth floor. He strode along the hotel corridor as if he owned the place. Lotus tottered on her heels beside him. He stopped in front of a door, opened it with a swipe of the card, and gestured for her to enter.

Lotus inched forward. Lit by two gentle wall lamps, the room was

lovelier and more spacious than anything she had ever seen before, with
white linens, antique decorations, and pretty paintings on the walls.
She had been in many hotel rooms, but usually cheap ones hidden in the
shadows of train or bus stations, or on the outskirts of town. Some
charged an hourly rate.

The air conditioner was on, even though the outside temperature
was perfect. Lotus hugged her arms, partly because she was cold and
partly because she felt uneasy about this highly unusual client, even
frightened of him. At the same time, she was drawn to him. She wasn't
sure how the night with him would unfold.

Funny Eye walked straight in and kicked off his shiny leather shoes.
"It's okay, isn't it?" he said, looking about the room.

"Very nice," Lotus said, touching the golden silk brocade on the
king-size bed.

Funny Eye came over to her and rubbed her bare arms. "Are you
cold? Why don't you take a hot shower? You'll feel better," he said softly,
then switched on the bathroom light for her.

Lotus went in and stared. How extravagant it was! The tiled floor was
polished as if it had been licked clean and the room gleamed with white,
fluffy towels. She took off her jade bracelet, undressed, and stepped into
the shower stall. The pipes and faucets confused her and it took a few minutes to get the shower working. As she washed herself, she considered
whether she ought to play a more passive role for him, like an inexperi-
enced, recently fallen girl, or a more aggressive role, like an experienced
seducer. Judging by his wealth and his assertive manner, she decided to
take the safe bet and let him take the lead.

After she got out of the shower, Lotus wrapped herself up in one thick
white towel, the way she had seen ladies do in films, and walked back
into the room. In the glow of a bedside lamp, Funny Eye was sitting on
the bed, punching a text message into his phone. He was half covered by
the duvet, showing his bare and toned chest. As she approached the bed,
she noticed the dense hair on his strong arms. She somehow felt embarrassed. She had seen hundreds of men's naked bodies. But usually the
whole thing was hurried and businesslike.

"Come over here, my little beauty." He patted the empty side of the bed.

Lotus picked up her bag but walked toward him.

"G-u-g-c-i." He read the label on her bag, and burst out laughing. "Ha! They should at least get the spelling right. You don't need this, sweetie. I actually prefer to use my own condom," he said, taking the bag from her and setting it aside.

Lotus perched on the edge of the massive bed, and he reached over and took away her towel.

"You have a lovely body," he said, caressing her waist. "You'd look even sexier if you held your posture better."

Lotus turned toward him. "Thank you. You do know how to sweet-talk."

"I certainly appreciate beautiful women," he said smugly. "Your friend, what's her name, said you can perform any service required. Is that the case?"

He wanted to play sex games! Lotus's skull tightened at the memory of that hateful man who had tied her to the bed frame and then soiled her breasts with his sperm. She had wiped most of it off on his expensive suit when he went to the toilet. And if that was the case here, then it could be tricky with Funny Eye, Lotus thought, as she remembered how hard he had squeezed her hand.

"It all depends on what you offer me," she said as coyly as she could, in spite of her concerns.

"How about a thousand?"

"Fifteen hundred."

"Okay, then." He took her chin in his hand and looked into her eyes. "You intrigue me."

"Really?" Lotus asked, tilting her head.

"You seem to be tough and vulnerable at the same time."

Lotus smiled, not really taking in his words. She was thinking about the moment when she would hold those fifteen hundred-yuan notes in her hand. She'd put up with whatever she had to endure tonight.

She leaned forward and rested her head on his broad shoulder. "Would you like me to lie down?" she whispered. "Faceup or facedown?"

"Please lie down. Faceup and legs as open as possible."

Lotus complied, legs open and eyes closed. After a few moments she opened her eyes again and saw him lean over her, so close that she could feel his hot breath on her cheek and smell sweet tobacco, liquor, and cologne. She instinctively turned her face away, thinking he was going to kiss her. Then she remembered that this was a rich client she had to please. She stroked his thick chest. "*Shuaige*," she said, using a popular term for "handsome young man." "What a body you have."

He smiled a self-satisfied smile. "I go to the gym most days."

He continued to watch her intently, in the same way a farmer would stare at the teeth of a mule he wanted to buy in the market.

Something soft touched her breast, which made her squirm. She looked down and saw him teasing her with a goose feather.

"Relax, my little beauty."

Lotus laid her head back down, wondering if this man always carried a feather around. She found the light from the bedside lamp harsh. "Can we turn the light off, please?"

"But I'd like to look at you. You should know that men are visual." He softened his tone. "All right." He then reached out to dim the lamp. "You see, nothing gives me more pleasure than watching a woman enjoy making love with me."

Lotus shut her eyes again, but she was unable to shut off her senses. As he stroked, circled, and toyed with her breasts using the soft, soft feather, she couldn't help raising her chest as she felt her nipples hardening. The feather then snaked all the way down her body and she found her senses following it.

"Open your jade gate, my beauty. Open your gate of pleasure for me. Just for me," he said in a raspy whisper.

She opened up her legs wider. There, the feather lightly tickled and teased her lips, outside at first and then inside, arousing a sensation in her that she had never before experienced. Her breath quickened. She remembered her boss Moon's teaching. "Make nice noises and moan, the louder the better. It's the best music in the world for men." And for once, she didn't want to stay silent. His other hand and the feather were now both at work. Before she knew it, one of his fingers was moving in and out of her back entrance. She opened her eyes and looked straight into his, the good eye fixed on her calmly even though his "gun" had risen between his legs. She wanted to push his hand away, but was unable to move, as if she were under some kind of spell.

Almost at the same time, her private part began to tremble. This was something that had never happened to her before, not in this intense way. Most of her clients never stayed inside her for more than five minutes. The trembling pleasure shocked and confused her. She bit her lips as the contraction continued.

"Here we go," Funny Eye sang.

He pulled out a condom from somewhere and held it out on his palm. "Do you mind?" he asked politely.

Gathering herself, Lotus sat up and picked up the condom. Expertly she opened it and with her fingertips she slid the ribbed condom onto his enlarged cock.

He entered her with ease and rocked back and forth inside her like no other man had done. As he intensified his thrusts, he panted loudly. Then he shuddered and collapsed on top of her with a deep, satisfied groan. When he pulled back, she realized that her legs were still wrapped tightly around his lower body.

Lotus let go of him quickly and got out of the bed. Standing there, she became acutely aware of her nakedness. She dashed to the bathroom.

Sitting on the toilet, she felt dazed. She couldn't urinate, feeling some kind of sensation in her rectum, as if a finger were still probing there. In the mirror across from her, she saw her flushed face and bleeding lip.

She picked up another towel to cover her naked body.

CHAPTER 4

佛争一炷香，人争一口气

❖━━━━━━━━━━━━━━━━━━━━━━━━━━━━━━━━❖

As Buddha Needs Incense, So a Man
Needs Self-respect

Bing darted another look out the window. Scorched by the sun, the day already felt ancient. But it was only 11:30 a.m., and it was a half hour before Lotus was due.

He started to unpack the rolls of photos he had taken earlier that morning at a press release for a new product—an energy-saving light-bulb that allowed one to adjust its brightness. Luckily the factory was only a short taxi ride east from his home. As soon as he had snapped a few close-ups of the product and a few shots of the general scene, he left as quickly as a gust of wind, clutching his gift bag, which contained the product and the press release, as well as three hundred yuan in cash wrapped in a red envelope—the usual little bribe for journalists and photographers. Sometimes it depressed Bing to think that he had become unfazed by such practice. But he quieted his conscience by telling himself that such small-scale corruption was really nothing compared to the level of corruption he had seen in the business world.

In the beginning, Bing had been rather pleased with such assignments. Now they grew tiresome, allowing little outlet for creativity. Sometimes he asked himself: "I've given up the business world, with its money and comfort, just for this?" And how would people view him? He consoled himself with a quotation from Dante: "Follow your own course, and let people talk." There was no need to explain to everyone his high goal.

Bing had first picked up a camera at the end of 1984, after being assigned a job in Beijing at a state-owned factory making Forever Clean soap, and he began to explore the city. When one of his black-and-white images of *hutong*s, the narrow lanes with enchanting hidden courtyard houses, won the photo competition organized by his factory's weekly journal, he began to take his hobby more seriously. However, it wasn't until 1989 that he saw the real power of photography. Like many patriotic youths, he had enthusiastically participated in the democratic movement that erupted during that extraordinary spring. In the animated faces in Tiananmen Square, he detected the defiance of the students and the hope of the nation. He felt such an urge to record them with his camera. Later, when he developed the images in his dark room, he realized with a sense of inner jubilation that he had at last produced images worthy of a real photographer.

Just as Bing was about to check his watch again, he heard a familiar sound from Lotus. She spat a lot, usually accompanied by the unpleasant noises of snorting, throat clearing, and coughing.

He buttoned up his white shirt and smoothed his hair as he walked over to the door.

Lotus stood outside, one hand holding a plastic takeout bag and the other a green plastic net with bottles of shampoo and shower gel. Her hair, still damp, fell over her shoulders like a gentle waterfall.

"I can always tell when you're coming," Bing teased her with a smile.

"Sorry," Lotus said, covering her mouth with a hand.

"No need to apologize. Please, come on in."

She took off her flip-flops and stepped onto the bamboo mat covering the floor.

"I treated myself to an herbal bath at the bath house. So nice to soak in a proper bathtub," Lotus said as she lightly stepped over to the desk. "Have you eaten, Hu Laoshi?"

"Not yet." Bing moved his computer to make space on the desk.

"Good, I've got some goodies!" She put her washing bag down on the floor and took out two lunch boxes from the takeout bag, containing roast duck and steamed bread rolls.

"You're too kind, Lotus."

"The duck is freshly made." Still standing by the desk, she split apart a pair of disposable wooden chopsticks and rubbed one against the other to shave off the splinters. Occasionally when Lotus came around, she would bring inexpensive foods like duck feet braised in soy sauce or spicy dishes she cooked herself: the two of them shared a craving for spicy food. And Lotus wasn't the only girl who brought him meals. All the girls took pity on him, thinking that a single man couldn't possibly take care of himself. Mimi wasn't so much of a cook, but whenever she cooked something, she'd insist on sharing it with him. This had given Bing excuses to take the girls out for meals—sometimes just Lotus and Mimi, at other times all four together. Their favorites were KFC and McDonald's. Bing knew it was foreign junk food, but he understood that eating and drinking slices of America made the girls feel urban and modern. Such outings had not only deepened their friendship but also provided him insight into their lives. Bing was fascinated by what the girls shared in unguarded moments over the dinner table, from funny stories with clients and problems with boyfriends to their obsession with fortune-telling.

"Why still standing? Sit, sit down, please," Bing said, motioning for her to sit on his high-backed wooden chair, the only proper chair in the room. He settled himself onto a plastic folding chair, mindful of keeping a comfortable distance between them. He felt slightly embarrassed by the austerity of his room, which contained a double bed, a desk, and some homemade bookshelves.

Bing broke a bread roll in half and placed a piece of duck inside. As a northerner, he preferred wheat-based food to rice. Lotus had remembered.

She picked up a piece of duck meat with her chopsticks and ate enthusiastically. "Hu Laoshi," she began, talking with her mouth full. "You had once asked me what the best thing was about living in the city. It's got to be the food."

"Oh, yeah?"

Lotus sent another piece of duck into her mouth. "Look, I am having roast duck for lunch! Back at home, my poor little brother gets by eating plain rice and pickles, to save a few pennies on dishes."

"Before coming to Beijing, I only had roast duck once—at a wedding," Bing said.

"I sometimes ask myself: 'What I am doing here?'" Lotus carried on. "Then you asked me this question. I realized that there are many good things about the city, really. You know what? I like all the nice things money can buy: roast duck, dresses, perfume, and food I didn't know existed, like jam on toasted bread!" She struck Bing as more lively than usual. Perhaps she was now more relaxed with him.

"Hu Laoshi, I like talking to you. You make me think about things," she said, looking up at him, a bright smile on her lips.

Bing shifted in his plastic chair, beaming. "I am so glad to hear you say that. I enjoy talking to you, too."

Lotus wore a white T-shirt with "I Love Snoopy Dog" written in English underneath the image of the iconic canine.

"You look lovely today," he said to flatter her.

She uttered the standard polite reply: *"Nali, nali"*—"Not at all." Her fresh pink face blossomed into a flower of smiles, revealing her protruding "tiger teeth" on either side of the front teeth.

Lotus reminded Bing of Pearl, the woman who, during a brief romantic encounter a little more than two years ago, had given him his first taste of the power and pleasure of being a real man. Not because Lotus resembled Pearl physically. It was something more subtle: it had to do with their charm and beauty, and the way the two women looked at him, which sent his heart soaring.

Sitting in his large chair, her feet hardly touching the ground, Lotus had the petite figure of a typical southern girl. Looking closer, Bing noticed that she had dark circles under her eyes.

"Was last night all right?" he asked.

"It was okay," she mumbled as she chewed; then she told him about the banquet. "But Little Jade had a funny experience. This old man, Boss Jiang, took her home. He . . ." Lotus twisted her mouth but left her sentence incomplete.

"What about him?"

She stopped her chewing.

"Never mind," Bing added quickly, wiping away his sweat with a facial towel. He often found himself drawn to the details of Lotus's stories, especially in recent months after she had become a little more open with him. She had told him how she was once stalked by a well-dressed young man; how she used to linger in front of the South cinema, offering migrant workers her "first half" (men were only allowed to touch the top part of her body, once they were inside the dark cinema) and the "second half" (their hands could venture under her skirt if they paid double); how one middle-aged architect didn't want sex, but to complain about his terrible wife; and how an official insisted that she dress up as a soldier from the People's Liberation Army . . . Afterward, Bing would often feel embarrassed by his questioning, though he justified it as part of his research.

Looking up at a crumbling section of the wall, Lotus said: "Well, this dirty old man stuck a date into Little Jade's"—she hesitated for the right word, and chose the clinical option—"her vagina, and then . . ." She paused, tittering and shaking her head.

"Go on."

"This morning he took the date out, you know from down there, and, ha-ha, ate it!" She laughed heartily, her shallow dimples dancing on her cheeks.

Bing couldn't help laughing as well.

"Isn't he so disgusting!" she remarked.

"Utterly revolting!" Bing agreed. "You know, it's a traditional belief that older men can gain virility from young girls by doing things like that."

"Really?" Lotus said, tilting her head. "Hu Laoshi, you have an explanation for everything."

"Not really."

"Of course you do!"

Bing coughed to suppress a smile and leaned back against his chair. The ceiling fan blew loose strands of Lotus's hair, the breeze swaying her white flowing skirt and wafting the fragrance of shampoo around the room.

"Such a mountain of books!" Lotus said, eyeing his bookshelves. She stood up to survey his books and CDs. A certificate of bravery from Tsinghua University, half hidden between a blue-and-white vase and a projector, attracted her attention. She picked it up. "What's this?"

"Oh, just some old certificate."

Lotus studied it and gazed at his face. "*Wasai*, Hu Laoshi, so you saved a boy's life?"

"Oh, that was many years ago." Bing began to recount the story. In early November 1981, two months into his second year at university, he had gone on a school outing to Longqing Gorge, north of Beijing. At noon, as they were hiking along the winding mountain path, they suddenly heard desperate cries for help. The students all leaned over the edge and saw someone struggling in the water below. It took Bing only a few seconds to make up his mind. He threw off his down jacket, shoes, and glasses, and dived straight into the shimmering surface some eighty feet below. The water was so cold that he felt he had fallen into a pool of needles. A strong swimmer, he soon reached the drowning person, a teenage boy, and pulled him to safety.

"It was my first life-and-death experience," Bing said, recalling the big moment—remembering how, as he pulled his jacket back on against the chilly wind, his teeth chattering, he felt alive and exhilarated for the first time since stumbling into his university.

"*Wasai,* so brave of you to dive into the gorge," Lotus said admiringly. "My knees turn to noodles just thinking about it."

"I guess I just didn't think too much before I jumped." Bing finished his duck bun and sprang up. "Now, Lotus, let's go to the temple. I'd really like a shot of you praying there."

She knitted her eyebrows.

"Come on! It won't take long. Please."

"Okay then. You lock up. I'll go first."

Before Bing had a chance to protest, Lotus had already gathered her net bag and dashed out like a startled deer.

He picked up the certificate from the desk and gazed at it. What he hadn't told her was the fact that his roommate Yuejin had been the first to jump off the cliff, but he was a poor swimmer and needed saving himself. After dragging the teenager to dry land, Bing then jumped back into the river and helped Yuejin to safety. However, without Yuejin's heroic action, Bing wasn't sure he would have taken the leap.

He carefully placed the battered certificate back on the shelf and set off.

The golden-cheeked spring day, so full of promise, cheered Bing up. In the warm sunshine, he strode along a mud path beside a smelly ditch full of rotten vegetables, bits and pieces of Styrofoam, plastic bottles, and discarded tires. A few ducks waddled by, sucking water from the puddles. A fat pig was rooting through a large open bag of rubbish on the roadside. White plastic bags, caught on trees and shrubs, flapped in the wind, like nature's flags of surrender.

Before Shenzhen was turned into a Special Economic Zone in the 1980s, a place to experiment with capitalism, Miaocun had been a sleepy farming village. Before long, the city had encroached, bringing with it high-rises, eyesores against the sky. Bit by bit, fields and forests were sold to property developers. Although still called a village, Miaocun had lost the charm the word evoked and now sat at the blurred intersection between rural and urban. With cash from selling the land, the locals had traded their traditional courtyard houses for new apartment buildings several stories high, all finished in brutally ugly blue glass and white ceramic tiles, which they saw as modern. Many rented out the spare rooms, often to poor working girls.

Graffiti crawled over the walls of houses, competing for space with slogans. "We Insist on the Socialist Path!" "Family Planning Policy Is

Good!" or "Firmly Crack Down on Prostitution!" Some of the red char-acters were plastered over by tattered fliers, promising "Effective Cure for Gonorrhea with Secret Family Remedy" and "Magic One-Injection Cure for All STDs."

The scenery became much more pleasant after Bing turned a corner and started to trudge up a steep path. Rooster Crowing Temple stood on a hill near Miaocun. A tall whitewashed wall, streaked with black mold, circled the temple compound. In the distance, Hong Kong's soar-ing skyline emerged from the clouds.

Bing walked inside the temple through the red wooden gate. These days, only small community temples like this one were still open to the public free of charge. Passing through the forecourt, he came to the main courtyard that housed the Great Hall of the Buddha.

Only half an hour's walk away from Miaocun, the temple might as well have been another world. The noise of the village dropped away. A string of tiny bronze bells clanged in the breeze. The smell of burning incense was everywhere, its smoke curling up through the exquisite brickwork that decorated the temple eaves.

Bing took a few shots of the eaves and the beautiful sloping roof made from yellow glazed tiles.

Most of the worshipers were local Hakka grandmas from the neigh-borhood, wearing wide-brimmed bamboo hats trimmed with black cot-ton lace, and traditional blue or black cotton jackets buttoned up on the right side. Though labeled a subgroup of Han Chinese, the Hakkas had their own tradition and customs, which they were struggling to pre-serve. And there seemed to be a higher percentage of Buddhists in their community.

A few businessmen in their smart suits were also lingering, incense in hand, presumably praying for the success of their enterprises, and for more wealth.

What Bing found interesting was the startling gap between Buddhist philosophy and the pragmatic way Buddhism was practiced by many in China. For them, the religion often became a platform to demand favors from divinity. Yet according to Buddha's teaching, desire was the root of all suffering. All cravings for pleasure and material goods could never be satisfied.

Inside the hall, Bing could see Lotus kowtowing on a round hassock in front of the giant Shakyamuni statue, her body bending so far forward that her forehead touched the hassock. Photographing the interior was prohibited, so he sat down on the ledge of the main hall and thought about Lotus and her faith with some envy.

Bing had searched for his own spirituality in his early days at university. A top student at his hometown school, he suddenly found himself struggling to get by at Tsinghua. He would have been motivated to work harder if he had been studying literature, his own choice, instead of chemical engineering. However, his father had been adamant that Bing must pick a science subject, as it was politically less risky. At university, he attempted to change departments but wasn't allowed.

After arriving on campus, Bing longed to romance a girl, but few took notice of him, an awkward student from the provinces, with cropped hair. At the university's dance parties, the pretty girls had swirled around only the good-looking boys, the brilliant dancers, or the Beijing residents who were more likely to be assigned a job in the capital.

In Beijing, Bing had no one to turn to, and little family pride. His grandfather, an educated landowner, was targeted and tortured to death by the Red Guards during the Cultural Revolution. And his grandmother hanged herself after her past as a concubine was exposed. Before Bing's departure from home, his father had disclosed the family stories. The most shocking detail was how the Red Guards dug out his great-grandfather's body from his grave, then chopped off the head and kicked it among them like a soccer ball. The revelation had made Bing lose faith in the Party and in Chairman Mao.

At Tsinghua, the bewildered young man had experienced his first existential crisis. For the first time in his life, he took an interest in religion as he searched for something to believe in, something to fill the void inside him. He spent hours in the university library studying the Bible, the Quran, and books on Buddhism. In the end, none of the religions completely satisfied him. It was then that he had picked up smoking, as if it could make him feel less lonely and confused.

After a while, Bing spotted Lotus coming out of the main hall into the yard, holding three joss sticks. He clicked away as she carried on with her ritual. After lighting the sticks from the row of red candles on metal spikes, she walked over to a massive bronze incense burner in the middle of the yard, pregnant with years of incense ash. She held the sticks high above her forehead, her face veiled by the smoke that snaked out of the burner.

With a simple motion, Lotus dropped the joss sticks into the burner and made a final bow.

She perched on the stone ledge of the main building. Bing sat next to her.

"This is my favorite place in the whole of Shenzhen," Lotus declared.

"When did you become a Buddhist?"

"When I became a *ji*." She made an attempt to smile.

Bing wanted to ask her how she had gotten into the trade, and the words leaped to his throat. That story held the key to really understanding the girl, he was convinced of it. But it was not the right moment. He swallowed his question and listened on.

"You see, my grandma is a Buddhist, murmuring *amitabha* all day long," Lotus said. "I used to laugh at her for being superstitious. Now look at me, praying to the Guanyin Buddha every day."

Lotus's Snoopy T-shirt looked out of place in the temple. Bing peered at her and wondered how this working girl reconciled her profession and her religion. "Why did you convert to Buddhism?" he asked.

"Why not?" She raised her voice. She glanced up at the sky as if consulting with her deity and then turned to Bing, her face now red with irritation. "Life is very bitter. Why can't I have something that makes me feel better?"

Bing was taken aback by her vicious tone. He nodded and flashed an encouraging smile. "I am just so glad you've found your spiritual home."

"Spiritual home?" Lotus repeated, knitting her brows slightly, trying to digest the meaning of the term. She rested her chin on her clasped hands, watching people praying in the yard. "Hu Laoshi, do you think sins can be cleansed by doing good deeds and pleasing the Buddha?"

He thought it would be harsh to answer her with a simple no. After some deliberation, Bing replied: "The concept of redemption exists in most religions. One of the key concepts in Buddhism is 'cause and effect,' right?"

Lotus looked at him quizzically.

"So, every effect arises from a cause. What you are doing now determines your future. In theory, if you accumulate good karma now, then . . ."

Lotus cut in. "But do you think it really works?"

"Well, it may if you truly believe in it."

Lotus held his gaze. "You don't believe in it, do you?"

"Not really. Sometimes, I do wish I could believe in something." His voice softened. "I actually like several aspects of Buddhism. There is no supreme god in Buddhism and every being is equal."

But Lotus was absorbed in her thoughts and not really listening. It became clear to Bing that she didn't understand Buddhism and had no intention of studying the faith. She only saw it as a vehicle to serve her need to cleanse herself.

Why not? he said to himself. Yet he felt a slight dejection and stopped talking.

For a while, they sat together silently. After a few minutes, Lotus began again, a slender finger of hers pointing at the kapok tree in the far corner. "Look at those flowers, like tongues of a fire. Now I know why the locals call it red cotton tree."

Bing's eyes followed her finger. The tree was already flowering in March, its large flowers clustered on bare branches, bright red, dazzling, like dancing flames in the sunlight.

"Kapok has another popular name—the hero tree," Bing said. Looking at the majestic kapok, he thought about the poplar trees, also tall and straight, that lined the roads in his region in the north. When he was ten, his father had bought a bicycle, a luxury item at the time, and taken him for a ride. They rode along a path shaded by poplar trees, the thick trunks dotted with black marks that looked like large inquisitive eyes. He mentioned this to his father, who praised Bing for being so observant. His father got off his bicycle and patted the trunk of a big tree and said: "It's a great tree, the poplar. It can survive in any kind of harsh conditions. We must learn from this tree." Bing now realized that his father had actually been encouraging him.

He picked up his camera and took a few shots of kapok flowers and then shifted his lens to Lotus.

She began clearing her throat to spit. He put down his camera.

"Your university fee, Hu Laoshi. How did you pay for it?" Lotus inquired.

"Education was completely free back then. On top of that, poor students, like myself, received grants from the government."

"Free university?" she cried. "*Wasai!* It sounds too good to be true!"

"I was born at the right time," Bing said. He explained that, at that time, China had just opened up and desperately needed talented graduates.

"Why do people have to pay now?"

"Well, the market economy," said Bing, reveling in his authority. "Education has been turned into an industry, like everything else. Plenty of people can afford to pay for higher education. The better a university is, the more expensive it is. It means few students from poor farming backgrounds can get into decent universities."

Before Bing could finish his social commentary, Lotus forcefully squeezed the word "unfair" from between her teeth. "But no matter what, I'll send my brother to university."

"Your brother? Is he taking the examination this year?"

"Next year." Her voice dripped with pride. "He is really smart, that brother of mine. Hu Laoshi, how expensive are the university fees exactly?"

"On average, about six or seven thousand yuan a year."

"*Tamade!* That is expensive."

"Do you plan to cover all of the costs?"

"Yes, I will," she replied, emphasizing the word "I." "All of it. My family has no money."

"I can see that you are very fond of your brother, Lotus. But don't you think that it is too high a price to pay?"

"High price to pay? What do you mean?"

The majority of the working girls Bing had come across helped out their families financially, out of love, filial piety, and perhaps to some degree, a feel-good factor. Yet Lotus's sacrifice seemed beyond reason. "You didn't get into the trade because of your brother, did you?" he ventured to ask.

"No," Lotus said curtly. "I have to go." She stood up, brushed the dust off her skirt, and then picked up her net bag and started to walk out.

Bing trailed behind her. "Hope you won't be late for work today."

"I'll be okay." At the entrance, she stopped. "I'll go first, Hu Laoshi. People may talk if they see you spending too much time with someone like me."

Bing was moved by her thoughtfulness. "I don't mind what people say. But go ahead if you like," he said, waving goodbye.

He stood by the red gate of the temple and watched her slender body walk down the shade-strewn path, her long hair, totally dry now, flying in the wind and her skirt billowing. He imagined the joy of walking by her side. He kicked a stone and scolded himself for not insisting on walking with her. Coward. Hypocrite.

The large bronze bell in the main hall rang. Someone had just made a cash donation. Bing thought about how Karl Marx referred to religion as the opiate of the masses. "Opium," he murmured to himself as he walked back to the temple. "Sometimes it's just what you need."

CHAPTER 5

同病相怜

*Those Who Have the Same Illness
Sympathize with Each Other*

The Shenzhen spring lasted as long as a snap of fingers. By late July, the city felt like the inside of a bamboo steamer.

Lotus woke up, agitated, from a deep dream. She closed her eyes again, hearing the muffled noise of the traffic drifting in from behind the closed window.

After a few moments, she crawled out of bed, tied the mosquito net into a knot, and turned off the air conditioner. When it was on, she felt trapped by the cold air. But it was hard to survive Shenzhen's summer without it. She drew back the thick red velvet curtain, made from the same material as the curtain in the front of the massage parlor—one of Boss Moon's efforts to make the establishment look classier than it actually was. It felt more out of place in her room, but it served the purpose of blocking out light and reality. She slid open the window that sat behind protective metal bars. The hot air from the sun-grilled world oozed in.

Lotus headed out to the bathroom that stood at the end of the corridor, still wearing her white silk negligee. The nightdress was one of the new things in her life that she had come to like. She was particularly fond of this one. The soft and shining fabric clung to her body, making her feel sexy and modern. Nai wouldn't have approved of such a showy thing, but too many things made Grandma tut her disapproval. No matter. She was now living in a city, free from the shackles of the village.

The dark corridor linked to four rooms, Lotus and Mimi's on one side of the bathroom and Xia and Little Jade's on the other. It was quiet for the moment.

In the bathroom, Lotus started to wash, using the electric shower installed on the concrete wall. She slapped on shower gel generously and took her time rubbing her body. These days she wasted a ridiculous amount of time cleaning herself. In her village, water had to be carried from a well. Before retiring to bed every night, she would usually wash her feet in one basin and her face in another. But that was another era, another life.

After her long shower, Lotus went to the kitchen and reached into the fridge for a carton of milk, which she drank for breakfast. When she was a child, milk was something she had only read about in books, something foreigners drank. Only in recent years, when a few extra coins tinkled in her pocket, had she started to experiment with new foods.

Back in her room, she carefully applied Olay body lotion to moisturize herself. She had to take care of her skin. Her obsessive cleaning had made it very dry.

After putting on a comfortable white cotton dress without her padded bra, she began her ritual of worship. She lit some incense in the copper pot, and bowed several times in front of the portrait of Guanyin, clasping her hands together as she begged for forgiveness. "I know this is wrong," she said silently to her goddess. "I hate myself for this. But I made a stupid decision at a time when I felt totally lost. But I'll get out as soon as I can. And I am trying to be a good filial daughter by helping out my family." She always began by asking for forgiveness and ended up defending herself. Finally she prayed that her deity would bestow a good day on her, with good earnings. During working hours, she had trained herself not to look at Guanyin. Since her room was usually dark, few clients noticed the portrait.

It was now time to deal with the earnings from the night before. Lotus cleaned each note with a wet wipe, then separated the small notes from the big ones and counted them. Three hundred and sixty-five yuan, from two "big jobs" and two "small jobs." Not too bad. But it could have been better if the last guy, the one in a floral shirt, had been more generous. He kept going forever, so much so that she was half asleep underneath him. Then he asked her to get on all fours, to play "mandarin ducks in spring water" with him. She refused and told him to hurry up. He did, and left without tipping a penny. What a cheap dog! For the straight massage service, the charge was fifty yuan per hour, double for a sexual massage, and another fifty yuan on top for full-fledged sexual intercourse. If a client wanted to take a girl away from the premises, they had to pay a little more. Thirty percent went to Moon's pocket, and the girls kept the rest plus tips. Lotus put aside ninety yuan for her boss and stashed the rest in a half-empty bag of sanitary napkins and hid it in a corner of the wardrobe. At the end of the week, she would deposit the accumulation. The bank was always infested with irritable and irritating people, and she could have gone much less often. But when she saw the figures in her bank book climb, her soul would fly up to heaven.

Having finished counting, Lotus carefully wiped her hands and turned on the electric fan crouched in the corner. She lay back down on her bed. From under the pillow, she pulled out the latest letter from her brother and began to read it for the tenth time. Written neatly on lined exercise pages, his characters all slanted toward the right, as if being blown by gusts of wind. She found the handwriting endearing. She liked to place a few recent letters under the pillow. That little connection with home made her feel less lonely.

Shadan had informed her that, in preparation for the university entrance exams next year, his class was divided into two groups: a fast stream, with a few students likely to pass the exams, and a main stream for the others.

There were only two dozen of us in the fast group, selected from four classes of nearly two hundred students. It was an honor and I now get more glances from girls. I have to say I enjoy the attention. (Don't worry, sister. I am not dating, just as you told me.)

The thing is that the students from our group will have to pay more since we'll get more attention from our teachers. Yet this extra cost is nothing compared to the huge university fees. If I pass the exam, how can we afford the cost?

Good on you for getting a better job, Chouchou. This new restaurant sounds great! Do you get to eat fancy dishes such as sea cucumber or bird's nest soup? I imagine even the leftovers would be tasty. And do rich customers give you tips? Wasai, I've never heard of such a thing. (Then again, what do I know about things in the city.) How wonderful that the restaurant also pays you for extra hours! But please, my good sister, don't work too hard. You are so far away, all on your own. If you don't look after yourself, who will?

Her brother's kind words melted her heart. Of course, she would cover the extra costs. Each time she sent money home, she had the same uplifting feeling as when she donated money to a temple. Naturally, she was far more generous with the home donation.

Ba's vision of life was as short as that of a rat. If he had had his way, he would have taken Shadan out of the school, just as he had done to her. Foolish man!

Lotus tried to think how much taller the seventeen-year-old had grown in the past three years. Ever since the death of their mother, the boy had wanted desperately to grow up, to be in a position to protect his big sister. She recalled how one night, when Ba had returned home drunk again, he discovered there was no food left. Lotus, having recently been dragged out of school, said coldly: "Stay at home at dinnertime if you want food." Her enraged father started to hit her. Suddenly Shadan charged at Ba, a long broomstick in his hand. Ba stood there, stupefied, without resisting his son's beating. Since then, their father rarely hit his children, but only grew more distant from them while the siblings grew closer.

I must help my brother, Lotus told herself, to give him the great life his loud cry at birth had predicted.

Next July, Shadan would surely pass the university entrance exams. That would make him the first university student from Mulberry Gully. One summer, a neighbor's boy had been accepted to a professional school in Chengdu, their provincial capital. The village head organized and sent a procession, with trumpets, gongs, drums, and all, to the boy's family home to celebrate the news.

What would the celebration for a proper university student be like? Lotus wondered. And what would the long-tongued women in the village say when they'd learned that it was she who had paid for her brother's university education? Then she would once again command the sort of respect and admiration she had once enjoyed. In the wake of her mother's death, her fellow villagers had been so impressed by the way the young girl had shouldered responsibility for the family. When she took her little brother to his school in the village or when she weeded the cornfields, people would click their tongues in admiration. "What a good girl! Whoever becomes her husband will be a very lucky man." In fact, Lotus had become such a model that parents often said to their daughters: "Why can't you be more like Chouchou?"

After sorting out her brother, Lotus had a plan for herself, too. Having become accustomed to life in a city, she wouldn't want to return to her village. She would like to start a shop in Phoenix, the nearest town to Mulberry Gully, selling stylish dresses, skirts, and perhaps fashion accessories, all bought from Shenzhen.

Lotus liked to dream about the future. Bing had found out that tuition, plus the cost of books, administration fees, and so on would come up to 7,500 yuan a year. Then there were also living expenses. And four years of study. Her savings weren't enough yet to cover the total expenses, but they were certainly enough to get Shadan started on the golden path.

How good it would be to have a few rich clients, Lotus thought. The image of Funny Eye floated into her mind again. She had been half dreading and half longing that he would turn up unexpectedly, like last time. That she had enjoyed the night with him made her uneasy. Lotus hadn't experienced any sexual pleasure before entering the trade, and had learned most of what she knew about sex from working at Moon-flower. When she had first arrived at Moon's little empire, the boss ordered her to watch dozens of porn movies. She was fascinated, aroused even, but also repulsed by them, especially by oral sex scenes. When she timidly shared her thoughts with Moon, the boss said, with an arch smile: "I didn't ask you to watch those movies for nothing! You'd better learn to like to 'play the flute.' More clients are demanding it, because more Chinese men are watching porn."

Lotus sensed that there must be something amazing about making love with a man one liked. But being aroused in such a way by a client? Was it normal? Was it decent? Since the night with Funny Eye, she had caught herself replaying again and again in her mind the scene on that soft king-size bed, and the sensations he had stirred with his feather and the trembling between her legs. That was more than four months ago.

Lotus turned on her side. I am doing this job for the greater good, which should atone for some of the wrongs I've done, she reasoned with herself. Then again, you never really knew until you stood in front of the King of Hell, with his bloody red face and his fangs as long as chopsticks. He would reward the good people with fortunate future lives and send those who misbehaved to one of the eighteen hells. She had once seen sculptures in a temple in Phoenix, depicting scenes from hell, with gossips having their tongues cut off, thieves having their hands cut off, and adulterers getting grilled over a roaring fire. What was the treatment for a prostitute? What about a reformed one?

To expel these hellish scenes from her mind, she closed her eyes and decided to sleep.

———

A loud banging woke Lotus up. She rolled out of bed and opened the door. There stood Mimi. Her eyeliner was black and heavy around her red eyes, her hair messier than usual.

"*Tamade*, unlucky again . . ." Mimi began. "I just did the test!"

"Oh, no, Mimi!" Lotus covered her mouth with a hand. "You forgot your pills?"

"I guess so," Mimi mumbled.

Lotus leaned over and wiped a lipstick smudge off Mimi's lower lip with her thumb. "Use condoms, heavens above, Mimi! How many times have I told you?"

"Using condoms with my guy? Never!" Mimi's messy curls trembled as she shook her head. "He doesn't like them. Besides, it feels like fucking a client."

So many working girls had abortions; it almost seemed like a required credential. Two years ago, Xia had had one. Although Lotus hadn't experienced one herself, she had heard enough horror stories.

"How many have you had?" Lotus asked.

Mimi counted with her fingers. "Five, I think. Four by him." She glanced up at the portrait of Guanyin. "Let's talk outside."

They walked to the small yard through the back door. Lotus frowned as she spotted the other two women there. In the shade of a banyan tree, Little Jade was sitting on a low stool, playing cards on a piece of newspaper, to predict her fortune. Beside her, Xia was lying on a reclining bamboo chair, knitting, her face covered by cucumber slices.

Despite herself, Mimi cackled. "Sister Xia, you look so funny."

Xia gave them a sideways glance without disturbing a single slice. "My facial. Cucumber slices dipped in egg whites make your face nice and white."

"Sorry, sisters, I need to talk to Mimi privately," Lotus said.

A couple of cucumber slices slid off Xia's face as she sat up. She took a long look at the girls. "All right, then," Xia said, nodding knowingly. She removed the remaining slices from her face and popped them into her mouth. Turning to Little Jade, she said: "Come on, good girl. Let's play inside."

Little Jade picked up the cards. "In my old age, I'll have five grand-children."

"Good for you," Lotus said under her breath.

Little Jade had joined Moonflower Parlor a few months after Lotus, replacing a girl who had run away with a client. In the beginning, Lotus made an effort to be friendly, but the girl, upset and withdrawn at the time, didn't want to talk. Like a mother hen, Xia took Little Jade under her wing. Since then, two camps had formed: Lotus and Mimi versus Xia and Little Jade.

Lotus led Mimi to the chair and sat herself down on the stool. "What are you going to do?"

"What else? Get rid of it," she said, the thick wings of her nostrils flaring. "Lanzai . . ." She paused.

"Well?" Lotus asked, trying not to let her contempt for Mimi's boy-friend show on her face. She understood why some girls needed boyfriends. After so much false intimacy and so many fake smiles, one would naturally long for some genuine affection and someone who could hug you at the end of an exhausting day. Lotus wouldn't have minded having a man herself. Looking around, however, she discov-ered most of these "boyfriends" were either hooligans or pimps or use-less men like Lanzai who were only good at "eating soft rice," living off women.

"You know what he's like." Mimi sniffed loudly. "So, Sister Lotus, could you come with me tomorrow, too?"

"If I have to."

Mimi and Lotus had met nearly three years ago when they both had been street girls. Lotus had needed a friend, someone to fill the hole left by the death of her cousin. It was also safer to team up with another girl. Together, they hung out around the train station. Sometimes they ven-tured to Lichee Park in the city center. The popular park, dotted with exotic trees, a pond, and arched bridges, was also a pickup spot. While the city's senior citizens sang revolutionary songs in the shadow of a giant portrait of Deng Xiaoping near the main entrance, scantily dressed working girls offered their services for a fee. Their business was sometimes carried out in the shade of the low-hanging branches behind the pond in a densely wooded area.

Once in the early days, Lotus had been picked up by a thuggish-looking client who offered a high price. Mimi had a bad feeling about him. So she followed them into the bushes. After the business, the man refused to pay. When Lotus, outraged, grabbed his collar and wouldn't let go, the man started to hit her. Hiding behind a tree, Mimi had a flash of inspiration. "The police are coming!" she screamed. It scared the man away. When Mimi picked her up from the ground, Lotus burst into sobs in her friend's arms, her pride even more bruised than her body. After that, they were inseparable. When Lotus found work at the Moonflower Massage Parlor, she brought Mimi, too. It was much safer to work under the protective umbrella of a parlor.

"Also, Sister Lotus," Mimi asked, squinting one eye.

Lotus knew that Mimi always put on this weird expression when she felt uncomfortable. She sighed. "How much do you need?"

"Three hundred?"

Lotus didn't approve of the way Mimi borrowed money readily from people around her, especially Bing, but didn't always repay it. "Sure. But listen, Mimi: don't let Lanzai take all your money."

Just then, Xia returned. "Leave that dogshit boyfriend of yours, Mimi!" she said in her loud voice. "If you can't live without a man, then find a good one, half-brain!" Xia had obviously been eavesdropping.

Stung by Xia's harsh words, Mimi shot up, her red eyes turning into two flames. "Dog fart!" she spat. "I may be a half-brain, but at least I have my standards. I'd never blow the flute for any man!"

Xia made a dismissive noise. "We are all whores, aren't we? What-ever men want, as long as they pay."

"Calm your tits, both of you!" Lotus pushed Mimi away from Xia. "Come on. I'll get you the money."

"At least I have a man who loves me," Mimi said over her shoulder in a parting shot at Xia.

The word "love" bothered Lotus. Without saying anything, she dragged her friend back inside the parlor.

——————

At eleven o'clock sharp the next morning, Lotus stood outside Mimi's room, bearing a thermos of ginger tea with brown sugar, the best drink for a woman who has lost blood.

She tapped on the wooden door. "Mimi, it's me. Are you ready or not?"

"Oh, almost, Lotus," came Mimi's reply.

"Hurry up. I don't have all day!" She walked to the shadow of a chinaberry tree in front of the house and waited. Her gaze shifted left to the heavy brass lock blocking the way to Bing's room. Good for him that he had won a photography award. Lotus was glad she had made the effort to be friends with this gentleman. When the magazine had published his photo documentary, he brought a copy to her, smiling so broadly that his mouth split nearly to the ears. Lotus didn't really want to see her own pictures. Persuaded by Bing, however, she opened up the magazine. It had been her conscious decision to allow him to photograph her. But Lotus was nevertheless startled to see herself all over the glossy pages, especially in the photo of her on the bed. She looked haggard and sad. Do I always look so pathetic? The question crossed her mind. Gathering herself, Lotus mumbled congratulations and decided to push the whole matter out of her mind. Now with this success, would he pack up and leave? she wondered.

Ten minutes later, Mimi and Lanzai emerged from the house. Mimi wore a black polyester dress with white dots. Her eyes were a little swollen, but she seemed to be calm. The trio set off for a clinic on East Station Road.

Mimi leaned heavily on Lanzai, a stocky man in his early twenties with bearlike, thick arms. His hair, oiled and combed back, was so slick that a fly couldn't have landed on it. As usual, his tight black sleeveless T-shirt was rolled halfway up, revealing the dragon tattoo on his stomach. Lanzai, his nickname, meant Rotten Lad, a good-humored local slang term for a good-for-nothing man. No one knew his real name. A little more than two years ago, Mimi had met him at the roadside pool table in Miaocun. She fell hard for Lanzai's masculine looks.

Silly Mimi. Sometimes Lotus wondered why she had become good friends with such a thoughtless girl who always got herself into trouble. But then Mimi was also bitter-fated, which made Lotus feel both sympathetic and superior. And she enjoyed the position of bossing someone around.

The July sun radiated over their heads as they made their way down the street. In the unbearable heat, the public toilet by the gate of the school, which stood in the center of Miaocun, stank to the sky. Untroubled by the smell, half a dozen children were playing on top of the school's redbrick wall, on which a white-painted slogan read: "Uphold the Government's Policy of Nine-Year Compulsory Education."

Lotus sneered at it. That was only for city kids. The kids of migrant workers didn't count. Because the schools charged non-local residents extra fees, most migrant families couldn't afford to send their children to school. As their parents collected rubbish or sold vegetables in the market, the children would while away the day in the street, playing, fighting, or even stealing. Lotus felt sorry for them.

One night when Lotus was fifteen, Ba had said to her: "No need to go back to school next term. No money." Ba delivered the news in the same way he'd announce that he was popping out to have a drink with Little Red's father. She screamed and protested but Ba didn't even bother to respond. Plenty of poor families in the village had taken their girls out of school early. They saw no point in wasting money on a daughter's education, because girls had to be married off and "a married girl is like spilled water," as the saying went. Lotus had hoped that her excellent academic record and behavior would extend her schooling. Her pencil was homemade, simply the broken end of a pencil's lead discarded by her classmates, stabbed into a piece of soft wood. Did Ba ever notice that she needed money for stationery? Did he care? Grudgingly, Lotus spent long hours tilling the land, plotting ways to get out of the village.

The pain of having her education cut short had never faded. It hurt now, as Lotus watched the street kids playing.

"Sister Lotus, where are you going?" a boy of about eleven shouted from the top of the wall.

Lotus glanced at Mimi and replied vaguely: "We're going out, Big Head."

The boy got his nickname because his egg-shaped head looked too large for his thin body. He was one of the few friends Lotus had in Miaocun. Unlike most of the street kids, he was from a poor local Hakka family.

Big Head sprang off the wall, which was twice as tall as he was, and started to follow them, tugging at his oversized shorts. "Could you take us with you?" he asked hopefully. His younger brother Laoer, "Number Two," joined in.

Mimi tried to shush them, but the boys persisted.

"Sister Lotus, when will you have time to read us a few stories?" Big Head begged with wide eyes.

Lotus always found it hard to say no to those big shining eyes; they reminded her of her brother's. "Not today, but soon. Okay? Here are some coins, now go. Be good boys."

"*Wasai,* go!" The boys cheered and dashed toward the village square to Cripple Kong's grocery.

"Lotus, you've become friends with your number one enemy," Mimi said. "Why bother?"

When Lotus had first settled in the village, she rented a room in a new apartment building across the street from Big Head's courtyard house. Back then, the very sight of that big head would drain the color from her face. The energetic boy and his brother would mimic chickens, flapping their arms and laughing their teeth out, whenever they saw a *ji*. Sometimes Lotus wished she could slap his big head, but she couldn't afford to upset the locals. She relied on them to tip her off ahead of an official inspection or police raid.

In time, Lotus had won over Big Head by sewing up his torn shorts, teaching him a few basic characters, and helping him cook: on the days his parents, who made a living selling vegetables at the market, forgot to leave any lunch, the boy had to prepare meals for his two younger siblings. In turn, he taught Lotus some of the Hakka dialect, which proved to be useful for talking with local clients. More important, she improved her relationship with his family and the other neighbors.

"I like to teach them a few characters," Lotus explained to Mimi. "It somehow cheers me up. Why not? These days, there are not that many things that make me feel good about myself."

Mimi glanced at Lotus and clung closer to her boyfriend.

"Reputable Doctor Zhang, Schooled in Traditional Chinese and Western Medicine," read a black wooden sign above the glass front of a clinic, a one-story structure encased in white ceramic tiles, like any other shop front at the far end of East Station Road. The smaller print stated that the establishment specialized in gynecology, obstetrics, and hymen restructuring.

Inside the clinic, the sharp tang of disinfectant filled the cool air. To the left side of the square room, a middle-aged woman in a white coat sat behind a desk, doing paperwork. Her hair was covered in a net, making her narrow face look even smaller. Lotus wasn't sure if she was a doctor or nurse. Behind her, through half-drawn plastic curtains, she could see a full-figured young mother sitting on a chair, breast-feeding a baby. On a long wooden bench set against the wall, a couple in their late twenties were talking intimately between themselves.

"What's the problem?" demanded the woman in the white coat.

Mimi stared at the baby, who was making faint noises of satisfaction. Beside her, Lanzai looked at himself admiringly in the mirror above the bench.

Lotus threw a disgusted look at him and then led Mimi to a stool in front of White Coat.

"I need an abortion," said Mimi, her voice flat.

White Coat produced a patient record. "Fill out the form, then sit and wait for your turn," she said, pointing at the long bench.

The three sat down, next to the couple. Lotus started to fill out the form for Mimi. She put down "Li Mimi" as the name, "19" as the age, and "service" as the profession.

"I'm scared," said the young woman on the bench, her head turning toward the closed operation room.

Her man wrapped an arm around her and said lovingly: "Don't worry, Little Heart."

Sandwiched between the two couples, Lotus felt a little uncomfortable. She looked ahead. On the wall, beside a medical certificate, a graphic poster displayed vaginas and penises that had been ravaged by syphilis, gonorrhea, and other sexually transmitted diseases, all red and close-up. She had seen the poster before, at the drugstores dotted along the street, but she was nevertheless disgusted by its gruesomeness at close range.

Lotus thought about her first hand job, at a hotel room. She had just started at Moonflower. Sitting on the edge of the bed, a middle-aged businessman with pathetically thin legs and a potbelly had placed her hand on his erection. The brutal afternoon sun streamed in through a gap in the curtains. By then she had had a man's cock go in and out of her countless times, but she had never really looked at one in the bright daylight. It was red and shining, especially its turtle head. Her whole body started to shake. After five minutes, which seemed like an eternity for Lotus, the client gave up. "You'll get used to it," he said good-naturedly. He then finished the job himself.

That client had been right. Before long, Lotus had gotten used to "shooting down the plane" and much, much more.

A shrill scream erupted from the operation room, which made everyone turn their heads.

Mimi sat up, as if waking from a nightmare. "I'm going home!"

"Come on, honey," said Lanzai.

"I want a daughter, so I'll always have someone to be with me," Mimi declared.

Lotus shook Mimi's arm. "For Buddha's sake, Mimi! Having a baby is a big deal."

"I know. But I may never be able to get pregnant again," Mimi said, spitting the words out. "Don't you want a baby, Sister Lotus?"

"Yes, one day, with a worthy man."

"You are young and beautiful now, Mimi," Lanzai chimed in. "But if you start to have babies, you will soon get fat and ugly. Besides, we have no money."

"Money, money! Why can't you work like a man?" Mimi retorted.

Lanzai jumped to his feet. "Okay, you choose. Either it goes or I go."

Mimi shook. Big tears streamed down her face. She started to hit him with her fists. "I hate you. Hate you!"

White Coat raised her voice: "Quiet or get out!"

Mimi's drumming slowly lost its intensity and she collapsed on Lanzai's chest, whimpering.

Soon enough, it was Mimi's turn. Lotus held Mimi and brought her to the operating table. Beside the table on a white enamel tray, steel instruments glimmered like ice.

Returning to the waiting room, Lotus found the young couple had gone. So had Lanzai.

Lotus lowered herself onto the bench. As Mimi's painful cries grated her ears, she prayed for her friend, twisting the bracelet beads on her wrist faster and faster. Would Mimi ever become a mother? she wondered. Could a *ji* ever return to a normal life?

The cloud of doubt wrapped around Lotus as she sat opposite the gruesome poster.

CHAPTER 6

藕断丝连

The Lotus Root Snaps, but Its Fibers Stay Joined

In the moonlight, the pair of stone lions guarding the Beijing Bamboo Hotel seemed to grin at Bing as he stepped out of a taxi. It had been by a stroke of luck, years ago, that he had discovered this courtyard lodging where the shadows of tall bamboo danced in the spacious central yard. On that Sunday afternoon, with his daughter perched on the back of his bicycle, he was cycling around the maze of *hutong*s to photograph and document the carved stone blocks that stood on either side of the front doors of traditional houses. The designs on the stones, which indicated the status and wealth of the residence owners, had always intrigued him. He loved to explore the capital with his daughter. She laughed easily back then, and was full of childish questions. When she was tired, she would rest her head against him as they rode along, her breath warming his back.

When he was invited up to Beijing to receive his photography award, Bing had requested that the organizers put him up at this unusual hotel.

Now the stone lions had grown back their missing paws and the red paint glowed on the double wooden doors. Yet once inside the reception's arched moon gate, the establishment retained its charm.

Bing tottered toward his room, letting out hiccups along the way. He had just spent his last night in town with Yuejin, his old classmate from Tsinghua and now a high-flying official with the government. Yuejin was one of the few Beijing friends he had left. Bing's failed business and his divorce had led to a dramatic decrease in the number of his friends. His photo project had raised more than a few eyebrows and sparked unsavory rumors about his personal life.

In his room, Bing ran a hot bath. What a luxury! In Miaocun, there wasn't even a proper shower in the house. As he sank deep in the tub, his body relaxed and thoughts flooded his mind.

If his prayers at Rooster Crowing Temple had been answered, it had taken some time to take effect. After sending off his photos to *Photography* by express delivery, he spent three anxious months waiting for a reply. Every day he looked forward to the postman's arrival, but every day he brought nothing. Just as Bing was about to give up hope, he received an email from an editor, asking him to clarify some photo captions. Three weeks later, his photos prominently emerged in the publication.

Shortly afterward, he won "Photographer of the Year," a competition sponsored by *Photography* and Kodak. It wasn't that prestigious an award, but an award nevertheless. While Bing was in the capital for the ceremony, Yuejin had drummed up a massive amount of publicity for him. After an initial polite refusal, Bing played along. Journalists from newspapers, magazines, radio, and TV shows clamored to interview him. He was now on the receiving end of the cameras' clicks and flashes. During his fortnight in Beijing, he often felt he was floating up in the sky.

He must have dozed off in the tub. He awoke to the sound of the doorbell. When no apologetic chambermaid's voice followed, he knew it wasn't room service. Another prostitute? Back on his first night in the hotel, he had been jostled awake by a call propositioning him. With tip-offs from the hotel receptionist or security guards, local *ji* targeted single male guests.

"Are you alone, boss?" a young woman had said on the line, her voice thick with smoke and sex.

"Please, I just want to sleep," Bing had said.

"I can make you sleep like a dream."

"Leave me alone, please."

"Come on, baby. I know you want it. Only a hundred yuan."

"Get lost," he had snapped. He had been annoyed with her and annoyed with himself for bothering to talk to her. "The last thing I want is a cheap *ji* like you!" He had slammed the phone down. Lying back in bed, he had felt embarrassed that he had lost his temper at a working girl.

Who could it be this time? Bing wondered as he climbed out of the tub. Probably a ding-dong girl, a prostitute who frequented hotels and delivered the goods right to your door. They sometimes flashed their bare breasts to persuade hesitant buyers.

"Who is it?" he asked as he wrapped a towel around his waist.

No answer but another ringing of the doorbell. He went to the door and opened it a crack.

No bare breasts but a familiar, made-up face.

"Mei!"

"Not welcome?" Mei raised one eyebrow, groomed to the shape of a willow leaf. She wore a low-cut floral-patterned Laura Ashley dress, which emphasized her long, elegant neck. He used to refer to it fondly as her swan neck.

"Of course you are. Just let me get dressed first."

Bing was about to shut the door, but his ex-wife pushed it open. "It's nothing that I haven't seen before," she said, and glided into the room.

Bing retreated to the bathroom to get dressed. When he reemerged, he saw Mei looking at his gold-plated award on the bedside table.

"You know, I was a little surprised to have won it," he said.

"Why?"

"Well, Mr. Liao, the editor from the magazine, said I was lucky because the foreign judges from Kodak didn't care about the sensitivity of this issue inside China."

"One makes one's own luck, I believe."

Bing smiled broadly at her remark. The overhead fluorescent light illuminated the fine fish-tail wrinkles around her eyes. Still, no one would guess that she was actually three years older than Bing. She had gained back the weight she had lost during the divorce and her waistline had noticeably thickened. Yet she looked as elegant as she always did.

Aware of the messiness of the room, he started to pick up his clothes from the armchair. After their divorce, he had forsaken Mei's training in tidiness.

"Sit down, please." He gestured toward the now empty armchair. "Why didn't you call?"

On his first Sunday back in Beijing, they had taken their eleven-year-old daughter to Beihai Park, the first time the family had been together since the divorce two years previously. It was a sunny afternoon and crepe myrtle blossoms weighed down the branches. As they strolled by the lake dotted with water lilies, Little Li asked to be lifted up, like she used to when she was a small child. Her parents struggled, weakened by their own laughter. When they parted later that day, Mei had said that they should have more outings together while Bing was in Beijing, and she said that she would call.

"I thought it would be better to meet in person." She produced a measured smile, which showed her teeth but not too much of them. "Little Li is still raving about the outing."

"I loved every minute of it myself," Bing mused.

Mei settled into the armchair. "First of all, thank you so kindly for sending us the money," she began.

"That's the least I could do." One week after their park outing, when Bing had heard nothing from Mei, he decided to wire half of his award money of fifty thousand yuan to her, with a note: "With all my love."

"A cup of tea? The hotel only has jasmine tea," Bing offered. He knew Mei cared little for blossom tea, claiming that the flowers were there to cover up the poor taste. Every spring, she would get friends to buy freshly picked young tea leaves from the lower Yangtze region, and then she'd store them in the freezer to preserve moisture.

"That would be lovely."

Bing scooped tea leaves mixed with dried jasmine petals from a tin into two cups and added hot water from a thermos provided by the hotel.

"Hmm, smells nice." Mei sipped her tea, surveying the room. "We don't need such bright light, do we, darling?"

Darling? She had started to call him that after the historic night of their first bedding together. Bing had never felt comfortable saying "darling" in English, which, in his northern accent, always came out sounding like *da ling*, or "big general" in Chinese—an appropriate term but lacking the intended intimacy.

Bing switched off the overhead lights and turned on the soft lamps on the wall, then sat down in the other armchair across the small table from her.

Mei scooped a bottle of champagne out of her large Prada bag. "Now, let's celebrate. Have you got glasses?"

Bing went to the bathroom and brought back two tumblers.

"Not quite classy, but they'll do," said Mei with a smile. She undid the wire, popped the cork, and poured the champagne into the glass in Bing's hand. Bubbles instantly overflowed the edge and a few drops fell onto his hand.

Mei leaned over and wiped up the drops with a finger, which she then popped into her mouth.

The skin tightened on the back of Bing's hand.

"Delicious," she purred. Her finger rested on her lips, painted rose red today, matching the flowers on her dress. She poured a glass of champagne for herself and raised her glass. "Cheers!"

"Cheers!" They clinked the edges of their glasses. Bing didn't like the fancy drink even when he didn't have a bellyful of beer, but he didn't want to dampen her spirits. He took a small sip.

During their afternoon in the park, Bing had noticed signs of the ice thawing between them. He wondered what had made his ex-wife soften her attitude toward him. For two years after the finalization of their divorce, he and Mei had barely spoken.

The scene at a Beijing courtroom invaded his mind. To sign the papers officially terminating their ten years of marriage, Mei had turned up elegantly dressed in a lilac Chanel suit. Though originally well tailored, it looked loose on her that day. And her back was more erect than usual. When she took off her dark glasses to sign the paper, Bing noticed that her eyes were red. Weighed down by a biting sense of guilt and humiliation, Bing could hardly stand straight. He tried to make eye contact with her, but she turned and marched out of the courtroom, never looking at him once, as if he were invisible. He had never felt so small and sad.

Mei's voice brought Bing back to the room. "Many congratulations!" she gushed, her face wreathed in smiles.

His heart glowed with a deep satisfaction. "Well done yourself. You've become the deputy head of your school, so I hear."

"That's nothing compared to your achievement," Mei said. She raised her glass to take another sip, her little finger curled elegantly. "What a creative man you are! I always said you had a 'magic talent for releasing flowers under your pen.' You know how much I cherish the poems you wrote to me."

The verses had come straight from his heart. Mei, short for Chunmei, Spring Rose, was the first woman he had ever slept with. They had been introduced in 1987 by an old colleague of Bing's, who could not bear to see people turn into "old unmarried youth." Bing was twenty-six, and still a virgin, which wasn't very unusual for a man of his generation back then.

Bing had immediately taken to Mei, a middle school English teacher, when they met at Old Zhao's cramped apartment inside the soap factory's run-down residential compound. In her well-tailored silk dress, heels, and pearl necklace, Mei was like a phoenix that had mistakenly landed in a poultry farm.

For their first proper date, Mei had chosen a western restaurant in Beijing. The candles, fresh roses, white tablecloths, and live piano music elevated Bing to unfamiliar territory. Mei had to show him how to cut his steak with a knife and fork. As the evening went on, Bing, a ferocious reader, grew more at ease as they talked about literature. He didn't care for the foreign wine but was drunk on the English teacher's sophistication and charm. She seemed so self-assured, so certain about who she was and what she wanted from life.

When Bing returned to his dormitory, he composed his first love poems to her. He described her waist as slender as a willow and her temperament as gentle as a spring rose. His love-letter offensive—what her mother called "sugar-coated bullets"—worked.

One night, four months into their courtship, Bing invited Mei to his empty dormitory room. His best friend, Yuejin, had kindly dragged Bing's other two roommates out to the cinema. It was a balmy day in early May. The white fluff from the poplar trees floated in the air like spring snow. As Bing lay in his bunk bed, with Mei in his arms, his hand went under her shirt to play with the strap of her bra. The world of women had, until that point, remained a mystery to him. Then his hand inched downward. She stopped him only to ask him to swear he would never betray her, which he dutifully promised. To his disappointment, he discovered she wasn't a virgin. But he decided not to hold this against her. She was already too good for him.

Now his ex-wife was smiling at him almost coquettishly.

Bing changed the subject. "Lili is doing well at school, isn't she?" He paused to sip the drink he didn't care for. He had wanted to raise the possibility of visiting his daughter more frequently. But he hated confrontation, especially confrontation with his combative ex-wife.

"Yes, she is. I'm really sorry that you haven't seen that much of her. Well, Mother felt you were a bad influence, living with hordes of whores and all that."

Mei had touched a sore point. Bing went silent.

She ranted on about her mother, or the Dowager, as he secretly used to call her. "You know Mother is a bit overbearing. You can't believe how she has been nagging me to find a new husband."

Bing gazed at his ex-wife. Now she looked her age, if not more.

Mei abruptly stopped talking. There was a long pause. "You resented me for pushing you into business, didn't you?" she asked.

"No, not really."

"You know why I did it."

"For our daughter, I know," Bing said, feeling a sense of déjà vu. The couple had argued over their daughter's education before. Mei had insisted, despite their modest income, on sending Little Li to an expensive private school.

"I know that life has been hard for you," she said, and her voice was unusually soft.

"It can't be easy, your life. All on your own," he replied with equal gentleness.

"To tell you the truth, darling, 'having sailed the ocean, how can one be content with a little stream?'" Back in their courting days, they used to enjoy competing with each other in their use of idioms and sayings. Today her words seemed to have touched Bing as well as Mei herself. She began to tear up, and covered her face with her hands.

"Do you hate me?"

"Hate you? No, Mei. Never!" He got up, inched toward her, and rested a hand on her shoulder.

Mei composed herself. "Thank you for sending the magazine. I was so moved," Mei said. "Eye-opening images. I had no idea about the lives of these, er, these girls."

"My pleasure." A smile dawned on Bing's face. He wasn't entirely sure why he had wanted to trumpet his achievement in front of his ex-wife. To share his glory with her? To score points? She had always poured cold water on his childlike enthusiasm for photography, arguing that it would never lead to anything.

Still sitting in the armchair, Mei pressed her head against his stomach. "*Ai,* why can't everything just return to normal?"

Bing didn't know what to say. He caressed Mei's short hair.

"Why have you stayed so distant from us these past years?" She sounded more sad than bitter.

Bing's hands stopped. "I thought you wanted me to stay away."

Mei's head swayed back and forth. "I was hurt and angry. That woman . . . but I loved you." She straightened herself, took off her glasses, and wiped them with a handkerchief.

"I'm so very sorry," Bing murmured. He was starting to feel awkward, standing in front of her like this, but he needed to find the right moment to pull away.

"I'm sorry, too," Mei said, looking up at him with her sad eyes. "I do blame myself, too, for what happened. I wish I hadn't been so demanding."

Mei apologizing? Bing was surprised and touched by this rare show of vulnerability.

She started to cry again. Bing's heart had never been tear-proof. In the past, her tears had ended many of their disputes—on the rare occasions when he had dared to allow disagreements to escalate into disputes. Bing embraced her tenderly.

Mei stood up and wrapped her arms tightly around his waist, her wet face touching his, her warm breath and alluring fragrance enveloping him. He began gently stroking her back.

"I've been missing you terribly," Mei whispered. Before long, her hand found its way under his T-shirt.

"Have you?" Bing froze for a moment but didn't object. He felt her hand move across his back, cool on his bare skin. It felt good. How could dry wood resist a spark? When Mei sought his mouth, kissing him with the eagerness of a thirsty woman, he kissed her back.

She tasted of champagne. Bing couldn't remember the last time they had kissed so passionately. Toward the end of their marriage, they didn't seem to kiss that much at all.

They fell onto his bed. Mei slid off her dress. Bing kissed her long neck and then buried his head in her breasts.

Mei unfastened his trousers, then lay back on the bed, her legs wide open. "Now," she said, pulling him toward her.

Bing entered her. Mei moaned.

In the dim wall light, Bing looked down at this naked woman, his ex-wife. She had often been the subject of his fantasies, especially in the early days after his divorce. It felt surreal that he was actually making love to her.

Under him, Mei was grinding more aggressively than he could ever remember, her pelvic bones digging into his body.

"Wait," he pleaded. "Wait."

But the excitement was too much. He came inside her.

After Mei went into the bathroom, Bing sat up on the edge of the bed. His brain seemed to be on pause. He was still staring blankly in front of him when Mei returned. His eyes followed his ex-wife as she switched on the main light and searched for her scattered clothes. She darted a look at him, which somehow brought back his senses. He held his head with both hands, not sure whether he was blocking out the light or covering up his own shame.

Mei had never demonstrated much enthusiasm for sex, which she described dryly as "the bedroom business." Once—it must have been halfway through their married life—right in the middle of the "business," his wife had suddenly muttered: "Dammit! I almost forgot!" As soon as they were done, she jumped off the bed and dug out her ID card from a cabinet. "I need this for Lili's kindergarten transfer," she said, shaking the ID card.

"Are you all right?" Mei asked.

Bing looked up abruptly. "I'm sorry, Mei," he began. During their marriage he had learned that when in doubt, he should apologize. It would never go wrong.

"It's all right," she replied, granting him a gracious smile.

He put his shorts and T-shirt back on. "I've been living like a monk for too long, you know."

Mei raised a well-groomed eyebrow. "Monk? You haven't slept with any women since our divorce?"

"I haven't."

Mei took a good look at him. After she got dressed, she sat back in the armchair, fully poised. "I've been thinking that things would have been different if we hadn't lived with my parents all that time."

"Possibly, quite possibly, Mei," Bing said as he came over and lowered himself into his chair.

After their wedding, they had moved in with his in-laws in a three-room place inside a courtyard house in a *hutong* just north of the Forbidden City. The stay was meant to be temporary, but as his state-owned factory continued to churn out soap no one wanted, they stayed on.

No doubt things would have been easier if they had had their own place, free from his mother-in-law's suffocating interest in their lives. But how much easier? After their wedding, Mei's spring rose gentleness slowly withered. She was a very good wife, to be fair. She organized their lives efficiently to a degree that both shamed and amazed him. He tried hard to be a good husband by taking up most of the house chores—cleaning, caring for their daughter, and shopping in the market, a grocery list from Mei in hand. But that wasn't enough. Mei also wanted him to achieve something remarkable, to rise up the management ranks at his factory or to become a rich entrepreneur or a best-selling writer. Bing knew that Mei was under pressure to push him to be successful and to show her mother that he was a worthy choice. Very driven herself, Mei took evening classes to get certified as a translator and moonlighted as a freelance interpreter. Bing would have liked to write something creative, but nothing would come, even when he could snatch a quiet moment in the evening, after washing up. It pained him. He conjured up ideas to make something out of his life but he lacked the will, energy, and time to execute them. After his daughter came along, she made more demands on his time, but also eased the pain in his soul. Meanwhile his wife complained ever more bitterly about him, calling him "*meichuxi*" and "a pile of mud that will never be turned into gold."

Bing wondered what Mei thought of him now.

"Look, to be honest, darling, the reason I came here tonight was to try to take you home with me," she said with a matter-of-fact calmness, as if she were certain of the outcome.

Bing got up from his chair. "I need a beer," he declared. He went to the minibar, took out a cold one, opened it, and glugged directly from the bottle. When it occurred to him that Mei wouldn't approve of such "buffalo style" drinking, he slowly moved the bottle away from his mouth.

"I need time to think about this," he said at last.

Mei nodded, her long fingers tapping on the table. "Now, how about your future. A stable job, perhaps in Beijing?"

"I am not sure yet." Bing drained his beer. From the corner of his eyes, he noticed that she looked surprised and agitated.

He took refuge in silence; it felt just like the old days under the Dowager's roof.

"What is keeping you down there? Is there a woman?" Words fired out of Mei's mouth like clips of ammunition. She rose, looked around the room, and seated herself again. Her lips disappeared into a thinner line. "Why are you so obsessed with those whores? What did that Pearl woman do to you?"

Pearl. The fox fairy. A fading dream.

"Please, Mei. There is no point in dragging us into the murky water of the past."

She took a sip of her tea, which must have gone cold by now. "I need to know so we can put it behind us and look to the future."

Bing fixed his eyes on the woman who was once the center of his universe. His heart was heavy with mixed emotions; regret, guilt, resentment, pity for her suffering, and above all an unbearable sadness. He got on his feet and walked over to the window. Feeling oppressed by the atmosphere in the room, he pulled the curtain and looked out into the yard. In the darkness, bamboo leaves shivered in the gathering wind.

Bing's words bubbled up in his throat. "I'm terribly sorry for what I've done, Mei. But by the time the thing with Pearl happened, you and I had drifted apart."

"My God, I haven't heard this before!" Mei snapped, her voice climbing to a higher pitch. To give her voice more authority in the classroom, she had deliberately trained herself to lower it. When she became angry, it slipped into shrillness. "Drift apart? It was you who drifted into that whore's arms. You're just trying to find excuses for yourself," she said, jabbing an accusing finger at him.

"Please, Mei." Bing turned around and saw that Mei's face was taut with anger and pain. "It's late. You need to rest and I need to pack."

A silence fell heavily between them.

"I . . . I thought," she stammered. "I thought you'd want to be a family again."

"Not really," Bing said in a barely audible voice.

Mei began to gather up her belongings. "Sure, let's not get stuck in the past. Let's look forward." She made an effort to sound lighthearted.

"Yes, let's look forward." Bing echoed her words without knowing exactly what they implied.

She smiled with a nod and slowly walked toward the door, her shoulders slumping slightly.

He followed her.

At the door, Mei stood face-to-face with him. "We've gone through plenty of wind and rain together," she said in a quavering voice. "That's a great deal to throw away. Think about it, please, for the sake of our family."

A lump rose in Bing's throat as he watched his ex-wife struggling to keep her dignity and conceal her disappointment. Fighting back his own tears, he said: "I will. You take care, Mei."

The rest of the night was depressingly quiet. For hours, Bing flopped in the armchair, listening to the rustling of bamboo leaves. But nothing could soothe his mind, now filled by thorny questions.

How did I end up sleeping with my ex-wife? he kept asking himself. Why? To regain the lost ground from Mei? To assert a new sense of his own power? Or was it purely sexual hunger?

Bing had never expected that Mei would want to repair their shattered marriage.

He had indeed resented his wife for pushing him "into the sea of business"—a popular expression at the time referring to people leaving a stable job and venturing into the business world—even though he understood that she was just trying to hoist him up in life, doing what

a good Chinese wife should do. Looking back, that move was the starting point of their alienation.

Almost from the start of their married life, Mei used to report, with
envious enthusiasm, tales of success of people around them, in particular a relative named Wang Zhigang. The humble salesman with a ready
smile had profited lucratively from under-the-table kickbacks. Wang
was among the first who had flocked to Shenzhen after Deng Xiaoping
had made his famous "Southern Tour" to the city back in 1992, in a bid
to revive the economic reforms that had stalled in the wake of the government's brutal crackdown on the democratic movement in 1989.

Increasingly Deng's maxim "To get rich is glorious" had become a
new national mantra. But Bing, who usually found it difficult to say no,
especially to his willful wife, had launched a quiet war of resistance with
Mei until Wang Zhigang proposed setting up a company together in
early 1993 to produce scented bar soap. Some state-owned enterprise
had gone bankrupt, and with his connections at the city's State Asset
Management Bureau, Wang could buy the factory, with its machines
and buildings, for the ridiculously low price of one hundred thousand
yuan. "Once-in-a-lifetime opportunity!" Wang had enthused. During
China's transformation from a planned economy to a market economy,
plenty of state property had slipped, through murky gray channels, into
the hands of individuals with power and connections. Bing wouldn't
dream of being part of this sly game. Mei, however, issued an ultimatum
to her husband: embrace Wang's proposal or divorce her. Bing surren-
dered.

With the four hundred thousand yuan the family had struggled to
pool together, he followed Wang down south.

A giant building site. That was Bing's first impression of Shenzhen.
There was dust everywhere, dancing in the hot, humid air, dressing the
city in a hazy veil. And everywhere the noise of construction grated
on the ear. New companies sprang up daily, like mushrooms after
spring rain.

Bing was in charge of production and Wang handled marketing and everything else. In his early thirties, Wang had a stammer, potentially a fatal flaw in a salesman. Somehow he managed to compensate for his lack of eloquence with his disarming charm. Wang dealt with all the paperwork efficiently, soon obtaining the business license, and operations started.

Even with cheap labor and the tax rebates of the Special Economic Zone, the company didn't do well at first. International brands such as Safeguard, Hazeline, and Lux had already dominated the middle-range and luxury markets.

After one fiscal year, when Bing checked the accounts—one for official inspection and the other for private use—he was horrified at the large amounts spent on banquets and bribes for buyers, sales agents, and government officials.

"But this is just the way it works in China," Wang argued.

Wang also checked the consolidated account and decided that they needed a novelty product, like a fat-reducing seaweed soap. Seaweed had a reputation as a weight-loss product, containing naturally nutritious and fat-emulsifying properties, he claimed. There were heaps of fat men and women around, all of whom were too busy making money to do any exercise. They were all looking for a way to magically solve their weight problems.

Bing knew that soap made from deep-water seaweed could indeed lead to healthier and softer skin, but he pointed out that weight-loss effects were a stretch. While he hesitated, his partner threatened to pull out of his share.

Bing couldn't return to Beijing empty-handed. He consulted Mei, as he always did on important matters. She instructed him to go ahead and keep his doubts to himself. He sighed. Looking around, the shelves of China's shops were filled with pirated goods, fake spirits made from industrial alcohol, edible oils extracted from gutters, and milk mixed with poisonous chemicals. Seaweed soap would be a good beauty product, to say the least.

Thus, Slim and Fragrant soap was born. An expensive marketing campaign followed, using real-life examples to demonstrate how people had magically shrunk—with the help of Photoshop—after rubbing themselves with the seaweed soap.

Slim and Fragrant spread far and wide across the four oceans and brought in fat profits.

Would he still have been in business if he had just stuck to seaweed soap? Bing sank deeper into the armchair. It was hard to say. Life's journey was always packed with unexpected twists and turns. Realizing the dawn was creeping in, he decided to sleep. As he climbed into bed, he mused on the seemingly insignificant events that ultimately altered the direction of his life. And one of them was meeting Pearl.

CHAPTER 7

矮子里拔将军

Choose a General from Among the Dwarfs

Aware that she was very late for work, Lotus quickened her pace as soon as she spotted her boss standing in front of Moonflower.

Moon laughed her coarse laugh as she watched Lotus walk over. "*Aiyah*, look, look. Our star's back," called out the owner of the parlor, throwing a jewelry-laden arm up in the air. She stood elegantly with Xia and Little Jade on either side of her, her colorful pleated skirt flapping in the wind like a magnificent peacock's tail.

"Star? What do you mean?" Lotus asked, trying to catch her breath. She gazed at her boss, whose big eyes with their double-folded eyelids had come courtesy of a cosmetic surgeon. The effect lent her a permanently shocked look. Lotus was afraid to meet those eyes, especially when they were angry.

Moon ignored the question. "Did you let anyone know that you might be late?"

Lotus turned to Xia hopefully, but the normally talkative woman stayed silent, looking the other way. The tapping of her feet against the concrete ground made a nerve-racking noise.

Moon placed a sandaled foot on Xia's thin calf. "Stop being such a peasant."

Xia stuck out her tongue and stopped shaking her legs.

The boss referred to her charges collectively as peasants, even though she hailed from a small provincial town herself. But her curvy body and smooth tongue had pulled her up from a mere good-time girl to mama-san of a song-and-dance hall—these places were also commonly fronts for brothels—and then to the owner of a massage parlor. Lotus feared and envied her boss in equal measure. Moon would always find fault with the girls, criticizing them and bossing them around as if she found pleasure in doing so. On the other hand, Moon wasn't as harsh as her language suggested. In the hair salon next door, the girls had to work from ten in the morning until three the next morning, whether they had clients or not.

"Sorry, boss. I—"

Moon cut her short. "You've become such a star, Lotus, getting pictures published in a magazine and attracting admirers." Blowing smoke through the side of her mouth, she flicked the ash off her slim cigarette. Her fingernails were varnished, but with clear polish, to distinguish herself from the common flock of *ji*.

Lotus could feel her face burning. "Boss, sorry I'm late," she said humbly. "I took Mimi to a clinic today. Well, you know her problem."

Having taken Mimi home, Lotus had been obligated to stay since Lanzai had simply disappeared. If Mimi hadn't begged her to stay, she would have felt offended: she secretly loved the sense of being needed. Feeling physically and emotionally drained, she rested beside her friend and fell asleep. When she woke up, the day had gone.

The smile evaporated from Moon's lips while the smoke lingered. "Tell your half-brain friend: if she ever dares to get her belly big again, she'll be a fried squid!"

"Fried squid": what an ugly phrase, Lotus thought. In her factory days, the bosses had often used this expression when they threatened to fire a worker. She had only understood the meaning after she saw one of the sacked girls leaving the dormitory with her tightly rolled bedding looking like squid tentacles curling up in a hot wok.

"Mimi is a little careless sometimes. But she does attract a lot of business," said Lotus.

Moon's lips curled upward. "Sure, with '*boba*' tits like hers." As she talked, Moon started to massage her own large breasts, a habit of hers. In the beginning, Lotus had thought it was rather strange. Then Xia said that Moon had gotten implants. Lotus wasn't sure she believed Xia until she saw Moon's breasts in a changing room during a beach party, when they were celebrating the boss's birthday: one of her nipples pointed sideways. Moon must have gone to a back-alley clinic in her early days, before she had fattened her wallet enough to afford a decent place.

"Still, Mimi is probably not as popular as you are," Moon said as she stroked Lotus's face with a soft, damp hand.

Moon often fussed about their appearance, straightening their dresses and even putting on makeup for them. The other girls didn't seem to mind the hands-on approach of their boss, but Lotus did. She edged away from Moon's hand.

The boss pretended not to notice. "This afternoon, during your absence, a man with a thin mustache came to look for you."

Lotus knew it must be Jiabao—Family Treasure. He was a regular client of hers and a fellow Sichuanese.

Moon tossed her cigarette onto the street. "Your mustache man said he'd come back later as he has got some news for you." She looked at Lotus expectantly.

The younger woman simply nodded and wondered if Family Treasure was going to offer her the position of *ernai*—his second wife.

The boss seemed to be reading her mind. "Let me tell you something, young lady," Moon said, jabbing a ringed finger. As always, she enjoyed snatching any opportunity to lecture her girls. "Being tied down to one man may not be the best option for a *ji*. If I were you, Lotus, I would focus my energy on the big fish like Mr. Gao. You have no idea how loaded he is. I heard he isn't happy at all with his current girlfriend."

"That sounds like a big delicious fish," Xia sneered.

Lotus shot a fierce look at Xia, checking if the woman was mocking her. Then she said to her boss: "I don't have Mr. Gao's number." Clients like Funny Eye, with money or power, rarely bothered to leave behind their numbers.

"I'll see what I can do," Moon said.

Lotus expressed thanks and went inside. In the bathroom, as she stood under the hot shower, she wondered what it would be like to have a rich man as a regular or even as a patron. No, no. She splashed some hot water onto her face and scolded herself. "Don't be the 'ugly toad that dreams of eating swan's meat.'"

If she did, she wasn't the only working girl to do so. All of them loved to circulate fairy tales, of how a Hong Kong businessman married his *ernai* or how a senior government official bought a fancy apartment for his prostitute-turned-mistress. Lotus had slowly learned to be cautious with her imagination. Family Treasure would be more realistic.

Thinking that he might return at any minute, Lotus finished her shower. On the back of the wooden door, two rows of pillow-sized towels hung neatly on two racks. She picked her white face towel from the top row to dry her face and top. Then she snatched Xia's blue face towel and used it on the lower part of her body. "You old hag!" she muttered to herself as she rubbed. "Why couldn't you put in a good word for me in front of the boss? Haven't I done enough favors for you?" She didn't exactly know why Xia aggravated her so much. True, her colleague had said nothing to help Lotus out just now. But out of all the girls, Xia was the one most afraid of becoming a fried squid. Lotus sighed. How could she be so mean to poor Xia? She carefully washed Xia's towel and put it back.

In her room, she slipped into a two-piece outfit that Family Treasure had once praised. As she squatted down by the bedside to put on her makeup, she caught the reflection in the mirror of Guanyin behind her. She shifted to a different angle. The face looking back from the pink plastic-framed mirror looked pale. She added more rouge to her cheeks.

Lotus strode to the front door in her high-heeled sandals and joined the other girls. She put on her working hours smile. It was no wonder that people called the work of *jis* "selling smiles." Her eyes scanned the darkening street. Above their heads, the neon light flashed "Moonflower Massage Parlor," competing with all the other lights and lanterns that had glimmered into life. The restaurant opposite the parlor had set up tables on the sidewalk; in the window, large pieces of barbecued pork and freshly roasted ducks, hanging by their necks, were displayed. Red flames from an oil-drum stove leaped high into the air, mixing with rising steam from large pots. Diners slurped noodles, sweating in the heat, their T-shirts and pants cuffs rolled up like spring rolls. The night had just begun.

Family Treasure swung open the front door and turned on a fluorescent light. "Come, come, see with your own eyes, Lotus. Our home!" the young migrant said excitedly in Sichuan dialect. He had indeed turned up at the parlor and taken Lotus by taxi to his newly rented place on the other side of the city.

Lotus followed him into the unfurnished apartment. It smelled moldy. Under the crude light, the room's bareness lent it a sad air, like an old man embarrassed by his nakedness.

Family Treasure obviously didn't share her sentiments. "We've got everything: a kitchen and a bathroom with a sit-down toilet . . ." His voice boomed like a loudspeaker, and he pointed to the bathroom with one hand while stroking his thin mustache with a long-nailed little finger.

Family Treasure was a man of about thirty and a bundle of nervous energy, with thick, cropped hair that rose from his scalp like a scrubbing brush. He had first entered Lotus's life just over a year ago. Halfway through a massage, he grew restless and asked if she offered "that" service. Back in her room, he became quite flustered. He squeezed her breasts for a moment and then knelt down to smell her. He quickly came, even before getting his thing out of his fly. "I never had such a problem, *meinu,* never!" Holding his soiled trousers, he sobbed like a child. "I haven't smelled a woman for two years." She gently assured him that she believed him. Men were just like little children, Lotus often thought. So weak and so controlled by their bodily needs. Family Treasure soon returned afterward, and became a regular. There were no more "accidents," but sex with him never lasted long, a fact she never minded. Not in the slightest.

Standing in the middle of the bare hallway, Family Treasure was as talkative as ever, his thin eyes shining. "Sorry, Little Heart. I haven't had time to buy furniture yet. But I just couldn't wait to bring you here."

As his dark face descended toward her, Lotus tilted her head to avoid his mouth. The wet kiss landed on her chin.

Lotus looked about the apartment. She knew that when he first arrived in Shenzhen, he used to share a makeshift room with a dozen other construction workers. "How nice to have one's own place. Good for you, *laogong*." The working girls often called their clients the slang word for "husband." Lotus usually didn't feel comfortable using it. But this man was generous with his tips, and had flair, ambition, and a restless energy. Family Treasure had tried his hand at so many things: starting out as a construction worker, then cleaning car windows at road junctions, and later on collecting rubbish. Not long ago, he had rented a stall inside a commercial building and had started selling clothes and fashion accessories. He might prove to be a "treasure" yet, Lotus thought.

Through the open window, she spotted a woman cooking in the opposite building—so close that Lotus could see the bald patch on the back of her head. This must be one of the so-called handshake buildings she had heard people talking about.

Family Treasure dragged her into his arms, one hand going under her miniskirt to grab her bottom. "Oh, I love your round butt, good for childbearing."

"Be careful. People can see us." She pointed at the opposite building.

"Let them," he replied. Still, he turned off the light and led her to the bedroom.

In the darkness, Lotus staggered along on her high heels before stumbling into something. *"Aiyah!"*

In the dim light filtering through a bed sheet that was strung up as a halfhearted curtain, she saw a row of duffel bags lined up against the wall.

"Sorry, my goods. Nylon T-shirts." Family Treasure guided her over to the mattress on the floor. "Come this way. I'll get a bed frame soon." He started to peel off his clothes.

Lotus sat down on the edge of the mattress and began to undress. While he struggled to remove his nylon shirt, she quickly spat on her fingers and sent them down between her legs: there wouldn't be any foreplay.

Family Treasure was now stark naked. Men were such funny creatures, Lotus thought, with all their bits and pieces hanging out there, appearing all the more ridiculous when they got excited.

"Oh, my Little Heart, I spent the whole day looking forward to this." He pounced on her, like a hungry dog jumping on a piece of juicy meat, and planted more wet kisses on her face and neck. "Now tell me: am I your first for today?" he asked.

Lying under his hairless, lean body, Lotus wondered why so many men would ask this stupid question. "Of course, my *laogong*. You know I was away from the parlor this afternoon. Then I waited, just for you."

"Oh, yes, yes! I'm your real *laogong* from now on!" Family Treasure chuckled. "Let's make a son." His hands busily explored her body. When he squeezed her bottom, his long fingernail scratched her, enough to give her goose bumps. Earlier in the taxi, he had picked his nose and wiped the results under the seat, at the same time boasting about how he had made a good deal that morning and netted ten thousand yuan profit in a matter of minutes.

"I haven't seen you for a few weeks, *laogong*. I thought you'd forgotten about me," Lotus said coyly, one hand stroking his back. She wore only her bra. She never bothered taking it off unless clients insisted.

"I went to Zhejiang to buy these nylon T-shirts," Family Treasure replied as he tried awkwardly to undo her bra. "This *tamade* stupid thing! My wife never used one." He began to pull at the snap with both hands.

"Please don't. Let me." Lotus reached over and unhooked the bra and placed it on top of her pile of clothes.

Kneeling there, he opened up her legs and poised to enter.

She rolled sideways to take out a condom from her bag. "Wait, wait. What's the hurry?" In the sweetest voice she could muster, she continued. "It's called Golden Gun—Never Flops. It makes you hard for the whole night!" The "special" condom was Lotus's last resort, applied whenever men tried to wriggle out of using one.

"You're not laughing at me, Lotus?" he said humorlessly.

"How could I dare?" She used her teeth to open the package, pulled out the condom with the tips of her fingers and slid it on. She hated the slimy and greasy piece of rubber. She stroked his balls to make him harder.

Hurriedly, Family Treasure mounted her. Maybe the condom did boast some magic powers, or maybe he just felt more relaxed in his own home; the session lasted markedly longer than usual.

Lotus dutifully produced a moaning sound but her mind was filled with numbers. How much would he offer her for monthly maintenance? How much should she accept? She had to save enough for Shadan, no matter what. "Oh, yes, yes!" she shouted.

"Oh, *tamade* good." Family Treasure collapsed on top of her, his scrubbing-brush hair tickling her chin. Lotus turned her head aside.

He rolled off, turned on the light, and lifted off the condom. "This motherfucking condom is great. Where did you get it? Very expensive?"

"Pretty expensive," Lotus said, shutting her eyes to avoid the glare of the light. When she opened them again, she saw him walking out of the room, holding the soiled condom like a prize catch.

"I'll wash it and keep it for later. Too good to throw away," he announced.

Lotus got dressed, and went to the bathroom with her bag. There she took out her hygiene kit, using a rubber bulb attached to a tiny glass tube to squeeze a few drops of antibacterial liquid inside herself. Before Boss Moon had shown her how to do this, she used to wash herself with vinegar before going to bed every night.

Lotus returned to the bright-lit room first and perched on the edge of the mattress. Overhead hung a mosquito net, wrapped over itself. It was gray and dusty, as if it had grown a beard. The whitewashed wall was already run through with cracks, dotted in grease, and covered in scribbled telephone numbers and calculations. She simply could not imagine herself living here, even with furniture. Still, she'd hear the offer first. It sounded as though Family Treasure did intend to take her as his *ernai*—a glorified term for mistress. An upmarket residential compound close to the Hong Kong border was packed with such women. Once she had gone there with Mimi to take a look at the "gold canaries" of rich and powerful men, many of them from Hong Kong, and spotted finely dressed young women leisurely walking their dogs in the street. Moon liked to call their patrons the "classy clients." In truth, any man with some extra cash to throw around liked to take an *ernai,* even Family Treasure.

The migrant laborer, clad only in his underpants, trotted back as he sang a Sichuan folk song. He had brought back a plate of sliced watermelon, a bottle of beer, and a can of Coke. He handed the can to Lotus.

She took a sip even though she didn't care for the strange foreign drink, which she had tried several times.

Family Treasure opened the bottle of beer with his strong, long teeth, and took a gulp. He then wiped his face with a hand and slumped down on a duffel bag. He slapped the bag. "They look like nothing, those bags, but they made me ten thousand yuan richer!"

Lotus had heard the story several times, but she still flattered him with a smile. "You're so clever, my treasure."

"No one calls me stupid." He took another mouthful of beer and stroked his thin mustache with his little finger.

Lotus didn't understand why he bothered to keep a mustache. It was so thin that one could count the number of hairs on his top lip on both hands. Still, there were many more unbearable things she had to put up with in life. "*Laogong,* you've just started your business. Be careful with your money," she said in a honey-coated voice.

"No, I want an *ernai*. It's too risky to fuck any *ji* these days, with AIDS and everything. And I'm earning enough."

"Are you really?" Lotus said, smiling more sweetly.

"Really! I may still be a country bumpkin. But my pocket is *tamade* deeper than that of many of the city folks."

"Good on you!"

"But I still get treated like dog shit sometimes! The other day, I went to a shop with air-conditioning, just to cool myself down. This goddamn security guard came over and asked me to leave, because of my flip-flops. But plenty of others were wearing flip-flops."

"How dare he pick on you!" Lotus said with half-genuine indignation.

"Fuck his ancestors!" Family Treasure spat the words out with beer-laced spittle.

"Don't mind that low worm."

"I like you very much, sweet Lotus. I'm thinking of giving you three thousand yuan a month. Not bad, huh?"

Lotus had another sip of Coke. She grimaced.

Three thousand was lower than her average monthly income. Yet the life of an *ernai* meant security and safety. Such offers didn't come about every day. Lotus didn't want to let an opportunity slip through her fingers, but she didn't want to accept the first offer that came along, either.

She wiggled her body in the same ridiculous way that Mimi always did in front of Lanzai. "Put your hand on your heart, my *laogong,* and tell me how much you love me."

"I'd marry you if I were single." He put a hand on his heart to show his sincerity. "But I'm married and my wife has to look after my parents at home."

"I have to look after my poor family, too," Lotus said, leaning closer to stroke his bare legs. "And you haven't tasted the spicy food I can cook."

"Listen, how about thirty-five hundred yuan—but only if you give me a son! I only have two girls," he said somewhat mournfully. After a big sip, he cheered himself up and a flood of words poured out of his mouth. "You aren't a stunning beauty, Lotus, to be honest. But I need a woman who can cook and give birth to a son. Come and live with me. My shop isn't far. You can bring me home-cooked lunches." He let out a guffaw. "The other guys' eyes will turn red with envy, I bet!"

Lotus thought about laughing with him but she hid her lips behind her can of Coke instead.

Lotus felt his gaze before she saw him. She was leaning against the glass front of the Moonflower, mulling over Family Treasure and last night's offer. Mimi stood guard by the door while the others were having an early supper. The sun was grudgingly retiring behind the mountains and East Station Road was alive again with human activities. Two men from the restaurant across the street were splashing the pavement with water, to cool things down and to get ready to set up tables. A short distance away, Lotus caught sight of Funny Eye. Wearing a well-ironed white linen shirt and dark glasses, he was stationed there like a tall statue, studying her.

Lotus stood straight and watched him striding over, her heart beating fast. She wondered if her boss had said something to provoke his visit or if he had come there of his own accord. And after so long?

Funny Eye stopped inches away from Lotus, radiating his distinctive smell, a mixture of cologne and aromatic tobacco. "How are you, my little beauty," he greeted her in his rich voice, and placed his glasses on top of his head. "Long time, no see." Briefly, he turned to Mimi and bowed slightly. Mimi gawked at him as if Princess Huan Zhu's husband had suddenly materialized in front of them.

"Okay, okay-la," Lotus said, summoning her sweetest smile. "I thought you'd long forgotten about me, *shuaige*!"

"Oh, no! Didn't I tell you that I was intrigued by you? I don't normally look for girls from parlors, you know. But high-class prostitutes are too savvy with men and too smooth-tongued. I find them boring," he said unhurriedly. Towering over her, he stood with his muscled arms crossed. "A project took me away for quite a long while. My life is not quite as free as you may imagine."

Lotus felt an urge to pat his chest. The first three buttons of his shirt were open, revealing plenty of his muscular chest. She patted his arm instead. "Your life? I imagine you fly up in the heavens while we crawl on the ground," she said playfully.

Funny Eye burst out laughing, throwing his head back. "I had the impression that you were rather reserved. Maybe I was wrong," he said, wearing a lopsided smile. "Now listen, my beauty. I have a proposition. Next week, I have to go to Hainan Island for work. Fancy coming along for a week and enjoying the beach? Of course, I'll compensate you and your boss. Isn't Moon deliciously curvy?"

"Of course I'd like to come!" Lotus replied, looking up at Funny Eye. Though she still thought of him as Funny Eye, his lazy eye didn't seem to be that disturbing or even prominent, perhaps because he was standing against the light. He struck her, more than ever, as handsome.

"You lucky thing!" Mimi nudged Lotus with her elbow.

Lotus turned and flashed a brief smile at her friend. Maybe Guanyin had heard her prayers and decided to show some mercy, Lotus thought. Occasionally some girls would get lucky and be taken on trips. Such gigs were much better paid and there was usually a big tip toward the end. Though Lotus sensed that this man might not be as nice as his manner suggested, she was willing to take a little risk.

"Good, you're game! I'll come again in a few days."

Lotus nodded with a smile. She was tempted to ask for his number but refrained: she mustn't appear too keen.

Then he reached out to grab her hand.

She instinctively pulled it back.

Funny Eye let out a strained laugh. "I just wanted to check your nails, sweetie."

Lotus blushed and felt obliged to hold out her hands. Immediately she was embarrassed by the unflattering appearance of her self-painted red nails.

Funny Eye tutted as he examined her nails. He fished some notes from his pocket and pushed them into her hand. "Go to a decent nail salon tomorrow, will you?" he said. Then he put his dark glasses back on and bowed to both of the girls. "Now, please excuse me. I have commitments tonight."

Lotus watched him until his figure was swallowed by the sea of people in the street. She clutched the money in her hand and pressed it to her chest as if trying to calm her heart that was threatening to leap out of her throat.

CHAPTER 8

闭月羞花

Her Beauty Outshines the Moon and
Puts the Flowers to Shame

A sky full of stars. Standing in his backyard in Miaocun, Bing looked up. Under the moonlight, the intricate brickwork, curved eaves, and tall grass sprouting between broken tiles on the roof all possessed a melancholic charm. The humid air was thick with the smell of green moss that had gathered in the yard during his absence.

He started to bathe himself with a bucket of cold water, soaping himself from head to toe and scratching his body like a monkey. When he tipped the whole bucketful of water over his head, he gave a satisfied cry. *"Aiyah!"*

Just that morning, he had been under the hot water of the shower in the Bamboo Hotel in Beijing. Now he was back in his austere home in Miaocun. Back in another time, it seemed.

He returned to his room, still infused with its familiar musty smell. Patches of the wall had gone moldy from the rain that constantly bombarded the city in summertime. He sat down in front of his desk, exhausted but not at all sleepy.

Through the open doors and windows, the sounds of the night drifted in. A neighbor's TV spat out costume melodramas; mosquitoes hummed their nightly choir in the backyard and a street cat meowed. In the distance, Bing could hear a baby crying and a couple arguing. He recognized Lanzai's voice: "*Wasai,* good shot!" He must be playing pool at the outdoor pool table around the corner. Bing found the familiar sounds comforting.

Under the glow of the lamp, he started sorting through his camera bag and picked out a few rolls of film to be developed. Without intending to, he found himself cleaning his equipment, blowing on the lenses and dusting the camera body. The camera felt solid in his hand.

Playing with his camera always had a calming effect on him. Fresh bubbles of memory from the night before still surfaced and disturbed him. In his mind, he saw Mei's face, distorted in pain. He knew he was partly responsible for her bitter disappointment. True, his ex-wife had made the first move, but how could he be so weak willed as to allow her to drag him to bed?

It wasn't the first time a woman had seduced him, though he certainly had no regrets about Pearl. He often wondered if the beguiling girl who had crashed into his life and then vanished just as quickly had ever existed. But of course she had. Without her, he wouldn't have been there now, living among the working girls.

Bing's eyes had followed Pearl's tall, curvy form from the moment she walked into the dining room. She was wearing a cream silk cheongsam, brightened by an embroidered red butterfly on her left breast. The high mandarin collar of her dress covered her front and neck, yet her long white legs flashed between the deep slits from thigh to ankle. She wasn't, perhaps, a beauty in the conventional sense. Her eyes, though spirited, were deeply set and not very large. The lines on her face lacked gentleness but she radiated sexuality. Her long shining hair was tied up on her head, leaving a black curtain of bangs across her forehead.

Pearl slid down in the empty seat reserved for her, next to the pipe-smoking Mr. Gao, a successful business friend of Wang's. He had his long hands in everything from construction materials to property development. From their body language, Bing could tell that Gao and Pearl were familiar with each other. When Gao made the introduction, he referred to her simply as Pearl, and she smiled charmingly, nodding at each guest who was presented to her, including two senior male managers from the company and Wang's secretary, who was also his mistress.

When it came to Bing, he fancied that Pearl's gaze rested on him a moment longer than the others.

Bing ordered himself to focus on the food. He was a married man, after all, even though his wife was far away. Yet he couldn't help but be keenly aware of Pearl's presence. He wondered if she was a working girl. Business deals in China were mostly done over dinner tables. And prostitutes, an essential part of the business landscape, were often hired to entertain men, to grease deals, and to bribe whoever needed to be bribed. A little over a year ago, Wang, pained by the taxes the company had to pay for its profitable business, had organized an outing to an expensive karaoke TV establishment on the seafront to court the favor of an official from the tax bureau in the hope of being granted a 15 percent tax deduction, a policy reserved for enterprises using high-tech facilities. Six hostesses were booked for six men. Afterward, all the men, except Bing, had taken their girls to the rooms upstairs. Bing had fled and spent a restless night imagining what would have happened had he stayed. But his conscience wouldn't allow him to sink so low and so blatantly. He later asked to be excused from such frivolities in the future, and Wang agreed. He had been mindful not to upset Bing ever since their major argument over the weight-loss soap.

The banquet graced by Pearl had taken place near the end of July 1997; Bing remembered this time clearly. Their seaweed slimming soap was still expanding its market share, though at a slower pace. Yet Wang had recently come up with another idea: to take over an amusement park project, another "once-in-a-lifetime opportunity" because he could secure the deal at an extremely favorable price. Bing felt it was too ambitious and too risky. There were plenty of theme parks already in

Shenzhen: Splendid China, which boasted miniature versions of China's famous sites; Window of the World, which re-created famous sites from around the globe; and a newly developed water park. So this time, he had firmly put his foot down.

Bing figured that Wang had organized the banquet to persuade him to go along with his new plan. To his surprise, Wang didn't raise the issue even once over dinner. Their conversation was dominated by the Asian financial crisis that was spreading across the region, following the collapse of the Thai baht. The businessmen wondered if it might lead to a world economic meltdown and if China's currency, the renminbi, would be devalued, like the baht, and how they could turn this into a money-making opportunity.

"Devalue the renminbi? You're dreaming!" Pearl cut in. After making sure that everyone's eyes were focused on her, she pursed her red lips and released smoke rings in perfect circles. "How big is the Thai market? And how big is ours?" she continued with the cool assurance of an economist. "Besides, our leaders love this golden opportunity to show off our strong economy."

"Yes, exactly, well said," Gao cheered.

"Are you in finance, Pearl?" Bing ventured.

"Finance? How dull would that be?" She cracked a smile. "I'm in PR."

"And indeed, an e-expert at it," crowed Wang, flattering her as he always did.

That night Bing got rather drunk. This wasn't typical of him, and he grew animated and talkative. The alcohol burned away his inhibition and fueled his ego. When Wang requested that he recite a poem, Bing jumped up and recited his favorite, "Bring in the Wine," by the Tang Dynasty poet Li Bai. After he sang out the final line, "Just let me be forever drunk, and never again awake," the table erupted in applause. He bowed and raised a glass in Pearl's direction. "The wine can't make me drunk, but your beauty makes my heart tipsy."

She laughed brightly. Her full bosom heaved so much that the butterfly on her chest fluttered as if about to take flight. Bing had the urge to catch it.

His recollection of the rest of the night was somewhat murky. When a plate of large "dragon eyes" turned up, the people around the table started to peel off the leathery skin of the fruit and passed around the slippery eyeball-like flesh. When Pearl leaned in to pass him the fruit, he remembered the closeness of her cherry-red mouth. Why had she decided to sit next to him?

After the banquet, Wang pushed Bing and Pearl into the company car. Bing was to take her home first.

"May I?" she said, resting her head on his shoulder. "I feel a little drunk."

"Please," Bing murmured.

"I've never met a businessman who can recite poems. I didn't know such a species existed." She lifted her head slightly and blew the words into his ear.

"Really?" That was all he had energy for. He caressed a nipple-like knotted button on her mandarin collar, controlling his impulse to suck it. He remained silent, but inside him his nervousness was battling with a longing for an adventure.

When they passed by his compound, Bing pointed it out to her. Pearl requested a toilet stop.

Bing lived alone. His wife and daughter joined him only during holidays. He had tried to persuade his family to move in with him, but Mei was too settled in her life in Beijing to decamp. In the meantime, he had gotten used to his freedom in Shenzhen. So he just visited Beijing regularly.

Up in his apartment, Pearl made a lengthy visit to the bathroom, and he heard her gasping, as if she might throw up, and later he heard her splashing water on her face. When they were walking over, she had still seemed woozy with drink. As he paced restlessly in the sitting room, he caught sight of a photo of his wife and daughter on a table. When Pearl came out from the bathroom after a long while, he went over. "Are you all right?" he asked.

"Fine. I just had a little too much to drink," she replied feebly, her head leaning against the wall. Her long hair was now down and a floral fragrance wafted from her body.

"Well, if you are not feeling well, you are most welcome to stay," he said rather flatly. "Use my daughter's room."

"That's so kind of you."

Bing helped Pearl to settle down in his daughter's room. When he covered her up with a blanket, he caught himself stealing a look at the flesh of her bare thighs.

In his double bed, he slept restlessly that night, amid wild dreams of the fox fairies. His mother had told him tales about them on the starry nights of his childhood. The fox fairies turned into beautiful girls in order to seduce lonely scholars. The good ones fell in love with the scholars and bore them sons, while the evil fairies cut open their victims' hearts at the moment of climax, revealing their true animal form and feasting on the scholar's immortal souls.

Bing's sleep was disturbed by a tickling sensation on his face, and he turned his head to avoid it. When he opened his eyes, he saw Pearl's smiling face, with no trace of a hangover, radiant in the glorious morning light seeping through the curtain. Lying on her side next to him, she was lightly brushing her long hair against his face. Her white, full-figured body was adorned by nothing but a red string around her waist, tied to a tiny piece of green jade, an ornament some women wore as a lucky charm in their *benmingnian*—the year of their Chinese zodiac sign.

"Why didn't you come to me last night?" she whispered.

"I'm married, you know, married," Bing stammered, holding on to his marital status like a drowning man clutching at a rice straw.

"What a shame, I was just about to propose!" she said sarcastically, smirking.

Bing tried to shift away but her hand went to his groin.

"Not a bad tool!"

There was a flash of red and Bing found himself a drowned man.

He felt as if he was still in a dream as he watched this naked beauty rocking on top of him, her full breasts dancing as if they had a life of their own. He kept touching them and her face—as if to check that she was real.

Bing was surprised but delighted by the way she moaned. Pearl's unrestrained manner liberated him. He responded to her every move with equal passion. As his confidence grew, he became the dominant lover, initiating the positions that he had seen on pirated pornography DVDs but had never explored with his wife. "Bend down over the edge of the bed," he demanded as he stood behind her. As he entered her, one hand grabbing her long hair, he felt he was the master of the world. He let himself go only after he felt a spasm between her legs and she cried out in ecstasy.

For a long while after, lying beside her, Bing gazed at her naked body, soft, smooth, and dazzlingly white. He caressed the red string around her wasp waist.

She opened her eyes and flashed a smile. "You know, I've rarely met a man with such a tiger's energy, my Mr. Brilliant!" She teased his manhood with her fingertips and rubbed a foot against his legs.

Bing grabbed her foot and tickled it. Pearl giggled and tried to pull her foot back but he held it firmly.

"Shall I give you a foot massage?" he offered.

"I'd love it!" Pearl sat up in bed.

Bing went to the kitchen and returned with a basin full of warm water. He soaked her feet in it, and sat down on a low stool in front of her. When he was a child, he used to wash his mother's feet every night, a task he used to hate. His mother's feet were flat and coarse, full of calluses. Pearl had perfect slim feet with slim toes and high arches. Her toenails, painted bright red, shone against her skin. He picked up one foot, dried it, and placed it on his knee. He pressed the points on her feet with his thumbs, rubbed and massaged her foot. Pearl relaxed on the bed, her eyes closed.

Afterward, they cuddled together in bed.

"I like this," he said, fingering the jade piece. "This is your *benmingnian*?"

Pearl nodded.

"You are twenty-four, born in an ox year. What's your big wish for the year?"

Pearl confided that she planned to go to America to get an MBA.

"You must be making decent money from your PR job then."

Pearl smiled and went on talking about how she was considering a university in California, for its warm, sunny weather and vineyards. She added that she would also visit Disneyland, to make up for the fun she had missed as a child.

"Do you think people would go to a new amusement park in Shenzhen?" Bing asked. He told her about the amusement park project.

"I, for one, would love to visit anything you erect, theme park or otherwise." Pearl winked at him. "Seriously, I'm no businesswoman, but I should imagine that as people get richer, they'll spend more money amusing themselves. Also, remember this is Shenzhen. There's not much else to do other than go to theme parks."

"That's true. But I think it is too risky."

"Great men are those who are willing to take great risks."

Maybe the park project wasn't so bad an idea after all, thought Bing. If it became successful, he would slip out of the seaweed soap business, something he had never felt completely at ease with.

That Sunday with Pearl, Bing had a taste of the ninth heaven as they indulged in more sessions of "cloud and rain." What a brilliant Chinese euphemism for lovemaking, he thought. So graphic yet poetic, with a hint of humor.

In the late afternoon, Pearl readied herself to leave.

"Oh, do you have to?"

She looked about the room as if trying to take mental pictures of the place. She studied his photos hanging on the wall and asked: "Why don't you take some pictures of me? I heard that you are an accomplished photographer."

Bing grabbed his camera and had Pearl stand by the window. He moved around her, talking and joking with her, all the while taking photos. Natural light from the window lit her striking face. He wanted to eternalize the image.

After that Sunday, Bing spent many nights mulling over what had happened. Guilt gnawed at his conscience. Yet the memory of her, spiced by his own imagination, became better by the day. For hours, he stared at the high-contrast portrait of Pearl. The image looked as engaging as she had been in real life: it had caught her captivating and mysterious smile. Before long, he penned a beautifully crafted letter to her, expressing his longing for her and sent it, together with her portrait, to a post office box address she had given to him. Like a stone sinking into the sea, his letter went unanswered.

Depressed and confused, Bing retreated into his work. It dawned on him that he might have been unhappy with his wife for a long time. Otherwise how could he have been tempted by another woman? he reasoned.

Two months later, Bing went to Beijing to visit his family. He tried to behave as normally as he could. The couple, in fact, enjoyed a much better and active sex life during his stay.

One morning, he woke up to find Mei sitting in front of the dressing table, staring at herself in the mirror, naked beneath her open bathrobe.

"Are you all right?" Bing asked and put on his glasses.

"I had this terrible dream," she said, a disturbed look in her eyes.

"About what?"

"I dreamed about death, about me dying." Before Bing could react, Mei got up and turned around, her hands closing the bathrobe. She glared at him so intensely that he felt heat rising on his cheeks. "Are you having an affair?" she asked.

Bing's body jerked upright on the bed. He then clutched a large pillow in his arms and buried his head in it. The moment he had been dreading had finally come.

"No, not . . ." Bing heard his own muffled voice. "Not an affair as such," he mumbled.

"What?"

He repeated his words.

Mei came over and tried to snatch the pillow from him. He held on tight, but the expression on his wife's face frightened him. He let go of the pillow.

Mei nearly fell over. She regained her balance and stood in front of him, panting.

Through her open robe, Bing glimpsed the horizontal cesarean-section scar on her stomach. He was besieged by panic, afraid of losing her and his family. He confessed everything.

"Why?"

"Well, you . . . you sent me to Shenzhen . . . "

Mei was dumbfounded for a moment. Then she carefully placed the pillow back on the bed, and turned and stood with her back to Bing for a long while. "Get out. Now!" she ordered in a low voice.

Bing got up. "Please, please forgive me, Mei. I promise this will never happen again."

He tried to embrace her but Mei squirmed away from him. She stuffed some of his clothes into his suitcase and shoved it outside the door, and with a force powerful enough to move a mountain, she pushed him out of the bedroom and then out of her parents' house. "You fucking bastard! Get out of my sight!"

The door slammed and Bing, dressed only in his underpants, found himself standing alone in the communal courtyard, next to his suitcase. "Please, Mei, you can't treat me like this," he pleaded in front of the closed door. Silence. Conscious that the neighbors were poking their heads out, he pulled out some clothes from his suitcase, put them on, and left hurriedly.

Yet beneath Mei's iron mask, Bing knew how much his wife must have suffered. He returned to Shenzhen, but the nagging sense of guilt, shame, and failure kept him awake night after night. He lost half of the weight accumulated over years of heavy dining and drinking.

Then almost overnight, his business venture collapsed. At first when Bing had given consent to the amusement park project, it kicked off like a rocket. He suspected that Wang had done all the necessary preparation before he had said yes. Within five months, the project ran out of funds, much sooner than Bing had anticipated. It started when the construction company they hired took them to court for two months' back pay. This was the first time he became aware of a cash-flow problem. He checked the accounts and was alarmed by the massive amount spent on machinery and construction materials. Yet for every purchase, there was a contract, a commercial invoice, and the proof of payment. But Bing knew Wang and his creative accounting only too well. He would have liked to go through all the major items with his partner. But Wang's priority was to take out another bank loan. It just so happened that China was tightening its economy in the wake of the Asian financial crisis. After assessing their financial situation, the bank not only refused to lend them any more money but also applied to the local court to freeze the company's assets. Bing was deeply disappointed that Wang, with all his connections, failed to raise sufficient funds to meet the bank's tight new deadline. The bank took the company as collateral, in accordance with a mortgage contract the partners had signed. They were forced to declare bankruptcy.

The bankruptcy was perhaps the tipping point for Mei. She filed for a formal divorce as soon as the news became public. Bing had no choice but to accept. Once Mei made up her mind about something, a four-horse carriage wouldn't be able to pull her back. One piece of good luck stood out among all the misfortunes: Bing's sizable personal savings, kept in an account under Mei's name, hadn't been swept away by the tsunami of bankruptcy. He gave most of it to his ex-wife in the financial settlement after the divorce and offered to pay her fifteen hundred yuan per month in child support.

After finalizing his divorce in Beijing, he flew back to Shenzhen, where he still had a rented apartment. He was now a free man, yet a broken one in every sense.

Once again, he reached out to Pearl, reporting to her the happenings in his life, and requesting a meeting. When he heard nothing in return, he felt unbearably disappointed, even though he had half expected her silence.

However, Pearl started to send her friends to Bing. The girls all wanted glamorous and flattering photos of themselves. It soon became obvious to him that these girls were prostitutes serving the high end of the market. His conversations with them confirmed his assumption.

So Pearl must be a high-class prostitute herself. As Bing's world had already been turned upside down, this revelation added only a few more ripples. Nevertheless, he stubbornly clung to his rose-colored image of Pearl.

The photo sessions proved to be Bing's first freelance assignments. More important, they woke him from his hibernation and enabled him to discover the therapeutic value of photography. Then it became a passion at a time when he was searching again for meaning in his life. Looking back over his path, he realized that his life had always been carved out by others: in his early years by his parents, then by the government that had allocated him the factory job, and finally by his wife. He made up his mind to pursue photography, something that afforded him some control over his interpretation of the world around him.

Bing grew curious about the girls he had photographed. How did they end up that way? Did they have any moral qualms about their profession? It was at this point that he decided to undertake a photo documentary on prostitutes, not high-class ones, but those on the lower end of the ranks who made up the majority of the working girls.

He gave up his comfortable apartment and started working freelance, slowly establishing contacts with various media and advertising companies, using his old business connections. To match his new identity, he bought a photographer's vest and started to grow his hair long.

Bing underestimated the courage and discipline required to live an unstructured life. The days seemed to fly by without him achieving anything. Several times he nearly beat the retreat drum. Then he would see, in his mind, his ex-wife's contemptuous look. So he had held out in his hovel in Miaocun.

———

Where was Pearl now? In America, most likely. From her friends, Bing had heard scraps of rumors about her: how she had returned to her hometown, Shanghai, to prepare for the TOEFL exam required by American universities, and how she was dating a rich American. Then even the rumors about her dissipated, and it was as if she had returned to the underworld of the fox fairies.

No need to worry about that girl, Bing told himself. She knew how to take care of herself.

He put his camera back in the bag, and patted it like a soldier thanking a horse that had performed bravely in battle. Perhaps he could follow Lotus to her impoverished home village and shoot a session there. This trip could provide a good opportunity to get to know her and obtain invaluable details for his book on prostitution. After winning the Kodak award, he had decided to pursue a book project on prostitution in China.

Would Lotus like to go home? Earlier that year on lunar New Year's Eve, he had taken her and Little Jade, the two girls who stayed at the parlor over the holiday, out for the reunion dinner. At the end of the meal, while they ate sweet round dumplings, a symbol of family reunion, they burst into a reunion song, with exaggerated cheerfulness. Bing spied tears in Lotus's eyes. He became curious about her relationship with her family.

Bing continued unpacking and reached into his suitcase to retrieve the gold-plated award cup, safely wrapped in some clothes. He placed it on the bookshelf.

Next, he took out an alarm clock featuring a Red Guard waving Chairman Mao's Little Red Book. He had bought it at the "dirt market" in Beijing, which was full of interesting reminders of history. He placed the clock on the desk. After twelve hours, or around half a million waves of the Little Red Book, he would see Lotus again. He would surprise her with the Beijing delicacy he had brought back: vacuum-packed roast duck, with pickled plums and dried persimmons. In the whirlwind of the past few weeks, whenever he could steal a moment, his thoughts had automatically turned to her, wondering what she was doing. Without him realizing it, Lotus had become an important part of his life.

Bing lit a cigarette, inhaled deeply, and blew the smoke out with a hard sigh, watching the small cloud slowly dissolve into nothingness.

He loved the feelings evoked by smoking. They had a simplicity and certainty that life didn't have.

CHAPTER 9

弱肉强食

The Weak Are the Prey of the Strong

This parlor feels like a mouse hole, Lotus thought as she massaged a client one evening in mid-August. The only source of light came from two timid wall lamps. Between them, above the TV set, a map of acupuncture points quietly gathered dust on the wall. A fashion accessory of massage parlors, it could only be seen when the red velvet curtain across the glass front went up. The main room was crowded with three massage beds, two of which were empty at the moment. Lotus had never learned to massage properly, let alone in the Thai style as advertised in the glass front. But few customers ever complained about her technique. Her touch would arouse some or put others to sleep, like the fat man she was working on now. He was lying facedown, snoring through the round padded hole cut in the massage bed so clients could breathe.

Sitting by the man's side, Lotus massaged his leg halfheartedly while she brooded. A bad luck ghost must be haunting her. First of all, there was Funny Eye. Ever since his unexpected visit two weeks ago, a balloon of anticipation had started to inflate. The day after his visit, she had her nails painted deep red at a nail salon up the road and cut and styled her hair. She bought a colorful swimsuit. She waited anxiously. After a week, the anxiety gave way to disappointment and her fascination with him turned into resentment. Lotus also lost face in front of her colleagues. Mimi, of course, had told everyone about Funny Eye's offer.

To make matters worse, her brother was now causing her some anxiety. She had just received a letter from Shadan in which he had expressed his wish to study law instead of computer science as she had instructed. She couldn't recall her little brother ever disobeying her before. Now what? He thought his wings had grown strong enough to fly on his own? But how could he make a living fighting lawsuits for his fellow villagers? Was she spending her blood and sweat and money on him just for this? And his future ought to be in the city. Did he have enough sense to see it? The more she dwelled on this, the angrier she became.

Xia's scream from outside the parlor made Lotus jump. There were unusual noises and a commotion in the street. Lotus was about to head out to take a look when the door slid open and a blur of uniforms burst in, together with glaring flashlights. Her customer woke up with a start, with drool around his mouth. Once he realized what was happening, he tried to hide his massive body under the massage bed. Lotus simply stood there, awestruck.

The next thing Lotus knew, she was squatting in a police van, crammed in with several girls. From the back of the van, she saw a police car block one end of the street. The sirens moaned like crazed animals. It looked as though all the parlors and salons on the street were being raided. She realized that they must have gotten caught in a so-called "sweeping away the yellow" campaign. She never understood why "yellow" was the byword for prostitution and pornography. Such campaigns had struck before, like odd storms in the summer. But Moon would usually catch wind beforehand and shut the parlor for a few days to avoid any trouble.

Lotus remembered her last brush with the police and how she had shivered as if running a fever when she was arrested. But that experience had made her calmer now. She also took comfort in the fact that she wasn't alone this time.

Little Jade, who had been resting in the back room because of a stomach problem, was the last to be hurled into the vehicle. Under the spinning light of the police van, Lotus spotted her petrified face.

As the back door slammed shut, Little Jade screamed: "My hand, my hand is caught!"

"Open up!" Lotus banged on the metal door. Other girls joined in to no avail. The van charged ahead.

"*Aiyah,* my hand's broken. Help me!" Panic-stricken, Little Jade's voice was more of a whine than ever.

Xia took charge immediately. "We'll have to pull her hand out. Lotus, you pull the door to the left and Mimi, you push to the right."

Lotus hesitated for a fleeting moment, then joined hands with the other girls. "One, two, three!" Xia counted, and they leaned in.

Little Jade gave another loud cry and pulled her right hand out of the door. "*Aiyah,* blood, heavens, blood," she wailed, her left hand holding the right.

In the light seeping in through the back door's windows, Lotus could see the sticky liquid dripping onto the floor. The bleeding had to be stopped. With a flash of inspiration, she took off her T-shirt, undid her bra and quickly bandaged Little Jade's hand with the bra.

Xia wrapped her arm around the girl and cooed: "There, there."

Little Jade rested her head on Xia's shoulder and wailed and wailed.

The next morning, Lotus found herself sitting on a corner of an army mattress stained with dried blood and urine, inside a gloomy cell at Zhangmutou Detention Center. The tiny steel window was too high up to allow a view of the outside world. Still she could tell that it was raining again. Exhausted, she rested her head against the cracked whitewashed wall. She closed her eyes, trying to doze. Flies were buzzing around. On the concrete floor, columns of ants rushed in all directions, as if on a military drill. There were about twenty women in her cell, mostly girls in their late teens and early twenties. They lay on mattresses, sat on the floor, leaned against the wall or against each other. Everyone looked as haggard as leaves after frost.

Upon arriving at the center last night, Lotus had recognized the low rectangular brick compound within the high walls trimmed with barbed wire—it was the same place where she had been locked up some eight months ago. They were herded into a greasy-floored hall, which was already crowded with dozens of people. All were made to squat down, their hands on their heads. After a breakfast of watery porridge earlier in the morning, they were given a general health checkup and then taken to different cells where they were told to wait for interrogation.

The cell was hot and suffocating. No one had the energy to talk or move. Only when the warden shouted a detainee's name, his voice thundering in the corridor, did the concerned one turn her head to stare through the iron bars.

Lotus fingered her bracelet beads. Inside her head, worries buzzed like flies around her. Her fear of the police had been deeply rooted. When she was a child, adults would often threaten to call the cops if she didn't stop crying.

One of the most humiliating experiences Lotus had suffered as a *ji* was at the hands of a police officer of certain ranking. A special guest of Moon's—which meant there was no payment—the imposing man in his late thirties had turned up in civilian clothes. There was half a circle of flattened hair on the back of his head, obviously the result of constantly wearing his police hat. In her room, he stood there and ordered her to kneel in front of him and "play the flute" for him. Lotus had no choice but to obey, even though she always felt there was something fundamentally wrong in the job: a girl's mouth was meant for eating rice, not for hosting a man's flute. After a few minutes, Lotus, on her bare knees, looked up at the policeman, hoping he would give the signal to move on to the main course of "hole-digging," but he yelled angrily in a thick Cantonese accent: "*Tamade,* two and a half sucks. Are you trying to fool me?" As the words shot out of his mouth like bullets, he grabbed her hair and thrust his manhood into her mouth. Ever since then, Lotus had hated both playing the flute and policemen in general with renewed intensity.

Am I really a "broomstick star"? Lotus asked herself. Her recent disappointments with Funny Eye and her brother had paled into insignificance compared to the trouble she was in now. She knew that there were several possible outcomes, all of them terrible. She could be released with a fine of several thousand yuan—if she was lucky. Or she might get the punishment of *qiansong*—being sent back to her home region, with her family then responsible for paying the fine. Or she would be sent to a so-called custody and education center, a labor camp of a sort, if the authorities found enough evidence against her. Lotus feared being sent back home even more than to a labor camp.

She looked over to Little Jade, who was hunched in the corner beside Xia. The teenager was rocking back and forth, her left hand clutching the right, bandaged by the bloodstained bra, one loose strap dangling down. Her eyes were nearly swollen shut.

Lotus went over to her. "Come on, Little Jade, let me bandage your hand properly."

"No," said the girl, drawing both hands closer to her body. "Ma, Ma, I want Mama," she kept murmuring.

Lotus knew almost nothing about Little Jade. She pulled Xia aside. "Where is her mama?" she whispered.

"*Ai*, bitter-fated girl," Xia started with a sigh. "Her family gave her away when she was three or four. Imagine, giving away your own flesh and blood?"

"Because her family wanted a boy?" Lotus had heard of such stories in her village. She glanced at the pitiful sight of Little Jade and had a rush of genuine sympathy for the girl.

"I guess so," Xia continued in a low voice. "Anyway, her adoptive family treated her like a dog. Then one day a man turned up in her village and said that he could find her own mama for her. She swallowed that line and followed his tail. Guess what? He sold her, not to Moonflower but to another place." Xia darted a look at Little Jade. "Hush, hush. Don't mention it to her. She's very ashamed her family gave her away like a piece of trash."

Xia clicked her tongue, her eyes gleaming with maternal tenderness. "One day, I'll take her home to the Mongolian steppe. I don't want her to end up an old wreck like me."

Xia inched closer to Little Jade and began smoothing the girl's messy hair. Startled by the touch, Little Jade opened her swollen eyes briefly and then resumed her crying.

"There, there. Good girl," Xia cooed softly. "We'll get you out of this dogshit place and find your mama."

"We'll find a way," Lotus chipped in. "The important thing is to call our boss. The guards will let us use a cell phone, if we can pay."

Mimi came over. She dropped down on the floor, paying no heed to the filth. "How about our photographer friend? He's back, I know. I saw the light was on in his room when I got home the other night."

"I hope he can help us, too," Lotus said. She hadn't thought much about the photographer lately, but now the mere mention of his name made her feel better. "Listen, has anyone got any money?"

Xia's hand went down to a zippered pocket on her underwear. "I've only got a condom. Well, it may be useful."

"Condom?" A woman in her thirties overheard their conversation and leaned over. "Get rid of it, this minute," she said to Xia in her foghorn voice. "Don't you know? A condom can be used as hard evidence against you. Last time when the police raided our parlor, I quickly swallowed the condom I had on me. Otherwise, I would have been in a labor camp by now."

Xia stuck out her tongue. "Thank you," she said, grabbing her zipped pocket.

Lotus also mumbled thanks. She then turned to Mimi, eyeing her friend's robust chest, the spot where the girl often hid her earnings from her boyfriend. "How about the hidden money?"

"That?" Mimi raised an arm as if to protect her chest. "But that's for emergencies."

"We are in an emergency right now, Mimi!"

"Don't worry. We'll pay you back," Xia promised.

"Okay, okay-la," Mimi grumbled.

Just then, the iron door clanked open. The first girl had returned from interrogation: her face was bloody and her hair and her pink T-shirt were wet. Two guards pushed her inside the cell and she fell onto the concrete floor.

Lotus and several women rushed over and helped her onto a mattress. The girl smelled of mustard, and bits of green stuff were caked around her red, wet nose. Someone gently wiped the girl's injured face with her shirt. Lotus recognized the battered girl as the new arrival at a beauty salon a few doors down the street. Between sobs, the girl told them how the policemen had beat her when she refused to admit that she was a *ji*. After she lost consciousness, they filled her nose with water laced with mustard to wake her up. Unable to cope with the torture, she made a false confession and signed the paper. As she talked, blood bubbled around her mouth. "But I'm not a *ji*," she insisted.

" 'Killing a bird to scare the monkey,' " Xia said, drumming a foot against the concrete floor. "The cops always treat the first badly—to scare the rest. Stinky dogshit, *pei*!" She spat on the floor.

"Sister Xia is right," Lotus said. Now that they were grasshoppers tied to the same string, the ice between them had melted. "We have to work together and stick to the same story."

"I won't be able to stand the beating," Mimi stated.

"For Buddha's sake, Mimi!" snapped Lotus.

"You half-brain!" Xia joined in. "Once in the labor camp, you'll never see your Lanzai again."

"No!" Mimi started to cry, her thick nostrils flaring.

The next woman returned to the cell. She was untouched but crying openly. "They caught me red-handed. I'm ruined!"

Before long Xia's name was called. She jumped up, tidied her hair, and spat on her fingers, using the spit to fix a signature tease on her forehead. "How do I look?" she asked her friends.

"Good, very good," Lotus said, even though Xia looked terrible without her makeup.

As she walked toward the door, Xia desperately bit her lips in an effort to make them redder.

The iron door banged shut behind her, sending a shiver through the rest of them. Little Jade rocked more violently than before. Lotus wrapped an arm around her.

Ten minutes later, Xia returned. Although half of her dark face was swollen, she pulled her mouth into a grin. "Ha, ha, I said to them: who would want to sleep with old bones like me? One guy punched me. Fuck that bastard! *Pei!*" She spat. "Hold out, girls." She paced around the crowded room excitedly for a few minutes before sinking to the floor. "*Tamade,* wish I could get a drink!"

Lotus was the next one to be summoned. Trailing behind a guard in a gray uniform, she made her way through the dim corridor, praying desperately to Guanyin Buddha. On both sides, the detainees craned their necks through the iron bars to watch as she went by. When she entered a brightly lit interrogation room, she had to squint to adjust her eyes. Then a large red banner on the wall came into view: "Leniency to Those Who Confess and Severity to Those Who Do Not."

She straightened her back.

"Sit down," ordered one of the two policemen who were sitting behind a desk beneath the banner. A guard stood on either side of them.

Lotus sat on a low stool positioned in front of the policemen.

The older policeman asked Lotus's name and home province. The younger one took notes.

"Where do you work?"

"Moonflower Massage Parlor," Lotus replied.

"The one on East Station Road?"

"Yes."

"And you live in the back of the parlor?"

"Yes."

"I am familiar with that sort of arrangement." A knowing smile played on the policeman's lips. Eyeing her chest, he asked: "And you call yourself a masseuse?"

Lotus looked down and saw how her tight white top highlighted the contours of her breasts, her nipples pointing through.

"Do you always massage clients without your underwear?"

The men burst out with a shriek of laughter. Their stares burned her cheeks. She crossed her arms to block their view.

"I used my bra to bandage my friend's hand. It got caught—"

The older policeman struck the desk so hard that the lid of his porcelain teacup bounced off. "Don't change the topic. You're a prostitute, aren't you?"

"No, I'm a masseuse."

"Where did you get your training? Which medical college?" The policeman's voice was sour.

"I was trained at the parlor."

"Masseuse!? Specializing in massaging the part between men's legs, right?"

Lotus said nothing.

The policeman took off his cap. He scratched his head and sighed. "Why don't we just get on with it? I've got so many of you to get through. I don't want to go home late again tonight. My wife has been complaining so much!"

Lotus didn't know what to say. Just then she heard footsteps and a cheerful voice called out as the door swung open. "Guys! Almost lunchtime."

"We won't be a minute. We've got a granite-brain here. Masseuse? Just look at her," the policeman said, waving at Lotus.

"Let's have a look. Come on, look up. Don't be shy." The newcomer officer tapped her on her shoulder.

Lotus looked up and saw a young broad face with large thick earlobes. It was the policeman who had arrested her that first time.

A look of surprise crossed his face. "We've met before, haven't we?"

Lotus tried to shift her body away from him but he just stood there, scrutinizing her. After a while, he turned to his colleagues. "I know her. Let her go for now, I'll handle her myself."

"Okay-la, if you say so," said the older policeman. After another scratch of his head, he put his cap back on.

CHAPTER 10

仁者见仁，智者见智

The Benevolent See Benevolence and the Wise See Wisdom

Goose bumps rose on Bing's arms as he entered the air-conditioned lobby of the International Trade Center. Uniformed security guards fended off the flocks of poor who sought the cool air within the automatic doors. A stern sign—"Those Not Appropriately Dressed Will Not Be Admitted"—stood propped up on the shining floor.

As he headed for the lift, Bing passed the glitzy cosmetic counters displaying Christian Dior, Estée Lauder, and Chanel products. Who would spend five hundred yuan on a little lipstick? he thought. The nouveau riche and high-class prostitutes would. Pearl would.

Bing was annoyed that he had overslept the day before. "Overslept" was putting it mildly. He had woken up just as the sun was slipping down into the hills, and he had missed his chance to see Lotus. He wanted to make sure he could see her today before she started to work.

He checked his watch. Five minutes to go before his lunch appointment in the revolving restaurant on the top floor. He was meeting *The*

Southern Window's Zhang Jianguo, who had tracked him down with an interview request. Bing had readily agreed. Zhang was a well-established journalist who had made a name for himself exposing sensitive social issues. *The Southern Window,* a weekly newspaper based in Shenzhen, was the most popular publication in the country. The paper's investigative stories frequently pushed the line of what was considered acceptable by the authorities.

Bing stepped into the lift and pressed the button for the forty-ninth floor. The International Trade Center was one of the first sights he had visited in Shenzhen. Built at the incredible rate of three stories a day in the early 1990s, the center had once been the tallest building in the country, and a symbol of the economic miracle of the Special Economic Zone. Now it was dwarfed by other taller buildings around it. As he ascended, he looked out through the glass panels at the high-rises mushrooming around the city center, competing with each other in height and design. China's manifesto of modernity, Bing thought.

As he entered the restaurant, a broad-shouldered man strode over. "Are you Mr. Hu?" he asked rather loudly. His eyes, slightly obscured under jutting eyebrows, glowed like high-voltage bulbs. He looked a few years younger than Bing and a good deal more energetic.

"Yes," Bing replied.

The man grabbed his hand and gave him a bone-crushing handshake. "I'm Zhang Jianguo. I've long heard your name, it thunders in my ears." He uttered this obsequious cliché with such sincerity that Bing felt his ego flattered.

"Oh, you are very kind." Bing shook the man's big hand with equal warmth. "Mr. Zhang, your name isn't unknown either."

The journalist smiled, showing neat white teeth. "This is our photographer Little Wang." He pointed to a floppy-haired young photographer holding a tripod.

Bing greeted the photographer with a nod.

"Do you mind sitting by the window?" Zhang said, gesturing with a strong arm.

Bing was glad to have the opportunity to appreciate the bird's-eye view of the city. It occurred to him how rarely he went out these days, taking little advantage of the huge variety of restaurants on offer. This one was airy and bright, with light pouring in from the glass walls. Groups of tourists took photos of the changing scenery outside as the restaurant revolved. Businessmen negotiated over the dining tables. Young couples took refuge in the cool interior, feeding each other ice cream or singing along to the love songs of Canto-pop queen Faye Wong, which were playing over the background speakers. Young couples? More like kids, Bing thought. Each time he ventured out of his room, he was struck by how young the faces were in this migrant city.

A pimple-faced waitress in a yellow-and-red uniform came over and handed them a menu.

"What would you like to eat?" Zhang asked.

"I am easy. Why don't you order? One spicy dish would be great."

"Okay, fish head on a bed of hot chili and prickly ashes. Please throw in a few more chilies." Zhang made the order. Then his eyes flicked across to Bing. "And we'll take the shrimp dumplings and durian pie. Both are specialties here."

While Zhang ordered bottles of local Jingwei beer and a few other dishes, Bing watched the photographer set up his tripod. Journalists could be aggressive at times, but he had to admit he had been enjoying their attention lately. Conscious of the lens that was pointed at him, Bing flicked some hair back from his forehead with his fingers.

Within minutes, beer was brought to the table. The journalist poured it into two glasses.

"Congratulations on your recent award," Zhang said in his booming voice, raising his glass. "Your photos are both telling and unexpected."

Bing also raised his glass and took a large sip. The compliment went down as smoothly as the beer. He savored the words as well as the sensation of the cold beer as it spread inside him. There was nothing more satisfying than that first mouthful.

"Now, I trust you've read some of our profiles before?"

"I shall feel flattered to be among the outstanding people you've profiled," Bing said with a smile.

Zhang turned on a pen-size recorder and began by asking about his family background, education, and his business experiences. The journalist had apparently done his homework. "I'm sure you're tired of this question, but how did you become interested in 'willow trees on the roadside and flowers on the wall'?" He used an old poetic term for prostitutes.

Back when he had been confronted with this question for the first time, Bing hadn't known how to answer. Now, after a few interviews, he had grown more confident about articulating his interest. Clearing his throat, his words poured out in a steady flow. "In China, prostitution is a blurred dirty word. Nobody talks about it, but it affects the lives of millions of mostly uneducated young girls. My aim is to show a more human side of the lives of these working girls. Through my photos, I hope to help people understand this issue in order to better address it."

Instead of taking notes, Zhang fired off another question: "Was there a personal experience that inspired you to take up this project?"

Bing knew he was talking to a veteran journalist who wouldn't be fooled by any bluffing. "For me, prostitution is a window through which to see the changes in this country," he stated. "It has to do with the tension brought by the economic reforms, right? And I do believe photography can make a difference. People need to see it as well as read about it."

Zhang nodded. "Sure, I think we can all agree with that. Prostitution touches on all those hot-button issues—migration, the income gap, corruption, sex, morals, you name it."

Bing eased into his chair. He and the journalist were on the same page. He made a mental note to borrow some of the journalist's phrases for future interviews.

"I'd like to write a book about prostitution, myself, if I had the time. It'd probably be a best seller!" Zhang declared, his chiseled face cracking into a smile. Then he resumed his questioning mode, straight-faced. "But I'm still curious about the particular reason behind your interest. I get the feeling it's not just some kind of sociological thing. Am I right?"

Bing shifted in his chair as he felt uncomfortably transparent. "Well,

I mean we're all fascinated by prostitution, right? I confess I'm no exception."

Zhang chuckled. "Sure we are, but for most men, an occasional visit to a brothel or a little Internet porn would satisfy that itch. I think it means something more to you, no?"

Bing looked out of the window without answering. When his gaze returned, he noticed that Zhang was leaning back in his chair and glancing down at his notebook.

"I read an interview with you in which you mentioned that the American photographer Jacob Riis is your role model. Why is that?" the journalist asked.

Bing's facial muscles relaxed. "Yes, Riis's work influenced my photography. He wasn't just a social documentary photographer. He was a social reformer, as well."

Less than two years earlier, Bing had spent hours in the Shenzhen library, studying photography books. It was there that he came across Riis's works. Riis, a police reporter turned pioneer in social photojournalism, had captured the desperate poverty of the nineteenth-century New York slums in his book *How the Other Half Lives,* and his writings and photography had aroused public interest in social change.

Bing dreamed that his own works might have some kind of impact, too. It was after his discovery of Riis that he had decided to move into the slums and record the lives of the prostitutes who lived there.

The waitress brought food to the table. For a while, they focused on eating.

Soon Zhang restarted his probing. "You mentioned social responsibility. You're a Communist Party member, right?" he asked, half a smile hanging on his lips. "My editor will love me for asking this question," he added, dryly.

"Yes, I'm a Party member," Bing replied, and then paused to take a sip of beer. He had not paid his Party membership dues since leaving the soap factory. As a teenager, he had indeed naïvely believed in the glorious cause of communism. At university, as he investigated the world's religious belief systems, he had started to resent the way the

Party used communism as a form of religion. He nevertheless became a member, following Yuejin's steps, because everyone said the Party membership was useful, even though he had no longer believed in the Party or communism. But Zhang didn't need to know that.

"I think my generation was brought up believing that one should make some contribution to society," Bing said after some deliberation.

"Interesting!"

Bing sipped his beer, watching the journalist in action. In his notebook, scribbles emerged on the page like dancing oracle-bone inscriptions. He gathered that Zhang was using some kind of shorthand. He wondered what it would be like to be a journalist. Maybe he could have been a good one. Too late for that now, though. In any case, becoming an author was a better bet.

"How did you become a journalist?" Bing asked.

Zhang looked up at him and put down his pen. "I was an academic. I lost my job after 1989."

"You were in the student movement?"

"Actively," Zhang replied, taking a grilled prawn.

Feeling a bond of solidarity, Bing held out his hand. "We probably crossed paths on the square. Glad to meet you."

Zhang shook his hand firmly and continued his story. "It was probably for the best. Anyway, after leaving my university, I worked as a freelance journalist, and after I got married I accepted an offer from the newspaper. Stable income, but less freedom!" He shrugged his shoulders and smiled ruefully.

Zhang's square-shaped face and angular jaw gave him the confident appearance of someone who knew his place in the world and felt comfortable filling it. Bing imagined that his large presence and his assertiveness would make him very popular with women, more so than the pretty-faced young photographer, who had left a little while earlier.

"It seems I've taken the opposite path," said Bing.

He noticed that the journalist was about to make a comment, but after consulting his notebook, Zhang changed the topic. "So what's your relationship with these working girls? Do you pay them for their time?"

Bing was slightly startled. Was this a clever double entendre? Zhang's face betrayed no ironic intent. "Well, no! No money changes hands." He could feel his face reddening. "It's reciprocal and we help each other out. They sometimes come to me for advice, asking me to write letters home, that kind of thing."

The journalist flashed an impudent smile. "So, just like Gabriel Garcia Marquez in his youth? Didn't he make a living by writing letters for his prostitute friends?"

"Indeed, yes, he lived in a brothel for a while."

Zhang made a circle in his notebook and asked: "Now, this Girl A, why did you choose her?"

"Oh, Girl A. Of course," Bing said. "I once helped to get her out of detention."

"What happened?"

"The usual crackdown on migrants," Bing said. Given a chance to explain the entire background story, he opened up, telling Zhang about the migrants from the countryside, how they were always subject to police scrutiny, how the government needed their cheap labor but wanted to keep them under control.

As he spoke, Bing realized how much he missed such intellectual discussions, and Zhang, nodding and listening intently, struck him as a kindred spirit. The journalist reminded him of his old classmate Yuejin. A son of a ranking leader, Yuejin had the confident air of someone favored by fate, which Bing had taken at first as arrogance. But the incident of saving the drowning boy had changed their relationship. Born in 1957, the year Chairman Mao had launched the disastrous Great Leap Forward, or the Great Yuejin in Chinese, the young man was as politically charged as his name. Yuejin was a few years older and a lot more worldly, and he introduced Bing to a group of liberal-minded, idealistic friends, all self-styled social commentators. Bing found a community he felt he belonged to, and his opinionated friend found a firm supporter. Over beer and peanuts, they would analyze the latest corruption scandal, discuss books by Nietzsche and Freud, debate endlessly if the government would allow real political reforms, and argue whether western-style democracy was the answer to China's future. After graduation, the group continued to meet, but less and less frequently over the years as demands from career and family increased. Since moving south, Bing had made only "meat and alcohol" acquaintances. Maybe today he had finally found his intellectual equal.

"Did you know that violence is the biggest threat faced by the working girls, especially for those from the lower end of the market?" Bing asked.

"I can imagine that."

"From what I understand, usually it's not the clients who rough them up. It's the cops."

"That, I didn't know, but I'm not too surprised," Zhang replied as he took notes. "Do you know why Girl A got into the trade?"

"Not exactly. She's a very private person."

"Really?" Zhang's jutting eyebrows jumped. "Somehow, I thought you were good friends already."

"Well, sure, but it's not a topic that just comes up naturally," said Bing, suddenly feeling both defensive and embarrassed. "But I'll find out, for sure. In fact, I've been thinking of following her back to her home village in Sichuan, to see her in her own setting. It may shed some light on her past."

"Showing the relationship between her and her family would make a good photo essay."

Bing saw the opportunity he had been waiting for. "Would your paper be interested?"

"I'll have a word with my editor to see if we can fund the trip—providing you'll give us exclusive use of your photos."

"I can also write a short article to go with it."

"That would be great. Hopefully we'll find a way to work together," Zhang said with a businesslike smile.

Bing took a sip of beer, secretly congratulating himself.

The soaring Emperor Building came into view once again, reminding Bing that they had been in the revolving restaurant for an hour. It was just completing a full circle. "I should get going," he announced.

"I'll probably have to call you for some follow-up questions, if that's okay."

"Of course." Bing rose.

Zhang also stood up and bowed, presenting his name card with both hands. "It's a real pleasure to have met you. Here in Shenzhen one doesn't get to meet such interesting people every day."

Bing took the name card with both hands. "I sincerely hope that we can meet again."

"You go ahead. I'll take care of the bill."

Bing nodded and took his leave. As he walked out of the restaurant, he could feel his back burning. He knew the journalist's sharp eyes were following him.

CHAPTER 11

站在屋檐下，不得不低头

⊰———————————————————————————⊱

Standing Under the Eaves, You Have to Lower Your Head

"*Wei,* who is this?"

Hearing Moon's hoarse voice hissing over the cell phone, Lotus cried with relief. "Boss, it's Lotus."

"Thank heaven you've finally called. Where are you? Zhangmutou Detention Center?"

"Yes, yes, we are."

"Those fucking cops! I've paid so much money to get them to leave us alone. Why didn't they warn me about this campaign?"

"Boss, could you get us out of here?"

"Of course! I'll have to. Do you expect me to sleep with those peasants myself?"

"Also, Boss, could you tell Hu Laoshi, I mean the photographer, about this?"

Before Lotus got an answer, the guard snatched the phone from her hand. "Time is up. It'll cost another ten yuan if you want to continue."

Lotus's eyes followed the guard as he started to bargain with another woman.

Xia tapped her shoulder. "What did the boss say? She'll get us out of this dogshit prison?"

"She will," Lotus said, her voice unnecessarily loud.

On the second night, Lotus lay on the mattress, struggling to grab hold of a corner of a sheet, the only thing that could shield her against swarms of fat mosquitoes. The bed was too crowded for her to lie on her back, so she slept on her side. The cell had cooled down a little. Mosquitoes whined and the girls occasionally broke into squabbles over the sheets— there was only one sheet for every three women. Next to her, Mimi snored. Xia and Little Jade were asleep on another mattress.

Lotus couldn't sleep. Ever since her interrogation that morning, she had been like a nervous bird, startled by the slightest sounds. Whenever she heard footsteps, her heart would jump into her throat, and she feared each time that she would be dragged out again. And what had the broad-faced policeman meant when he said that he would deal with her himself?

Earlier that day, the women in her cell had competed to tell the worst horror stories they knew: how one well-dressed *ji* was robbed and her bank account emptied, and how one young girl was tricked into the woods, where she was raped and then brutally murdered.

After her disappointment with Funny Eye, Lotus had been more inclined to accept Family Treasure's offer. The arrest had driven her to make up her mind. The prospect of living with the man, with his scrubbing-brush hair and that bare apartment, its walls crawling with grease, didn't entice her. But she would be safer, with a steady income.

I could have been the proper wife of a well-to-do farmer if I had stayed in the village, she thought bitterly.

Lotus might have married Luo Yijun, a neighbor and a classmate, if she hadn't met Little Zhao, the first city person she'd ever known. Little Zhao was a young government official who had been sent to her village to research rural living conditions.

With his checkered shirt, his backpack, and his scholarly manner, Little Zhao was a new breed of person to Lotus. Every night, he would sit on the millstone outside his host family's house, gluing his ears to his radio, which blasted foreign sounds or music.

One day she gathered up her courage and presented him with some juicy plums carefully wrapped in a pretty handkerchief. Little Zhao was taken by surprise. After some hesitation, he took the fruit and asked which grade she was in school. Her face turned the color of the plums and she replied that she had dropped out.

"What a shame," he said. "You should know that education is the best way to change one's fate."

She didn't reply but never forgot his remark.

Little Zhao left after a month. Lotus began to dream of him and the world beyond Mulberry Gully with growing eagerness. Those who had made it in the cities always sent money home. Their families bought TV sets and knocked down mud houses to build brick ones. Cities seemed so exciting. In contrast, life in the village was like a pool of stagnant water.

Then, four months later, an opportunity presented itself.

It was the second day of the Spring Festival, in 1995. Lotus had been silently making sweet dumplings with Grandma Nai at home. Just then Hua, one of the few girls who had dared to leave the village, came to visit. By Buddha, how Hua had changed! Instead of her long pigtails, there was a bird's nest on her head with frizzy curls, and her lips were redder than the New Year paper decorations stuck on doors and windows around the village. Her thick, fur-trimmed platform leather boots made her taller. Hua boasted that she had been working at a factory in Shenzhen, making shoes for export to foreign countries.

She sounded different and so savvy, too. "Shenzhen, you know, right next to Hong Kong, the British colony."

"Oh, that place by the sea, with palm trees and towering buildings?" Lotus asked, grabbing Hua's arms.

"Exactly!" Hua let out a whistle. "Why don't you come with me? My factory needs more hands."

Lotus needed no persuasion. She dusted off the flour from her hands. "I'm coming."

Just a few days earlier, Lotus's father, without consulting her, had accepted a marriage proposal from Luo Yijun's family, along with the betrothal money, a thick wad of twenty thousand yuan wrapped in a piece of red paper. She and Yijun had grown up together, skipping ropes and catching shrimp in the river. He was sweet-natured and good-looking enough, and she had enjoyed his attentions at first, and the privilege of watching TV with his family. But his eyes didn't see far ahead and his chest didn't hold ambitions. All he wanted was to get married early and start a family. He didn't need to venture out, since his family had already made enough money running a transportation business. In addition to the TV set, they had even bought a washing machine, which they used for storing rice.

Lotus's decision to leave for Shenzhen instead of marrying Yijun led to an all-out war at home. Nai cried and hit her own chest as if it were a drum. Ba shouted out a string of hateful words in one long breath: "I need to whip you into shape, you little unfilial beast, Chouchou! We brought you up by feeding you rice. And this is how you pay us back, by letting us lose face!" He picked up a stick, ready to beat his daughter into submission, but Shadan held him back. Ba then opened a trunk and fished a thick wad of notes from inside. He threw the money at Lotus's feet.

The notes, in fifties and hundreds, spilled out of the red paper wrapping. Lotus had never seen so much money in her life. In the countryside, the betrothal money was the reward for the bride's family for bringing up the girl. She squatted down and picked the notes up from the mud floor. "I owe you, Ba. I'll make money and pay you back," she declared.

On the dirty mattress of the detention cell, Lotus used her fingers and figured out that the dribs and drabs of money she had sent home had exceeded twenty thousand yuan. A pang of sweet pride, tinged with bitterness, spread through her.

Call me unfilial, if you like, Ba, Lotus said in her heart. But I am the one who is holding up this family! She had learned from her brother how fellow villagers laughed at Ba for his inability to control his own daughter. His anger slowly diminished as time went by and as more and more money flowed into his hand.

Mimi stirred in her sleep. She scratched her arms, which were speckled with mosquito bites, and turned, pulling the sheet away. Lotus gently pulled it back. When Mimi had been interrogated that afternoon, she had started to cry even before the questioning, saying she couldn't stand any pain. The policeman laughed, gave her a hard kick on the backside and told her to get lost.

Lotus almost wished she had been beaten. Convinced that she had to suffer for the *zuo nei,* the bad or evil things she had committed in this or her previous life, she always expected some kind of disaster. Physical suffering was the least of her fears.

Lotus stared at the iron bars and wriggled closer to Mimi's warm body.

The detention center seemed to operate on its own time. One day ticked by without any news; then another. Lotus spent another ten yuan to call Moon again, but she learned that they would have to wait for a bit longer. A nationwide "sweeping away the yellow" campaign was still in full swing.

On the third night, Lotus dreamed that she was losing her teeth. In the dream, she pulled out her teeth one by one, with her rubbery fingers, and threw them into a white porcelain rice bowl. The first few teeth skidded inside, then settled. The bowl slowly filled, each tooth bright and white, like a larger grain of rice.

She woke with a start. She felt her teeth with her tongue. Thank Buddha, they were still there.

The jangle of the rusty iron door yanked her from her thoughts. A guard called out her official name, Luo Xiangzhu. She stayed on the mattress for a few seconds to collect herself before she scrambled up.

When Lotus arrived in the interrogation room, she found the young policeman, sitting behind the desk, his broad face shining in the glare of a single lamp. The door creaked. She saw a flash of gray at the door and the guard was gone. She crossed her arms in front of her but could not stop her body from shaking.

"Sit down, please," the policeman said.

Lotus lowered herself onto the stool.

"I would have brought you out earlier if I had managed to get my shift changed." He spoke in a soothing voice, as if talking to a demanding girlfriend. "I was very happy to see you again. Do you know why?"

She shook her head.

"Because I knew I was *tamade* right! You are a *ji*! I knew that when I first laid eyes on you at the embankment." A threat lay just under his gentle voice. "Not only by the way you were dressed. I saw how nervous you were when you saw me."

The policeman stood up and came over to Lotus.

She hung her head. She saw his fat feet bursting out of his leather shoes.

"You have no idea how much you pissed me off last time." He raised his voice. "They let you—a wild *ji*—fly out of this place without even letting me know beforehand. One colleague even said that I arrested you because I took a fancy to you. I lost face for nothing!"

Some drops of spittle landed on Lotus. She didn't dare wipe them off.

"Do you think I enjoy my job? The salary is shitty and the job hard. We have a fucking quota to meet, you know. So we have to arrest a certain number of *ji* and send some to the labor camp. If they don't confess, we just have to beat it out of them. What can we do?" As he talked, the policeman paced up and down the room, his leather shoes making a percussive tapping sound against the concrete floor.

Each sound hit a nerve in Lotus. She held her breath, her hand holding tight to the edges of the stool.

He returned to his desk. "It seems like the friend who rescued you last time has been busy on your behalf. Thanks to him, I have some evidence against you." A smile spread on his fleshy face.

The policeman opened his drawer and took out a copy of *Photography* magazine.

She recognized it at once and felt her head start to spin.

"Nice pictures. Girl A," he said as he flicked through the pages.

Lotus cast down her eyes.

"How did you become a *ji*? I am curious."

"I was raped," she said flatly.

"Raped? Haha! You lot always come up with excuses. You were raped, dumped by husbands, or tricked by human traffickers. It's never your own fault, is it?" In a lower voice, the policeman continued. "Apart from the money, do you enjoy sleeping with men? Do you like men with big dicks or small ones?"

She said nothing.

"How much did the photographer pay to get you to pose?"

"Nothing. The photographer is a friend."

"A f-r-i-e-n-d?" He spelled out the word. "Well, he must be a friend of some sort, because he is trying hard to get you out. I am just curious about what kind of friend a prostitute has. That was why I did a bit of research on him."

She stared at the floor, her fingers digging deeper into the stool.

"So why did you let him, this so-called friend of yours, photograph you naked? You just love to get your clothes off, don't you?" he said as he tapped the picture with his fingertips. Silhouetted against the light, Lotus could see the black hairs on his fingers.

She noticed that his hand was shaking. Why was he nervous? Lotus looked up and saw that his face was also tense.

"Take off your clothes," he demanded.

After a moment, she said: "If I do that, will you let me go?"

"That depends on whether or not I am pleased with the show."

Gritting her teeth, Lotus took off her T-shirt, but crossed her arms over her chest.

"Strip, I said a strip show."

She let her arms fall.

There was no answer from him, only labored breathing.

Lotus glanced at him and caught sight of the bulge in his uniform pants. His face was now the color of a pig's liver.

She opened her mouth to speak but there was a frog in her throat. She coughed and said: "We can fuck if you like."

"'If you like,'" he repeated, mimicking her voice.

He stood there, panting heavily. "You have no shame! When I saw you, you looked like a fairy fallen down to earth from heaven. Now I see that you are just a common dirty whore. Get out, now!" he ordered. A muscle twitched in his jaw.

Lotus hurriedly put on her T-shirt and ran for the door.

When he spoke again, the ferocity of his voice startled her. "If you dare utter a word to anyone, I'll have you brought back in and fuck you to death. I promise."

Lotus slammed the door shut behind her. She began to vomit violently, the bitter taste stinging her throat.

The next morning, when her friends questioned her about what had happened during the night, Lotus remained silent. She went through the day as if in a trance.

The following afternoon, a guard turned up, holding a piece of paper.

"Wang Junxia," he shouted.

Xia leaped up. "Yes, sir?"

"Ji Xiaoyu."

Little Jade got to her feet with Xia's help.

"Li Ming."

Mimi got up. "Me too?"

Lotus stood up, too, fixing her eyes on the guard's mouth.

"Out," he ordered.

"We're free then, my brother?" Xia asked again, tugging at the warden's gray sleeves. "What about our friend here?" She pointed at Lotus.

He pushed Xia away. "How would I know? Just get out."

Xia touched Lotus's hand. "Lotus, don't worry, okay? We'll talk to our boss and get you out."

Lotus's eyes followed her friends as they walked out behind the guard. When the iron door slammed shut, the loud bang hit her like a physical blow.

CHAPTER 12

云开见日

The Clouds Disperse and the Sun Starts to Shine

At long last, the metal jaws of the detention center opened and Lotus walked out.

Bing flicked his cigarette into the air and strode toward her from under the shade of a tree where he had been waiting. In a filthy white top, she looked pale and thin, her arms bruised and dotted with mosquito bites. There was a bloodstained bandage on her forehead. She hunched her shoulders as if to ward off the cold, although a fireball was burning in the August sky. He was rather alarmed when he noticed that she didn't seem to be wearing a bra.

"How are you, Lotus?" Bing said, taking her arm.

"Okay," she replied, her voice barely above a whisper.

"Come on, let's go. You'll stay with me for a few days. That's the least I can do."

Without a word, Lotus followed him, like an obedient child, into a waiting taxi.

On the way back to Bing's house, she slept in the back of the taxi, resting her head on the window. He wondered what had happened to her head. He noticed for the first time the fine hair on the side of her face, like down on a fresh peach.

While Lotus was detained, he had worked with Boss Moon, trying to get her out. They hoped that bribes would do the trick. The detention authorities, however, used the photographs of her as evidence of her crime, rendering bribes useless. In desperation, Bing turned to Zhang Jianguo for help. Thanks to the journalist's powerful connections, Lotus was eventually released, four days after the other girls.

When they arrived at Bing's place, she announced that she needed a wash. He had already bought a large plastic bathtub, a nightdress, and other necessities for her. He made her a bath. While she was cleaning herself in his room, Bing waited in the backyard, smoking. He heard her painful groans when the water first touched her wounds. He paced in the yard, beset by a sense of trepidation. He was filled with a tender desire to look after her.

After an hour-long soak, Lotus emerged wearing a cotton nightdress printed with pink daisies. Her hair was wet and she had removed the dirty bandage from her forehead.

Bing invited her to sit down on his chair. Standing behind her, he began hesitantly: "Er, Lotus. I have to ask you. Did they touch you? I mean, violate you?"

"No."

Thank heaven for that, Bing thought. He applied a new bandage to cover the cut on her forehead. "How did this happen?"

"I did it myself. The last time I was called in for questioning, I banged my head against the wall."

He nearly jumped up. "What? Lotus! You could have killed yourself!"

She darted a look at him. "I didn't want to go through the interrogation again, but I didn't want to kill myself either."

Bing patted her arm. "You poor thing!"

"Not a big deal," she said with no emotion.

He shook his head. "Now, you need a good rest." He tidied up his double bed for her, stacking the books against the wall.

That night, Lotus agreed to sleep on Bing's bed, but insisted that he sleep on the floor beside it rather than in the darkroom. She said she would feel safer that way.

Bing had a sleepless night, and not just because of the hard ground beneath the bamboo mat. Listening to Lotus's regular breathing, his heart was suffocated with tender feelings for the girl; guilt, pity for her suffering, and a longing to know her better.

Lotus spent the rest of the day sleeping. On the morning of the second day, she woke up in much better spirits. Color had returned to her face, which still bore the imprint of the soft bamboo pillow cover.

"I'm going to make you some breakfast," Bing announced, and dashed to the kitchen.

When he returned with a tray laden with food, he found Lotus, still in her nightdress, sitting at the desk and looking about the room. Her hair was tied back with a white cotton handkerchief.

Bing placed the meal in front of her—congee, a savory rice porridge, with chicken, pickles, and tea.

She looked at him, then at the food. Suddenly her face turned rose red.

"What's the matter?"

"I don't deserve all this, Hu Laoshi," she said, reddening more. "You are too kind to me."

"Stop talking nonsense, please," Bing scolded softly. "Now, eat your breakfast." He sat down in a folding chair beside her and picked up his own bowl of porridge.

Lotus started to eat, demurely at first, picking a small amount of congee with her chopsticks. As the food cooled down and her appetite grew, she sucked on the porridge noisily and then lifted the bowl to her mouth and shoveled it all down.

"Delicious," Lotus said. She burped and then smiled with embarrassment, covering her mouth with her hand.

Bing smiled along with her.

Lotus took out her handkerchief and started to comb her hair with a wooden comb, one of the few items she had asked Mimi to bring over from the parlor. Her soft hair had tangled up a little.

"Ma left this comb to me," she said as she removed some loose strands of hair from the comb and placed it back on the table. It was dark and shining from years of use, with one and a half teeth missing in the middle.

"I haven't gone home for three years," Lotus suddenly stated.

"We are two of a kind," Bing said, taking pleasure in finding connections with her. The fact that he had traveled a long way from the world he was from had also alienated him from his family. After Bing's father died, his younger sister was left to take care of their mother, and to compensate for Bing's absence he sent them money. He felt guilty for not being a better son. He knew his mother had pinned all her hopes on him and he knew how she had loved him, in her suffocating fashion.

The sun had climbed high, shining through the south-facing window. Bing walked over to let down the blinds and cleared the table.

Then he propped Lotus up in bed with pillows and sat down on the edge of the bed. He could see her breasts through the thin cotton of her nightdress. He looked away.

"Tell me about your mother," Bing asked.

"Ma was very beautiful, and very smart," Lotus said in her soft voice. "When I was little, she taught me songs and traditional poems by drawing the characters in the mud with a stick."

"My father also made me recite traditional poems as soon as I could talk."

"Hu Laoshi, I envy that you had an educated father. Do you think that him being a city man made it easier for you to become one?"

Bing pondered on this. "My life in the city was far from easy at first," he said. "But looking back, I realize that I owe so much to my old man. It was he who taught me to love books."

"My mother wasn't that well educated, but she would never have taken me out of school." Lotus sighed. "*Ai,* but she died of cancer when I was twelve."

"That must have been hard." Bing waited for her to talk more about her mother, but Lotus simply sat there, as a shadow of sadness settled on her face. He started to tell her the story of his mother in the hope that she'd open up to him about her family. Although her family were farmers, his mother was strong-willed and lucky enough to marry a schoolteacher with a salary.

"Have you heard about 'the three natural disasters'?" Bing asked.

She blinked her eyes, thinking hard, but shook her head in the end.

"Never mind. After the Great Leap Forward, there was a widespread famine in China. Millions died. In fact, it was actually more of a man-made disaster."

"Why man-made?" She looked at him innocently.

"Bad economic policies, false claims of harvest yields and such. It's complicated." Bing waved a hand. "Anyway, in 1961, the year I was born, our neighbors were reduced to eating tree bark, duckweed, and even leather belts, and many babies died. Thanks to my father's salary and his ration, we at least had some thin rice porridge to eat. My mother became determined to make me another salaryman with an 'iron rice bowl'—a proper government job in the city. Well, as you know, the only way for people like us to get there was through education. Ah, Lotus, you can't imagine how strict she was. Each time I drew a wrong character, she would rap my hand with a bamboo stick."

"My mother was the nicest mother ever," Lotus declared. "I don't think she ever laid a finger on me."

"Lucky you." Bing shifted in his seat. "As for my mother, I suppose it was her way of showing her love."

"And she can be proud of you. But I—"

A large fly landed on the window by the bed and snatched her attention. In the sunlight, its large greenish head looked almost transparent. Lotus stared at the fly for a good while and then said: "While in jail, I began to wonder if I am really a broomstick star."

Bing knew she was referring to the traditional term for a female jinx.

He was taken aback by the bitterness in her voice. "Lotus, do you know what a broomstick star is?"

"An unlucky woman who is born under a broomstick star—the unlucky star."

Bing twisted the corner of his mouth and shook his head. "Well, 'broomstick star' refers to a comet. It got the name because of its shape. You know, it usually has a tail, like a broomstick." He explained that the ancient Chinese had considered comets to be inauspicious because when a comet emerged, it outshone the moon, the symbol of luck and happiness. "So when ancient people couldn't explain such a natural phenomenon, they labeled it as inauspicious."

Lotus rested her chin on her knees. "Some women in my village called me a broomstick star after . . ." She faltered. "So many unlucky things have happened in my life. Yet I don't want to be resigned to my fate. I just don't," she said, pursing her lips. Her voice was filled with sadness, and defiance.

Tears began to roll down her cheeks. Bing controlled his urge to wipe them off. He put a hand on her shoulder. "Broomstick star? You, who brought me such good luck?"

She didn't respond.

He persuaded her to rest. After he helped her to get back into bed, he stepped into the yard, closing the door gently behind him.

Bing sat down in the tired wicker chair under the Dragon Eye tree and started to smoke. As he puffed, he watched the smoke swirl slowly in front of him.

A breeze brought about a sweet smell from the tree, which was bearing plenty of small round fruit. The leaves were shining in the sun like coins. Holding the cigarette butt in his mouth, he stood up to pick a dragon eye and shelled it. The black seed showed through the translucent flesh, like an eyeball. He dropped the cigarette and ate the fruit.

Bing sank back in the wicker chair, his eyes shut.

The image of Lotus's thin shoulder blades flooded his mind. He wondered how much trauma they had borne. He found himself increasingly attached to her. A few days earlier, he had been invited out to dinner by his former manager, a widowed southern beauty. He used to have a soft spot for her, but over the dinner, he found her smart talk about the economy pretentious, and her flirtatious smiles irritating. Lotus was all he could think about.

How about Mei? After that night, Mei had continued to call him. They chatted about their daughter and what was happening in their lives, and before Bing knew it, Mei had started offering her advice again. For example, she had advised him to turn down the offer of a staff position from the *Special Economic Zone Herald*. Perhaps she still secretly harbored the hope of getting back together, even though, to his relief, she hadn't raised the issue again. Or perhaps she simply had the good intention of maintaining a better relationship. He found himself enjoying her attention: he had always appreciated her intelligence and energy. But for Bing, there was no way back—"No spirited horse would return to graze on an old pasture," as people say.

Suddenly, he felt light breaking in his cloudy mind. Why was he clinging on to his life here? Lotus. She was the reason.

Bing stared at his photos of the girls, published in the *Southern Window*. As requested, he had sent some photos of himself to Zhang Jianguo as well, thinking they were going to accompany his profile. But there was no profile. Why not? Was the subject too sensitive? Or perhaps the journalist didn't really believe his story?

Standing by his desk, Lotus peered at the paper. "That's Mimi, isn't it?" she said, pointing at a photo that showed a girl, her face half covered by her messy hair, pretending to breast-feed a white cat with a bow tie.

"Indeed, Mimi and Little White."

"You know, Hu Laoshi, Mimi always called Little White her daughter." She giggled but only briefly. "Poor Mimi, she wants to become a mother so badly!"

"Perhaps she's in love. Women in love often want children with their loved ones," Bing suggested.

Lotus pondered this. "Maybe Mimi doesn't want to be lonely. She often says that she's afraid to end up alone."

"Maybe." Bing carefully folded up the newspaper. "What are you reading?"

"One of your books." She held it out for him to see. "Look, what a beautiful hat!"

She was holding *The Portrait of a Lady* by Henry James. The girl on the cover was wearing a large hat, decorated with flowers and feathers.

"That's a great book. It's about a young lady confronting her destiny," he replied, and was immediately embarrassed by his pompous language. "This young American lady goes to Europe. She wants to determine her own fate; to decide her own life."

Lotus went silent for a moment before sitting down on the bed, still clutching the book. "I don't understand this whole thing about fate. I remember when Ma died, my grandma kept saying: 'No matter how strong you are, you just can't win over fate.'" She gazed into the distance, as if communicating with some divine force in the sky.

Bing could tell that this troubled her. He searched for a good answer that was convincing to both of them. "From what I can gather, Buddhism, at least modern Buddhism, is a positive philosophy. That is: one's fate is determined by oneself, and not some god."

Lotus frowned, seemingly unable or unwilling to digest Bing's words.

She focused her attention on the book again. "Is it a love story?"

"Yes, it is."

Lotus flipped through the book. "I've never read a foreign book before."

Bing took the book from her hands. "I'll read it to you, if you like."

"*Yaodei!*" Lotus replied—*yes* in the Sichuan dialect, which Bing found delightful, much more expressive and musical than standard Mandarin. She sat back on the bed, against the wall, with the simple delight of a child awaiting a bedtime story.

He had always been very fond of reading aloud. Back in his university days, he had spent hours imitating the China Central Television presenters' standard Mandarin in a bid to get rid of his rural accent.

Now Bing pulled his chair closer to the bed, cleared his throat, and once again put on his CCTV presenter voice.

Lotus listened attentively, leaning against the wall.

For the next few days, Bing read *The Portrait of a Lady* for Lotus, explaining things when necessary. She was both captivated and puzzled at the same time.

"Do Europeans look down on Americans?" she asked.

"Not exactly. Isabel Archer doesn't know about or care for the social conventions of Europe."

"Those people do nothing but talk and talk," she observed.

As they made their way through the book, Lotus asked more and more questions: "Isabel says no to the rich lord? Mad! Does she know how poor she really is?"

"Not really. But she is a free spirit, self-assured, and she's willing to live with the consequences of her choice."

"If she were as poor as me, she wouldn't have said no," she asserted.

"Perhaps. 'Poverty stifles dignity,' as people say." He quoted the saying but immediately regretted it. He glanced at her and noticed the color rising on her cheeks.

He closed the book. "It's time for you to get some rest."

Mimi had been popping over every day, for lunch, and to complain about her boyfriend. In a bossy tone that surprised Bing, Lotus advised her friend to get rid of Lanzai once and for all, but Mimi said she couldn't.

Then one day, all the girls from the parlor paid a visit, bringing bundles of snacks: roasted chestnuts, salty duck's stomach, and kebabs on skewers. As if to declare her closeness to Lotus, Mimi was the first to climb onto the bed with her, and she started to comb her hair. Little Jade followed, and Xia perched on the bedside.

They examined Lotus's wounds.

"Will there be a scar on my forehead?" Lotus asked her friends clustered around her, though she didn't look particularly worried.

Moon studied Lotus's face and stroked her chin. "No, there won't be," she assured Lotus. The boss then made herself comfortable in the only proper chair in the room, throwing her white silk scarf over her shoulder. "But you must avoid soy sauce. Otherwise the dark color may seep through the skin."

Bing sat in the folding chair, watching the dynamics among the girls with great interest.

Little Jade pressed a small plastic bag into Lotus's hand and winked. "This is for you, Sister Lotus."

"What is it? Why so mysterious?"

"A gift from me. Thank you, my good sister, for saving my life," Little Jade said, bowing toward Lotus.

"Of course, you wouldn't have died. How is your hand?" Lotus asked, bending over to check out the girl's hand.

"No problem. You see." Little Jade wiggled her fingers, though there was a raw-looking scar on the back of her hand.

Bing had heard that Xia had nursed Little Jade back to health. He could usually distinguish a prostitute from ordinary girls—the way her eyes would always be searching, calculating, and demanding. But in Little Jade's eyes, he couldn't read any of that. She had probably been numbed by her traumas, preferring instead to focus on the small pleasures of life.

"Open the gift!" Xia called out.

Under the watchful eyes of her friends, Lotus took out a fancy fluffy bra, trimmed with bright red down, from the bag. "*Wasai*, look at this!"

"My idea," Xia said. "Isn't it great?"

"Put it on then. You can charge an extra hundred yuan just for letting the customer look at it," Moon joked.

"A hundred yuan? If only!" Lotus placed the bra in front of her chest, giggling.

"I'll make some tea," Bing announced, and headed toward the kitchen. When he returned, he knocked on the door.

"Come in," the girls all called out.

He stepped in with a tea tray, with exaggerated pomp and ceremony, like an imperial servant.

"My brother, why do you knock on your own door?" Xia asked with a smirk.

"Why? Just in case Lotus was wearing that sexy bra! I'd have to pay a hundred."

More gales of laughter followed.

"Free of charge, only for you," cracked Moon with a wave of her hand, the heavy gold bracelets clanking.

"Thank you, Boss Lady," Bing said, bowing chivalrously before her. Even in informal situations, Moon carried the poised air of someone in charge. She was a very attractive woman with a striking Barbie-doll-like figure: thin long legs, tiny waist, and a large chest. But her beauty had a hard edge to it, and he found the way she stared at people, with her unnatural eyes, quite off-putting. After befriending Mimi, Bing had invited her boss out for a drink, to explain his photo project and to ask her permission to photograph her charges. Moon gave him the go-ahead, on the condition that he ensure that business would continue undisturbed. Fueled by the alcohol, she had started to complain about the difficulties of keeping her business going: dealing with the police, gangsters, clients, and all the fish and dragons swimming in the murky waters of Shenzhen, and how men often tried to take advantage of her, as if she were a common *ji*.

At one point, Bing had interrupted her tirade. "Why don't you just get out of it and leave?"

Moon gulped down some beer in a not so ladylike fashion. "Leave? Where the fuck would I go? My hometown is still as backward as the goddamn Qing Dynasty. I tried to live in Shanghai but people there treated me like a peasant. And anyone who knows anything about my past simply doesn't respect me in the least. Besides, this is the only line of business I know."

It was then that Bing suddenly understood why Moon enjoyed bossing her girls around.

Presently, a jolly mood filled Bing's room. The girls drank tea and beer while munching on melon seeds, pickled plums, and dried persimmons that Bing had brought back from Beijing. As for the roast duck, knowing it wouldn't last, he had offered it to Mimi.

They started to joke, at their clients' expense, as usual. Xia got up, and with surprising comic flair, began to mimic a hesitant client. The man had walked up and down the street half a dozen times before eventually surrendering to her come-ons. "I know his type: wanting to have fun but he doesn't have the balls to just ask for it. So I said: 'Hey, honey, I'm a crack shot, good at "shooting down the airplane" by hand.'" Xia laughed, pumping her hand up and down over an imaginary cock. "And I reeled the bastard in!"

The girls all burst out laughing. Little Jade laughed so hard that she slid down in the bed, kicking her feet like an overturned turtle.

"You're so right, Xia, 'the oldest ginger is the hottest.'" The Boss hacked her coarse laugh, which soon turned into a fit of coughing.

Bing, himself a little tipsy from the alcohol, picked up his camera. "My dear ladies, you all look so lovely together. May I?"

All heads turned to Moon.

Boss Moon blew the smoke sideways through her glittering lips. "Sure. Why not?"

"Not me, I look so ugly," Lotus said.

"Oh, no no! We can't keep our little heroine out of the shots," said Moon, taking off her silk scarf. "Use this to cover your pretty little head. You, ugly? That mustache man came to see you again the other day, with some jars of pickles. He was in a suit. A suit in this hot weather! And the label still on its sleeve!" She cackled.

Bing watched Lotus through the viewfinder as she fiddled with the scarf. He wondered who this "mustache man" was. Someone special?

Xia, her face red, shouted: "Come on, you beautiful virgins. Let's look good for the photo."

Like giddy teenagers, they reapplied their lipstick and assembled for a pose.

Bing took half a dozen shots. The girls all made pouty kissy faces, vying for the attention of the camera. But all he could see was Lotus's face, the scarf emphasizing her soft beauty. He shot a close-up of her.

Moon stumbled over and wrested the camera from Bing's hands. "Let me take a picture of you all."

Dragged and pushed by the girls, Bing sat next to Lotus on the bed. His shoulder touched hers.

Moon clicked her tongue. "*Tse, tse,* photographer. Have you met a man who isn't happy surrounded by so many pretty girls with such nice tits?"

"He would have been a silly monk," Bing said, and grinned at the camera amid fresh bursts of laughter.

CHAPTER 13

归心似箭

Speeding Back Home with the Swiftness of an Arrow

Lotus watched Bing moving restlessly about the room, reading a book one minute, cleaning his camera lens the next, rooting around aimlessly. He had been like an ant on a hot pan ever since the girls' visit. She wondered if he had overheard her conversation with Moon about Family Treasure. The Boss had stayed behind, demanding to know her plan. Lotus admitted that she intended to accept Family Treasure's *ernai* offer.

After her release, Mimi had told Lotus, in an aside, that Funny Eye had come to look for her again. When he heard that Lotus was still in jail, he swore that he would never set foot in the parlor again. Lotus then mulled over the information but decided to push it aside: that business-man was simply too unreliable. All things considered, Family Treasure was her best bet for the moment.

She pondered how Bing would react. Her week-long stay had deep-ened their friendship. He might miss her as a friend, and he might lose one of his models. Beyond that, she couldn't foresee any other impact on his life.

After her nap, Bing started to read aloud from *Portrait of a Lady*, but without his usual expression. He shut the book with relief when Mimi turned up with Lotus's address book, as requested.

After Mimi waddled out, Lotus asked to borrow Bing's phone.

"Sure." He checked his cell phone. "Actually, the battery is dead. Let me charge it up. Is it urgent? Who do you want to call?"

"Family Treasure. He is one of my regulars."

"I gather you are going to marry him?" Bing let out, his face turning the color of a ripe radish. He wiped his face with his white towel but that seemed only to redden it more.

"Marry? No such luck. He's married already. He wants me to be his *ernai*."

"His *ernai*?" he asked, his eyebrows raising questioningly.

She gave him a wary smile. "I am no Princess Huan Zhu."

Bing grabbed the folding chair and seated himself by the bed. "Listen to me. Please don't rush into anything. What kind of guy is he? Is he trustworthy?"

"He's okay, I guess."

"But, Lotus, you're too good to be anyone's mistress!" He took her arm and shook it, as if trying to wake her from a nightmare.

Lotus looked down at his hands, surprised: Bing usually avoided physical contact with the girls around him. She gently pulled away from his grasp. "At least I'll be safe with him," she said.

"Would you ever consider giving it up?" he asked. It was more a plea than a question.

"Giving up being a *ji*? Who wouldn't?" The tangle of the past was too long and too complicated to explain. Lotus raised her voice. "I don't want to look back. Right now, I need the money."

Bing leaned forward. "Look, I can support you and contribute toward your brother's university costs. Will you accept that?"

Lotus listened, in stunned silence.

"I want to change your life."

The words, though softly spoken, carried such weight that she could almost hear them thump on the ground.

She spoke again after a while. "You just feel sorry for me, don't you, Hu Laoshi?"

"Lotus, you are willing to accept Family Treasure's offer. Why not mine?"

She couldn't answer.

"Why can't we be more than friends?" Bing asked, his eyes locking on hers.

Lotus just stared.

Bing bent down and planted kisses on her hands and arms. His unshaven beard, sparse but prickly, irritated her skin. She hadn't even noticed that he had a beard. She recoiled, withdrawing her hands and pulling up the sheet to cover herself. Her own sudden movements fueled her rising anger. How dare he! she thought. He was supposed to be her friend, the only man in her life who didn't want to sleep with her or take advantage of her.

Lotus glanced at him. He was still leaning forward, his hands, holding her own a minute ago, were now resting awkwardly on the edge of the bed. His expression was that of a child who had made a grave mistake.

Confusion swirled inside Lotus. She looked out into the yard, biting her lip.

"I'm sorry," he muttered.

"It's okay." She continued to gaze out through the open window, feeling his eyes on her face.

Outside in the yard, the light of the evening sun had lost its sharpness. A swarm of red-tailed dragonflies gathered, their transparent wings moving gently. The humid air was thick and oppressive.

Lotus smelled a coming storm.

Later that night, Lotus lay in bed, staring up at the dark contours of the wooden beam overhead. It was cooler after the downpour. For the past week, whenever she had awoken at night, Bing's snoring from the floor would soothe her back to sleep. Tonight, however, he had moved to the darkroom, probably feeling awkward about sharing the room after his proposal earlier that afternoon.

She rubbed her temples, trying to ease the pain in her head, which was jammed with too many thoughts. Her fingers moved to the scab on her forehead. Most of her injuries had been self-inflicted. She thought how he had made such a fuss over her and how he had showed such care, as if she were the only thing that mattered under heaven.

Here she was, Lotus thought, lying in his bed. The pillow had his smell. Upon her release, she had accepted his invitation to stay because she looked upon him as a friend.

Like a pebble dropping into a pond, his proposal had caused endless ripples in her heart. She had often wondered why a man of Bing's class would devote so much attention to a girl like herself. She had attributed it to his kindness and his professional needs. But Bing as her husband? Wasn't he a little old? Then again, age wasn't really the issue. What was the real issue? She couldn't pinpoint it. Could he possibly marry her, a *ji*?

In the darkness Lotus rubbed her arm where he had planted the kisses. He had never looked at her as if she were a mule at a market, like the other men did.

What luck, this offer. A pancake fallen from the sky, as her grandma would say! But could he, a freelancer without a steady income, really afford it? And would it be right to accept such an offer, one made out of charity and kindness?

Bing had suggested that they make a trip together to her home village. The *Southern Window*, which had commissioned him, would cover the travel expenses. He pointed out that there was no newspaper around in the village, let alone a publication such as the *Southern Window*. She hadn't yet agreed, as she was now wary about being photographed. Now, all of sudden, she became unbearably homesick.

How simple life had been when she played with white butterflies in the fields as a child. She and Shadan would cut a piece of white paper into the shape of a butterfly and tie it to a string. Real butterflies would chase and dance with the paper one. The siblings would spend a whole afternoon out there, until the evening smoke snaked out of their mud house.

A free trip home. Why not? She was going to get out of the game anyway.

The "fire wagon" charged ahead. Back in her village days, Lotus had dreamed so much about the train—the wagon pulled by a fire. Presently she sat on her lower bunk bed in a carriage full of bunk beds and looked out of the window, watching the lights from the lampposts along the railway fly by.

As soon as she had nodded her agreement to return to her village, Bing made the necessary arrangements. A few days later, they boarded a northbound train. Beyond a river that ran beside the train were the shapes of ragged mountains in the semi-darkness. Listening to the rhythmic rumble of the wheels, she wished the train could fly like a fire dragon and reach her home in an instant.

Lotus felt a gentle tap on her shoulder and turned to see Bing standing in the narrow space between the bunk beds. Clean-shaven, he looked younger and more energetic than usual.

"Some tea?" he offered. "We have another fifteen hours of journey ahead of us."

"Yes, tea, please."

Bing scooped up a metal thermos from under the small table, which was crowded with boxes of dry noodles, fruit, hard-boiled tea eggs, and assorted teacups. He poured water into an empty Nescafé jar, in which he had already placed plenty of green tea leaves.

Excited about the prospect of her home visit over the past few days, Lotus had been chattering cheerfully nonstop, and the awkwardness between them receded somewhat.

She rested against her folded-up bedding and said: "I can't believe traveling by train is so comfortable, and air-conditioned as well."

"Wait until you see the soft sleeper. The attendants make your tea for you," Bing said, ceremoniously setting the teacup down with a respectful bow. "Madam, your tea!" He sat down on the end of the bed by the aisle.

"Thank you!" Lotus giggled. She had to admit that she enjoyed having Bing look after her.

"Boss, here, have a cigarette," said a middle-aged man, sitting by the aisle window. He thrust a cigarette into Bing's face. He had a huge belly as if he had just swallowed a watermelon.

"No thanks. I believe this is a no-smoking compartment." Bing pointed at the sign.

"Don't worry about that, boss." The man shook the cigarette in the air a couple of times, as if it were bait. "Everyone smokes here."

Bing gently pushed away the man's hand. "It's better to obey the rule. Besides, there are female comrades around."

"Female comrades." Lotus wanted to laugh whenever Bing uttered the antique term, which few would use anymore. Yet she liked its respectful connotation.

"It's okay if you smoke," Lotus said.

"All right, then." The businessman lit his cigarette. His big bull eyes darted between Bing and Lotus. "Is this young lady your secretary, boss?" The man addressed Bing, his plump yellow finger pointing at Lotus.

"I am actually a photographer, not a boss," said Bing. "I am following her to her home village to take some pictures for a newspaper."

"*Aiyah,* you a village girl? I would never have guessed." The businessman opened his mouth to smile and revealed smoke-stained yellow teeth.

She felt obliged to smile back. She was never sure whether her urban outfits were successful in concealing her rural origins.

The businessman dragged on. "Lots of peasants bring their dirty habits into the cities. Their quality is too low, those migrants." The criticisms tumbled from his mouth, thick with cigarette smoke. He spat on the floor.

When Bing gave him a disgusted look, the man started to rub the phlegm into the ground with his fake leather shoe, as if trying to make it disappear.

Lotus rose. "I'm going to the toilet."

Inside the train, the loudspeaker blasted news and pop songs. You could order your favorite music track, for a fee, of course. As she made her way along the aisle, she passed sleeping passengers, while others smoked, drank tea or beer, and chatted.

After relieving herself, Lotus was about to return to her bunk, but stopped in the passageway instead. She leaned against the wall, staring at the empty space between the carriages and listening to the clanging of the steel rods underneath the train. The noise plucked her last train ride from the recesses of her memory.

It had been a little more than three years ago when Lotus was taking her cousin Little Red home, in a box. On that trip, she sat close to the toilet—the only place she could find in the packed carriage—and hunched over the box of ashes. She had hidden it under a cloth, so as not to scare other passengers: it was an unlucky thing to bump into something containing ashes of a dead person.

The compartment door slid open and Bing emerged.

"Are you all right?" he asked.

"I was just thinking about my last journey. I brought my cousin home. I . . ." Lotus faltered. She gathered herself. She found it comforting to talk openly to a sympathetic listener like Bing. "Did I tell you about my sweet cousin Little Red?"

"Not yet. Please do tell me."

"She died in a fire at the factory. It's my fault."

"So sorry to hear that. But how was it your fault?"

"I dragged my cousin out to the city. She was happy enough in the village. You see, I was secretly quite afraid to leave on my own, even though I'd never admit that to my family." Lotus let out a shuddering sigh. "If not for me, Little Red would still be alive, probably married with a couple of kids crawling under her feet."

Lotus turned her face away, biting her lip to fight back her tears. But they leaked out anyway.

Bing pushed a handkerchief into her hand.

Lotus took it gratefully and mopped her face with it. She decided to tell Bing something lighthearted. "Do you know what persuaded my cousin to leave the village?"

"What?"

"You'll never guess. Bananas!" Little Red's father had once brought her a banana from Phoenix town. She had bitten into the whole thing, skin and all! But she soon discovered the heavenly taste underneath. "So, when Hua promised us all the bananas we could eat in Shenzhen, Little Red was ready to go."

"I see."

The door to the carriage swung open, and out came the watermelon belly. The businessman stared at them as he passed by, a fixed smile on his face. More passengers streamed out, heading to the toilet and getting ready to turn in for the night.

Bing checked his watch. "Nearly ten o'clock. The lights will be out in a minute. Are you tired?"

The concerned look in his eyes warmed Lotus's heart. "Yes, I'm a bit tired," she said.

A moment later, the train was plunged into darkness. In the dim glow of the floor-level nightlights, they made their way to their bunk beds.

Lotus settled in her bunk. It always took her a while to fall asleep in a new place. Curling up on her side, she thought about the excitement she and her cousin had felt when they arrived at the main railway station in Chengdu, the provincial capital, full of anticipation about their first ride on the fire wagon.

Chengdu station was a bewildering chaos of people, motion, and sound. It was the end of the Spring Festival, and millions of migrants were returning to their jobs in the cities after visiting home. After pushing and shoving her way to the front of the line, Hua managed to buy three tickets, standing only, for the train leaving for Shenzhen at midnight.

Having survived the stampede to board, the cousins stood in the aisle, jostled and pushed about by the crowds around them. Still, nothing could dampen the high spirits of the young girls setting out for their big adventure. When their empty stomachs started to complain, they took out the savory pancakes Nai had made with scallions and a healthy dose of tears. Right up to the last minute, the old woman had tried to stop her granddaughter from leaving. "The city is a place where dragons and fish jumble together. Not a safe place for a young girl."

She responded with Chairman Mao's quotation. "'Women can hold up half of the sky.'"

Nai shook her head and wiped away a fresh bout of tears.

After his initial outburst, Ba had refused to speak a word to her. But Lotus noticed how he had to hold back tears as the time approached for her to leave.

"Soon, I'll buy a down jacket for Nai, the same type Hua bought for her grandma," Lotus announced as she chewed her pancake.

"I want a photograph of myself, with lipstick, but not as red as Hua's." Little Red burst into merry laughter, loud and clear like the ringing of a silver bell. Cheerful-natured, the girl always looked for something to laugh at.

Lotus shushed Little Red. They turned to peer at Hua, who was sitting on her luggage, dozing, her head hanging low. Ever since leaving home, the older girl had suddenly become rather quiet and dispirited.

"Hua said she'll take us to the beach," Lotus said joyfully.

"Beach!? What fun! But we can't swim."

"It'll be great fun just to play in the sea!"

As they traveled farther south, their plan grew grander and grander.

After a full day and night of travel, the trio arrived in Guangzhou, fatigue wrenching at their bones. It was so warm that they had to peel off their padded jackets and knitted woolen trousers. The cousins trailed behind Hua as they left the train station. Outside, the streets were packed with people, bicycles, and cars. Each car horn made Lotus jump, yet people walked in the middle of the road among the moving vehicles. City people are not afraid of traffic, just as country people are not afraid of dogs, Lotus concluded.

They boarded a minibus to Dongguan. But weren't they heading to Shenzhen? Lotus asked. "Dongguan's only an hour away," said Hua. "It's almost a suburb of Shenzhen." These new names and places were all too confusing, and the cousins were too tired to care.

The bus took them farther and farther away from the city, onto a main road. For miles, factory after factory lined both sides of the highway: Prosperous Toy Factory, Shenkong Machinery Factory, Beautiful Fashion Accessory Factory.

They soon fell asleep. When Lotus woke up again, she spotted a factory with a garden in front. Incredibly, it had a swimming pool and manicured green lawns.

Lotus woke up Hua. "Look, look, Hua. What's that?"

Hua rubbed her eyes and looked out. "Oh, that's a high-tech foreign factory. But without plenty of ink in your belly—at least a university degree—you can't get into a place like that." She rested her head on the window and went back to sleep.

High-tech? There were so many things about the city she had to learn, Lotus thought, now wide awake.

Waking up the next day in the dormitory, Lotus didn't know where she was at first. Instead of the usual singing of birds, she heard traffic, and the constant honking of horns rattled her nerves. The dormitory was dark, and the other girls—there were eleven of them—were still sleeping on four bunk beds, each with three levels. The air was stale. She climbed out of her bed.

Lotus used the toilet down the corridor and then stood before the open window. Looking down from the seventh floor, she felt dizzy.

She had never been inside a high-rise building before. Below, she saw paved driveways framed by a dozen rectangular shacks, made from a corrugated material she couldn't name. People here called the shacks workshops. Everything was gray. There were few trees.

Was this really the factory Hua had raved about?

After breakfast, wearing her uniform—a sleeveless green smock that went down to her knees—Lotus was taken to Workshop Number 7. Once inside, her nostrils smarted at the pungent stench. She sneezed. Some workers raised their heads, smiling or nodding at her, but only briefly. In the center of the room, a moving belt carried leather shoes, and several dozen workers at their tables huddled around the belt.

The head of the workshop explained Lotus's job to her: she was to fix shoes that had not been glued together properly. This meant she had to find the splits, often more than one per shoe, then coat the opening with glue and press the edges together. After a few minutes, she would rub off the excess glue with a piece of rubber. The task was simple and the movements robotic. After a couple of hours, her fingers began to ache. But she didn't dare slow down. Her boss had warned that her pay would be docked if she failed to meet her target of a hundred and fifty pairs per day. While waiting for the glue to dry on one shoe, she had to move on to the next. Since there were no windows, long strips of electric lights sizzled overhead all day. As the temperature rose, the workshop felt like a bamboo steamer. Four industrial-size fans blasted the thick foul air around, bringing little relief. Apart from toilet breaks, one in the morning and one in the afternoon, and a lunch break, the door to the workshop was kept locked. And any non-work-related talking was strictly forbidden.

Thank Buddha her cousin was around. Little Red was assigned to Shack Number 6, next to Lotus's, and her job was to paint glue on the shoes and put them on a moving belt to be dried by powerful lights before machines pressed on the soles. The girls spent all their spare time together, comparing the blisters on their fingers, and chatting endlessly, as if to compensate for the lack of freedom to talk during the working hours.

Before long, they learned that Hua, their fellow villager, had received commissions for recruiting them. Still they were grateful, as the older girl took care of them and introduced them to fellow Sichuanese.

In the third month, they received their salaries for the first time. The factory customarily held back the first two months' pay to prevent the workers from running away. The cousins caressed the three one-hundred-yuan notes imprinted with the portrait of Chairman Mao. Lotus couldn't help but feel a little discouraged, thinking about how long it would take at this rate to earn back the thick wad of money that she had returned to Luo Yijun's family. But she also knew that her father couldn't earn much more than three hundred yuan in cash in an entire year.

Little Red treated herself to some bananas. She allowed herself only half a banana at a time, while Lotus, having long felt sickened by the bland factory food, wolfed down a bowl of spicy glass noodles at a night market.

At first, Lotus sent most of her salary home, keeping a little bit of money for bare necessities. Slowly as she made extra money from over-time, she started to buy herself lipsticks and pretty but affordable dresses, like all the other girls.

Many young people paired up. Life was so hard and dull. They needed sweeteners and excitement.

Lotus remained single. The workers who filled up the production lines were mostly migrant women like herself. Among the five dozen or so male workers, a few did express interest in Lotus, especially one lively young man named Little Qian, who worked maintaining the equipment. She liked when he turned up at her workshop from time to time, oiling the machine joints while humming songs and stealing lengthy looks at her. But sitting on the high romantic fence elevated by Little Zhao, she refused to be seduced by a man of common stock.

Lotus took a fancy to the manager of the sales department. He always wore a white shirt and a tie when he whizzed in and out of the factory. One day, she stopped him to present him with an embroidered hand-kerchief that had taken her a week to complete. He was visibly startled. "I have no need for such a thing," he said curtly, before turning away. Lotus stood for a moment, then spat after him. She took out her hairpin and started to unpick the colored threads that formed the embroidered mandarin ducks on the handkerchief.

One Sunday evening, Hua took the cousins to Shenzhen's city center. Sitting by a fountain in a square, they watched the nightly light show. Lasers sliced through the sky, creating a changing pattern of shapes and colors, accompanied by music blasted from a speaker. Little Red, always easy to please, jumped for joy, clapping her hands. Lotus, on the other hand, was besieged by mixed emotions. She was glad to see the spectacle but she also felt that Shenzhen, with all its glamour, was too far removed from her confined life at the shoe factory in Dongguang. When Lotus shared her sentiments, Hua said: "Money. To enjoy life in a city, you need money." Hua revealed that she was planning to move to Shenzhen.

With no boyfriends to wander the streets with after work, the cousins looked forward to visiting the nearby street market together. Every day after sunset, the small road in front of the factory would burst into life. On top of newspapers, peddlers sold lipsticks, pictures of film stars, and pretty little accessories. It was here that the girls bought their first bras to replace their homemade vests. But mostly they just looked. However, even this little pleasure was not guaranteed. When rush orders dropped in from overseas, they found themselves glued to their posts, working until late at night.

Lotus became very good at her job. She was given a raise, then promoted to the head of a group. But even so, her life in the factory felt as stagnant as a pool of dead water. She felt as stifled here as she had back in the village, just in a different way.

For a year and a half, the cousins repeated their daily routine within the gray confines of the factory, conducting their work under the two banners that bore the slogans "Happy, Happy Come to Work" and "Safe, Safe Return Home."

"Safe, Safe Return Home": Lotus shivered as she saw the banner again in her mind. She tossed in her bunk bed.

The train shuddered to a halt at a station. Bing was asleep on the top bunk. Lotus got up, slipped out of the train, and stepped out onto the platform. She stretched her legs and breathed in the fresh warm air. A young couple tried to sneak into her carriage but the attendant checked their tickets and sent them away. The couple hurried back toward their hard-seat section, their heavy bags making a scratching sound as they dragged them along the concrete. Lotus could see a crowd of people at a nearby train door, some fighting to get on, others pushing to get off.

How lucky to have a bed in the sleeper section, she thought. She rarely felt a notch above others. It was just one of the benefits of being associated with Bing. One of the benefits? Do I expect more? Lotus asked herself.

A whistle blew loudly. It startled her. She scrambled aboard and found her way back. As she lay still in the bunk bed, she heard the sound of a whistle in her head. It transported her back to the event that had shipwrecked her life.

The screams had started before the alarm went off. It was a normal day in August in 1997, sunny and hot—maybe a little hotter than usual. Lotus stopped working, listened carefully, and determined that the cries were coming from Shack Number 6. These were the sort of screams people let out when confronted by white-boned demons.

"Little Red!" she cried and dashed for the door.

The shack had no windows, so she couldn't see what was happening outside. But she sensed a major crisis.

"Open the door," Lotus begged, banging on the locked door of their workshop like a possessed woman. Other girls soon joined her, shouting for help. The cries from the neighboring workshop became more desperate. All of a sudden, the door of their workshop swung open. She rushed out and a powerful burning smell hit her nose. The factory was a scene of terror. The alarm was now deafening. Workers in green smocks were running in all directions. Black smoke was billowing out from Shack Number 6.

Little Red! Where was she? She stood there, looking for her cousin among the frantic crowd.

Flames erupted from Shack Number 6, followed by a huge explosion. A wave of heat knocked her out.

A sudden jolt of the train brought Lotus back to reality. She could feel cold tears on her cheeks and dried them with Bing's handkerchief. It had a faint smoky smell, the same as his pillow.

Lotus had tried her best never to think about that tragic day. She didn't sleep for days following her cousin's death. Falling asleep meant waking up and confronting the painful truth all over again. Little Red was gone, and she was partly responsible.

Lotus stretched her legs on the bed. The carriage was quiet except for the businessman's snoring. Even in his sleep, he refused to be quiet. She remembered his earlier remarks and then thought about Bing's kind face. He was a city man with a bellyful of ink and great prospects for the future. In contrast, Family Treasure was a peasant, only hiring her as his mistress.

She grimaced at the recollection of the last time she had spent at Family Treasure's apartment, shortly before this trip. He had worn a gold watch and dark glasses—his latest effort to look like a city gentle-man. A gentleman he wasn't. He had taken her to an all-you-can-eat buffet, where he devoured prawns and pork ribs—vegetables were not worth his while—as if his stomach were a bottomless bucket. "We must get our money's worth," he mumbled through a mouthful of food.

Guided by the same principle, that night he had bounced on top of her again and again.

Ever since she was a little girl who couldn't put two and two together, Nai had lectured her about the ultimate importance of finding a man to marry, because a husband was a woman's *guisu*—her final destination.

And Bing wouldn't be a bad *guisu* for her, Lotus thought. He was sixteen years older than her. So what? He wasn't that bad-looking, and quite tall. She hadn't really rejected him. She had simply been too shocked to give him an answer, and he had taken her reaction as a no. She peered up at his bunk. He was snoring gently.

I guess I could get used to that noise, she mused. The thought made her blush. A woman like her would get used to anything.

Unable to sleep, Lotus pulled back the curtains to look out. The street lamps whizzed by in the darkness, looking like the streaks of fireworks. She knew she was getting closer to home. Her heart felt as if it were flying.

CHAPTER 14

初生牛犊不怕虎

A Newborn Calf Isn't Afraid of Tigers

"Look, they've widened the roads!" Lotus shouted, pointing out of the window as she rode next to Bing in a bright yellow van.

"Like everywhere in China," Bing remarked.

Her eyes scoured the scenery, her cheeks crimson with excitement. The horrible cut on her forehead had healed, leaving only a slight scar—"a speck in white jade that doesn't obscure its virtues," as the old saying went. She wore a white sequined shirt. Upon arrival at Chengdu station earlier in the afternoon, she had gone to the washroom and swapped her comfortable T-shirt for the fancy top. Bing thought she was a little overdressed but understood that she wanted to put on a good show for her fellow villagers.

They were sitting together in the back of a "bread loaf," a minivan resembling a loaf of bread. It was cheaper but not as fast or as safe as a taxi.

"See the old pagoda over there?" She tugged at Bing's vest for attention.

He admired the elegant six-sided pagoda standing in the middle of a rice field. "It looks exquisite."

"I heard it's been haunted ever since a young woman hanged herself there. Hu Laoshi, do you believe in ghosts?"

"Not really."

"Nainai says that the thing about ghosts is that you can't completely believe in them, but you can't rule out their existence, either."

Like fate? Bing smiled at her ambivalent attitude.

Lotus chatted for a while before drifting off to sleep, her arms still cradling the plastic bag, containing a large bunch of green bananas, on her lap. He was a little surprised but delighted when she rested her head on his shoulder. Hot wind from the open window blew the loose strands of her ponytail onto his face, tickling and teasing him. Several times Bing buried his nose in her smooth hair to catch its faint scent. But each time he withdrew quickly, like a thief.

If Mei were still his counselor—one of the many roles she used to take on—she would definitely describe his offer as "an impulsive act." He certainly hadn't planned it. In the moment he was so overwhelmed with emotion that he felt he had to open his heart to Lotus.

If Lotus got out of prostitution, would she really want to become the *ernai* of a small-time businessman? To his mind, an *ernai* was still a prostitute, since the relationship was based on money rather than an emotional connection. Bing thought about his concubine grandmother. He knew next to nothing about her life, but didn't imagine it being an easy one. He never fully comprehended the appeal of keeping multiple wives. In any case, he was convinced that the tradition must have contributed to the flourishing sex industry in today's China.

Lotus's rejection had spurred his longing for her. This morning on the train, Bing had yearned to hold her in his arms and comfort her. The fire that had killed Little Red had started when a shoe got caught in a conveyer belt. Several dozen flower-aged girls, locked up in the workshop, all burned to death. He often read newspaper reports of similar incidents, hidden in the back pages. But this time the story moved him deeply.

The pain of losing her cousin together with her survivor's guilt must weigh like a mountain on Lotus, Bing thought. He tilted his head to look at her peaceful face resting on his shoulder, so close that he could count the fine hair on it.

With a jerk, the bread loaf stopped. "Get out now! Out! My van can only go this far," the driver yelled back at them.

"Lotus, wake up," Bing said softly, patting her arm.

Lotus's almond eyes opened and looked at him. She then sat up straight and wiped her mouth. "*Aiyah,* I've been drooling like an idiot."

"Yes, you have."

Lotus giggled, covering her mouth. She checked her watch. "It's five thirty. We'll get to Mulberry Gully before dark, if we hurry."

Once out of the minivan, Lotus slung her fake Gucci bag over her shoulder and started to lead Bing along a mud path. She carried her bag of bananas in one hand, and in the other a large red-and-white-checked plastic sack of the kind nicknamed a snakeskin bag, its woven texture reflecting the sun, like the skin of a snake. "Let me carry your bags for you," Bing offered, somewhat breathless as he struggled to keep up with her.

"No, I'm fine."

"Come on." He took the bag of bananas from her.

As they trudged along the path, Bing stopped occasionally to photograph the view. In the distance, he could see a forest of bamboo, fir, and pine trees. Small plots of cultivated land dotted the mountain slope. The scene spoke volumes about the diligence of the folks in this densely populated province, Bing thought. Arable land was very scarce, and farmers had learned to make use of every patch of ground. It was almost harvest time. Sweet corn stalks grinned yellow toothy smiles, tender soybeans hung from plants, and scarecrows watched over the fields. The light from the summer sun had dyed the rice fields gold.

The path turned right, revealing a village nestled in the side of the mountain. Columns of smoke rose from the rooftops of houses scattered around the slope.

Lotus stopped. She took off her plastic sandals and fished out a pair of shining black leather high heels from her sack and put them on. She charged ahead in her high heels, like a skilled acrobat on stilts.

Bing followed close behind. At the village entrance, he spotted a tall thin figure, standing on a millstone, silhouetted against the setting sun. His skinny long legs resembled a drawing compass.

"Shadan!" Lotus dropped her sack and flew toward him.

Bing put down his luggage and the bananas, took his camera out and started to photograph the reunion. He managed to catch the moment when the siblings met by the millstone.

Lotus playfully punched her brother's chest. "Look at you. You've grown into a tall bamboo pole!" she said in her local dialect.

Her brother grinned at his sister.

"Did you get my telegram?" the sister asked.

"Of course; otherwise, I'd still be at school. I rushed home and didn't have time to tell Ba ahead of time—when I showed up it gave him such a fright that he nearly wet his pants."

They both laughed. People were starting to come out of their houses and a crowd quickly formed around the siblings.

"Dumb Luo's daughter?" Bing heard someone in the crowd say. "Look, she's turned out so pretty, like her mother." Another one said: "Look at her fancy outfit. She's done well in the city, then."

Bing was about to introduce himself to Shadan when a woman in her sixties, clad in a traditional-style cotton shirt, tottered over. "Chouchou, is she here already?" she called out in a thick Sichuan accent.

"Nainai, Nainai!" Lotus cried.

The old woman's gnarled hands cupped the girl's smooth face. "*Amitabha*, you're back, my girl, thank Guanyin Buddha. Back at last, at long last." Her voice grew weak as tears covered her walnut face. "I haven't seen my little heart for three years. Three long years!"

"Nai, how I've missed you!" Lotus held the old woman's hand.

Bing continued to take photos until Lotus pulled him over to introduce him.

"Nainai, this is Hu Laoshi, a photographer. He is doing research on migrants," she said.

Bing bowed to the old woman. "Nainai."

The old woman took a good look at him and his camera. "Good, good," she mumbled. Bing bet that she hadn't really registered her granddaughter's words and she didn't care. Once she had established that he didn't seem like a marriage candidate for her girl, the old woman shifted her attention back to her granddaughter.

"Are you hungry? Tired, my good girl? *Aiyah,* what happened to your forehead?" Nai touched Lotus's scab.

"I tripped. Nothing." Flustered, Lotus pushed away her grandma's hand. She reached into her bag and took out a tiny red velvet box. "A gift for you, Nai."

"A gift for me? What is it?"

"Open it."

Nai opened it with her shaking hands. A gold ring sat in the pretty box, glistening in the setting sun. All the onlookers lengthened their necks for a better view. Some clicked their tongues in admiration.

"Pure gold?" someone asked.

"Pure gold, one hundred percent!" Lotus replied loudly as she helped her grandma to squeeze a thick, knotted finger through the ring.

Nai held up her rough hand, admiring the gift. "My Buddha, what fortune! To wear a gold ring before I slip into the yellow earth."

Lotus smiled broadly, her tiger teeth flashing and her eyes scanning the admiring crowds.

Bing made sure to catch the moment with his camera.

By the time Lotus's family and Bing made their way to the Luos' family home, all the village dogs and more than half of the children were trailing behind them. The children sucked noisily on the hard candy Lotus had handed out, savoring a treat usually reserved for Spring Festival. They mimicked the way Lotus called Bing "Hu Laoshi." A few pointed at his camera and even tried to touch it with their sticky hands.

If a UFO had landed in the village, it could hardly have caused more excitement.

Later in the evening, Bing lay motionless in bed, afraid he would disturb Lotus's father, who was sleeping beside him, if he tossed and turned too much. Shadan, who usually slept in this bed, had gone to his cousin's house for the night. It was not yet midnight and the family had been in bed since ten. For centuries, farmers had been following nature's timetable. An urban dweller for too long, Bing couldn't possibly sleep before the clock struck one. The small pillow, filled with millet husks—he could tell by pinching it—was too hard. He wished he could read, but the only light in the house was a dim, naked bulb hanging in the hallway. From time to time, he heard pigs grunting from the pigpen in the backyard. Old Luo gave a drunken snore, a queer shuddering sound, and then faded to near silence before snoring again.

A mountain draft wound its way in through cracks in the earthen walls. While Chengdu was still blazing hot in early September, here the nights were starting to get cold. The mud house was made from unfired clay and looked as if it would collapse in the next strong gust of wind. Bing couldn't recall any family from his own village being as impoverished as the Luos. Then again, his hometown was in a fertile grain region, not as isolated as it was here.

Nevertheless Lotus's family had been very hospitable, offering him a pork dish cooked in a thick bed of red chili peppers. It was deliciously spicy. Old Luo also served some strong grain alcohol, which Bing was obliged to accept. Whenever he finished the rice in his large bowl, a refill would appear instantly, topped by another ladleful of pork and peppers. Everyone else only touched the meat symbolically, eating only the vegetables. The oily pork and bowls of rice now moored in his stomach, making it difficult to sleep.

Bing turned, trying not to kick his bed mate. He guessed Old Luo must be only a few years older than himself. But life had worn him out, making him old before his time. Lotus had mentioned that her father was rather good-looking in his youth and a very good singer.

A craving for a cigarette forced Bing to get up. With his cigarette and lighter in hand, he tiptoed toward the door and quietly let himself out.

Outside, a symphony of croaking frogs broke an otherwise peaceful night. In the glow of a half moon, Bing could just make out the outline of hills in the distance, the peaks like the arched backs of animals.

He lit his cigarette, drew in a deep breath, and exhaled with satisfaction. Then he heard a splash from a pond a short distance away. The photographer's instinct drove him back into the house for his camera, and he then headed toward the noise. As he approached, he saw someone with a flashlight tied to his head, wading in the shallow pond. He was holding a long bamboo pole with a net at the end. Bing shot a few frames. The person in the water jumped at the sudden flash.

Bing recognized the confused face. "Shadan, it's me, the photographer. Sorry if I scared you."

"Oh, Hu Laoshi. Why aren't you asleep?" The youngster tried to speak standard Mandarin but his accent seeped into his speech.

"It's a little early for me. What are you doing, anyway?"

"I'm catching eels for our lunch, and some frogs, too. Look, there's one." He focused the flashlight on a frog. Dazed by the light, the little green creature went motionless, only its chin shivering.

"You really shouldn't trouble yourself so much," Bing said.

"No trouble." Shadan scooped up the frog with the net and put the catch into a bamboo basket tied to his waist. "Before I go back to school, I'd like to give our guest this treat." He switched off the flashlight, and trudged over to Bing's side of the pond and sat down.

Bing joined him, squatting next to the young man. "Your exams are coming up. How are you feeling?"

"Nervous," Shadan said, scooping up water with his net as he talked. "And very worried. Each time I close my eyes, I see Sichuan University in my head. But how can we afford it? But if I fail the exam, my sister will probably hang herself!"

"I don't think your sister is the type who would choose suicide easily," Bing said, letting out a short laugh. "As for you, there's always a way. You can make money tutoring other students in math, or something else. Just do your best. 'The planning lies with man, the outcome with Heaven.'" Bing quoted the ancient idiom. He looked up at the star-studded sky. When did I start playing the Old Wise Man? he thought. Would it feel right to be this boy's brother-in-law?

Slowly in his substandard Mandarin, Shadan told Bing his troubles. His sister had been forced to give up her schooling, and yet she was the provider of the family. He wished he could be more like a real man and contribute more.

"Don't worry too much," Bing said. "I think helping the family gives her a deep sense of fulfillment."

"There's another thing, Hu Laoshi." As he talked, he continued to fiddle with his fishing pole. "You know, my sister wants me to study computer science, but I'm very interested in law. Now that I've got a few drops of ink in my belly, neighbors—some of them illiterate—often come to ask my advice about rules and regulations."

"Like what?"

"Like how much agriculture tax they have to pay, tax exemptions for handicapped people and things." He started to explain how he had become interested in law. Once a blind old man from the village came to him and inquired about the law regarding the tax reduction for disabled people. Shadan went to the local library and learned that people with disabilities were entitled to an exemption from the agriculture tax. With the photocopied law at hand, the blind man brought his case to the county officials and was reimbursed for the tax he had been forced to pay.

Bing was impressed. He patted Shadan's shoulder. "Good job! China is working to improve its legal system, and we'll need more lawyers."

"But my sister says I can make good money in the city if I study computer science."

Bing recalled that Lotus had once asked him what kind of degree was needed in order to get a job at one of the grand high-tech factories. "Computer science," he had said.

"A lawyer can be highly paid as well. At the end of the day, I think you have to go for what really interests you," he advised. "What is it about the law that interests you so much?"

"With a law degree, I can help farmers to fight corrupt officials and protect their rights," Shadan said with a touching enthusiasm. "I want to help my family but I also want to do things I like."

Bing was becoming fond of Shadan. He saw shades of his own youthful idealism in him.

"Did you tell your sister what you want?"

"Yes. It didn't change her mind. She's pig-headed." He paused, biting his lips in the same way Lotus did when she tried to control her emotions.

"Is she?"

"Yes," Shadan said with a nod. "Once, years ago, my sister got into a competition with some boys—to jump off a big wall. I begged her not to do it, but she jumped anyway. She fell and scraped her knees badly. She could have died!"

Bing was amused to hear the story, as he recalled seeing the scars on her knees. "Interesting."

The youngster then added quickly, "Don't get me wrong. I am extremely grateful to my sister." Shadan whipped the water with his pole and changed the subject. "Chouchou told me a lot about you. She said I should learn from you. How did you meet my sister?"

"My next-door neighbor Mimi, a good friend of your sister's, introduced us."

"Why are you so interested in migrants, Hu Laoshi?"

"Well, you see, I'm originally from a village. And migrant workers are China's unsung heroes. Without their cheap labor, their contribution—taking over the heavy, dirty jobs in the city—there would not be China's economic miracle." Bing let loose a torrent of words as if his big talk could conceal his private intentions toward this youngster's sister.

The young man was silent for a minute. He gazed into the pond. "Hu Laoshi, I hope you don't mind me asking you questions."

"Not at all."

"My sister never tells us about any of her problems. What kind of restaurant does she work for?"

"Well, it is just an ordinary Sichuan restaurant." Bing wished that he and Lotus had worked out the details beforehand.

"Ordinary? It can't be ordinary if she gets extra pay for extra work and tips."

Bing nearly blurted out that tipping was uncommon in China; then he realized that Lotus must have exaggerated her income to her family. "She does work very hard. But don't worry. Just do your best and make her proud."

"I will," said Shadan. "It's the least I can do."

Bing woke to the sound of chopping in the backyard. It took him a few seconds to orient himself. Old Luo had gone. Bing stretched luxuriously, rose and went outside.

The sunlight flooded the yard. Bing held up a hand to shade his eyes and spotted Lotus, her hair braided, with her brother; both of them were squatting by the pigpen. They were chopping some leaves, talking animatedly, and giggling.

"Good morning," Bing greeted them.

"How did you sleep, Hu Laoshi?" Lotus inquired, raising her sweat-beaded face.

"Very well, thank you," Bing replied, and walked toward her. "Let me help you. I used to make pig feed when I was a boy."

"No, no. Nearly done." She wiped her face against her shoulder, then got up, gathered bits of leaves and chucked them into a large boiling wok sitting on a wood fire. She did everything so naturally, it was as if she had never left the village. "Please, Hu Laoshi, head back into the house, breakfast is ready. I'll just pour some maize flour into the feed here and I'll be done. We need to fatten up our pigs." Lotus pointed at the pigpen behind her. A big pig stood by the wooden fence, its nose poking out, snorting impatiently for its meal. "Aren't they cute? Only a little skinny," she said affectionately, as if talking about her children.

She stirred the concoction with a long bamboo stick, steam rising around her.

"Let me take a few shots of you," Bing said.

But Lotus put up her hand. "Plenty of chances later. Breakfast now." "*Yaodei.*"

They went back into the house. Old Luo was waiting in the hall. "Hu Laoshi, eat. Nothing good, sorry. Eat, eat." He gestured for Bing to sit down on the chair facing the door. Old Luo's thin body, clad in a coarse cotton peasant jacket, never stood straight. A worn-out blue hat slumped on his head. His dark yellow face seemed to have endured a hundred years of hardship.

"Thank you." Before taking his assigned seat, Bing cast a look at a large portrait of Chairman Mao on the mud wall. It was dusty and fading, the mole under the Chairman's chin looking more sinister than ever. He had noticed the portrait last night. Now, in the bright morning sun, it appeared so outdated that one could almost smell the mold. A memorial tablet for the ancestors and a porcelain statue of Guanyin made up a little shrine underneath the picture. What a strange combination of worship, Bing thought.

Lotus put down a clay teapot and a bowl of grapes on the wooden table. Glancing at the portrait, she said in a harsh tone: "Ba, do you know which dynasty it is? Even Chairman Mao's successor has died. When are you going to change the picture?"

Lotus seemed to speak faster in Sichuan dialect, lending her an air of confidence. Bing was simultaneously surprised and amused to see the other side of her. As soon as she had arrived home, she started urging her father to smoke less, lecturing him about his health and criticizing her grandma for casually throwing garbage over the wall of their house. She complained about how dark the village was as soon as night fell. Last night before bedtime, Bing, smoking in the yard, had overheard her making some kind of threat to her family in a bossy tone he hadn't heard from her before.

"Change the picture, why?" her father countered. "Chairman Mao was the best emperor China ever had. Don't you agree, Hu Laoshi?" His bleary eyes flicked toward Bing.

As in many parts of rural China, farmers often displayed Mao's portrait in their houses, worshiping him like a god, without fully knowing the grave mistakes he had committed. They only saw him as the man who had united China and made the Chinese stand up in the world.

"Chairman Mao did a great deal for the Chinese people. But it was Deng Xiaoping who introduced the economic reforms and dramatically improved millions of people's lives," Bing answered diplomatically.

"Economic reforms?" Old Luo pushed his crumpled hat farther back. "What reforms? The rich are getting richer and the poor poorer."

It was obvious to Bing that the Luo family had gained little from the new private farming system. They would have been better off muddling along in the old collective commune system.

Aware the conversation would not go far, Bing changed the topic. "You've been out to the field already?" He had noticed the wet patches on Old Luo's cheap rubber army shoes, the same sort that he himself grew up wearing.

"Yes, I have. To harvest corn. There are only a few hands in our family. Eat, eat." He gestured with his chopsticks, and then sucked up his porridge with gusto.

Shadan came in and joined them at the table. "Ba, I'll help you after breakfast," he volunteered. He wore a worn-out white shirt two sizes too small and a pair of fading army trousers that ended way above his thin ankles. Lotus always fondly talked about how smart and handsome her brother was. The youngster did boast a handsome face; his almond-shaped eyes shone under his thick, ink-black eyebrows. But he was too tall, and was obviously conscious of this fact as he often stood in a slight crouch. And he was very skinny, with a thin, long neck.

"You stupid egg!" Lotus said in a sharp voice that startled Bing. "Focus on your studies."

"Right, right, you study, my boy," his grandma echoed.

Bing picked up some dried tiger lilies dressed in soy sauce and sesame oil. "Delicious!" he said to the grandma, who was still making pancakes on a traditional brick cooking range. "Nainai, please join us for breakfast."

The old woman waved her hands. Now and then, she would feed the fire some corn stalks. Her wrinkled face perspired heavily.

"Don't worry about Nainai," said Lotus. "She never eats at the table when we have guests."

Bing didn't insist. Living in the city, it was easy to forget how traditional country folks could be.

Nainai brought over a pile of pancakes in a bamboo basket. "Eat, eat."

Bing took one. "Are there some crushed walnuts in these pancakes? It tastes wonderful!"

"Eat more," urged Nainai, smiling. She tapped Bing's back. "Hu Laoshi, you're a wise man. You help me to . . ." A strongly accented sentence fell out of her toothless mouth.

"Sorry?"

"Persuade me to come home and get married," Lotus interpreted, her tone ironic.

"Yes, get married. Chouchou is a big girl, almost twenty-five."

Bing knew for the country folks, a child was one year old at birth.

"That nice boy Yijun, why didn't you want him?" the grandma grumbled. "Even if you search the world with the brightest lantern, you may not find such a good husband!"

"Don't bring up the old millet and stale sesame, Nai!" Lotus retorted, her face red.

"Chouchou!" She clicked her tongue. "What has the city done to you, my girl?" Nai said to Bing: "Chouchou was the sweetest girl in the village. You look at her now. What does she eat in the city? Rice, or gunpowder?"

Bing listened, smiling politely.

Lotus stood up to refill the water in the teapot, still fuming.

Nai continued to talk about how other girls Lotus's age all had husbands and babies, and how she longed to have a great-grandson.

"You will. You look healthy," Bing assured her.

"Not healthy." The old woman pursed her wrinkled lips. "I nearly died from a heart attack two years ago. *Amitabha*." Turning to her granddaughter, she said: "Having children is your duty. You can't disgrace our ancestors."

"Nainai!" Shadan reproached his grandma. "Chouchou has done so much for our family."

Nai started to carefully scrape off some dried flour from her new ring. "I know, I know. But she needs to know that a woman is nothing without a man."

Old Luo was oblivious to his family's conversation. He held his bowl to his mouth and twisted the bowl with one hand as he finished his porridge with one long, noisy slurp. He smacked his lips in satisfaction and wiped them on his sleeves. Then he squatted down in one corner and began to work on a half-finished bamboo basket as he smoked his pipe. The slanting rays of the sun, where the smoke dissolved and the dust danced, lit up his dark face.

Nai blew gently on her ring and began again: "Return home or not, Chouchou, I don't want you to end up an old virgin."

Bing thought he spotted a slight smile crossing Lotus's lips. As if sensing he was watching her, she looked up. Their eyes locked.

CHAPTER 15

晴天霹雳

A Thunderbolt from a Clear Sky

Tongues of flames darted upward, swallowing the fake paper money. One by one, Lotus fed the fire with the yellow "banknotes for the next world." The notes burned quickly, the edges curling up, breaking into pieces, like a swarm of black butterflies.

"Little Red, I've come to see you," she said, kneeling in front of the modest grave. The headstone, partially covered in shade, simply read: "Our Beloved Daughter Luo Xiaohong (1980–1997)."

"Good cousin, here is a gold ingot for you." Lotus cast a piece of gold-colored foil into the fire, then a tinfoil replica of a cell phone and a small model house. "With all of these things, I hope you'll be happy in heaven."

Tomb Sweeping Festival, the day to honor the dead each spring, was long gone. But Lotus wished to carry out her own ceremony. With a trowel, she dug out a pile of earth, placed it on top of the grave, and carefully smoothed it into a round shape. Only neglected graves were shapeless and "hairy" with grass on top.

The graveyard was set on a slope filled with bamboo trees, some fifteen minutes' walk from her village. Black crows squawked in the wind, their cries echoing in the trees, like whimpers from those no longer able to speak.

From a bamboo basket Lotus took out the bunch of bananas she had brought back from the train station, and laid them by the tombstone. Next she offered a bowl of rice, poking a pair of chopsticks into the rice so the ends pointed toward the sky. "Here's some food for you," she said, bowing three times, her head nearly touching the tombstone.

Bing stepped closer and put his hand on her shoulder. She would have felt uneasy at the graveyard without him. His presence warmed her back like a hot-water bottle. The other day, in the bread loaf van, she had rested her head on his shoulder, pretending to be asleep before really drifting off. She had felt him gently smelling her hair and was touched by the gesture.

Poor Little Red: she had never experienced a man's love in her life, Lotus thought.

Lotus turned to face Bing. "Thank you for coming with me."

"Sure," he said, withdrawing his hand.

Bing was wearing a blue cotton shirt underneath his photographer's vest, and a checkered scarf around his neck. His clothes and longish hair gave him an air of sophistication that seemed out of place in the village. His eyes protruded slightly—too much reading, perhaps.

Lotus sat down on the grass and Bing seated himself close by. As she gazed at the tombstone before her, the burial scene from three years ago flashed through her mind. Since Little Red had died young and unmarried, no proper funeral rites were performed for her. Her family, wearing black banners on their arms as a symbol of grief, buried the box of ash without ceremony.

"Right in front of her tomb, I promised Little Red that I would look after her mother," she told Bing. "And that I would try to become a better person." She bit her lip.

Lotus paused and started to pull at the grass in front of her. When she became calmer, she began to describe life after Little Red.

"I didn't know what to do," Lotus said. "For a month after the funeral I stayed at home, thinking of what to do next."

One early evening, about two weeks after the funeral, she went to the well to draw water. Several women were washing clothes on boards while chatting and, no doubt, gossiping. They all stopped when she approached. One of the women was Luo Yijun's aunt, the number one gossip in the village, who had a grudge against Lotus ever since her refusal of the marriage. The woman was also a self-styled witch doctor, who treated her patients with chanting, trance dance, and concoctions she made from incense ashes and virgin boys' urine.

Silently Lotus drew her water and walked away. Before she was out of earshot, she heard the gossip say: "Look, that girl must be born under a broomstick star, a jinx! No less. She cursed her grandpa and mother to death, and now Little Red. I am so glad she didn't marry my favorite nephew."

Lotus began to notice some of her fellow villagers looking at her with cold suspicion. Once again, she decided to flee the village. She vowed to herself that she would never return unless she was covered in fine silk and radiating glory.

Lotus returned to the factory, but only for two months. Her heart jumped painfully inside her chest when she first saw the burnt ground where Shack Number 6 had stood. She could think about nothing but the fire. Nightmares haunted her. She would dream that she was trapped inside a fire, and would wake up screaming, with a burning sting in her nostrils.

Little Qian, her suitor at the factory, sought her out. Unbearably lonely, she agreed to go out with him one night. They slurped noodles together at a nearby cheap eatery. Afterward, she went with him to the so-called lovers' corner behind the factory, which consisted of a pond and some stone benches around it, where young couples fumbled with each other in the darkness. When he wrapped an arm around her shoulder, she didn't push him away. To cheer her up, he sang happy tunes, and his mouth inched closer and closer to hers . . .

But nothing could warm Lotus's heart, which felt like a block of lead inside her chest. After that night out with Little Qian, she didn't want to bother with him again. Anger tormented her and consumed her. Ten thousand yuan compensation for a young girl's life? A good cow could fetch a few thousand at the market, easily. She decided to take action.

One evening at supper time, when many of the worker ants were crawling around the compound, Lotus climbed up to the roof of her dormitory, where she unfurled a white banner covered in red characters: "Justice for the Dead and Proper Compensation for the Family of the Dead." She yelled that she wanted forty thousand yuan extra for her dead cousin. Otherwise, she would jump off the building. In a matter of minutes, she was overpowered by a few security guards and locked up in a dark room.

The next day, an envelope containing five thousand yuan in cash was pushed into her hand and she was shoved outside the factory gate, with her few belongings. She became a fried squid.

After wiring the money to Little Red's mother, Lotus boarded a bus to Shenzhen, with Hua's address in her pocket. Her fellow villager had indeed deserted the factory for glittering Shenzhen. Little Red hadn't really lived, Lotus thought. She, on the other hand, was going to live life to the fullest, for both of them. She would leave her past behind and start anew.

In Shenzhen, Lotus found Hua dozing in a hairdresser's chair in a rather fancy hair salon. Her old friend had, once again, transformed herself. Her bird's-nest hair had given way to a spiky look, unevenly cut on one side. A short dress clung to her plumper body. She looked like a real city girl and smelled like a flower.

Lotus gently woke her friend, and Hua let out one of her whistles to express her pleasant surprise. She took Lotus in a taxi to her apartment on the outskirts of the city, in an area called Miaocun.

At home, Hua poured herself a small shot of fire water and offered

Lotus a bottle of iced tea, which she gulped down. It was sweet, refreshing, and such a novelty.

Lotus asked Hua to help her get a job.

"What kind of job are you looking for?"

"I don't know. Something with good pay, ideally."

"Good pay? Get real, Chouchou! For peasant girls like us, there aren't many choices."

"Anything will do. Please, Sister Hua."

"I'll try, for the sake of Little Red. After all, it was me who brought you two to the factory." Hua went silent for a bit. "How is her mother?"

"I don't know. Not good . . ." Lotus paused, her face like a stone. "Please, let's not talk about it. I need a job."

"I only know jobs like mine. It's not the right dish for everyone."

"What's wrong with being a hairdresser?"

"Well, a hairdresser of some sort." Hua wrinkled her flat nose. "You have to massage men's heads and they may try to touch you."

"I won't let them touch me, but I don't mind washing their hair. I often washed my grandma's hair."

"Okay, I'll see what I can do."

Staying with Hua was an eye-opening experience. The following day, Hua called her hair salon, saying she had got her period and wouldn't be going in to work. She explained that her working hours were flexible.

Hua took Lotus shopping at a Hong Kong supermarket called Park'n'Shop. "I came all the way to the city. I want to live like city people. Even better than them," Hua declared. The prices were expensive, but the huge varieties of goods displayed on the shelves were a feast to the eye. Lotus picked up and smelled all sorts of exotic fruits before carefully putting them back.

After a few days, Hua arranged for Lotus to work at a hair salon owned by a man called Dragon. His place was in a rough part of town, near the long-distance bus station, not as fancy as where Hua worked. Out of five young girls working there, only one really knew how to cut hair. Their clients, mostly bus drivers, didn't seem to care about the haircut.

For the first few days at work, Lotus handled only the simplest task: rinsing the shampoo after a head massage. The rest of the time, she watched how the other girls pampered their clients, applying shampoo, massaging men's scalps, and sticking their little fingers into men's ears to twist the wax out, something Lotus found repulsive.

When the men left the salon, they sometimes took the girls with them. They would reach some kind of agreement beforehand. Instinctively Lotus knew they were up to no good, but she tried not to think too much about it.

Two weeks later, Hua didn't come home one night. Alone in the apartment, Lotus curled up on a bamboo mattress on the floor and gauged her situation. She didn't feel comfortable living in Miaocun. It was so chaotic, with women in revealing dresses parading the dirty streets and all sorts of men coming and going. There were no street-lights. At night, fights often broke out in the total darkness. The only place with lights was the village square, where mah-jongg players bat-tled until the small hours.

Didn't Hua dress up just as slutty as the other girls on the street? Lotus asked herself. In the quiet of night, Lotus realized that the signs were everywhere. She had chosen not to see them.

The next morning when Hua stumbled into the apartment, Lotus went up to confront her. "Where have you been?"

"In some shitty hotel, digging hole with a man, of course," Hua admitted freely as she kicked off her heels. "I'm sure you've already guessed. I've been a wild *ji* ever since coming to Shenzhen."

"A prostitute?" Lotus said, stepping out of Hua's way as the older girl walked in.

Hua poured herself a drink. "So what? It's a lot more fun than work-ing at the shitty factory. A lot more money, too." She smiled, waving her fat purse. "Last night, I earned almost a thousand yuan, plus this jade bracelet!" She shoved her wrist in front of her friend.

Lotus could hardly conceal her disgust.

"No big deal. I wasn't a virgin, as you know," Hua added.

Lotus couldn't see any connection between being a nonvirgin and the choice of the profession. Hua had no qualms about it? "So the girls at the hair salon, they are all dirty *ji* like you?" Lotus asked, her voice stern.

"Same, same."

"Why did you bring me into this dirty business?"

"Why? Because you begged me to."

"When I asked for a job, of course I meant an honest one!"

Lotus decided to quit as soon as she had her first month's wages in hand. "*Ji*": the word gave her goose bumps just thinking about it. And how humiliating that she had to live off the charity of such a woman! She would have left Hua's apartment if she had had anyplace to go.

Secretly, though, Lotus envied the life of her fellow villager: Hua had time and money to do what she liked. And Hua even received gifts from men, despite the fact that she wasn't so pretty. In the long evenings when Lotus was alone in the apartment, she sometimes put on Hua's pearl rings or golden necklaces, her gut tightening with jealousy.

Lotus was also disturbed by her feelings of envy. Where was her sense of right and wrong? To make a statement, she dashed out to buy her own rice bowl—one less shared thing, uncontaminated by her roommate.

Two days before payday, while Lotus was sweeping hair from the floor and getting ready to go home for the night, Dragon came to the salon with a man who wanted a head massage. Before she started the job, her boss offered her a bottle of iced tea as an apology for keeping her late.

She could still taste the tea when she woke up, hours later, alone on the sofa in the salon, naked apart from her bra. She felt dizzy, disoriented, with a pounding headache. When she moved she felt a sharp pain between her legs. She crawled off the sofa and turned on the light by the door. Then she noticed the hundred-yuan note sticking out of her bra. She collapsed back onto the sofa.

Lotus didn't know how she got back to Hua's place.

Hua, furious over the injustice, went to the salon the next day and extracted a five-hundred-yuan "virginity fee" from Dragon.

For a month, Lotus hardly left her friend's apartment, sleeping mostly. One night, Hua asked if she was going to go back to Dragon's salon. Lotus shuddered but didn't reply. Hua kicked the furniture, shrieked, and swore, but Lotus ignored her and went to sleep. She slept on even when Hua brought a man home.

One day when Hua returned home at noon, Lotus was still sleeping. Having had enough, her old friend dragged her up and kicked her out of the apartment.

Lotus walked along the streets like a sleepwalker. It was bright, chaotic, and noisy as usual. To avoid the crowds, she headed toward the hill, and then stumbled across Rooster Crowing Temple. She went in. In the main hall, she bowed in front of the giant statue of Shakyamuni.

Lotus thought about what her grandma used to say about *zuo nei*—committing sins. Was what had happened to her retribution for sins committed in her previous life?

What should I do now? Lotus asked herself. Go back home, poor and broken? Admit to the gossips that she was an inauspicious broomstick star, just like they said? No, she thought, she'd rather die. Stay here? Doing what? Another factory job with pathetic pay? Or following in Hua's footsteps, making good money but with no face or dignity? But why should she care about face and dignity after all that had happened? She might as well use what was left of her. "A cracked jar doesn't mind being smashed again."

Kneeling down on a hassock, Lotus decided to let a one-yuan coin decide her fate. The side with a large "1" in the middle would mean she'd pack up and go home. The other side, with a chrysanthemum, meant she would stay and follow Hua's path. She dropped the coin ever so gently. It landed with the flower facing up. She repeated the process and got the same result.

Lotus still held the coin as she walked down the hill. She decided that she wouldn't use her name, Xiangzhu, Fragrant Bamboo, anymore. From now on, she would simply be known as Lotus. "The lotus grows out of the mud yet remains pure and unstained." She still remembered the lyrics from an old poem.

She rented a matchbox-sized room in Miaocun, around the corner from Hua's place. Her first client was a short migrant worker in his twenties. He didn't say much but smiled a lot, a shy and apologetic smile. At the hair salon, they agreed on eighty yuan and then went back to her room. She lay down on the bed and shut her eyes. The man took off her underpants, opened her legs like a pair of scissors, and climbed on top of her. It hurt. She grabbed the edge of the bed. Moments later, the man let out a short and high-pitched groan and collapsed on top of her. He smelled of sweat, cigarettes, and grease Lotus recognized from her days at the factory. He rolled off her and turned on the light. She opened her eyes and saw him standing in front of her bed looking at her, wearing only his shining nylon T-shirt and nylon socks. Before he left, the man said sheepishly that this was the only bit of fun he could have in the city and he could allow himself the pleasure only once or twice a year. He left another fifty-yuan note on the table.

Lotus took the note and watched this stranger walk out of the room. He moved awkwardly on his bowlegs, and for a moment, she almost felt sorry for him.

At the hair salon, she smiled more and got picked up more often. Late at night, however, her dreams were haunted by the King of Hell, his face as green as spinach and his fangs as long as chopsticks. She made frequent visits to the temple to pray and burn incense. Gradually the nightmares became fewer and fewer.

After several months, Hua and Dragon became lovers and ran away together. His hair salon went bust.

"So I became a street *ji*," Lotus said, pulling the grass from the ground. It gave forth a delicate fragrance. She rarely talked to anyone about her past. Now she found unexpected relief and even pleasure in opening up to this understanding man.

Bing heaved a long, shuddering sigh. "What a story, Lotus, you poor thing." When he turned to look at her, she saw his wet eyes. "But I don't understand you. Why don't you do something for yourself?"

"I did plenty of things for myself, buying myself pretty dresses, exotic fruits and things. But they didn't make me feel any better." She rested her chin on her pulled-up knees.

"I meant you could've used the money to improve your situation in life," he said gently.

"Can you make a carving out of a piece of rotten wood?" Lotus asked, pursing her lips. She grabbed a handful of loose bits of grass and threw them up in the air.

Bing shook his head and patted her shoulder. "You mustn't think so poorly of yourself."

"What is there to think well of?"

Bing shifted his position so that he could see her face better. "Your family has to take you seriously now, don't they? They completely rely on you."

"They do rely on me," said Lotus, knitting her brow. "But I am not sure they take me seriously. Did you ever hear a word of thanks from my family? Never! After all I've done for them."

"I am sure that they are deeply grateful," Bing said, staring into her eyes. "But people in the countryside don't tend to express thanks in words, especially to their own family members. You know that, don't you?"

Lotus mumbled, "Maybe," and dropped her eyes.

Her home visit had been a stir-fry mixture of bitter and sweet. She had missed home unbearably. And she was genuinely happy to see her family again. Yet once the excitement was over, she was filled with resentment toward them. She was the one who was feeding them all. Yet Nai lectured her all the time as if she were still a child, and Ba rarely asked her any questions or even noticed her. What would they do without her? Lotus asked herself.

How would her life have turned out if her father were more capable and her family less poor? The more Lotus asked herself such questions, the more irritable she became.

So far, she had managed to control her anger in front of Bing. In fact, she had been making a conscious effort to appear cheerful in the village, partly for his sake and partly to show the villagers that she was doing well.

The crows cawed more loudly. A wind started to blow as the warm light began to fade. The shadows of trees swayed on the ground like dancing ghosts.

Lotus shivered and leaned back on Bing once more, resting her head lightly on his shoulder. It felt natural to do so. He wrapped a warm arm around her.

She closed her eyes, savoring this cozy silence and a sense of peace.

After a long while, Bing stirred. "The sun is sinking. Shall we?" He stood up first and offered her his hand.

Lotus took his hand and pulled herself up. She had been enjoying having him on this trip to her village. In the past week, he had helped to harvest the corn and chop feed for the pigs. He photographed her and life around her as if these were the only things that mattered under heaven. And her fellow villagers were duly impressed. When she had bumped into Luo Yijun's aunt in the street, the gossip had flashed an eager smile and asked about her and the photographer. Lotus deliberately didn't reveal much, though she was certain that whatever she had bluffed about him to others would have already reached the long-tongued woman's ear.

Lotus knew that her fellow villagers had started to see her in a new light, not only because of her association with the photographer but also the successful image she had deliberately cultivated. Yet no one would really know her earning power, she mused, until the day came when they learned that it was she who sent her brother to university. By then she would, once again, become the model daughter that all families aspired to have.

They stood closely side by side for a while. Then Bing started to gather up their things. "If we've been gone for too long, won't the villagers talk?"

"No," Lotus answered. "No one would ever match us together."

CHAPTER 16

天高皇帝远

❖⟡————————————————————————————————⟡❖

Heaven Is High and the Emperor
Is Far Away

In Mulberry Gully, Bing felt at home. The landscape was beautiful, with pristine mountains, limpid waters, and an azure sky he had never photographed before. No city noise, no pollution, no plastic bags flapping on trees. Life in the city had taken him away from nature. Now he was part of it once again. Many rustic objects—wooden ladles, gourd buckets, and twig baskets—all inspired his creative impulses.

The quality and quantity of his host's food had declined. But Bing didn't mind as long as he could devour the crust of rice cooked in the bottom of the Luos' great iron wok. Modern rice cookers never produced the same crispy effect. In that crust, he tasted his own childhood.

From time to time, Little Red's mother would bring in a red-cooked fish or date paste buns. Auntie was a tall, big-boned woman, yet she was soft-spoken. Before entering the house, she would call out in her melodious voice. "Chouchou, Chouchou, are you at home?"

Lotus would always scold her for bringing food. "Auntie, how much did this cost you? You must stop."

A few days after her visit to the tomb, Lotus sat Nai on a stool in the middle of the yard and started to wash her grandma's hair. When Lotus applied shampoo, Nai touched the lather with her fingers. "What is this, Chouchou?" she asked. "Will it turn my hair totally white?"

Lotus giggled. "It's shampoo. I brought it with me to wash my hair. It's much better than soap."

Bing was sitting nearby, and he chuckled at the scene. Lotus flashed a bright smile at him. It sparked a rush of happiness in him. Ever since the tomb visit, he felt that they had been seeking each other's eyes whenever possible, trying to read the meaning in them and delighting in the signals they sent out.

Nai nodded and closed her eyes. As Lotus's fingers worked into her grandma's thinning roots, the old woman groaned with pleasure. "Scratch harder, my girl," she demanded. "So itchy! I haven't washed my hair for a month."

"*Yaodei!*"

The afternoon sun warmed the old woman's face, which was carved with deep lines from old age. Her expression was a picture of divine contentment, her head tilting back.

Bing picked up his camera. He remembered how his sister Sufang used to wash their mother's hair, a ritual enjoyed by both women. Bing was sure that Lotus and Nai were enjoying this special bonding just as much.

"Is Hu Laoshi in?" a voice called, interrupting Bing's thoughts. There were visitors at the house.

Old Luo accompanied half a dozen men who filed into the yard. They nodded to Lotus but went directly to Bing. "We heard you are a journalist. Hu Laoshi, is that so?" inquired a man in his thirties, who wore an army uniform without any badges. His skin was as dark and coarse as the bottom of a well-used wok.

Bing waved his hands. "No, not exactly. But let's talk. Have a cigarette." He handed his pack around.

Nai shouted an order: "Father of Stupid Egg, bring our guests fresh loquats."

Old Luo plodded into the house and came out holding a small basket full of bright yellow fruit. He offered it to the visitors, his red-rimmed eyes flitting from one to another.

"We heard that you've published stuff in newspapers and that you are famous," said the man in uniform.

Bing glanced at Lotus, wondering if Lotus had been bragging about him, but she focused on Nai's hair.

"I'm actually a photographer. Still, how can I help?"

The man rolled up his army jacket sleeves and started to complain. The more he talked, the angrier he became and the faster his words spilled from his mouth.

"What? What? Slow down," Bing pleaded.

"He's saying that terrible things are happening here and he hopes you'll expose them in the newspaper," Lotus stepped in.

All eyes turned to her as she meticulously combed the lather through her grandma's hair with her wooden comb.

"Thank you," Bing said to Lotus.

She gave a twinkling self-satisfied smile.

"I can try," Bing said to the uniformed man. Remembering his journalist friend's request, he took out a pen and notebook from his camera bag and sat down on the millstone under the shadow of an elm tree. The rest stood around him.

A small black pig was scratching his round body against the tree, grunting in satisfaction, its thin curly tail swinging as it moved.

"Big brother Luo, speak slowly," Lotus urged.

"*Yaodei,*" the man agreed.

"What's your name?" Bing began.

"Luo Kecheng."

Bing wrote it down. He had noticed that most of the families in the small village shared the same surname.

Luo Kecheng pushed his sleeves farther up, as if ready for a fight. "In this place, 'heaven is high and the emperor is far away.' The local officials are all corrupt. They build grand office buildings for themselves and always have lavish banquets. Where's the money from? From us, from our blood and sweat. This *sui* is worse than a fierce tiger. *Sui*, do you understand?"

Bing didn't. He turned to Lotus.

"*Shui*," she said: "tax" in Mandarin.

The others all joined in, listing the taxes they had to pay: agriculture tax, irrigation taxes, family planning administration fees, and "donations" for a road that had never been built . . .

Luo Kecheng continued to talk, the veins in his neck bulging. "I served in the army and I've seen a bit of the world. The tax should be less than five percent of our total income. The government document, black characters on white paper, says it clearly, right? But we are being forced to pay a lot more. When I refused to pay the extra tax earlier this year, guess what happened? The village officials sent thugs to beat me up, as if I were a criminal. Those *tamade* turtles!"

He spat hard on the ground. His phlegm rolled into a dust dumpling. "Hu Laoshi, please look, look." From his breast pocket, Luo fished out a few pictures and handed them to Bing. The amateurish shots showed the man's bloodied face and severely bruised back.

Looking at the pictures, Bing's heart ached with sympathy. The sad truth was that these stories of peasants being overtaxed, then receiving such brutal treatment at the hands of local officials, were all too common in China's vast countryside.

"This is terrible. But are there any more serious cases?" Bing asked.

They all pointed to a sturdy young man. "Him, the third brother of the Li family." Several of the men began to tell the story at the same time. When they finished, Lotus summarized for Bing. Last year, when Li's wife couldn't come up with the tax imposed on her family, the cadres had come to her home to humiliate her and confiscate her TV set, the family's most cherished item. In desperation, she drank a bottle of pesticide, killing herself and leaving two young children behind.

"*Ai*, my poor bitter-fated wife." As the tearful widower sniffed, his face twisted in sorrow. "If I had been at home, it would never have happened." He blew his nose on the ground, pressing each of his nostrils in turn.

Luo Kecheng waved a finger at him. "Brother Li, no regulation allows cadres to confiscate villagers' things. I know. I've been teaching myself law. I am going to sue those turtle bastards who beat me up."

Bing stood up and shook the ex-soldier's hand, acknowledging that in this country, one needed great courage to do anything that might upset the authorities. "How are you teaching yourself law?" he asked.

"I've signed up for a Teach Yourself University course."

"Very good!"

Luo Kecheng smiled shyly. "I often discuss legal matters with Shadan. We farmers have to arm ourselves with the weapon of the law."

After the interview, Bing followed the villagers to the Li family's house to take some pictures. When he parted from the farmers, they bowed and expressed a thousand thanks. He lit a cigarette and took a long drag, satisfied that he had done a decent reporting job. It would make a great feature piece. He might try to write it himself.

Bing walked back toward Lotus's house with an extra spring in his step. On the way, he spotted a fresh pile of cowpat and again remembered his ex-mother-in-law's remark: "A fresh flower wasted on a cowpat." He laughed to himself.

As he stepped into the yard, Bing spotted Lotus standing on a stool, picking grapes from the vines overhead. He took out his camera. The setting sun cast a golden luster on her fine-featured face. At home she sometimes braided her shoulder-length hair, like the other girls in the village. But she looked different with her deliberately chosen fancy outfits. And she even carried herself differently. The city had left its mark on her.

Lotus jumped down. "Hu Laoshi, you've brought lots of face for our family. We've never received so many guests before."

"Thank you for helping me out." He loved it when she interpreted for him. It felt as if they were sharing something her fellow villagers couldn't penetrate.

"It's nothing," Lotus, said, her face all smiles. She picked up a string of grapes from the basket and offered them to him. "Try some. They are delicious."

When he took the grapes from her hand, brushing it slightly, the sensation made his fingers tingle. He popped a grape into his mouth.

"Mm, very sweet," he said, resting his eyes on her.

Lotus held his gaze for a moment. She suddenly went crimson. She turned and skipped back into the house.

Watching her disappear into the house, Bing's heart throbbed with joy. In just over a week, her cheeks had become a little rounder and rosier. When she wasn't spending time with her family, she would play with the village children, combing their hair, singing songs, or teaching them some characters. And she laughed more loudly and readily than ever. Once again, she was full of youthful vitality and fun to be with. Remarkably, he hadn't heard her coughing or spitting even once.

Bing's affection for Lotus deepened further after she had bared her soul to him by Little Red's grave. What kind of society has China become? Bing wondered. "Big fish eat small fish, and small fish eat shrimps." The phrase that used to describe the dark years before China's liberation, came to mind. It wasn't any better nowadays. If you were weak or a woman, anyone with slightly more power could take advantage of you. Bing thought about Dragon, the salon owner, with disgust.

He now understood why Lotus had been guarded about her past. As someone who had also grown up in the countryside, he understood her conservative upbringing in Mulberry Gully, waist-deep in tradition. She wanted to break free from the shackles of convention but also wanted to be a filial daughter; she longed for modernity but could only struggle on the edge of the city instead of becoming part of it.

Life had taken on a new meaning for Bing. He would lift Lotus out of her sordid life, no matter what became of them. He felt energized by his resolution.

He sat on the millstone to watch the sunset. After the sun disappeared behind the western hills, evening smoke and mist in the valley curled heavenward. And the symphony of croaking frogs rose once again.

CHAPTER 17

大树底下好乘凉

A Big Tree Affords Good Shade

Half pulled by Bing, Lotus arrived at Chengdu train station in a fluster. The massive waiting room was packed with people and filled with the smells of spicy pot noodles, smoke, and sour human sweat. Before she had a chance to catch her breath, the loudspeaker boomed the announcement of the arrival of the fast train to Shenzhen. Upon hearing this, dozing travelers bolted awake, card players stopped playing, and noodle eaters stopped chewing. The chaotic mass of passengers turned instantly into soldiers, charging ahead, snakeskin sacks on their shoulders, pushing and shoving to get onto the platform. Caught in the advancing battle line, Lotus and Bing, their hands linked, were swept along to the narrow ticket checkpoint.

"Fake tickets! Get out of the way. Hurry up!" At the ticket checkpoint, a woman in a railway uniform snarled at them and thrust the tickets back at Bing.

They stepped aside to let the current of passengers flow through.

When the current thinned, the ticket woman turned to them and asked with a gleeful smile: "Tricked, were you?"

Lotus took the tickets from Bing's hands. They were thinner than the normal ones and the black print was slightly smudged. "Eight hundred yuan down the drain without a sound!" She pouted.

"I should have checked more carefully when I bought them from that tout. Never mind!" Bing said, adjusting Lotus's sack, which had slipped off his shoulder. "We'll just have to spend the night here. You must be exhausted, Lotus."

"I am." After hours of jolting up and down in a bread loaf van along the mountain roads, Lotus felt her bones were on the verge of snapping.

Out in the balmy evening air, they walked past a series of cheap, dirty-looking hostels before they found a two-story block building with a big red banner boasting "Home Away from Home."

Bing said, "This one looks all right."

"You decide."

They walked toward the front desk.

"Two rooms with a shower, please," Bing said, handing his ID card to the receptionist, a plump, bespectacled woman who was cracking sunflower seeds with her teeth.

"One room will do," Lotus cut in. She could feel Bing's gaze on her face but she fixed her eyes on the woman.

The receptionist screwed up her face to take a good look at them through her pickle-bottle lenses. As she shifted her attention from Bing to Lotus, her look turned from curiosity to disdain.

"Have you got a marriage certificate?" The woman threw her heavy key rings on the desk with an intimidating crash. "This is a decent hotel, I tell you." She popped another sunflower seed into her mouth.

Lotus put a twenty-yuan note on the desk. "Is this enough?"

The woman studied the note for a minute before accepting it. "Here is your room key. Fifty-yuan deposit. Here are your toiletries." She gave them two sachets of shampoo, two thumb-sized soaps, two tooth-brushes, and a very small roll of pink toilet paper.

Bing pushed away his share of the things. "No, thank you. I've got my own."

Lotus picked up hers. No point in wasting anything, she thought.

They arrived at their room at the far end of the ground floor. It took Bing a few tries to open the door.

The first things Lotus noticed were the twin beds. She somehow felt relieved there wasn't a double bed. The room had a damp smoky smell, typical of a cheap hotel. But the white sheets and the blankets on the bed looked clean enough.

A few hours later, Lotus and Bing found themselves at a hot pot stall at an open-air night market, a slingshot away from the hotel. Lotus watched the copper pot on a small burner. Inside the pot, the soup was bubbling with dollops of chili oil, prickly ashes, ginger, garlic, and poppy seeds. She inhaled greedily. The aroma of her home province.

It was creeping toward midnight but the market was still lively. From time to time, the cooks would bang their spatulas around their red-hot woks, tossing sizzling meat and vegetables in the air. Steam hissed from bamboo baskets, and the aroma of pork buns wafted into the street. There were plenty of diners, many of them with their luggage tucked between their feet, killing time before catching their trains. Every stall had its own bright lights strung overhead, and electric wires snaked under the greasy tables.

The smells and activity around her all filled Lotus with a sense of well-being that she had not felt in five years. She was giddy.

When the soup had begun to boil, she threw in slices of lamb, mushrooms, quail eggs, squares of tofu, and pig's blood. She picked out a thin slice of lamb from the boiling broth with her chopsticks and dipped it into some sesame sauce. "So tasty!" she raved. "Why aren't you eating, Hu Laoshi?"

He sat watching her and then took several shots. "I love the steam. It gives you a mysterious beauty."

"Me? I guess 'in the eyes of a lover, even a plain-looking girl becomes Xishi, the famous beauty.'" Lotus quoted the old saying but immediately felt her face heat up. She gave a dry cough. "Were you happy with the trip?"

Bing dipped a piece of lamb in the pot. "Extremely. Thank you so much, Lotus."

"I should thank you for taking me home."

"You should thank the *Southern Window*. Anyway, it was great to have met your family. Such nice folks."

"You really think so?"

"Of course! I was very impressed with your brother. He said he is very keen to study law and fight legal cases for the poor and needy."

"I'm sure he enjoyed talking to a worldly man like you and showing off his smart phrases, like 'upholding justice.'" Lotus burst out laughing. "Oh, my good brother! He's been interested in martial arts for years."

She giggled again and told Bing a story about her brother. One Spring Festival, they had all gone to Phoenix to see a temple fair. There, when some cheeky youngsters whistled at Lotus and her cousin, Little Red's older brother did a martial arts pose, which effectively scared off the youngsters. After that, Shadan started to learn kung fu from his cousin. Later he also developed a liking for martial arts novels. "As a boy, he dreamed that one day he'd become a swordsman performing chivalrous acts and upholding justice."

Lotus continued, "He became very interested in law after he managed to get a blind villager's tax exempted."

"Yes, he told me the story," Bing cut in. "I was struck by his strong sense of justice. It seems natural that he'd want to study law."

"Well, I'm afraid that he'll spend all his time helping those villagers with their cases. Then he'll never make any money."

"But, Lotus, isn't it important to listen to what he wants?"

Lotus stopped chewing. She was glad that he took an interest in her family, but she knew them better. "My brother is too young to know what is good for him." She soaked a piece of lamb in a small bowl full of sesame sauce and placed it on his plate. "Please, eat, eat!"

"What kind of restaurant did you tell your brother you worked in?"

"A fancy Cantonese restaurant. Why? I figured that an expensive restaurant would pay more."

"Oh, *tamade*!" Bing tapped his head with his chopsticks. "I told Shadan that it was an ordinary Sichuan restaurant."

Her brother had indeed asked her a basketful of questions about her life in the city. However, Lotus didn't get the impression that he was suspicious of anything. "Nai would probably hang herself if she ever found out."

Bing wiped his forehead with a tissue. "You don't have to go back to your old way of life," he said as he stirred the bubbling hot pot with his chopsticks. "No need to become that man's *ernai* if you don't want to."

Lotus stared at him.

Bing took her hand. "I know I don't deserve you. But I want to support you and your brother's studies. Please allow me to. I'd be honored."

He looked sincere and determined, like a soldier requesting his commander for a difficult but honorable task.

Lotus rested her hand on top of his. "Why do you like me?"

"I am a man, not a monk. A man can easily fall in love with a nice, beautiful girl," Bing said. "Besides, I'd really like to help you."

The heat from the fire fueling the hot pot made his face glow. The reflected flame danced on his glasses. Behind them, his eyes welled with sadness. Somehow, the sadness touched Lotus.

She picked up a quail's egg from the pot for him.

Bing ate it.

Lotus picked up another one. "Dip it in the sauce. It tastes better."

He complied. "I've become such a pig."

"Pigs don't like eggs."

They looked at each other and laughed.

Finally Bing asked for the bill. "It's getting late. Let's go back."

On the way back to the hotel, a fight erupted between two young thugs. They stood head to head in the middle of the narrow road, their necks lengthening as if the men were two belligerent roosters. Onlookers either tried to pull the two apart or joined in the boxing. The scene was as chaotic as a disturbed beehive.

"Lotus, you walk behind me," Bing said.

She held on to a corner of his vest. Before long, she was holding his hand as they hurried away from the fight. She knew she wasn't in any real danger but loved the feeling of being protected. Soon Lotus forgot all about the fight, only aware of his warm hand. She had a strange sensation, as if she were walking on clouds.

When they reached the hotel, still holding hands, they tiptoed through the foyer so that they wouldn't disturb the receptionist dozing behind the front desk, trying hard to suppress their giggles. On their way out, the receptionist had woken up from her sleep and cried: "Going out at such a late hour? Have fun!"

Once inside their room, Lotus threw herself onto her bed, laughing. "I half expected her to wake up and say to us, '*Hei,* you're back!'"

Bing laughed, too. "Home away from home. You surely feel at home with someone like her stationed at the gate and monitoring guests like a dog." He poked out his tongue and panted. Lotus burst into a loud laugh.

"Shush, Lotus. People are sleeping."

Lotus looked up and saw him bend down toward her. For a moment, she thought he was going to embrace her. She waited, feeling as if a little deer was kicking in her chest. But he only pulled her up.

"Why don't you use the bathroom first?" Bing suggested.

"Okay. Do we have to get up early tomorrow?"

"No, not at all."

Lotus took an extra-long shower, making sure every inch of her body was clean. Stepping out of the shower stall, she wiped away the mist on the mirror and spotted her pink face. She stood on tiptoes, wishing she were a palm taller, and her skin whiter.

The little deer started to dance inside her chest again. Lotus rested a hand on her left breast, trying to calm it. She cupped her breasts in her hands and pushed them to the middle. She let her hands drop, thinking that Bing was probably not the type who particularly cared for big waves.

She had never been truly in love with a man. Of course, there had been Luo Yijun from Mulberry Gully. But to be with him felt like cracking a plate of melon seeds—pleasant enough, but nothing too exciting. Then there was Little Zhao. But it wasn't really love, as she never had the chance to get to know him. She did get to know Little Qian from the factory physically, but he failed to move her heart. Then working as a *ji* over the past three years had destroyed any fantasies she had about men.

Lotus put on her nightgown and came out of the bathroom. "Your turn," she said to Bing.

He shot an uneasy look at her and dashed in.

Lotus switched off the main light, turned on the bedside lamp, and climbed into bed. Lying there, she listened to the water splashing against the concrete floor and imagined his naked body under the shower. She touched her nightgown, which Bing had bought for her, and smelled it. She took it off and tossed it onto a chair by the bed. Looking up, she could see a wet yellow patch on the ceiling and a spider web in the corner. The damp smell, mixed with stale smoke, felt stronger in the stillness of the night. She thought about the scenes she had seen in *Princess Huan Zhu,* of lovers whispering to each other under the moonlight, and the wedding night with flickering red candles. Never mind. What was it that her auntie used to say? "What is a good life, my girl? For a country woman, it's marrying the kind of man who doesn't lay a finger on her." Auntie herself was unfortunately married to a violent man, who would fly into a rage over reasons as trivial as finding a piece of garlic skin in his meal. He once beat her so badly he dislocated her shoulder. "Marry a dog, stay with a dog; marry a rooster, stay with a rooster": that was the iron rule for a woman in the countryside. Auntie had approved of Bing, predicting that his prominent forehead and thick earlobes were auspicious signs, indicating a prosperous future. Lotus knew there was no point in mentioning that she wasn't sure she loved him. "Love, what's the use in that?" her auntie would say.

Ah, the mystery of love. Lotus had never learned any of the facts of life from her family. When Lotus reached puberty, Nai had started to teach her that the most important thing for a girl was to keep her chastity. The lesson actually aroused her curiosity about sexuality. Knowing that she wouldn't get anything out of her grandma, she went to Auntie and asked how a baby was made and where it came out. Auntie replied that a baby came out of a mother's underarm and she would know the rest when she grew up. But there was no obvious hole in a woman's armpit!

Shortly before Lotus's schooling had come to an end, the mystery between men and women solved itself. The vibrant spring day bore into her mind. At the school's exercise ground, the girls skipped ropes in the setting sun. Soon they all got very hot. Eighteen-year-old Hua, the leader of their gang, took off her jacket. Her tight green sweater made from acrylic fiber emphasized the mounds on her chest.

"Sister Hua, have you eaten so much yeast recently that your breasts suddenly puffed up?" Little Red, still flat-chested, asked.

"I know why," cut in another girl. "It's your boyfriend!"

Hua let out a whistle.

In the village, it was very rare for an unmarried couple to have sex before marriage. Lotus knew that Hua would have denied it firmly if she hadn't crossed the line. In her view, Hua wasn't particularly attractive: she had a solid body and a flat nose as if she had been dropped face-down to the ground upon her arrival in the world. But she had a vivacious personality and skin as soft as egg white. Whatever the reason, Hua seemed popular with the boys.

Lotus pulled Hua's sleeves. "Please tell us. Aren't we all sworn sisters?"

"Why not! Young people in the city do it all the time." Hua began to unlock her secrets.

Lotus always admired Hua for having the guts to go for what she wanted. But she wouldn't give herself away lightly, Lotus had long decided. She would only do it with someone special.

At her hotel room, Lotus thought with a heavy heart how stupid she had been to have given her virginity away like a piece of weightless paper, to someone not special at all.

Bing was pretty special. This morning, her vanity had puffed up when half of the villagers came out to send them off and pressed eggs cooked in tea leaves, scallion pancakes, or dried tiger lilies into their hands.

The bathroom door creaked. Out walked Bing in his T-shirt and shorts, holding his black-framed glasses in one hand. Without the glasses, he looked different and slightly lost, Lotus noticed, as she half hid her face under the bedding. Before getting into bed, he narrowed his eyes, probably trying to have a better look at her nightgown on the chair.

"Lotus," Bing called out softly.

She pretended to be asleep.

He was quiet for some time. Lotus wanted to open her eyes to see what he was up to, but stopped herself.

"Good night, Lotus," Bing whispered and turned off the bedside lamp.

After a few minutes, Lotus unearthed her face from beneath the blanket and saw, in the dim light that filtered in through the thin curtain, Bing lying in his bed, his back toward her, motionless. But she knew that he wasn't sleeping.

The darkness lent Lotus the heightened nerves of a panther. She stepped out of her bed and slipped into his, moving toward him and resting her face on his neck. His skin was a little damp from the shower. She put her arm around his waist.

Bing took her hand and caressed it for a long while before turning toward her. "Are you sure about this, Lotus?"

"Sure, if I'm the first *ji* you've ever slept with."

There was a moment's pause before Bing answered. "Of course."

He pulled her toward him, hugging her tightly, rocking back and forth. Then, cupping her face in his hands, Bing pressed his mouth against hers. His tongue touched and teased hers. She could taste cigarettes in his mouth. She felt a little dizzy. No wonder lovers kissing in foreign films always seemed delirious, she thought.

Lotus opened her eyes and looked at his face, half hidden in shadow.

"Oh, Lotus, you are so beautiful!" he murmured.

Lotus laughed softly. "Look at you, with all your clothes on."

He rolled out of the narrow bed to undress, and while he was taking off his shirt, she poked at his big belly with a toe.

"*Aiyah!* You naughty girl!" He caught her foot and tickled the arch.

Lotus fell back on the bed, giggling. Kneeling by her side, Bing massaged her foot, making her laugh harder. Then, to her surprise, he lifted up her foot and kissed it. He moved up, planting kisses along her legs, her thighs, and her belly. He caressed her as if she were a precious, delicate object that could shatter under the slightest pressure.

Bing cupped a breast in each hand. He took turns kissing and sucking her nipples.

Lotus could feel them hardening, and a warm glow spread between her legs. She sat up, took his hardened manhood and circled it around a nipple, teasing it.

He let out a sigh of pleasure.

"Are you ready?" Lotus pulled out a condom from under her pillow.

Bing lowered his head to take a closer look. "I see you've come prepared."

"Did you forget my profession?"

He rolled on the condom awkwardly. Lotus lay down, opening her legs wide.

Bing slipped inside her and kissed her mouth deeply. When he lifted his head, resting his weight on his elbows, he looked straight into her eyes. "My lovely Lotus," he murmured.

He began to move, quickening his rhythm. Lotus lifted her hips to meet his, bringing him deep inside her.

Before long, she felt it tremble and cried out.

"I'm coming too!" Bing called out her name. "Oh, Lotus, my Lotus!"

It startled and moved her.

Bing rolled off. He murmured thanks as he leaned over to kiss her on the cheek. Then he got up and returned with a hot towel and wiped her ever so gently.

Lotus accepted with silent gratitude, feeling dreamy and surreal.

He then pushed the twin beds together and lay down next to her, wrapping an arm around her.

Lotus nestled against him, savoring the warm, secure feeling. He was no longer just "Hu Laoshi." He was her man and her *guisu*—her final destiny.

She soon felt his embrace soften as he drifted into sleep.

"Good night," she whispered.

Lotus paused in front of the Moonflower Massage Parlor. She thought about how she had spent hours of her life standing here, smiling her red smile at every passing man. Now, that life seemed far away. In the distance, she could hear a train pulling out of the station. She played with the gold ring Bing had bought her just before boarding the train back to Shenzhen. This would be her last visit to the parlor. Her smiles would no longer be for sale. For reasons she couldn't articulate, she had been dreading this final visit.

This morning, she had called Family Treasure with the news that she was washing her hands of the business. There was a pause before he began shouting. "I'll pay you thirty-five hundred yuan, all right? How about four thousand? I've told everyone about you! My friends will all laugh at me!"

Lotus mumbled "Sorry" as she hung up. Family Treasure wasn't a bad man. But she had to put her own interests first.

Lotus coughed to clear her throat, opened the sliding door, and called out: "Sister Moon."

The velvet curtains were pulled open in the smoky parlor, and the massage beds were pushed aside. The girls were playing mah-jongg on a folding table in the middle of the room. Unlike her charges, Boss Moon preferred this game to watching soap operas. Now, in Lotus's usual seat, sat a big-boned, fresh-faced young girl. The new recruit, most likely. Lotus saw that she was wearing one of Moon's dresses.

"Lotus, you're back!" The girls greeted her with delight.

"Don't sit there like a Buddha, girls, get a chair for our guest." Moon emphasized the last word.

There wasn't another chair.

The new girl looked around and stood up, pulling down her short silk dress. It was too tight for her. "Have my seat," she said in an accented voice. She rested her big hands on her belly, scratching the material nervously. Her nails were unkempt and dirty. The girl would get a telling-off by the boss soon, Lotus knew.

"No, thank you." Lotus dropped her snakeskin sack by her feet and stood awkwardly, playing with the ring again. She was constantly conscious of its presence and weight on her finger, as if the ring had become the center of her being. She rested her left hand on her waist.

"This is our new girl, Ayun." Moon pulled Ayun back to her seat and stroked the young girl's face with the back of her hand. "Rather sweet-looking, don't you think?"

Ayun squeezed out a smile.

Moon glanced at the ring and then at the sack on the floor. "What's the good news, Lotus? Look at your face, glowing like a red lantern!"

"Hu Laoshi—I mean, Bing—and I got together," Lotus began.

"Got together?" asked Xia. She burst into hysterical laughter and made a rude gesture of thrusting her right index finger through the circle formed by her left hand. "Ha-ha, his thing isn't just for pissing, then?"

Lotus lowered her head, blushing. "He's a real man, Xia."

Little Jade clapped her hands. "*Wasai!* Sister Lotus found a *guisu*!"

Mimi looked puzzled. "The photographer? But he's so old, too much of a . . ."

Lotus shot an angry look at her friend.

"Too much of a monk?" With exaggerated movement, Moon chucked a mah-jongg tile on the table and started massaging her breasts. "Why should I care? You were leaving us anyway."

Lotus had always been afraid of her boss and her glib tongue. But Moon wasn't her boss anymore, she reminded herself. She thought of something to say, words hard as a stone and sharp as a spear. But she couldn't come up with any retort. Instead, she glared at the owner of the parlor.

Xia nudged Lotus. "Money, has he given you any? I know one lucky girl got ten thousand yuan . . . "

"Xia! I'm not his mistress. And he isn't rich," Lotus said harshly. "But he did buy me a ring." She held out her hand to show them.

"It's so shiny," said Little Jade admiringly.

"Very nice," Mimi agreed. "I'd love to get one, too. But Lanzai won't let me."

"What's the percentage of gold in it?" asked Xia, examining the ring. "What's the gem?"

"The ring isn't cheap, actually," Lotus replied. If she had had her way, she would rather have had the cash. But Bing had insisted on the ring, a gesture of his commitment, he said. Naturally then, Lotus would have liked to have gotten a flashy one, to show off in front of the other girls. But a piece of very expensive jewelry would give Bing the impression that she was a gold-digger. In the end, she pointed at a 19-karat gold ring, set with a ruby stone.

"So when can we expect to eat your double happiness sweets then, Lotus?" Moon's voice croaked.

"We haven't really discussed the wedding date yet."

"*Tse, tse.*" The boss clicked her tongue.

"Make sure he marries you," Xia urged. Then she let out a long sigh. "Aha, Lotus, you're young and beautiful. And this man is taking you away for a good life. Look at me: I'll be stuck here forever!"

Lotus swallowed but didn't say a word. She hadn't known what reaction to expect from her friends, but certainly a better one than this.

As she got ready to leave, Moon spoke again. "Remember that rich boss, Mr. Gao? He was considering letting you replace his mistress. I discouraged him because I needed you to stay with me. I'm sorry. But it's not too late yet, you know." She stopped to draw on her slim cigarette as if to give Lotus time to consider.

Lotus said nothing.

"Mark my word, young lady," said Moon, holding up one finger decorated with a diamond ring. "If you meet a man on the job, he will always remember you as a *ji*. That's men!" A dismissive noise came out of her nose, along with the smoke.

"Thank you." Lotus stopped short of blurting out "Boss."

CHAPTER 18

芝麻开花节节高

*Shooting Higher and Higher Like
Sesame Flowers*

*I stumbled on the term "ji"—prostitute—in my dictionary when I was a
schoolboy. "Women who sell their bodies for a living," the dictionary
explained. When I asked my mother how a woman could sell her body, she
only scolded me, saying it was not a question for a child. As I grew older, I
realized that other terms relating to prostitution, such as "brothel," "whore,"
and "pimp," were absent from the dictionary. The Chinese Communist
Party has managed to elide not only the words from the dictionaries but
also the world's oldest profession itself. In the past two decades, however,
prostitution has become the fastest-growing industry in China, and all the
relevant words have resumed their places in the lexicon.*

*In the wake of my company's bankruptcy, I decided to pursue my long-
standing passion for photography. For two years I've been living in a slum
where prostitutes congregate, as a participant observer, if I may borrow
the anthropological term. I believe that once people become aware of these*

social problems and their root causes, they will be more willing to address them.

China is currently undergoing a dramatic social and economic transformation. The relaxed social control, growing wealth, widening income gap, and vast rural-to-urban migration have resulted in an increase of prostitution, especially in more developed coastal areas such as Shenzhen.

Who are the prostitutes? The majority of them are country girls from the impoverished hinterland, unskilled, poorly educated, and ill-prepared for life in the city. Only some who cater to the high end of the market are better-educated urban girls. According to my research, prostitution falls into a series of categories.

Ernai, the second wife, the modern version of a concubine, sits at the top of the prostitution hierarchy. Ernais are generally regarded as prostitutes because their main concern is financial gain rather than emotional connection. On the next tier are the high-end prostitutes who operate secretly, finding clients through connections or by frequenting posh hotels. The third tier consists of so-called "baopo," who are booked for days or weeks or even longer periods, when their clients come over on business trips. Then comes the "sanpei xiaojie," young girls who operate at karaoke bars, song and dance halls, or other entertainment venues. They accompany their clients to dine and drink, to dance and sing, and to have sexual intercourse upon request. The fifth tier is made up of the "hair salon girls" and "massage parlor girls." They use hair salons or massage parlors as fronts, offering on-the-spot sex or moving to a hotel once a deal is settled. This group comprises more than half of the total prostitutes, which is why I have focused my attention on them. Below them are "street women," who make do with clients they pick up in the streets, parks, bus or railway stations, and construction sites. Some of them are barely better off than beggars.

Contrary to popular belief, the evidence I've gathered suggests that the government does allocate massive resources and funds toward prostitution control. This effort, however, is hindered by corruption. Entertainment enterprises often work in collusion with local government. More important, the sex industry has become a significant part of the local

economy. After each major "sweeping away the yellow" campaign, Shen-
zhen's bank deposits drop as the working girls take their money to their
hometowns, waiting for the storm to blow over. All the song and dance
halls and karaoke bars stand nearly empty, with only a few carousing
tourists from Hong Kong or Taiwan.

Why do women enter the trade? For money, of course. A successful
prostitute can earn twenty times more than a factory worker. There are
many external causes, as well. Take Shenzhen as an example. The massive
influx of migrant workers to the Special Economic Zone, who lack the social
connections necessary for job hunting in China, find themselves struggling
in the already saturated labor market.

The jobs available to them are usually labor-intensive, poorly paid,
dirty, or low jobs that the locals don't bother with. Their positions are
further hindered by the hukou *household registration system that denies*
them equal status with the urban residents in terms of access to employ-
ment, health care, and education. The combination of a lack of job oppor-
tunities and the temptation of better pay persuades some migrant girls to
take up the trade.

Many working girls also have troubled personal histories or have run
into trouble for reasons beyond their control. In this respect, the stories of
the prostitutes featured in this book are paradigmatic of larger trends.

This book is a candid look into the everyday lives of sex workers oper-
ating out of massage parlors and hair salons in today's Shenzhen, featur-
ing Girl A and her fellow workers. It also explores the interplay between
prostitution and gender issues, the ongoing sexual revolution, a decline
in morality, and urbanization at a time when China is both delving into
the past and reaching into the future.

Bing typed furiously on his keyboard. He had been mulling over the
introduction to his book for weeks. Once he started writing, the words
flowed like a gushing stream.

Lotus made one of her half-coughing and half-throat-clearing noises.
He turned toward her. She was sitting on the bed, her back against the

wall, absorbed in a magazine article. He smiled to himself and returned to his computer.

Since their return from Lotus's village six weeks ago, Bing had been working steadily on his book. As the manuscript developed, so did his confidence. He labored to make sure that every word was a gem and every paragraph was thought-provoking.

He had finally come up with a possible title: *Smiles for Sale: A Glimpse into Prostitution in China.*

Bing automatically reached for his cigarettes but then checked himself. He had launched a healthy living campaign, smoking much less, usually just one after a good "cloud and rain" session, when he could still feel the reverberations of lovemaking, riding out the wave as he exhaled.

Above Lotus's head, a white mosquito net, tied up in a knot, swayed in the breeze blowing from the ceiling fan. This purchase was one of many new additions Lotus brought when she moved in. Her clothes hanging from a rack brightened up the room. His place even smelled better now, with her sweet presence. For the first time in many years, Bing felt that he was experiencing domestic bliss. Although he had been happy with Mei in the early years of their marriage, he was never the master of the house. Lotus, on the other hand, adored him, and never seemed tired of listening to him. Rather docile, she always went along happily with any plan he came up with. When he needed to write, she would be content to stay quiet for hours and amuse herself with reading or cooking. She had settled well into her new life, taking charge of the household chores. And he accepted her care like a seedling accepting spring rain. She seemed happy enough. Of course she was happy.

Bing had helped her set up her little shrine in one corner. Every day she burned incense, though not usually in front of him. But she no longer asked him questions about sin or redemption.

"Reading something interesting?" asked Bing, leaning over toward her.

"Hm?" Lotus looked up absent-mindedly from her magazine, the latest issue of *Migrant Workers' Literature*, a journal published by local migrant workers. He had bought her a subscription to the magazine and she couldn't stop reading it He, too, had been moved by the stories of displaced villagers struggling to improve their lives and put down roots in the city's often hostile environment.

"What a story!" Lotus exclaimed. She began to tell Bing about the article she had just read about a migrant girl's extraordinary journey from waiting tables to becoming a writer and a successful entrepreneur. While working at a restaurant to support herself, the girl, Ai Zhi, took evening classes to finish her senior middle school education. She then went on to study business management. "A migrant worker becoming a writer? Do you think it's a true story?" she asked.

"I've actually heard about her. And Shenzhen is certainly a land of opportunity."

"She must be extremely smart."

"She must be very clever and determined. You are also smart, my sweet."

Lotus shook her head. "I really wish I'd known about these magazines earlier. Or better, that I had met you earlier." She smiled up at him, revealing dimples on her cheeks.

He leaned over to kiss her cheek. "It was not your fault that you lived in a confined bubble. Most migrants live like you did."

Bing placed Lotus's hand flat on his palm. Her wheat-colored skin was just a shade lighter than his. As he caressed her hand, he could feel calluses on her fingers, traces of her farming past. Her palm was thicker than that of a city girl, but it was still deliciously soft.

"You know, Lotus, I've been curious about how working girls like you cope with your situation," Bing said. He was determined to fill the prostitution book with insights and vivid details.

"What do you mean?" Lotus looked at him quizzically, her head tilting toward him.

"Well, it's a tough life. Having to have sex with strangers, I mean."

"Oh, that." Lotus leaned back against the wall. "I just shut my eyes and hoped it'd be over soon. Or sometimes I touched their sensitive spots to help them to come faster. Lots of girls do the same, I guess," she said, attempting a smile.

Lotus went on to tell a joke, describing the growing industry of prostitution: pornography is the advertising department; the mama-sans and pimps work in sales; the chickens make up the production line; and the STD clinics offer after-sales service.

Although Bing had heard the joke many times, he laughed along with her. "What about Xia? She always talks dirty, telling dirty jokes and things."

"Poor old Xia. She used to get on my nerves." Lotus smiled wearily. "She's really street smart. One time, back in my early days at the parlor, a client insulted me. After he left, I cursed him for hours. Xia sat me down and told me that to survive in the game, we have to be thick-skinned and never let a client get us down. She said that we had to change our thinking. We aren't selling ourselves. Clients aren't men but tools to get what we want. They pay us and they can pleasure us." She released a nervous giggle. "I guess Xia has learned to squeeze pleasure out of the job. Xia once told me that she had never had an orgasm before coming to the business, not even with her husband. And they had three children! I'll never forget what she said."

This was precisely the insightful and authentic information Bing had been looking for. He took mental notes. "How about you, sweetie? Did you follow Xia's advice?"

"I tried, but I couldn't."

"Why not?"

Lotus's face reddened. "I don't know," she replied, turning her face aside. "For me, it feels, er, so wrong." It had been particularly hard in the beginning, she confessed. After each transaction, she still felt somehow that she got the short end of the bargain. She began to try harder to squeeze money out of clients. When she couldn't, she played little tricks on them, lacing their drinks with spit or snot, or not letting them dip inside her. Incredibly, a lot of the men didn't seem to notice that they were thrusting outside of her, between her legs.

Bing stroked her face. "People in vulnerable positions often come up with little tricks that allow them to feel they have some kind of control over their lives. Right?"

"Some control over my life?" she repeated, frowning. "I've never thought about it like that."

"So Xia could enjoy herself, but you couldn't really. Was that the reason Xia got on your nerves?"

Lotus's puzzled face was the color of peach blossoms. "I don't know . . . " She stopped, looking at him as if begging him to stop.

He did. "All right, enough about the past," he said, clapping his hands. "Now tell me. What would you like to do in the future, in an ideal world?"

She sat up straight. "I'd love to be a grade one teacher at a primary school," she responded after some deliberation. "I want to give the children a good start in life. I'd want to work with students who need me and respect me."

"You should go ahead and give it a try."

"How?"

"You've been teaching Big Head and his brother, haven't you? Take a few more students. I'll get a few books you can use to start." Bing patted her shoulder. "Now, could you please give me a massage?"

Lotus's face broke into smiles. *"Yaodei!"*

Bing lifted her up from the bed, peeled off her nightdress, and gathered her into his arms. He touched her slender waist and then moved his hand downward. He loved the perfect curves of her body. He knelt down and started to pull down her underpants with his teeth, very slowly. He loved her smells, talcum powder mixed with mango-scented shower gel.

He turned off the light. Together they let down the mosquito net and tucked it carefully under the mattress.

In the darkness, Bing undressed and lay facedown on the bed.

Lotus knelt beside him. She massaged his shoulders, pressing her thumbs deep into the muscles.

He groaned. "I didn't realize how tense my shoulders have become."

"You've been sitting in front of the computer for too long," she said as she pressed harder, using not only her fingers, but also the knuckles.

Gradually Bing felt his muscles relax. He was surprised at the strength of her hands, but then again she was a country girl who had tumbled in mud and soil.

The first time they had made love, he was anxious. Lotus had been with all kinds of men. But he was pleased to see her enjoying herself, even though she didn't produce the same loud, arousing noises that Pearl had made. At times Bing was embarrassed for desiring her so much. Resting after lunch had never been his habit. Now he found himself looking forward to a siesta every day so that he could make love to her inside their snow-white mosquito net, their sweat-lubricated bodies entwined together like eels. Then he would fall into a sound sleep with her soft, soft body in his arms.

Bing closed his eyes and followed the movement of her hands. This is the life, he thought.

CHAPTER 19

一石激起千层浪

❖————————————————————————————❖

A Stone Tossed into the Water Raises
a Thousand Ripples

Lotus had hung a small blackboard from the Dragon Eye tree, and she wrote out four characters that all were pronounced "ma," but with different tones. "This is *ma*—a flat tone means mother; this is *ma*—the tone going up means hemp; this is *ma*—the tone going down then up means horse; and this is *ma*—the tone going down means to curse." She pronounced each word loudly and deliberately, tapping her bamboo baton over each of the characters.

Her six pupils—Big Head, his brother, Laoer, and four others from the neighborhood—repeated the words after her, loudly and deliberately. They sat around the round plastic table. Even Big Head's toddler sister, Niuniu, joined in sometimes with her baby voice.

Lotus instructed them to compose sentences using the new words. She bent down, monitoring them as they completed their assignment.

"My mother doesn't ride a horse." Big Head wiggled his tongue from side to side as he wrote each stroke with care. "She rides a flatbed cart, with piles of hemp, cursing anyone in her way."

Lotus let out a laugh, as she could just imagine his mother riding her three-wheeled vehicle, showering curses on whoever was blocking her way.

"*Yaodei!*" Lotus ruffled his large head with her chalk-stained hand. The boy was as bright as a summer morning.

Big Head grinned, showing his uneven teeth and plenty of red gums.

"Teacher Lotus, how about me? Look at mine," Laoer said as he shoved his exercise book in front of her.

"Ah, not bad at all, Laoer."

"But he wrote 'hemp' in the wrong stroke order, I saw!" Big Head hissed about his brother.

"You stinky Big Head!" the younger brother retaliated.

"You stupid Rice Bucket, you only know how to eat rice!" Big Head raised his voice.

Laoer, red-faced now, raised his right fist.

"Stop it, you two. Otherwise, you won't get any popsicles," Lotus threatened.

That silenced the brothers. "Laoer, look. Write the dot before the horizontal stroke. Do you know that many characters look like the real objects? Take *ma*—horse—as an example." She walked up to the blackboard and drew a picture of a horse rearing up. Her students copied her and did their own pictures of a horse.

"*Wasai!* It really looks like a horse, Teacher Lotus!"

"Teacher Lotus." Lotus savored the sweetness of the words. Over one month ago, she had turned the backyard into an open-air classroom in the late mornings. Since moving in with Bing in mid-September, she had taken over the running of the household, buying food from the village market and cooking on the gas cylinder. Although she had always found satisfaction in caring for others, the domestic chores didn't consume all her time or energy. Sometimes she and Mimi would go to a massive indoor market to gaze at the colorful clothes and cheap jewelry. Lotus had once entertained the idea of opening a clothes shop in Phoenix, but not now, of course. What would Bing do in a provincial town? Serve as her cashier?

When the appeal of window-shopping had petered out, she felt lost. Meanwhile, Big Head and his siblings had started to spend more time with her. She played with them and taught them useful characters and basic mathematics. If they did well, she would reward them with little treats such as dried seaweed or sugar cane.

"You are such a natural-born teacher!" Bing had once remarked.

"You are putting a crown on a beggar's head," she replied, beaming.

Before long, Big Head and others had begun to call her "Teacher." Encouraged by Bing and inspired by the story of Ai Zhi, Lotus had finally set up the class, equipped with some primary school textbooks, a blackboard, and some chalk that Bing had bought for her. He also bought a book about the origins and development of Chinese characters, which was fun and useful. Several other children from the neighborhood soon joined the class. Her new students were used to running wild in the street and had difficulty sitting quiet in class, so Lotus had to impose and enforce the class rules. She very much enjoyed the authority she had over them.

Big Head's mother was a lioness of a woman who couldn't pass a recognizable *ji* without spitting on the ground. Now, she shifted 180 degrees in her attitude toward Lotus. In the evenings, the lioness would often bring over a dish of bitter melon stuffed with minced pork or Eight Treasure sticky rice pudding and fuss over Lotus in her Hakka dialect. "Not easy, you see, for us to make an honest living!"

Lotus knew her type: her "honest" work seemed to grant her the right to insult prostitutes.

Lotus had unexpectedly discovered a deep sense of fulfillment in teaching, and she savored the respect of her students. Every step of progress they made delighted her, and their reading aloud was the best music she had ever heard.

Sometimes when she stared at the portrait of Guanyin, she thought she saw a smile. She was probably accumulating some good karma, Lotus thought. More important, she felt good about herself. She felt lucky to be with Bing, her ticket to a secure future. She was now much less resentful toward the world.

"Little Flower, write your characters within the box. That's too big," Lotus told a girl in a dirty dress.

"Sing, Sister Lotus. Sing a song." Niuniu tugged at Lotus's skirt with her dimpled hands. The toddler had on only a pair of split cotton pants and a silver necklace with the character for "fortune" engraved on it. Maybe the talisman did work wonders after all, keeping her healthy despite all the filth that went into her mouth.

"*Yaodei, yaodei!*" Lotus fussed with Niuniu's tiny pigtails; then she sat and took the toddler onto her lap, and sang a song about a little swallow that her mother had taught her. The children sang along, drowning out the chirping of cicadas and the village noises. The music lingered for a long time in the air.

A familiar clicking sounded. Lotus looked up. "You are disturbing the class, Hu Laoshi, snapping away like that."

"Sorry."

"Teacher Lotus, why do you call him teacher? He isn't our teacher," Big Head said, his eyes flitting between the two.

"He's my teacher," Lotus said, smiling. The truth was that she didn't know how to address the man who shared her bed. In public, she continued to call him Hu Laoshi. When they were alone, however, the term sounded ridiculous. Bing continued to call her Lotus since he didn't like her nickname Chouchou—Ugly, Ugly. He also called her all sorts of affectionate names: baby, treasure, sweet melon, silly melon, and sometimes Princess Huan Zhu. She particularly liked this last title, even though she knew she would never become a princess. As for herself, she still couldn't bring herself to call him anything intimate. Luckily she could usually get by without calling him anything.

"It's nearly noon," Bing reminded Lotus, pointing to his watch.

She clapped her hands. "Children, we'll have to finish early today because Hu Laoshi and I are going to go out to celebrate Xia's birthday."

———

The group arrived at Small Plum Beach, out on the so-called Golden Coastline of the city. They stood on the pavement, looking at the crowds of people everywhere. Women hid under the shade of umbrellas while children risked the sun, shrieking excitedly in the rolling surf. Some swimmers floated on inner tubes, bobbing up and down amid the flotsam of plastic water bottles, ice cream wrappers, and watermelon rinds. It was late November but still warm enough for swimming and a perfect time to be at the beach.

"*Aiyah,* where can we rest our bums?" Mimi said.

"Especially a millstone like yours," Xia piped in.

Mimi wiggled her fleshy hips. "At least I've got one."

"Come on, stop it," Lotus pleaded with her friends. She turned to Bing. "Shall we stay here or go somewhere else?" She was keen to ensure the success of this rare outing. After all, it was her idea. She felt a little embarrassed that she had held a grudge against Xia for no good reason. When Xia had talked about her upcoming birthday, Lotus decided to invite her former workmates to the beach for a photo session, then treat them to lunch at a restaurant by the sea.

"Let's walk farther, away from the restaurants and crowds," Bing said and started to walk along a shady path sandwiched between rows of tall palm trees.

"Can we take a taxi?" cried Mimi, staggering in her high heels.

Lotus dragged her along. "Come on, Mimi. Some exercise is good for you."

"Walk in your bare feet, then," Bing suggested. "Lovely sand, imported, you know."

"Imported sand? Why?" Xia asked.

"To turn this place into a tourist attraction! The government reclaimed the land—filling up the bay and turning it into a beach," Bing explained.

The longer Lotus stayed with Bing, the more acutely she felt her ignorance. Once he had taken her to an ancient fort town called Dapeng, farther north of Shenzhen. She enjoyed visiting the fortress and walking around the winding narrow streets with their old-fashioned charm.

Another time, he had taken her to an artist village, where world-famous artworks were copied and produced in large quantities. She had had no idea such places existed. She wanted to learn more in order to lessen the gap between them, as wide as between heaven and earth.

After passing an empty private beach belonging to some government organization, they came to a much quieter bay where a crescent-shaped sandy beach hugged the sea. Arched over it was a vast blue sky, decorated with cotton-flower clouds.

"This is much better," announced Bing as he put down his camera bag. "We Chinese do love crowds."

As soon as the girls changed into their bathing suits, they flew toward the gentle waves of the gray-blue sea. All the girls were "dry ducks" who couldn't swim, but still they played in the waves and splashed each other with water and then posed in front of Bing's camera.

Lotus stayed behind and sat by the edge of the sea. The water was cool and refreshing, and she lifted her face to the sun, not bothering with a hat or sun cream as the city women did. What a lovely sensation when the waves rushed through her toes and pulled away the sand underneath as they retreated. Years ago, on the train down south for the first time, she and Little Red had dreamed about this. How much she wished her dear cousin could have lived to see this day.

Ever since she had placed her bet in Bing's hand, Lotus felt she had been taking a ride in a new territory. She didn't know where it was taking her or what to expect. She was a little anxious, but overall she enjoyed the unfamiliar landscape and the thrill of it, especially in the very early days.

Bing had started to buy her clothes, tight-fitting silk cheongsam or Chinese-style tops with knotted buttons on the side. She was flattered and pleased that he went out of his way for her, but she preferred modern clothes to traditional-style outfits. Lotus would put them on only when he took her out to fancy restaurants. She would sit there smiling politely, even though she found it difficult to breathe in her tight and formal dress, while he nearly drowned her in showers of lavish praise. Such dresses seemed to turn him on. Once back at home, he would take time undressing her, kissing her gently and kissing even the knotted buttons.

Two weeks ago, Bing had presented her with a bouquet of red roses for her birthday. Receiving flowers for the first time ever, she was overwhelmed with emotions, touched by his gesture but also worried that he might have spent too much money on an item without any practical use. Then he took her for dinner at the revolving restaurant on the top floor of the Emperor Building, the tallest building in town. She felt she had reached the nearest place to heaven.

There were other surprises. Bing, from time to time, would offer to wash her feet in the evening, just before retiring to bed. In her village, a husband would sometimes demand that his wife wash his feet. But a big man would never, ever clean a woman's feet. How incredible to be pampered like this, Lotus thought.

The first time they had gone to bed, she was nervous, but something in the way he had touched her soothed her. She was slightly surprised by his desire for her, but then it was difficult for her to judge what would be normal in a couple's sex life. Deep down, she always felt that a decent woman shouldn't be too interested in that. As a result, she wasn't totally relaxed in bed with Bing. But that was not her primary concern. Her priority was to please him so that he would eventually marry her. Only marriage could erase the stain of her past and secure her future, financially and socially.

Lotus half dozed and daydreamed until Bing and the girls came over and sat around her.

Xia stroked Bing's sleeve with a wet hand. "*Wasai*, my brother! More colorful than a peacock!"

Having changed into his swimming trunks, Bing still wore his bright shirt, though unbuttoned. He was probably trying to cover up his belly in front of the girls.

"Hawaiian shirt. Lotus bought it for me," Bing volunteered.

"You don't have to wear your photographer's vest all the time," Lotus said. She was worried that when people saw them together, they would notice the age gap and take her for Bing's mistress. To avoid this, whenever they went out she dressed more conservatively, while trying to dress Bing up.

"Last year, a man hired me to swim with him," said Mimi. "He forced me to do the business in the sea, saying that it wouldn't transmit diseases in that way, because of the salty seawater. Is that true?" she asked, staring at Bing.

Bing twisted the corners of his mouth, as if not sure whether to laugh or cry. "Of course it's not true. He can still pass his germs to you or make you pregnant."

Mimi stuck out her tongue. "Oh, *tamade!*"

Lotus listened to their chat. Familiar conversations, but they were so far removed now from her world.

The sound of a piano rose from Bing's camera bag.

He got up, wiped his hands on his shirt, and picked up his phone. "*Wei?*"

Lotus could make out a girl's voice, and judging by how Bing's face lit up, she knew it must be his daughter, Hu Li. He walked away, talking very patiently. "Good, well done. I'm glad you liked *Mulan* . . . That, I'm not sure . . ."

Lotus strained her ears to listen. Could they share the same roof? she asked herself. Would this girl accept her as her stepmother and respect her?

"Sorry," Bing said as he returned to Lotus's side. "It's my daughter, Lili."

"Is she okay?"

"Fine, fine. She just wants more DVDs."

"Do you miss your daughter, my brother?" Xia asked.

"Of course I do, very much."

Xia's hands played with the water; she was mindful not to wet her face. The birthday girl looked perky today with her face made up and tidy waves of hair surging up and down her head. "I miss my son, Bao-bao, like crazy," she said sadly. "He's twelve years old but looks like a child of six or seven. He used to be such a healthy boy. Then suddenly he stopped growing. An allergy to copper." Without her usual bright smile, deep lines fell on the corners of her mouth, revealing her true age. "Who has ever heard of such a strange problem? When he eats foods that have a tiny amount of copper in them, he gets poisoned by the copper. This copper business has ruined me, ruined my whole family." Tears worked their way down her powdered cheeks.

"Sister Xia!" Lotus had never seen Xia crying when she wasn't drunk.

Bing patted Xia's shoulder. "You are saving your son's life. That's the ultimate sacrifice for a mother."

Bing's kind words caused Xia more tears. She blew her nose. "Today's my birthday, I'm one year older. Under heaven, is there anything sadder than being an old *ji*?"

"Sister Xia, you still look young and . . ." Lotus paused to search for a suitable compliment. "Young and full of a tiger's energy." She felt Bing squeeze her hand. She turned to him but he just smiled, not his usual warm smile.

Little Jade, nestling beside Xia as always, seemed to be frightened by the tears. She grabbed the arm of her surrogate mother and rested her head on Xia's bony shoulder. "Sister Xia, you are a good woman and a great mother. Please don't cry."

"Thank you, good girl," Xia said, gently patting the young girl's head. "Every day I try to cheer myself up and try to enjoy myself. Otherwise, I would have been drowned by misery. I play the flute for men. Do I find it disgusting? Absolutely! It's the lowest of low. But without money, my son's going to die! Before I started to turn tricks, I was a peasant woman who slept with only one man—my poor husband." She drew a deep breath before continuing. "I had a nightmare the other day. In my dream, I saw my Baobao fighting for food with rats, and his face all bloody. I woke up and decided to bring my son here to live with me. Also, there are good hospitals here." She pulled Bing's sleeve. "By the way, thank you, Hu Laoshi, for finding out the information about the new medicine."

Xia hesitated, then fixed her eyes on Lotus. "Lotus, is it possible for you to teach my son a few characters?"

"Well, I'm not a teacher. Baobao needs to go to a proper school."

"Too expensive. Besides, he's weak. And you're so good with the kids."

"Sister Xia, I'd love to help you but . . ." Lotus glanced at Bing. "I don't even know where we are going to live."

Bing took her sandy hand. "We'll live wherever you want."

"If you help my Baobao, Lotus, I'd be happy to turn into a water buffalo in my next life and serve you forever," Xia offered sincerely.

Lotus stared at Xia's worried face, her heart filled with both sympathy and envy. It must feel good to have a child of your own to love, to care for and worry about, she thought.

"Well, when Baobao turns up, Lotus will teach him something, won't you?" Bing stroked Lotus's back. "You can take it from there."

Lotus nodded, grateful that she now had someone to turn to.

When the rest of the girls had gone to the toilet to reapply makeup for the next rounds of photography, Bing leaned over to kiss Lotus. "You look beautiful in your swim suit, my Princess Huan Zhu."

Lotus smiled her thanks.

"By the way, 'full of a tiger's energy' is usually used to describe men's sexual energy."

Lotus blushed as she murmured, "Sorry." She splashed water on her legs to cool herself down.

Bing kissed her again. "I love your rosy cheeks." He lowered his voice. "Speaking of sexual energy, have you had a checkup recently?"

"No. Why?" Lotus looked at his mouth. It took her a few moments to register his question. Then she felt new heat rising from her earlobes.

"It might not be a bad idea to have a proper checkup, to see a gynecologist, don't you think?" He spoke with extra gentleness. "I'll go with you, if you like."

"If you like," she replied mechanically.

Lotus stared back at the sea and started to draw circles in the sand. It was probably a simple suggestion without any major implication. Still, like a dish that didn't agree with her, Bing's suggestion sat uneasily for the rest of the day.

CHAPTER 20

近水知鱼性，近山识鸟音

❖————————————————————————————————❖

*Near to Rivers, We Recognize Fish, Near to
Mountains, We Recognize the Songs of Birds*

One Sunday afternoon in mid-January, Bing arrived at the Mission Hills
Golf Club to meet Zhang Jianguo. At the reception area, he found the
journalist, clad in a bright red polo shirt, sitting on a leather sofa and
reading a magazine. The massive chandelier in the room fractured the
sunlight, casting diamond patterns on the marble floor.

When he saw Bing, Zhang leaped up and reached for his hand, shaking it firmly. "Long time, no see, my friend. You look well." His loud
voice quivered in delight.

Bing nodded his greeting as he wiped sweat from his face with a
handkerchief.

"Sorry to drag you so far out," Zhang apologized.

"That's all right."

"It should be fun to play a round."

"I'm no golfer, but happy to keep you company. Are you a regular
here?"

"Not really. A businessman I once interviewed gave me a stack of free vouchers. I shouldn't have accepted, but . . ." Zhang let the sentence drop.

"Why not?" Bing said. The thing about corruption in China, he thought, was that everyone hated it but everyone was also a part of it. He didn't have a problem with a journalist enjoying a small benefit due to his position. Overworked, underpaid, and constrained by censorship, many Chinese journalists found it a struggle to live by their principles. Ever since their first meeting back in August, Bing had been very keen to make friends with the charismatic reporter. They had exchanged quite a few emails, but their schedules had kept them from meeting in person until now.

Zhang had already rented a set of golf clubs for Bing and had made the arrangements for two caddies.

Exiting the door framed by flowering bougainvillea vines, they walked toward the golf course. Having been cocooned in his cramped room day in and day out, Bing was intoxicated by the green openness. It was a world away from his shabby neighborhood. He breathed deeply, drinking in the fresh air.

The journalist swung his driver in a few practice swings, while chatting with his usual enthusiasm. "By the way, congratulations on the photo essay from Lotus's village. We've had a good response from readers. I think now's just the right time to do the profile on you. I still have a few more questions if you don't mind."

"Ask anything you like."

A few minutes later, two caddies turned up, carrying the clubs. The young women were covered from head to toe in white sportswear, with red headscarves pulled over their baseball caps.

"This is the biggest golf course in the world. You can easily get lost without a caddy," Zhang said with a flourish. He then headed toward the first hole, a downhill slope with two ponds on each side guarding the expanse of the green beyond.

Standing at the first tee, Zhang lined up his shot with the large-headed driver the caddy handed him. After a few practice swings, he launched the ball down the middle of the fairway.

"Good shot," his caddy cheered.

"Your turn." Zhang gestured.

Bing dried his hands against his shirt before taking his driver. He had played once before with a client, but that was more obligation than fun. Now in better company, he decided to give it a try by imitating the way Zhang hit the ball, but he missed the first two swings. The third time, he connected but sliced the ball far left into the next fairway.

"Hmm, good effort," the journalist said, leading the way to search for the ball.

Bing handed the driver back to the caddy and caught up with his companion. "It feels so surreal, to be playing golf out here."

"Why is that?"

"Well, this morning I was writing about Lotus's village, lost in dynastic times. Yet here I am, the same afternoon, in this massive golf course with the fancy clubhouse and all."

"Is this the book on prostitution you were talking about?"

"Yeah."

"Great! It'll make a fascinating read. And I can tell that you're an excellent writer. Your captions were well written, if a little long."

Bing had been very pleased with the pictures and the captions. They complemented each other like red flowers and green foliage. "Thank you," he said, bowing to Zhang slightly.

If Bing had brought his camera, he would have taken a few shots of the journalist in his red top and dark glasses stomping on the golf course. His confidence lent him a magnetic quality, especially now as he was bathed in the brilliant sunlight.

At the next tee, Zhang hit a long shot that landed just left of the green. "Oh, almost!" he shouted in frustration. Then his bright eyes wandered from the golf ball in the distance toward Bing beside him. "Come across any good stories in the village?"

"Yes, one story might interest you." Bing told the journalist about the tax issue and Brother Li's wife's suicide. He had actually attempted to write up the story himself but realized that the topic was too sensitive for a freelancer and might jeopardize his precarious position.

Zhang brushed the well-trimmed grass playfully with his iron and said: "Our premier has just called again for measures to ease the peasants' tax burden. This story could be quite timely. Did you take photos?"

"Of course! Oh, look out for a guy named Luo Kecheng, he's gutsy," Bing advised. "He's studying law and planning to sue the village officials who beat him up."

Zhang took off his sunglasses. "A barefoot lawyer!"

Bing laughed at the term, borrowed from "barefoot doctors"—farmers with basic training who provided basic medical services in villages in Chairman Mao's era. "Exactly. These guys may make a difference, just like the barefoot doctors."

"Absolutely. That'll make a great story," Zhang enthused, his eyes twinkling under his jutting eyebrows. "I'll have to put a positive spin on it, somehow." He slipped his sunglasses back on and slapped Bing's shoulder. "You should be a journalist yourself."

Bing smiled. Zhang's booming voice now sounded more appealing to him.

"Now, let's get on with the game. Watch me." Zhang demonstrated how to drive the ball straight up the fairway. Bing followed the advice and managed to keep the ball in play.

"Getting there," Zhang said encouragingly. "Shenzhen is such a cultural desert. Playing golf is one of my few hobbies here."

Once out on the fairway, Bing noticed two middle-aged men waiting to tee off. He gestured for them to play through. He and the journalist walked toward the shade of a palm tree. The caddies offered them water bottles and waited patiently nearby.

Zhang took a sip of water. "I thought a lot about our last conversation about 1989. Sadly, the younger generation isn't as idealistic as we were," he lamented.

Bing nodded and started to talk nostalgically about the 1980s, the era of his political awakening, filled with passion and ideology. He had not mentioned this part of his life to anyone in Shenzhen, but he knew Zhang would relate to his story.

His friend listened carefully, nodding at times, the laugh lines on his cheeks crinkling into deeper and deeper curves. "To be honest, when I first heard you talking about social responsibilities, I didn't know what to make of it. Now I know better where you're coming from."

"Well, thank you," Bing said with relief.

"Is there any chance our photographer Little Wang could take some shots of you at your home? I need something to show you in your natural environment. Maybe with some of the girls from your story."

Zhang had already requested a while ago to come around to his house with a photographer. But Bing refused because he didn't want anyone at that paper to know he was living with Lotus. He could send her out to the cinema or the market for a couple of hours, but there were traces of her everywhere in the room. It wouldn't be right to remove them; but if she had stayed, her presence would inevitably lead to the issue of their relationship. An award-winning photographer sleeping with one of the prostitutes he had been photographing? That would be a scandal.

"As I mentioned to you on the phone, my place is just too humble and dirty to receive any visitors." He tried to smooth things over as best he could. "I've already got a picture of me with some of the girls. I think it might work well for you."

After a pregnant pause, Zhang said, his tone natural: "All right then. I'll take a look."

Bing sensed the other man's disappointment, but was glad that Zhang hadn't pushed harder. He hated to let people down, and his mood darkened. He racked his brain, thinking of ways to compensate the journalist. Offering him more story ideas, perhaps?

"Shall we resume?" Zhang said, smiling graciously. Noticing that the middle-aged men had long since played through, they returned to the fairway.

Without warning, the weather suddenly changed. Black clouds blotted out the sky, like ink splashing from a giant bottle. The wind gathered strength.

Bing checked his watch, thinking about Lotus alone at the house. "I think I should be heading back," he pronounced.

"Someone expecting you for dinner?" Zhang asked, a faintly perceptible smile on his lips.

You nosy bastard, Bing muttered in his heart. "My roof will be leaking in this rain," he replied.

"Let me drive you home, then."

"That's so kind of you. I live in the village very close to East Station."

They hurried toward the clubhouse, followed by their caddies. By the
time they had returned Bing's clubs and picked up their bags, the low
sky was about to burst. The wind blew with desperation, battering flowers and pulling up leaves. Just before they reached Zhang's car, the rain
started to shoot down like water arrows, making dimples on the mud
as they hit the ground. They scrambled into his car, dripping wet.

"*Wasai,* heaven has sprung a leak!" Zhang dried his face with a handkerchief, then handed it to Bing.

Bing ran it over his head and neck. "I haven't thanked you properly
for rescuing Lotus," he said.

"Only a few phone calls. How is she? Has she gone back to the
parlor?"

"No."

"Oh! Has she left the trade?"

"Yes, I believe so."

"I'm glad to hear that. Where is—"

"Very nice car," Bing cut in, complimenting the white Citroën, looking grand and new. He touched the dashboard. "Yours?"

"Yes, mine. The paper subsidized it. It's nice to be taken care of. But
there's a price to pay."

"I'm sure." Bing buckled up and sat back comfortably in his seat,
pleased to have avoided an awkward question about Lotus's current situation. He handed the other man a brown envelope from his battered
leather case. "Before I forget, here are the photos."

The journalist switched on a light and took out the photos. He chuckled as he looked at the photo of Bing amidst a swarm of girls. There was
also an old picture of Bing in a Young Pioneers red scarf, and another
one as a businessman in a smart navy suit. "Perfect!" He carefully slid

the photos back into the envelope and started the engine and windshield wipers.

The sky darkened as their car sped along the road, cutting through the endless curtain of rain. Soon they arrived at the Outer Ring Road, where there was little traffic.

"I do love my job, even though I sometimes have to write stories I don't really believe in," Zhang began. "Aren't we all whores? Intellectual whores or working girls, where's the difference?" He laughed his infectious laugh.

Bing laughed, too. "Speak for yourself. I'm a freelancer."

They exited the ring road and drove east along wide Shennan Road, the main thoroughfare in Shenzhen. On both sides of the road, quite a few boys, most likely the children of migrants, were collecting mangoes thrown to the ground by the storm.

As the car turned south, grids of high-rises gave way to lower buildings constructed without a universal plan. The traffic thinned. The storm had calmed.

Bing watched the road ahead, shining under the headlights, and thought about his path in life. "I'm not sure how long I'll be staying in Shenzhen, actually." He had been thinking hard about the next move. Mei had suggested that he try for a staff position with *Photography*, and he was tempted. He needed a stable income as he now had to take care of Lotus. And of course, moving camp up to Beijing would mean he could see his daughter on a regular basis. But he had a feeling that Lotus would prefer to remain in Shenzhen.

The two men rode in silence for a while. "If you like, I can try to get some assignments for you," Zhang offered.

"I'd really appreciate that."

Bing was making good money at the moment benefiting from a few well-paid assignments from advertising companies. But he was aware that the job offers would trickle off once he fell back into obscurity. Besides, Mei had informed him of her plan to send their daughter to America for her university education and suggested they both save for this. Of course he would.

At the entrance of Miaocun, Bing asked to get out. "I need to pick up some stuff at the shop."

"Are you sure? Still raining."

"Sure. I live just around the corner."

Zhang pulled the car up to the curb. He drummed his fingers on his wheel, as if playing on an invisible keyboard, while Bing unbuckled himself. "How about your notes from Lotus's village?"

"I'll write up the notes and give them to you next time we meet."

"Next week?"

"Great."

Bing could hear the pitter-patter of the abacus before he walked into the convenience store. Cripple Kong was working on his accounts again, his thin body bent over the counter, like a dried old shrimp. "Here you are, the photographer." He stood up, smiling broadly.

"A box of cigarettes, Good Days, and half a dozen candles."

The old man limped to the end of the shop for the candles and returned to fetch the cigarettes from a shelf behind the counter. Every inch of the shop was jammed with goods. He provided twenty-four-hour service, sleeping in the middle of the shop at night and dozing over the counter after lunch. "Here you go."

Bing paid and was about to go.

"Wait a minute, photographer," Cripple Kong called out. He produced a piece of paper. "Mimi bought some stuff from here and said you would pay. Is it okay?" He eyed Bing as he scratched his balding head with a ballpoint pen.

"All right then." This wasn't the first time that Mimi left a bill for him to pay. Bing didn't mind too much. After all, Mimi was the one who had introduced him to Lotus.

With a quick jerk of the abacus, the shop owner cleared it for a fresh sum. His dark yellow fingers plucked the beads as if he were a musician plucking his stringed instrument. "Three packs of cigarettes, one bag of salty duck stomach, and two bags of haw jellies . . . 108.50 yuan. A hundred and eight will do."

Bing handed him the money.

"Mimi came here to telephone her mother this afternoon, in a flood of tears," Cripple Kong reported.

"The poor girl is going through a rough time," Bing said. He had heard from Lotus that Mimi was having trouble with her boyfriend again. He felt sorry for Mimi, but wasn't sure how he could be of any help to her.

"Thanks. See you later." Bing turned to walk out, waving goodbye.

"Go slowly," the Cripple Kong shouted behind him, as he did for every customer.

Bing stepped out into the rain, covering his head with his leather case. As he trudged along the muddy path, he could see the yellow glow from the window of his room. He imagined Lotus waiting for him, plates of quail's eggs and pickled cucumber already on the table. And on the stove would be his favorite pig-trotter stew. A candlelit dinner on this rainy night would lend a romantic air.

The thought of Lotus warmed his rain-soaked body. The other day at Small Plum Beach, when Bing had broached the idea of her checkup, he was afraid he might offend her. But she seemed to have taken it well. Such a sweet girl. He had thought of the idea one day when he noticed his genitals were itchy. He panicked, thinking he could have contracted some nasty disease. Apart from the first time, condoms hadn't slipped into their cloud and rain sessions, as Lotus took pills. Bing couldn't believe that he hadn't thought about getting tested earlier. A few years back, after he had realized that Pearl was a prostitute, he had gathered up the courage to have a thorough health checkup. Since setting up camp in Miaocun, several times he had felt compelled to go for a test, although he knew there was no chance of him contracting anything.

The latest checkup results, for both of them, had turned out fine. To make up for having her go through the tests, Bing had taken her out to an expensive restaurant on the seafront.

Outside his room, Bing mimicked Lotus's coughing noise, then waited for her to come and throw herself into his arms. But there was no response. Maybe the sound was drowned out by the rain. He pushed the door open. Through his rain-smeared glasses, he could see the blurry shape of Lotus kowtowing on the floor. The familiar smell of incense floated in the room. In the past few weeks, she seemed to be devoting more and more of her time to her worship. In the beginning, her faith had intrigued him. Now it bothered him a little. If she is truly happy with me, Bing reasoned, why would she still cling to her religion?

Bing coughed, louder this time. The shape sprang up and came into focus.

"You're back. Oh, look, you got soaked." Lotus went to fetch his towel and handed it to him.

Bing wiped his face and his glasses. In front of him, the pretty girl stood, her face creased in a smile, but her eyes looked swollen and sad.

"What happened?"

"Nothing!" she said, still smiling. "I'll get some dry clothes for you."

She dashed toward the rattan basket that Bing used as his wardrobe. On the way she tripped over the blue plastic tub that was catching rain from the leaking roof.

"We'll move to a better place with decent furniture as soon as I figure out where we're going to live," Bing said as he kicked off his muddy leather shoes.

Inside the room, he picked up the faint smell of an aromatic tobacco. "Did anyone come to visit?" he inquired.

Lotus hesitated for a moment. "Yes, just some guy," she said, her hands playing with the corner of her white blouse, all buttoned up.

"Some guy?" he repeated, in a voice louder than he intended. "Who was he? What did he want?"

"Just some guy trying to sell me something."

There was always some guy trying to sell something, Bing thought. But they wouldn't just walk into someone's house.

"Er, I was just washing my clothes," she said gingerly. "I forgot to shut the door, so . . ."

"All right." He softened his tone.

Lotus's hands dropped. "Supper will be ready in a minute," she announced, then hurried toward the kitchen.

Bing remained where he was, drying himself and sniffing the air.

CHAPTER 21

一失足成千古恨

❖————————————————————❖

A Single Slip May Become the Regret

of a Lifetime

It was spring again. But for some reason, the kapok trees had not blossomed yet.

In the fading sunlight, Lotus stood in the yard and watched the line of drying clothes dancing idly in the breeze. Bing's large black T-shirt was swelling with the wind. She grabbed it and smelled it. The T-shirt had the warmth of the sun, the fragrance of the detergent, and the unmistakable smell of the man himself. One by one, she took the clothes off the line.

Lotus went inside, folded the clothes neatly, and put them away. Without Bing's presence, the house felt bigger, and strangely quiet.

This evening he had gone to the Workers' Cultural Palace to teach a photography class, set up by his journalist friend. Returning home after the first class some five weeks ago, he had boasted, "You can really call me Hu Laoshi now."

Lotus would have liked to take some evening classes herself. But who would cook for Bing on the nights when she disappeared to the Cultural Palace on the other side of the city?

Throughout her life, Lotus had rarely spent any evenings on her own. She decided to write a letter home. As she settled into the chair in front of the desk, it felt like she was stepping into someone else's shoes. She pushed his laptop aside and took out a pen and paper.

This space was his. Lotus was conscious of that fact. At lunchtime when Mimi had come over to pour out her bitterness, they hadn't known where to go. They ended up sitting by the stone mah-jongg table in the village square. Poor Mimi. Lanzai was having an affair with an escort girl from a song and dance hall. The woman was a lot older but a lot richer, too. Mimi felt her heart was sliced into pieces but couldn't make up her mind to leave him. Why not?

Lotus knew she ought to feel lucky, yet she felt uneasy about her situation. Six months had flown out the window since she had bet her future on this man. Although every day had been garlanded by his fancy affectionate words, Bing had never elaborated on any plans for their wedding. Thinking about it, she wasn't even sure that he had actually promised that he would marry her, though it was understood that he would. Would he love her enough to marry her? Lotus had been taken aback when he had asked her for a medical checkup last November. Together they went to the Number 1 Municipal Hospital in Shenzhen. When a doctor asked if she would like to include an AIDS test, she and Bing exchanged an uneasy look and she nodded an agreement. So did he. It took a week for the results to come back. During that week, she waited like a criminal waiting for the sentence. She kept wondering and worrying what he would do if she had contracted some ugly disease like that. Thank heaven all the tests showed that she was free of any STDs, but she had secretly started to question whether Bing's love for her was conditional. She also questioned how much longer she would have to put up with the situation. She fretted that she was the weaker partner in the relationship, cooking food that suited his tastes, behaving in ways acceptable to him, and rarely voicing her opinions.

Was it all worth it? Lotus kept asking herself.

The relationship had not yet yielded much financial benefit for her. For their daily expenses, Bing simply stashed a couple thousand yuan in an empty tea tin. She could help herself anytime. To her disappointment, she had sensed that he wasn't exactly covered in gold dust. He had casually mentioned that he would like to support his daughter's university education in America. Lotus couldn't imagine how much that might cost. Would he be able to support her as well as her brother's education?

Only once, at Spring Festival, had Bing presented her with 4,400 yuan for her family. She put on a show of refusing before accepting it. She wired it home without even a note wishing them Happy New Year. Naturally she had not uttered a word about Bing to her family. She would only disclose their relationship to them when she was absolutely sure that they were to tie the knot.

Lotus found herself increasingly attached to this man. "Is this love?" she asked herself, but had no answer. She wished she could just love him the way a wife would love a husband, without expecting too much.

In her neat handwriting, Lotus started to compose a letter to her brother on one of Bing's lined papers. As usual, she began by asking after the health of Nai and Ba, and about Shandan's preparation for his university entrance exam, set for July 1, less than four months away.

Then she paused as she debated with herself whether to tell him now or later the story she had come up with, of winning the lottery. Might as well be now. Lottery. Hadn't she taken a little gamble in life lately? Her eyes rested on the waving hand of the Red Guard on the alarm clock. It felt as if the timepiece waved an accusing finger at her. She turned it to face the wall.

Lotus struggled to tell the lottery story. She looked out at the clouds in the evening sky, watching how the crimson was being slowly swallowed by darkness. Her thoughts drifted to one afternoon two months ago.

On that Sunday afternoon, she had been washing clothes at home, chewing over the unpleasant episode of the health checkup, when she heard a knock on the door. Bing had just left the house to meet his journalist friend. For a moment, she wondered if Bing had returned for a forgotten item. When she opened the door, she was surprised to see Funny Eye, dressed in a crisp blue shirt and tie, a black leather bag under his arm. He was smoking his pipe. Seeing her, he bowed. "Long time, no see, Lotus."

"You!" Her first reaction was to smooth her hair.

"May I come in?" he asked and started to walk in before she had the chance to reply.

As he passed by, their eyes met. She lowered her eyes first and shut the door behind her. "Sorry, could you take off your shoes, please?" she called out after him.

"Oh, I do beg your pardon." He put the pipe into his mouth, bent down to loosen up the silver buckles on his Italian shoes, and then he slipped them off. His eyes wandered from one corner of the room to another, his expression bemused. "In the olden days, gentlemen liked to keep their beauties in plush houses. Is this the best he can do?"

Lotus felt her face turning red. "This is only temporary."

"You imply that something better is to come?" The shadow of a smile flickered over his face.

Lotus used silence to shield herself from the verbal sting. Wiping her wet hands on her T-shirt, she sat on the bed but immediately jumped up again.

Funny Eye took a drag from his pipe. The smell of tobacco filled the room.

"Sorry, could you please not smoke in here?"

"Oh, that's not very considerate of me," he said in his rich voice. "It's not easy to see you, Lotus. Has anyone told you that I went to the parlor to look for you?"

She nodded.

"Now you've got this love nest. It's even harder to catch you alone." He walked over to the desk and emptied the tobacco onto a piece of blank paper. He then wiped the chair with his hand before sitting down.

"Why did you come here?" Lotus asked.

"First of all, I owe you an apology. I wasn't yanking you around when

I offered to take you to Hainan Island, but I ran into some unexpected trouble." He made an expansive sweep with his hand. "I don't want to elaborate, just to say that it couldn't have been helped."

"It's okay. All in the past now."

"No! Was it really all over between us? I have an offer to make."

"What offer?"

"I'd like you to be my girlfriend, living with me." He held out his long, elegant hand when he uttered the word "you," as if picking a winner.

"I'm engaged," she said, still standing awkwardly by the bed. She shifted her weight from one leg to the other as she played with the ring on her finger. "I am happy with him," she added rather loudly.

"Please don't turn down an offer before you know what it is. Why don't you sit down?"

Lotus perched on the bed.

"I liked you the first time I met you. I even asked Moon if you might like to be my woman," he said unhurriedly. "But your boss didn't like the idea, even though I was willing to compensate her. I then decided to go to see you and make the offer to you directly but you were detained. How irritating! Anyway, a few weeks ago I opened my newspaper and spotted your pictures in the *Southern Window,* and I said to myself, There's really something about this girl."

Lotus listened, watching this smartly dressed man in front of her. His blue shirt was shiny and expensive. It looked good on his tall, trim body.

Funny Eye's words poured out. "I thought to myself, Well, I have the power to change her fate. It'd give me great pleasure. Lotus, I'm happy to pay you a generous monthly fee of ten thousand yuan. Please say yes."

That was a lot of money. She needed it, badly, and Bing didn't have much to spare. But could she leave Bing, leave this life and the attention and respect he had been showing her? She shook her head.

"Why not? Are you really in love with him?"

Lotus cast down her eyes. When she looked up again, Funny Eye was standing in front of her. His particular smell washed over her. He reached over and caressed her face. "Such a lovely, tragic face. A beauty like you deserves beautiful things in life," he whispered.

Lotus knew she ought to push him away. But she couldn't move. She just sat there, her face slightly tilted back.

Funny Eye talked on. "You can think it over. In the meantime, let's reconnect, my beautiful."

She held his gaze. "I don't trust you," she said, pushing away his hand.

"Well, I have ten thousand yuan with me right now. It's yours if I can have one hour of your time."

Lotus envisioned the crisp bank notes, then Bing's kind face. "I can't. I just can't." She got on her feet and went to open the door. "Please leave, and leave me alone."

Funny Eye fished out a picture from his book-sized leather bag. "I have something interesting to show you. Your photographer may not be what you think he is."

Lotus looked at the picture, which showed Bing kissing a beautiful girl. "Who is this?" she asked as she held tighter to the doorknob.

"A prostitute," he said, watching her reaction. "A high-class one."

Lotus didn't say anything. Inside her, all sorts of emotions stirred.

"I'll never forgive Pearl for one thing: she told me that your photographer was more interesting than me. After that, I got rid of her." He smirked. "But for a man, being interesting isn't everything."

The sudden ringing of a cell phone startled them like a firecracker exploding. Lotus found the phone, which Bing obviously had forgotten to take when he rushed out, in the pocket of his shorts on the bed. Without thinking, she pulled it out. "*Wei*," she answered as she walked out to the backyard.

"Who is this?" A woman's bossy voice cracked from the phone.

"This is Lotus. Bing isn't here."

A pause. "This is Mei, the mother of his daughter. Lotus, are you the pretty girl Bing photographed? How are you?" Mei asked in an exaggerated friendly tone.

"I'm fine."

"You aren't working at the parlor anymore, are you?"

"Not anymore."

"Aha, he has not told me that you've moved in with him."

The cell phone was burning Lotus's ear. "I'll tell Bing that you called."

"Thank you, Lotus. Goodbye, then."

"Thank you. Goodbye," Lotus replied automatically, then felt ridiculous. Thanking Mei? For what? For meddling in their lives? Lotus felt the fire of anger leap inside her, powerful enough to light up the house. Why did Mei sound as if she still owned Bing? she wondered. Why hadn't he told Mei about her? And what about the photo of him with that sexy prostitute? Was Bing really not the honest and decent man she thought he was?

Lotus spat forcefully at the ground and marched back into the room. She saw Funny Eye fiddling with his cell phone. His profile, with his high-bridged nose, looked very attractive. She threw Bing's phone on top of the desk.

"You can have one hour. And I'd like to have the cash beforehand," she announced.

He jumped up from the chair and stood towering over her. "Good! Okay, cash first, on one condition—you do what I want."

Lotus gave a small nod and smoothed the loose strands of her hair behind her ear.

Later that evening, as she was cooking dinner, she felt an itch between her legs. In the pouring rain, she rushed out to buy a hygiene kit. Just touching the rubber bulb made her skin crawl as the memory of her old ritual came rushing back. After using it, she wrapped it up and buried it in the bottom of the rubbish bin. While waiting for Bing's return, she kowtowed in front of the shrine and wept. Again and again, she begged for forgiveness.

Lotus had tried to erase the memory of the episode, yet a ghost of it always managed to sneak out and sneer at her. Playing the flute with Funny Eye hadn't been as bad as she had dreaded. What had been haunting her was his loud groaning when he pushed his erection into her mouth. He seemed to be enjoying getting her to do things she hated.

Lotus began to dream of losing her teeth again. How could she have relapsed so easily, still behaving like a *ji,* thinking about money first and foremost? She was disgusted with herself for giving in like that. But it hadn't been just about money. Part of her had been flattered by the offer from a rich and powerful man; plus there was the matter of the photograph. Unreasonable though it was, seeing Bing with another *ji* aroused anger and a mad desire for revenge.

But how could she get angry with Bing over something he had done before they had become involved? If he had slept with other *ji* and lied about it, so what? Hadn't he been kind to her?

After that day, Lotus constantly worried that Funny Eye might turn up. She had made him swear not to get in touch or reveal anything to Bing. But she wasn't sure that man could be trusted.

Since then, she had treated Bing with extra loving care and had gone out of her way to cook his favorite dishes. She had also become oversensitive. If he had not made love to her for a few days, she worried that he might have discovered her betrayal. But Bing was as loving and kind as ever, which made her hate herself more.

Lotus switched on the desk lamp, only to realize that she had been drawing circles all over the page. She tore up the letter and decided to go to bed.

A bang on the door woke Lotus. She swung her legs off the bed and turned on the main light. Before she made it to the door, Bing stumbled in. On his heels was a broad-shouldered man. They smelled of alcohol.

The guest walked up to her and held out a hand. "You must be Lotus? I'm Zhang Jianguo, from the *Southern Window.*"

Lotus stretched out her hand. As he shook it, a little too eagerly, his sharp eyes scrutinized her. She darted a look at Bing and he grinned at her. This was new, she thought hopefully. He was introducing her to his friends.

"Sit down, my friend," Bing said joyfully. "Let's play some music. I am in a party mood." He started to go through the dust-covered CD collection stacked on one corner of the bookshelf. "Let's have some opera. Maria Callas, my favorite."

Bing put a CD into the player, and a woman started to sing in some foreign tongue, though it sounded more like a screaming cat than music.

"Come on, my brother," Zhang said, covering his ears. "It's too late for such sophisticated stuff. I'd like to talk."

"Sure." Bing blushed and turned off the music.

Lotus quietly let out a sigh of relief. "Some beer?"

"Yes, please," the visitor said.

She took a chilled bottle from the fridge and poured the beer into two glasses.

Zhang smiled kindly at her when she handed him his glass. He eased himself into a chair. "Bing told me that you are teaching migrant children. How good of you."

"Oh, just something to pass the time," Lotus replied timidly as she perched on the bed.

"She's too modest," Bing said. He brought Lotus a cup of tea and sat down in the folding chair.

Lotus took a sip of the tea. Inside her, a warm glow mingled with the spread of hot tea. She took an instant liking to this charming man who talked to her as if she were important. She was always impressed by Bing's smooth and agile tongue. His friend seemed to have the same gift.

"You know that I've just written a long feature—actually a follow-up of an earlier piece—on migrant children's education. I called it 'One City, Two Systems,'" Zhang said rather loudly.

"Great title, spot on!" Bing exclaimed. As usual, he was becoming more talkative after a few drinks, Lotus noticed. Bing started talking about a foreign book called *A Tale of Two Cities,* and comparing the British Industrial Revolution to today's society. This led to a discussion about China's fast-growing economy and its dream of becoming a leading world power, and also about China's spiritual vacuum and its moral decline. As Lotus watched the two men playing intellectual Ping-Pong, she realized she could never become part of their world.

The guest must have noticed her expression. "Sorry, Lotus." He turned to her. "I was talking about migrant children's education. You might be interested in this." Zhang unleashed a flow of eloquence. "With the great influx of populations from the countryside, schools for migrants started to emerge in cities across the country in the nineties. But some were shut down by the local authorities, who considered them illegal." He spoke in a formal tone, as if he was giving a lecture.

"Media reports on the shutdowns led to increased awareness of the issue. Two years ago, the central government responded and passed a law, which allowed the migrant children to attend local schools." He slapped Bing's knee for attention. "You know what, my brother? I was the first journalist to write about the plight of migrant children. Others followed like little lambs." He made a bleating sound and laughed his thunderous laugh, his Adam's apple shivering. "I was so happy to see the law, I tell you." He gulped down more beer and carried on in a louder voice. "That was one of the few occasions when I felt proud of being a journalist, truly proud: we can make a difference. Most of the time, I envy my friends in government or business. They are not any more talented than I am, but their pockets are deeper and their cars smarter and they all keep *ernai*s. Young women like men with money and power, don't you?" He pointed a finger at Lotus, dangerously close to her nose.

Lotus withdrew. She noticed that Zhang was breathing heavily, his reddened face aglow with sweat. She turned to Bing. He moved his lips a couple of times as if about to say something, but didn't.

She jumped up and announced: "I'm going to refill my tea."

This seemed to shake their guest from his drunken state. He struggled to his feet. "Sorry, I've outstayed my welcome." He nodded at Lotus, and turned to Bing to shake his hand. "A great night!" he said, and took his leave.

Bing walked to the door with him.

Lotus began to clear the table. In a minute, she felt Bing's arms wrapping around her waist.

"Stop it, sweet melon. I'll clean it up tomorrow," he said.

"*Yaodei.*"

"The journalist drank a bit too much, but he's a good guy and hugely helpful."

"It's okay. How was your class?"

"Very well. I'm not a bad teacher." Bing started to laugh, but he sounded strained. He stopped suddenly and said, "But it's all over now."

"Why?"

Bing slumped down to the chair. "Some bastards have complained that I don't have the professional qualifications to teach. So no more classes."

"No! What're you going to do?"

"Not to worry, Zhang said he would get me other jobs." After a pause, he said: "He has somehow sniffed something out about you. So I told him everything. He thinks our story is very romantic. And I am very lucky!"

"I'm the lucky one," Lotus said with a honey-coated smile and she perched on his lap.

CHAPTER 22

哀莫大于心死

❖━━━━━━━━━━━━━━━━━━━━━━━━━━━❖

No Sorrow Is Greater Than the Death
of the Heart

Her laugh was loud, high-pitched, and exaggerated, but it made Bing feel good. "Congratulations!" Mei gushed after she had laughed enough. "Such a long piece. It's so interesting and thought-provoking, too. I learned a lot."

As if to compensate Bing for the loss of his teaching position, a few days later the *Southern Window* had finally published his profile. He was receiving a congratulatory phone call from his ex-wife.

"Thank you, Mei," Bing said, grinning and leisurely pacing the room. Lotus was teaching out in the backyard. "There was some editorial debate about it. I almost gave up on seeing it in print. In the end, my journalist friend there pulled some strings."

"Good for him. Good for you, too," Mei enthused. "You know, the piece did get noticed by lots of people. Remember the editor-in-chief from *Photography*, Mr. Liao? I am now teaching his son English. He was wondering if you'd be interested in working for the magazine."

"Really?"

"Yes, he was very impressed."

"I'd be very interested, especially if they'd allow me the space to do what I want."

"Of course, I understand."

The conversation ended on a good note. For the past several months Bing had meant to tell Mei about Lotus, but he had always worried about Mei's reaction, and now he feared she might find out on her own. Several times during their conversation, he had been on the verge of mentioning Lotus, but knowing he would need strength to deliver this news to his ex, he remained silent.

Bing continued to pace around the room. New hope arose in his heart, but also new worries. Just as he had been thinking about his next move, Mei arrived with this new opportunity. Bing figured it wouldn't be a bad idea to have a steady job, plus benefits. But what about Lotus? Would she be happy in Beijing? He tried to push his worries aside, but he knew he'd have to talk to the girl about it soon.

At the Sunshine Bar on the fifth floor of the Grand Sunshine Hotel, Bing sat on a sofa by the window and waited anxiously for her to arrive. In the semi-darkness, he watched the women seated at the bar, their smooth legs hugging the high barstools, and imagined what Pearl would look like. He sipped his Carlsberg from a fancy glass. Bing couldn't believe the markup—a bottle cost sixty yuan here; for the same amount, he could get a whole case from Cripple Kong's. Luckily the *Southern Window* would reimburse all of his expenses. Zhang Jianguo had secured the assignment for him—a photo documentary on prostitutes serving the high end of the market.

Though he had heard of Shenzhen's Sunshine Bar, nicknamed "the high-class chicken coop," Bing had never set foot here. From the bar area, in the center of the spacious room, some girls twittered and darted flirtatious looks at him. They dressed more expensively and tastefully compared to the salon girls, and they were more subtle in their seduction. He checked his watch. She was already forty minutes late. Upon receiving the assignment, Bing had taken a chance and sent a letter to Pearl's postal address. Within days, her sexy voice had resonated through his cell phone.

But would Pearl really turn up?

Bing hummed along to the romantic song that was playing: "Love me tender, love me true." He had never been much of a singer. He stopped humming after a few notes and looked out the window at the activity below. The curtain of night had just fallen, and the city buzzed with a restless energy under flashing neon lights.

Bing's eyes drifted back to the women sitting at the bar, and his gaze lingered on their long legs. One woman wore a daring slit up the side of her black velvet cheongsam, and his eyes traveled upward and rested on a familiar face. His heart stopped beating for a moment.

"Pearl!" There she was, tall and elegant among the other girls, a crane towering over a bunch of chickens. But she couldn't hear him calling her name over the volume of the music at the bar. As she perched on a barstool, she cast a sweeping glance over the room, like a commander surveying a battleground.

Bing waved at her. Pearl saw him and sashayed over, white legs flashing between the slits, her high heels clicking against the marble floor.

Bing watched, as if in a trance, deafened by the drumming that now raged inside his chest.

"Sorry I'm late," she began.

"That's quite all right. Please sit down." He gestured to the armchair opposite him.

She lowered herself into the chair. "Well, my master photographer. 'Enemies and lovers are destined to meet again,'" she said, her fake eyelashes fluttering.

"Aren't we just friends?" Bing produced a smile. "What would you like to drink?"

"A shot of vodka, please."

"Vodka?" Bing raised his hand and a waiter appeared from nowhere. "Do you have vodka?"

"Of course we do, sir," replied the waiter in a black vest and bow tie. "For this *meinu*?"

"*Meinu*," instead of the more respectful term "lady"? Bing understood intuitively that the waiter knew Pearl well.

"Yes, for this *meinu*." She uttered the last word with emphasis and crossed her legs so that the slit in her dress faced Bing like a cheeky grin. A section of black lace in the front of her cheongsam revealed her deep cleavage. The black dress made her skin look white in contrast. Yet the porcelain had lost some of its sheen and her eyes some of their luster since they last met. Her face was still very attractive, but looked older, despite heavier makeup.

As soon as the waiter brought her drink, she took a sip. "My Mr. Brilliant. You are a celebrity now."

"Hardly, hardly." Bing offered her a cigarette, but she produced a slim one of her own. Bing lit it for her. She took a puff. Perfect smoke rings oozed out of her full cherry lips.

"Now, how can I help you?"

"Like I said on the phone, I'm working on a photo documentary for the *Southern Window*. Have you seen my pictures in the newspaper?"

"Of course. Who could have missed such a big splash?" As Pearl talked, she looked at Bing with her usual bold gaze.

Bing cleared his throat. "It's so lovely to see you. I thought you'd long gone to America."

"I did try. But my visa application was rejected for having the intent to immigrate. American devils! To be fair, I didn't score well on my TOEFL exam." She paused to rub her nose. "So I returned to Shenzhen and became the mistress of that turtle egg Mr. Gao. You know, that wealthy businessman." She stubbed out her half-smoked cigarette in an ashtray with force.

"Oh, I see. You had such a great golden mountain to lean on that you didn't even deign to reply to my letters."

Pearl blew him a kiss, which painted his cheek red. "Writing to someone you've shared a bed with is a form of intimacy. I wasn't allowed such a luxury then."

Bing worried his heart couldn't cope if he stared into her eyes any longer. He took a sip of his beer. "Please, tell me about your life."

In an unemotional tone, Pearl described her life as a lady of leisure, within the walls of a luxury villa. And the squint-eye didn't even have a wife. With the money he had given her, she could buy anything she liked. She didn't have to do anything except accompany him to banquets, as his beautiful decoration. But she was bored to death. To create some ripple of excitement, she played with younger boys. Having discovered her affairs, he tightened his control over her, and she started to experiment instead with white powder.

"How did you get into it, Pearl?" Bing knew some prostitutes took drugs and others fell into the trade because of their addiction.

She lifted her glass to take another sip. "Do you really want to know?" she asked, smiling. "Is it for your documentary?"

"Maybe."

Pearl began to tell Bing about her first encounter with drugs. One time, before she had become Gao's mistress, she was hired for a party thrown by a millionaire who had powerful connections with the central government. Naked girls were laid out and various exotic foods were arranged on their bodies for men to feast upon. Her belly was decorated with XO abalone and her nipples were dusted with powders. "So I helped myself," she said.

"Is your health okay?"

"Do I look ill to you?"

"Well, I guess it's fine if you only take coke occasionally."

"You sound like my father," she said coldly, lighting another cigarette. She lifted her head up toward the ceiling as she breathed in.

"I'm sorry."

"Shut up!" Sharp words shot out of her mouth, followed by a long plume of smoke. Her lovely deep-set eyes glared at him. "What, do you feel sorry for me? I have a great life and I can do whatever I want."

"Sorry, sorry! I didn't mean to upset you."

Pearl parted her lips in a smile, her teeth dazzlingly white in the dim light. "Okay."

Bing drank his beer. "How about Mr. Gao?"

"We said goodbye some months ago. I was fed up with him anyway. His good manners and his bedroom tricks are all for show." She uncrossed her legs and leaned forward. "Now, do you want to use me as your model?"

"'Use'? Yes, if you must use that word. Also, if you could introduce me to some of your friends, I'd be very grateful."

"I'll try, but I'm not sure how many will agree. As for me, I'd love to be photographed. It's rather exciting, I should think." Pearl posed as if in front of a camera. "Do you need to interview us as well?"

"Yes, if possible."

"I don't mind as long as you don't use my real name. But I have to say I am not a typical prostitute. I pick up men—interesting men in particular, not only for the money but also for the thrill." She boasted that she could afford to be picky, rejecting men she didn't fancy no matter how much they offered her.

Pearl told him about her last patron, a government official from a town outside Shenzhen. But having sex with him had been boring at first and later became a tedious chore, so she got rid of him despite his generous maintenance.

Bing listened, taking mental notes as he knew such stories could also enrich his book.

"But we had fun, didn't we, photographer? Remember?" Pearl kicked off her heels and ran her bare toes up and down his leg, looking at him with her half-narrowed eyes.

Bing drew his leg back. Remember? How could he forget the wildest and most fragrant flower he had ever come across? He shifted in his seat as if little thorns studded the armchair. He ought to go. But the thorns seemed to have stuck into him, pinning him in place.

"Listen, Pearl. If I can be of any help to you in any way, finding a decent job or such, please let me know," Bing offered.

She rewarded him with a smile. "You are so old-fashioned, my photographer. Decent job? Why should I burden myself with outdated morality? It's just a job, a highly paid one. I've never hurt anyone, have I?"

Pearl then sat straight, wearing a grave expression. "Now, let me ask you something. Where is your partner Wang Zhigang?"

"I heard he's gone to Hong Kong, running some big business there."

"That man is an evil smiling tiger! They didn't even pay me the full amount as promised. Cheap bastard!"

"Pay you for what?" Bing asked after a hard swallow.

"Well, I thought you had figured it out."

Bing sighed. Curiosity drove him to ask another question: "Why didn't they pay you the full amount?"

"You readily accepted the plan, so they didn't need me to go back to you, to work on you."

Bing stared at her.

Pearl stopped suddenly. She stroked his hand with the tips of her fingers. "I'm sorry," she mumbled.

He allowed himself a little smile.

She went on. Wang had received fat kickbacks when his friend offered him the amusement park project and later again when he contracted Gao for the construction.

Bing thought about Wang's eager smiles and understood why his relative had been so eager to form a partnership with him—for his expertise in technology and his naïveté about the business world. But Pearl's other news hurt more: she had been just a sex trap, who performed an act she was paid for. He went silent, nursing his injured pride. Deep inside him, he had known this all along but hadn't allowed himself to acknowledge it.

"Why don't you sue them?" she said viciously. "I'll be your witness."

Bing dismissed the suggestion with a wave of a hand. The last thing he wanted was to get involved in a hopeless legal battle.

"All right, let's forget about the past."

Bing nodded. When he caught himself stealing glances at Pearl's breasts pushing through the black lace, he looked out the window. The street was less busy now. Some shops were shut, though many restaurants remained noisy.

"My photographer, I dare say, you are my all-time favorite," Pearl cooed.

He didn't respond.

"Aha, have I really become yesterday's flower? Fancy playing dragon and phoenix with me again?"

"No, no, thank you. I'm actually with someone right now."

"You're with Girl A. Am I right?" A crooked smile flickered across her lips.

"Yes. How do you know?"

"Intuition." Her eyes suddenly lit up. "Yes, Lotus, Girl A!" she said excitedly, snapping her fingers. "Now, it all makes sense. The turtle egg dumped me because of this girl. *Wasai,* another gallant gentleman who wants to play the hero by rescuing a pretty fallen girl! One day, he showed me her photos in some newspaper and boasted that they were mandarin ducks for one night."

Bing felt a wave of fury surging inside him. "I don't think Lotus has anything to do with him now."

"Why are you so sure? How much are you paying her?"

"She's out of the trade and I'm not paying her anything."

"It's obvious that she's using you to get herself out of her sordid chicken coop." Pearl paused, letting her words register. "'Once bitten by a snake, one shies at the sight of a coiled rope for the next ten years.' But you don't seem to have learned your lesson, my photographer."

"I don't think you'd understand us, Lotus and me," Bing said.

She burst into laughter. "What you are having with Lotus is a man's ultimate sexual fantasy: the free offer of a pretty prostitute."

He glared at a crumpled napkin on the floor and imagined gagging the woman's red mouth with it.

"Listen to me, my Mr. Brilliant: never, ever trust a *ji*," Pearl said, her white hand caressing his. "Come to me, my dear photographer, I don't want anything from you but you."

As Bing withdrew his hand to wave at the waiter for the bill, her bare toes crawled farther up his leg.

"That'll be two thousand yuan," she announced.

"What?"

"We've just spent about one hour together."

Bing was speechless.

"Only joking."

He summoned a smile. "Thank you for coming. I'll be in touch." He grabbed the receipt and hurried toward the door.

Bing stomped along the street. A laser show projected from the top of the towering Emperor Building sliced the night sky, irritating him more than ever. When a beggar boy's dirty hand grabbed his sleeve, he pushed it away. A painted girl with a skirt hitched up to her thighs tried to pull him into a song and dance hall. This city is filled with filth, he thought with disgust.

Lotus and that squint-eyed, pipe-smoking Mr. Gao. It occurred to him that the tobacco he had smelled in his house on that rainy night must've been his. Was there something still going on between them?

Now that he thought about it, Lotus seemed more responsive in bed lately. Was it because she felt guilty? Bing asked himself. What kind of dodgy dealings was she having with a former client of hers? If she had nothing to hide, why had she lied about his visit? Would it be possible for her to make a clean cut from her messy past? Or would she always attract bees and butterflies? Would it be possible for her to remain faithful? Could she possibly love him? Even if she did, was this the woman he should marry? The enormous satisfaction he had experienced when he plucked her out of her sordid life had faded.

But then Bing felt ashamed that he even raised questions about Lotus. After all, she had played a positive role in his career advancement, and she continued to be helpful to his book project. Well, helpful to some degree. The truth was that he sometimes wasn't entirely sure that he ought to trust her stories. He had conducted some in-depth interviews with her in the past months. Before they had become romantically involved, she talked a fair amount about the sense of freedom she had experienced in the city and the pleasure and power money had brought, whereas nowadays, she seemed to focus on her role as a victim. It wasn't the nuanced insight he was looking for.

And recently Lotus seemed to have changed in the way she treated him. Exactly one month ago, on an impulse, he had suggested that they go out for a romantic dinner, taking advantage of the full moon. She pondered it, wearing a queer expression as if his request had pained her; then, with a sweet smile, she asked if it was okay to delay for a few days until the weekend, as she had to prepare for the next day's class that night. That was the first time Lotus had uttered no to him.

And her unpleasant habits such as spitting and her talking with her mouth full of food had bothered him a little bit. Having overcome provincial manners himself, he cared about such matters, though he had never raised them with her.

In the beginning, Bing had encouraged her to teach the children a few characters, just to keep herself occupied. He didn't expect that she would take up teaching so seriously, especially in the last two months, when she had embraced it with a sort of religious zeal. He ought to feel happy for Lotus that she had found something fulfilling and something she felt passionate about. But he didn't. Why not? Maybe he secretly feared that the same yardstick would magnify the gap between his ex-wife, a grade A teacher at a reputable middle school in Beijing, and a self-styled teacher to a bunch of migrant kids in Shenzhen. He felt shamed by his snobbery, but couldn't help himself.

Bing stumbled on a can of Coke lying on the ground. He gave it an almighty kick. The can rolled a far distance, staining the pavement with dark liquid.

CHAPTER 23

水有源 树有根

Every River Has Its Source and
Every Tree Its Roots

The lock clicked open and Bing stepped into the house.

Lotus looked up and saw him standing by the door, beads of sweat on his forehead, breathing heavily. He went out more frequently these days, usually with the journalist. Of course, a man like him needed intelligent company.

"You're back," she said in greeting, then fetched his face towel and went over to him.

"Thank you, my sweet melon." He took the towel, wiped his sweaty face, and continued to stand there, watching her intently.

"Why don't you come in?" She turned on the ceiling fan. It was a humid evening but she didn't mind the heat as much as he did. The pages of the exercise books on the desk began to flap in the wind.

He walked in and turned down the speed of the fan.

"You must be hungry. Let me heat up the spare rib soup for you." She was about to dash to the kitchen but he stopped her.

He looked deep into her eyes and said in a strangely gentle voice: "You are too kind."

Lotus usually liked his flattery but this time it somehow made her a little uneasy. So she just smiled and lowered her eyes.

Bing turned to the desk. "Were you marking homework?"

"Yes, I was." She went over to the table to tidy up the exercise books. Although he never complained about her teaching, she was mindful of trying not to make him feel sidelined by her expanding number of students.

"Would you like to take a stroll with me?"

Lotus had the sudden sensation of being lost in three miles of fog, unable to see clearly what was ahead of her. "Now? In the middle of the night?"

"Why not? There's a full moon in the sky."

"Where should we go?"

"Anywhere you like."

Lotus knitted her eyebrows. Usually, it was Bing who decided where to go and what to do. *"Yaodei,"* she said, but immediately wished she had responded more enthusiastically, with a kiss or a hug. She often found herself stuck between her reserved self and the person he wanted her to be—the woman who could stoke the fire in him. She envied Mimi, who could throw herself into her man's arms in public without any inhibitions.

At the village square, they failed to hail a taxi and ended up hiring a ground rat. Lotus told the driver to head to the Long Embankment.

As the ground rat hurtled ahead, Bing remained silent, slumping in his corner of the tin box. Lotus's brain raced, trying to work out the possible reasons for this unusual outing. She concluded there could be only one thing. She fingered her beads, bracing herself.

Upon reaching the destination, Bing told the driver to wait for half an hour. They climbed out of the vehicle and walked over to the seawall, without holding hands.

Lotus leaned against the seawall. It was her arrest at this spot over a year ago that had changed her relationship with this man. Maybe it would turn out to be the place where the relationship would also end?

The moon was a round silver plate up in the velvet sky. In its light, the sea gleamed like fish scales. Apart from the occasional car on the main road, all sounds were hushed. The delicate fragrance of flowers from the Chinese scholar trees permeated the air. There had also been plenty of such trees in Mulberry Gully. Her grandma used to make pancakes with the flowers.

"When I was still in the village, I always thought about the sea whenever I dreamed about the outside world," she began.

"Did you?" Bing mumbled as he shifted a fraction closer to her and rested a hand on her waist.

Lotus felt his warm hand. She turned toward him, waiting for him to begin.

"Lotus, Mr. Gao, the wealthy businessman, did he come to see you back in January?" he said after a long pause.

She felt her scalp tighten. "How did you know?" she asked, trying hard not to let her voice quiver too much.

His hand fell from her waist. "I just met the man's former mistress. She claimed that he dumped her because of you."

"Wait, wait. I thought you went out to have a drink with your journalist friend."

"Well, Zhang got me an assignment to shoot a documentary about high-class prostitutes. I didn't tell you who I was meeting with tonight because I thought you might feel uncomfortable about it. But I need the work, especially interesting work such as this."

So, you don't trust me: that was Lotus's first thought. Then she felt a pang of jealousy. So he seemed to have exhausted the topic of low-class *ji* and moved on to photograph the high-class ones. Would he become closely involved with one of those attractive and cultivated women?

"Who is this mistress? How did she know about me?" she said, affecting a calm tone.

"Her name is Pearl." Bing rubbed his hands as if he didn't know what to do with them. "Mr. Gao recognized your pictures in the *Southern Window* and showed it to her. He used to be her patron. Why did he come to see you?"

"Well, he was a former client. He came to ask me to be his mistress, offering a large sum as a monthly payment."

"*Tamade* scoundrel! He thinks he can make the devil push a grinding stone if he offers enough money." Bing paused. "And you didn't accept?"

"I've washed my hands of that."

After a pregnant pause, Bing continued: "How did he know where to find you? And he just turned up like that on a day I happened to be out?"

"I don't know," she said simply.

"Why didn't you tell me about his visit?"

"I didn't want to upset you. And now I just want to forget about it."

"Did he come again?"

Lotus felt as if she was being interrogated. "No, I don't think so."

Bing shifted his legs. "Do let me know next time. There shouldn't be any secrets between us."

"No secrets between us?" she said, glaring at him. "Haven't you kept secrets from me?"

"What secrets?"

"I wasn't the first *ji* you ever slept with, was I? Funny Eye showed me a photo of a girl kissing you and he said you were once a pair of mandarin ducks as well." She spoke fast, as if spitting out a fish bone that had been prickling her throat. Ever since Funny Eye's visit, she had intended to confront Bing and to hear his side of the story. But she hadn't, for fear of rocking the boat.

Bing shivered as if a basinful of cold water had been poured over him. "A photo? Well, I shouldn't be surprised," he muttered, shaking his head. "How stupid and naïve I was." Turning to Lotus, he said: "Look, I didn't exactly lie to you. When I went to bed with her, I had no idea she was a *ji*."

"She was a high-class one, I suppose?"

Bing nodded. "Yes, she is. I met up with her tonight because I thought she might be able to help me with the new assignment."

"Pearl? She looked like a film star in the photo, didn't she?"

"She is an attractive girl, and a perfect sex trap." Bing explained how

Wang and Gao had set him up. "It was just a one-night stand, not even an affair."

Lotus listened, recalling what Funny Eye had revealed about Bing's attempts to pursue Pearl. Funny Eye might have made it up. But even if he hadn't, what was the point of dwelling on it, anyway? All she needed to do was to make sure that girl wouldn't get too close to their life together. Cheap or expensive, a *ji* was a *ji*.

"I love you, my little treasure." Bing took her hand and kissed it. "I am willing to solve any issues between us. Believe me."

"I believe you," Lotus said with relief. His jealousy showed that he cared, she thought. But what about their future? She coughed drily, pondering how she might bring up the question. Catching herself making the unattractive noise, however, she stopped and swallowed the question.

Bing studied her face. "You look a little pale, Princess Huan Zhu. Are you okay?"

"You look pale, too, under the moonlight."

"You look beautiful, anyway," he said softly as he stroked her face.

Lotus stood on tiptoes to kiss Bing. He wrapped his hands around her back and pulled her close to himself. When they kissed, his ardor made her hot and giddy, as if drunk on the taste of the alcohol in his mouth.

She pulled herself away and said breathlessly: "Please can we go home?"

After their lovemaking, Lotus curled up in Bing's arms. She felt lucky that the storm that had threatened to blow apart their relationship had passed. Tonight, the fact that it had been Lotus who had initiated their cloud and rain session seemed to have turned them both on. She was in fact surprised by her sexual appetite these days. She let out a satisfied sigh and snuggled closer to Bing.

She was about to drift to sleep when he suddenly spoke in the darkness. "I may have to move up to Beijing."

The news left her speechless. Fully awake again, she turned to face him.

"Well, there may be an opportunity for me to work for *Photography* magazine in Beijing. It's a prestigious magazine and it'll be a staff position." His words tumbled out like those of a nervous schoolboy.

"Really? Good for you," Lotus murmured as she tried to think of the implications of this new situation. "What would I do?"

"I don't know yet," he said, then added quickly, "I'll certainly look out for opportunities for you in Beijing. Maybe you can study first."

After a long while, she began again: "Speaking of the future . . . " She sat up and looked at him in the dimness. "Would you, well, do you actually plan to marry me?" Lotus had rehearsed this question a thousand times in her head, but it still came out in a stammering burst.

Bing also sat up and grabbed her hands. "Of course, of course! It's just . . . " He heaved a sigh—in fact, his whole body seemed to sigh. "Well, please give me some time to establish myself so that I can be in a good position to provide for you and your family."

"I wish I was not such a burden."

"What nonsense, Lotus!" He cupped her face in his hands. She couldn't see his facial expression in the darkness but felt his sincerity. "Now, you go to sleep, my sweetie." He lay down again and pulled her into his arms.

Bing soon fell asleep and snored. Nestling still against him, Lotus stared into the darkness for hours.

A basket in her hand, Lotus bounded out of the house. She looked at the security lock Bing had installed before leaving town, but decided not to bother with it and left the front door unlocked: it was much too complicated. Apart from installing the lock, he had also hired someone to cement a row of broken glass on top of their back wall as some wealthier locals had done. As unnecessary as painting legs on a snake, Lotus thought. Who would try to break into their house? But he had insisted that these measures made him feel better.

Bing had left for a trip ten days ago. Days after their night outing to the embankment, he had received a call from the magazine in Beijing, offering him a photo assignment in mid-July. He had snatched it. Luckily, there wasn't a deadline for his photo documentary commissioned by the *Southern Window*. When Bing had raised the possibility of visiting his mother first, Lotus urged him to do so, sensing that he was too restless to stay at home. "Will you be all right on your own?" he kept asking.

Did a woman always need a man? Lotus asked herself. Mimi had finally split up with Lanzai. But while the smell of that good-for-nothing man still lingered in the house, one of his friends had stepped in to fill his shoes.

Ai Zhi, the waitress-turned-writer, didn't have a man. In her late thirties, she had never been married. Why not? Lotus had no idea. She certainly looked happy on her own. Lotus wondered if Ai Zhi ever felt the pressure to get married and to have her *guisu*.

In the slanting sun, Lotus walked toward the market in the village square, singing "Little Swallow" to herself. The sky was a vast blue and the world under it was coated in gold.

She had never felt so alive, and so busy as well. Back when she had worked as a *ji*, she always had a hollow feeling inside her. Each man came, had his way, then left, taking a tiny piece of her self away. Now, her teaching, and Bing's nurturing, had filled up that void. After his departure, Lotus had added afternoon teaching sessions—reading for the older ones and singing for the little ones. Keeping herself occupied expelled her worries about her future with Bing. She could have spent the afternoons watching more episodes of *Princess Huan Zhu*. But somehow she had lost interest in make-believe tales.

At the market Lotus took her time surveying the fresh vegetables, piled neatly in flat-bottomed bamboo baskets. The sellers were mostly local Hakka women who wore blue cotton tops and matching skirts, their faces hidden under wide-brimmed bamboo hats laced with black netting. She worked out her evening menu: pickled cucumber in garlic and soy sauce, spicy stir-fried eggplant, and egg and tomato soup. It was a lot easier to feed just herself. She was eating more and more vegetables.

Even though Bing said he would eat anything, she knew how much he enjoyed a hearty meat meal. She missed taking care of him. On the other hand, she enjoyed having the house all to herself and loved the freedom to do whatever she pleased. As a matter of fact, she felt she could finally breathe freely without Bing around.

Lotus thought about her brother and his very short recent letter, thanking her for the money she had sent to him. She couldn't believe that the large sum, earned with blood, sweat, and bitterness, hadn't won a warmer response. Had Shadan taken her financial support for granted, just like Ba and Nai? Or perhaps he had been too busy studying to express his gratitude properly.

Her thoughts turned to Baobao, Xia's son. The shy boy with sad eyes had been living with his mother in a rented apartment in Miaocun. Lotus bought a watermelon from a vendor who camped out in the square with his mountain of fruit. She decided she would drop in and give the watermelon to Baobao on her way home. Poor thing, he had so much to deal with. And Xia, too. How had she summoned the nerve to disclose her trade to her own son? Her concerns for his well-being must have overcome her sense of shame.

"Teacher Lotus, have you eaten yet?" a friendly voice asked from behind. She turned and saw a man in a pair of high rubber boots standing in front of her, grinning broadly, holding a big fish by its tail. He was the father of another new student.

"Oh, not yet," she replied with a polite smile.

"Mandarin fish, you take it. Take. Steam it, tasty, very tasty." As he talked, he tried to push the fish into Lotus's basket.

She tried to stop him. "You're too kind. Mandarin fish is very expensive."

"Take it, take. You're the one who is too kind. Teaching my unruly boy and not even charging any money."

"Well, okay-la. Thank you."

The fisherman bowed several times. "Whenever you want fish, just come here, Teacher Lotus." He pointed at a large plastic basin full of fish.

As Lotus was about to go, she felt something touch her backside. For a split second, she thought the fisherman had groped her. When she sprang around angrily, she saw an old woman push by with her over-sized basket. She sighed. Stop being paranoid, she told herself. You are a teacher, not a *ji* anymore.

Lotus was picking her way through a quiet stretch of the rubbish-littered path when the screech of a car startled her. She turned to see a shiny black car pull up beside her. When the back door opened, Funny Eye, in a white shirt and a red silk tie, emerged. The metal buckle of his belt glared in the setting sun.

His long legs brought him over. "Good afternoon, my lady teacher. Long time, no see," he greeted her cheerfully.

Lotus froze to the ground. She had considered calling him to tell him to leave her alone. After half a year went by without incident, she hoped that he would just vanish from her life.

Funny Eye peered into her basket. "Who are you going to cook for tonight?"

She looked over at the mah-jongg players at the square. They were too far away. "What do you want?" she asked.

"Why are you so hostile, my little beauty?" he said in his deep and rich voice. "You look beautiful and radiant. What happened? Did you win the lottery?"

"No." Lotus tightened her grasp on the basket.

"You told me not to come to your house, I obeyed. You said you would call me but you haven't. What should I do? I've sent my people around to keep an eye on you and they told me it's not always easy to catch you alone." While he spoke unhurriedly, his good eye stared at her with intensity.

Lotus stepped back from him.

"Am I so frightening?" Funny Eye asked. "Teacher Lotus, I trust you wouldn't want to cause a scene in public. All I want is to hear your answer to my proposal."

She put down the basket. "Please, Mr. Gao, I don't want to have any-thing to do with you anymore."

"Why? Last time, you gave me a different impression."

"Sorry, I've made up my mind that I'm staying with him."

"Can you name any way that your so-called photographer is better than me—well, apart from being more interesting?"

"I trust him," she said.

"I have a weakness, Lotus," Funny Eye said with a smirk. "My father had me at sixty. My parents indulged my every whim. Now that I have money, I tend to indulge my own whims."

Two elderly villagers passed by and stared at them.

As soon as they were out of earshot, Lotus pleaded: "Please, just leave me alone."

He carried on. "I have hundreds of people working for me. If I say go east, they wouldn't dare to go west. Now it seems that I can't handle a young working girl!" He paced a few steps, wringing his hands. Then he turned abruptly. "Listen, Lotus, I'll give you a good life, the kind you deserve. It'll give me pleasure."

She swung her head firmly from one side to another.

"Well, well, 'A butcher can become a Buddha after dropping his knife,' and a wild *ji* becomes a chaste lady overnight!" Funny Eye leaned back and laughed.

Lotus felt as if her nerves were on fire. She picked up the basket and shot back, "Who do you think you are? Look into a mirror and see yourself."

He gave a lopsided smile. "Yes, I have a squint eye. So what? That doesn't make me less of a man. I think you know my prowess." He winked at Lotus.

Trembling with rage, she spat on the ground, then started to walk away from him. She used to find his face handsome, but now she was disgusted by it, by his self-satisfied smile and the squint eye.

Funny Eye laughed and kept pace with her. "I like ladies with a bit of a temper."

Lotus strode ahead.

He followed her. "I'm a gentleman and I always treat my women generously. Pearl might have slung dirt at me, but can you trust a drug addict? She's begging me to take her back, but I can't. I want you, Lotus."

The heavy basket was weighing her down. She dropped it and started to run.

Lotus ran as fast as a startled deer until she suddenly felt nauseated. She had to stop.

Funny Eye caught up with her. "What's the matter?"

She took a deep breath. "I'm pregnant. And it's his child. Please, leave me alone."

CHAPTER 24

机不可失

Don't Let the Opportunity Slip Away

Bing poked his head out of the taxi window. Under a gray sky, an endless line of cars snaked like a metal dragon in front of him, jamming the second ring road. Young migrants hovered around in the midst of the traffic, offering to clean car windows or handing out flyers for new real estate. Beijing traffic certainly had taken a turn for the worse since his first days in the city. It would be quicker to walk.

He paid the driver, jumped out of the taxi, and headed for a nearby *hutong*. He always loved these narrow alleys where hawkers sold snacks and fruit, and kids rode on skateboards, while grandmas chopped vegetables on the stone steps outside their houses and grandpas played Chinese chess under elm trees. It felt far more alive and human here than around those concentric freeways circling the capital.

As Bing walked, he noticed buildings marked with chalk circles crossed with large Xs—the sign of demolition and the death sentence of an old way of life. Somewhere farther up the road, demolition had already started.

Turning a corner, he arrived at the headquarters of *Photography*. If he hadn't plucked up enough courage to visit the prestigious publication two years ago, he wouldn't have been asked back here today. He still thought it quite incredible that this state-owned magazine had actually published his photo documentary on prostitution. Then again, it had to manage its own finances, even though it was still part of the state propaganda machine. Money spoke volumes in every corner.

Bing paused in front of a gray brick wall that stood in front of the door, a "ghost screen" designed to keep away evil spirits. Staring at the large character "*fu*"—fortune or happiness—engraved in the middle of the wall, he tried to envision how this career shift would impact his fortune or happiness. He brushed his hair back with his fingers but it didn't have the same heft now that he had cut it short, on Mei's suggestion. He stepped around the wall and walked into a shaded yard. He knocked on the carved double door in front of him before entering the air-conditioned office. In the far corner of the oblong room, he could see a bald head behind a pile of papers. Its owner peered up at him.

"Aha, Mr. Hu, you're here. Come on in," the editor-in-chief warmly greeted his visitor as he took off his half-moon spectacles. He had bushy eyebrows, as if to compensate for the lack of hair on his head. He wore a pale blue shirt, a little wrinkled, with a faded collar.

"How are you, Mr. Liao?" Bing shook hands with the editor.

"My life isn't as exciting as yours, but I am fine." The editor turned around to call out to a young woman by the door. "Little Yu, tea for our visitor, please."

As they headed to a meeting area, several people looked at them and nodded. The young woman brought over tea in an enamel mug stamped with the magazine's logo.

"Little Yu is our administrator," Liao introduced her. "Get your supplies, films, and things from her later."

Bing nodded and smiled at the full-figured woman dressed in a flowing skirt. She smiled back, taking a good look at him, and turned away. Modern city women never shied away from anything, did they? Bing thought to himself. He sipped his tea and took in the office scene, wondering how he would fit into such a working environment. It would be interesting to have colleagues again. At present only four desks were occupied, out of a dozen.

Liao explained. "You see, some photographers are out on assignments or they are free to do whatever, moonlighting, for example—as long as they don't advertise it." He winked at Bing. "Don't tell anyone I said that."

Bing smiled a knowing smile, feeling grateful to the editor. "I see. Were you a photographer yourself?"

"Oh, yes, for years and years. I still fancy myself as one sometimes," Liao reminisced. "But photography is a young man's game, or men like you with a young man's energy."

As they drank their tea in silence, noise from the construction site outside drifted in.

"Will you have to move in the near future?" Bing asked. "This is such a delightful spot."

"We'll probably be fine for the moment, thanks to our ministry," the editor replied. He put down his mug. "Now, let's get down to business. Thank you for accepting the assignment." The editor hadn't told him the details of the job on the phone, only mentioning the pay, the fact that some travel was involved, and saying it was somewhat sensitive, though he promised that Bing would receive more details once he arrived at the office. "Our Party Secretary is waiting for you. Follow me, please."

Bing rose, smoothing his shirt. He knew that, as in any state-owned organization, the Party Secretary—supposedly only in charge of the publication's ideology—always held the most power in the end.

Liao knocked on the door to a side room.

"Come in," came a high-pitched voice. Bing couldn't tell if the speaker was a man or a woman.

They stepped in. The room was markedly colder. A man in his early fifties stood up from a massive leather chair.

"This is Party Secretary Wang and this is our award-winning photographer Comrade Hu Binbing. I'll leave you two to talk." The editor nodded to his boss respectfully and left the room.

The Party Secretary gave Bing a limp handshake. The man perfectly fit the image of a Communist Party official: his navy cotton Mao jacket had several pens in the breast pocket and his black mane was slicked back.

As the Party Secretary sank down into the sofa by his desk, he beckoned Bing to sit down in a chair opposite him.

"Comrade Liao showed me your profile," he began in his eunuch-like voice. "I agree with him: you are just the right type we are looking for. In this new era, we need to project a new image—a Communist Party member who cares about the plight of ordinary people." He spoke as if addressing an audience.

Speeches like this one used to grate on Bing at the soap factory's weekly Party member meeting. He had developed a technique of falling asleep while sitting bolt upright. Now he listened with feigned interest. Unlike the editor-in-chief's desk, which was buried under books, magazines, and papers, the Party Secretary's large rosewood desk was empty save for a notebook, a bottle of ink, and two telephones, one for internal use and one for outside calls; Bing knew the arrangement. Behind the Party Secretary, a national flag and a Party flag hung limply, next to a cupboard full of documents.

The Party Secretary took a sip of tea from the same kind of enamel mug, the inside stained brown. "There is an urgent and important assignment. China's space program, with the full support of the central government, has reached the most advanced level, which reflects our national strength. China is about to launch another satellite," he said, looking at Bing with grave solemnity.

Bing could hear the drumming starting inside his chest as the spectacular image of a satellite shooting into space burst into his head.

"Since it is an issue of national security, the photographer has to be trustworthy. If the launch is successful—and I trust it will be—then we'll run a set of the pictures. Do you feel you are up to the task?"

"Yes, I am!" Bing declared loudly. "Thank you, Party Secretary Wang, and thanks for the trust of the Party. I won't let you down."

A satisfied smile came across the Party Secretary's pale, puffy, hairless face. "It will be at the Xichang Satellite Launch Center in western Sichuan. Someone will come to pick you up from here at ten a.m. on Monday. Get whatever supplies you need from Little Yu."

"Do you want color slides?"

"For technical questions, you'll have to ask Comrade Liao."

"How long will the assignment be?"

"At least half a month, maybe longer. The launch site is a long way away from Beijing and you'll shoot some stock photos for the magazine as well. Are you restricted by time?"

"Oh, no, not at all."

The warm fresh air in the courtyard felt comforting. Under a Chinese scholar tree, the editor bade farewell to Bing. "Do a good job, Mr. Hu; I'm sure you will," he urged. "If the bosses are pleased with your work, you can start to work here straightaway."

"Thank you very much, Mr. Liao, for recommending me."

"That's quite all right. Mei has been an outstanding teacher. My son's English is improving rapidly."

"I heard he is a very clever, sweet-natured boy. He's got sharp ears. Perfect material for language study." Bing uttered the line scripted for him by Mei.

"Clever, yes. Sweet? No. He is a spoiled lazy boy who can't cope with the mountains of homework at his school. You know what Chinese schools are like." Liao glanced at his boss's room and lowered his voice. "That's why I'm thinking about sending my son to school in America. This isn't public knowledge yet, if you know what I mean." He resumed his normal volume. "I have a question for you."

"Go ahead, any question."

"Well, I understand that you've been very friendly with, with those working girls—you know what I mean." He rubbed his head. "That's why you got such fascinating pictures." He narrowed his thin eyes. "This Girl A, there isn't any special relationship between you and her, is there?"

Bing felt as though a fireball had hit him in the face. "Well, yes, Lotus is a friend, a very good friend. She . . ." He began slowly. Just then, a line of pigeons flew over their heads, creating a whistling sound that drowned out his voice. He looked up and watched the birds disappear behind the high-rises. "I have a closer relationship with her than with the other girls. That's all." He heard himself saying the words, astonished that he could lie so calmly. Then again, that wasn't a total lie, was it?

A broad smile narrowed the editor's eyes. "I'm glad to hear that. Our Party Secretary is such an orthodox Marxist. There is also a regulation from the central government that a Party member is to be stripped of his membership if he has any dealings with prostitutes."

"Yes, yes, of course," Bing replied as he started to move toward the front entrance.

Liao followed him. The editor's small hand climbed up to Bing's shoulder. "Please send my regards and gratitude to Mei. Quite a lady, isn't she? Very charming, intelligent, and yet so nice and gracious to everyone. You don't see many such ladies around these days," he gushed.

"Oh, yes. Mei is a special lady."

Liao's bushy eyebrows went up briefly as if waiting for Bing to elaborate further. When nothing more came, he waved a hand. "Goodbye, then. See you on Monday. Have a restful weekend."

Bing walked out of the courtyard and wandered deeper into the maze of *hutong*s. He heard a loud whistle, and another formation of pigeons flew overhead. He watched them sailing by in the gray sky. Their owners had attached tiny whistles to their legs so that the pigeons wouldn't get lost.

Bing suddenly remembered he needed to speak to Lotus. He'd be away a little longer than he initially thought he would be for this assignment.

CHAPTER 25

山雨欲来风满楼，

<hr>

The Wind Sweeping Through the Tower Heralds
a Rising Storm in the Mountain

After her afternoon class, Lotus headed straight to the kitchen to make some congee with leftover rice and cabbage. As she cooked, she nibbled on the fried dough her next-door neighbors had given her. Recently whenever she got hungry, she had to have something right away; otherwise she felt sick. She was only eight weeks pregnant and the morning sickness had started. Every day, the couple next door gave her the fried treats—their way of thanking her for teaching their girl, Little Chrysanthemum. Their eight-year-old daughter had, until recently, been living with her grandparents. Lotus wanted to call her Apple because of her apple-shaped face, decorated with rosy cheeks. How could the dough-maker couple bear to leave behind such a pretty girl? But it was a common arrangement among migrant workers.

When the congee was ready, she tipped it into a bowl. She blew on it and sucked along the edge of the bowl, the way her father always did, and finally lifted it to her mouth and shoved the food down her throat with her chopsticks. When she was done, she let out a satisfied burp. That was better! How wonderful that she could be herself again.

Lotus left the bowl in the sink, which was already crowded with Mimi's dirty bowls and plates. She would worry about washing up after her rest.

She returned to the room, let down the bamboo blinds and checked the locks on the door, grateful now that Bing had taken that measure. Funny Eye probably wouldn't bother her anymore. Yet you could never be sure.

Lotus climbed onto the bed. She needed a rest before preparing tomorrow's class. From under her pillow, she took out a book entitled *Everything You Need to Know About Pregnancy and Your Baby,* which she had bought at a large bookstore, with excitement and embarrassment. The cover of the thick book showed a pink-skinned Western woman holding a chubby blue-eyed baby.

Sometimes she wished that she could talk about her pregnancy openly with someone. What a shame that the person she had broken the news to was Funny Eye. She hadn't told Bing yet, not wishing to distract him while he was on his special assignment. She was concerned about his reaction. Once in a park a few months ago, they had bumped into a toddler. He was wobbling back and forth on his chubby little legs, making happy noises. Lotus couldn't help but stop and watch him, giggling. Bing gently pulled her away and said: "You'd like a cutie like that, wouldn't you?" She uttered a yes without hesitation, but he only smiled without voicing his stand on the matter. Her face turned red briefly before turning pale. She tried to comfort herself that it might not be the right time for him yet.

It had not exactly been an accident. What a cold word, "accident." She would rather view it as a gift from Guanyin Buddha, who oversaw fertility. She had been taking the pill but she recently allowed herself to lapse. Why? She couldn't explain exactly, even to herself. She simply had an overwhelming urge to have Bing's child.

Lotus read until her eyelids drooped. She rested her hands on her tummy, still flat, and fantasized about the baby. She pictured a boy with Bing's round face and a pair of bright eyes, like her brother's.

What a miracle, indeed. As soon as Lotus had learned that she was carrying a life inside her, she felt different, no longer dirty and unworthy. It had become unthinkable that she would ever fool around with another man.

A tapping on the door alarmed her. Funny Eye? She held her breath and listened. "Lotus, are you in?" A woman's voice, in standard Mandarin.

"Who is it?"

"Mei."

Her! Lotus shot up. "Just a second," she said. She hid the book under the pillow before she got up and went to the door. It took her a while to undo the safety lock. As soon as she opened the door, a powerful fragrance hit her like a wave and made her sneeze. She apologized and rested her eyes on the smartly dressed woman in front of her, holding a plucked duck by the neck.

"I came to see you and share this duck with you. See, freshly slaughtered at the market," said Mei, lifting up the bird.

Lotus managed a smile. "Oh, how kind of you. Please come in." She spoke slowly, trying to pronounce each word in standard Mandarin as properly as she could.

"Thank you, Lotus. I heard from Bing that you like duck." Mei stepped onto the bamboo mat. She wore a gray suit, brightened up by a gold necklace, matching earrings, and a bracelet. She looked formal, elegant, and expensive. In this humble room, she shone like a misplaced phoenix.

Smoothing her Snoopy T-shirt, Lotus wished that she was wearing a better outfit. "Is Hu Laoshi okay?" she asked.

"Hu Laoshi?" Mei's lips curled upward into a smile. "Oh, Bing. I trust he is. He should be on his way to Sichuan right now."

Lotus bit her lips to suppress the bubbles of regrets: she should have tried to call Bing after he sent her the telegram about his assignment, but it was expensive to call a cell phone from Cripple Kong's store. Besides, what was the point in making a call if there was nothing wrong to report?

Lotus noticed that blood had dripped onto the floor from the duck's hollow stomach. She found a piece of cloth and squatted down to wipe the mess off the bamboo mat.

Mei looked down. A few drops had landed on the pointed toe of her right shoe. "Oh, dear," she cried. "Let's deal with the duck first. Please show me where your kitchen is."

Lotus hesitated for a moment. What game was this woman playing? she wondered. "Just over here," she said, leading the way.

The visitor followed Lotus into the kitchen. Then she washed the duck in the sink and placed it on a chopping board. "Could you bring me a cleaver, please?"

Lotus handed the cleaver to her. Mei took it, raised it high in the air and chopped at the long neck of the duck with a loud bang. The head landed on the sticky concrete floor, inches away from Lotus's foot. She jumped back.

"Are you afraid of dead animals?" Mei asked, her expression reminding Lotus of a rooster relishing a good fight.

"No," Lotus replied, holding Mei's gaze. "Have you met many country girls who are afraid of animals, dead or alive?"

"I was afraid of them, I confess," Mei said, her tone now amicable. "My husband used to pluck the chickens; it was his job. Since he walked out on us, I have to do everything myself. You know what? I discovered that I can manage everything on my own, absolutely everything!" She laughed like someone who had just unexpectedly won a race. Lotus didn't know what to say as she watched this stranger take over her kitchen.

"May I use this?" Mei asked, pointing at a large clay pot sitting on the stove.

"Sure."

"I'll make us a nice duck soup." Mei stuffed the headless duck into the pot, filled it up with some water, and then added spices she had brought in a bag: ginger, garlic, scallion, wolfberry, and dates. She turned the burner to medium and clapped her hands with satisfaction. She washed her hands and turned to the younger woman. "It'll take a while. Shall we return to the room?"

Lotus nodded and headed out. This is my house, she reminded herself. She stepped inside the room barefoot, leaving her slippers by the door.

Mei strode straight in. The stains on her shoes were the only things marring her meticulous appearance. She was clearly a woman in control of her life, thought Lotus with certain envy. She felt short in front of the other woman in her high heels. She looked up at her uninvited guest and found plenty of wrinkles on Mei's made-up face. This consoled Lotus.

Mei glanced at her host's bare feet and apologized: "I am so sorry." She took off her shoes.

"Please sit down." Lotus gestured for Mei to sit on a chair while she perched on the bed. "Would you like some tea?"

"Oh, no, thank you."

Mei sat and surveyed the room, like a sharp-eyed inspector. "Hmm, not nearly as bad as I had imagined," she remarked, smiling graciously. "I flew down here to attend a trade fair and to do some high-level interpreting. It's my second job. Since I'm here, I thought why not stop by to see you, to make sure you are getting on fine without Bing."

"That's very kind of you."

Mei unzipped her black leather bag and took out a box of chocolates, wrapped in fancy gold wrapping. "For you."

"You are so polite. I don't really like chocolate. But I'm sure the children will love it."

"The children?"

"I teach some of the children in the neighborhood."

"Of course! Bing said you are brilliant with children." Mei looked at Lotus through her gold-rimmed glasses. "Actually, I've heard so much about you I feel like I know you already." She leaned in and briefly rested her hand on Lotus's.

Lotus replied with a polite smile. She didn't know Mei at all. Bing hardly talked about her. Had he really told this woman that much about herself?

Mei pulled back and said: "I've eaten quite a few more years' rice. I hope that puts me in a position to give you some advice, Lotus."

"I'll wash my ears and listen respectfully." Lotus borrowed one of Bing's sayings.

Mei laughed a brief, high-pitched laugh. "I trust he has told you about *Photography* magazine, right? They are very interested in him. One of the bosses there is a good friend of mine."

Lotus nodded.

"The magazine will open up many doors for him." Mei spoke with her natural authority. "But he may have to change his lifestyle a little. Let me explain. Bing has taken an interest in prostitutes for professional and noble reasons. However, if he gives people the impression that he is sexually involved with them, then they won't hire him."

When Mei paused, Lotus cut in. "As you know I am an uneducated country bumpkin. So if you have things you want to say to me, say them directly." She had been twirling around the ring on her finger. Suddenly conscious of this, she moved on to play with the beads of her bracelet.

"I am sure you are a smart girl." The shadow of a smile flickered over Mei's face. "Well, given that everyone knows who you are, I don't think it's appropriate if he takes you up to Beijing or, worse still, if he marries you, unless he is mad enough to give up his career." As Mei talked, she scratched her leg through her tights.

"Of course, he shouldn't give up his career," Lotus said, her voice barely louder than the humming of the mosquitoes.

"It's quite hot in here, isn't it?" Mei took off her suit jacket. Without the cover-up, Lotus noticed that the older woman wasn't as slim as she had thought, with a slightly bulging stomach.

Lotus turned on the ceiling fan.

"Please don't think that I'm trying to push you out of the picture so that I can have him back. To be honest with you, Lotus, I haven't really forgiven him and probably never will. Such betrayal." Lotus could see the bitterness in the woman's expression. "Still, I care about him, and he shouldn't throw away what he has been painstakingly building all these years." Mei talked faster as she scratched harder. "I've been bitten all over the place."

"Maybe your blood is sweeter than mine," Lotus said. She quickly scolded herself for taking pleasure in the suffering of her visitor. "Let me light the mosquito coil for you."

Lotus squatted down under the desk to put in a coil. She noticed Mei's legs were as thin and shapeless as the desk's. She sat back on the bed, her back upright.

"Lotus, do you see what I'm saying?" Mei sounded like a teacher questioning a student. "Right now, the Communists still run the show. In his situation, I think it's better for him to work within the system." She tapped two of her thin fingers on the desk to emphasize her point.

"Yes, better within the system," Lotus repeated. She looked up at the swirling fan that was casting ever-changing patterns on the ceiling.

"You two may not be that compatible, but . . ."

"Compatible?"

Mei flashed a smile. "Actually, a relationship is like a pair of shoes. Only those inside them can tell if they fit or not. You are young and beautiful, Lotus. Why not be his girlfriend in Shenzhen if you are happy with him?"

"You mean, I should be content to be his mistress?"

Mei shrugged, the way that foreigners did in films, showing her sharp shoulder blades. "Well, if Bing is so important to you, you shouldn't give him up altogether."

"Is he important to you?" Lotus said.

Mei raised her well-groomed eyebrows. "Yes, he meant more to me than he ever realized. It was Bing who revived my faith in men—well, for a while, anyway. I was in a bad relationship before I met Bing. I was engaged to a classmate, a man with a brilliant mind. To support him financially, I sacrificed my chance at further study and started working."

Lotus listened and wondered why the other woman would be so open. She doesn't care about me, the girl reasoned.

Some emotion entered Mei's voice. "This boyfriend left China for

America to further his studies and he was supposed to bring me over. But he changed his heart and married an American, a white woman. I had given him everything, absolutely everything, my youth, my love, and . . ." She paused for a second. "Even the most precious thing a woman can give."

Lotus's hands stopped playing with her beads as she thought about how she had given away the most precious thing of hers. She watched how Mei's gold necklace glittered in the glow of the desk lamp. Of course, it would be a whole different story for a lady of her social standing.

Mei went on with her story: It had taken her years to nurse her broken heart. Then she met Bing, who appeared to be talented, kind, and trust-worthy. "With all the books he had read, why hadn't he achieved more? That, I'll never understand. Worse still, how could he betray me for that whore?"

Lotus shifted on the bed and stared at the woman.

Mei stopped, gazing somewhere into the distance. Moments later, she continued in a calmer tone. "Heaven knows, I always had his best interests at heart. And I'd still like to watch out for him, because he isn't always sensible."

Lotus felt she had to defend her man—her man for the moment. "Hu Laoshi is someone who believes in helping others and making a contri-bution to society."

"I agree, totally! However, in today's society, people judge you by the depth of your pocket and the height of your social status." She tapped her fingers on the desk again. "Besides, well, how should I explain? My ex-boyfriend—he's now a professor at an American university—has been in touch with me. Actually, I got in touch with him. Anyway, he has promised to help my daughter go to America to study—the least he can do for me. I would hate it, more than anything in the world, if he thought that I was married to a man not as successful as he is."

"Hu Laoshi is successful." Lotus projected strength into each word.

"He can achieve greater success if we help him. We women always make sacrifices for men, don't we?"

Mei bent over to touch Lotus's hand again but Lotus withdrew.

The aroma of the duck wafted in. Lotus felt hungry and a little sick. "I should go and check the soup." She stood up.

Mei also got on her feet. "Yes, it's time to throw in some salt as well."

Suddenly Lotus's stomach began to pitch like the sea. She ran out into the yard and threw up violently. She straightened up, breathing in the warm humid air. The night had arrived unannounced.

Mei followed her and patted Lotus's back. "Are you okay?"

"Yes, I'm fine."

"You do strike me as a healthy young lady."

"I probably ate some leftovers that were a bit off."

Mei smiled, her white teeth flashing in the darkness. "Well, take care of yourself. Please think carefully about what I said, for his sake and for yours as well."

While Lotus collected herself, Mei went into the kitchen. She returned a minute later. "The soup is ready. Do have it while it is still hot. I'll have to get going now," she announced, clasping her hands.

Lotus closed the door behind Mei, then slumped in the chair, shutting her eyes, feeling tired to her bones. The lingering scent of Mei's perfume irritated her. What was Mei's game, coming here, making her soup? The soup! She jumped up and ran to the kitchen. When she took the lid off the clay pot, steam escaped. With a layer of yellow grease on top, it smelled sickly rich. She carefully picked up the pot, carried it out to the yard and poured it out into the gutter. Lotus felt better after that.

When she returned to the room, she noticed a fat envelope on the desk with her name on it. She picked it up and knew there was money inside. She took out the money and counted ten thousand yuan. Mei's bribe. Just like Funny Eye, she believed that "money could make the devil push a millstone."

Lotus collapsed onto the bed, her mind more restless than the chirping cicadas on the treetops. For some time now, she had felt that her association with Bing had elevated her status. The villagers' greeting, "Have you eaten?" came with more warmth, her friends envied her, and her students adored her. Yet, to Funny Eye and Mei, she remained a dirty little *ji*.

Ever since learning the news of Bing's possible relocation to Beijing, Lotus had worried about their future. Would he take her up to the capital? What would become of her if he did? Would he introduce her to his family and friends? Would he have to lie to them about her background? If not, how would they regard her? Now Mei's visit had clearly spelled out the gravity of her impact: she was nothing to him but a stumbling block.

Lotus also felt sorry to put Bing in this position. I don't want to ruin his future, she said to herself. But what can I do without him?

She huddled in bed, her hand resting on her stomach. At least she had her baby, someone who would always belong to her, she thought with gratitude. And, of course, her brother. There would be good news from him soon. Comforting herself with these thoughts, Lotus drifted off to sleep.

CHAPTER 26

在天愿作比翼鸟

Fly in the Sky Like the Legendary Birds
That Pair Off Wing to Wing

My Dearest Lotus,

I am writing to you from a Hakka restaurant by Houhai, a lovely lake in central Beijing.It serves authentic Hakka food, such as duck stuffed with sticky rice and fried pork belly with fermented tofu, cooked in a clay pot. You like both dishes, don't you?

I am sitting outside, watching the glitter of the water and enjoying the breeze. I wish you were with me, my sweet melon. I'll have to bring you here one day soon. You know the lake is actually part of a man-made canal, dug for the imperial court in order to bring goods from around China to the emperor in the Forbidden City just south of the lake. It used to be my favorite place. I simply can't believe that this sleepy neighborhood has become so touristy.

Bing looked up. Across the lake, diners and visitors crowded the rows of bars and restaurants that had sprung up along the shore. The wailing from a karaoke bar and the flashing neon signs shredded the calm of the evening. Many years ago, he used to bicycle leisurely by the lake, riding over those arched stone bridges, taking pictures and documenting the carved stones. The tackiness of the new shops had driven away much of the dreamy charm. Yet where else in Beijing could one find such a poetic open space as here in Houhai? On either side of the lake, the weeping willows trailed their green arms in the water like the long sleeves of the legendary beauty Xishi.

I hope you are well and taking good care of yourself. It's admirable that you are teaching the children, and I don't mind as long as you don't get calluses on your feather-soft hands! Seriously, please don't wear yourself out. I've been missing you more than I can say.

I very much enjoyed my trip home. My mother was very happy to see me. Each time I visit her, it strikes me how much older and more frail she has become. If—I mean if—we settle in Beijing, maybe my mother could stay with us for some time and you two could keep each other company? She is excited that I've found someone. And she can't wait to meet you.

Staring at the lake in front of him, Bing thought about his home visit. It occurred to him that he had just traveled the whole length of China, from Shenzhen, in the southernmost tip, to his mother's place, an overnight train ride north of Beijing. Since the death of his father, his mother had been living with Bing's sister, Sufang, in a small town near their ancestral village.

This trip home had been a joyful occasion, unlike previous ones in recent years, which had always been clouded by his mother's disappointment in his divorce, as well as in his choice of work. She felt his job as a freelance photographer was only marginally better than being a laid-off worker like his sister. Now, at long last, he was able to present his mother with some tangible achievements that qualified as *chuxi*. The old woman had caressed the little golden cup of the Kodak award and laughed so much that she couldn't shut her toothless mouth. The prospect of her son working for the government in Beijing also thrilled her. "Maybe I could live in our capital before I rest forever in my grave?" she let out at one point.

Why not? Bing thought. After all, without her pushing him as a child, he probably wouldn't have made it to university. Looking down at his leather shoes, he thought about one of his mother's pet phrases: "My boy, study hard and go to university. Then you can wear leather shoes. Otherwise, you'll rot away in the field in your straw sandals."

Bing laughed to himself. It was high time that he fulfilled his filial duty. His sister had done more than her fair share. Since losing her factory job, Sufang had been eking out a living delivering newspapers, while taking care of her own family and their increasingly embittered mother, all crammed into their two-room apartment.

As part of the new, successful image he was projecting for his mother, he revealed that he had found new love, but he avoided giving details and stressed it was still early days. If the old woman found out about Lotus's dubious background, it would send her straight to the grave.

Bing lit a cigarette and continued to write in the fading light. He could now fill Lotus in on additional details about the assignment, after he had first rushed off a hurried telegram in his initial excitement.

The meeting with the boss of the magazine went well. Tomorrow I'll be heading to a remote part of Sichuan, your province, Lotus, for the shooting assignment.

You may not be able to reach me on my cell phone once I get there. But please, my dearest, do try to call me. I was so happy when you called me last time. I should have bought you a cell phone before I left home.

I'll be there for about two weeks, maybe a little longer. I am sorry that the whole thing will take longer than I'd anticipated. But I'll head home, back to your arms, as soon as the assignment is over.

Last night, I met up with my old friend Yuejin, who is now a government official. He took me, in his chauffeur-driven car, to a very fancy private club, hidden inside an elegant courtyard house by the lake, not far from here, in fact. I don't think I've been to a more expensive place. A cup of green tea costs two hundred yuan! But at the end of the meal, he asked for a receipt, so I guess he could get the expense reimbursed somehow. And he looks like a corrupt official with his big "general's belly" and his gold Rolex wristwatch. Among our group of friends, he used to be the most critical of the government. After 1989, through his family connection—his father is some high-ranking leader—he joined in the Ministry of Chemical Industry. Yuejin said there's nothing wrong with enjoying the perks of his position as long as he does a good job. I imagine the perks are substantial. You may say it's corruption, but it is just the way it is with government officials. There is now no trace of the patriotic, pure-hearted ideological youth in Yuejin that had impressed me so much. I miss that old Yuejin, and resent this new version. Yet I envy him in some ways. Nevertheless, I am glad to have an old friend with whom I can talk about everything. He is very excited about the magazine's job offer and is urging me to take it.

This afternoon, I spent hours shopping on Palace Street for a telephoto lens, trying out this one, then that. In the end, I found what I was looking for.

After that I went to the main Xinhua bookstore next door. I love the mega-bookstores in Beijing where you can spend the whole day picking through books. Not like in Shenzhen.

Beijing and Shenzhen are dramatically different, I tell you. I think I'd prefer to live here. You'll like it, too, Lotus, I'm sure.

That afternoon, as Bing had wandered along Palace Street, he heard the chimes from the giant clock at the nearby railway station striking five, followed by the tune "The East Is Red." He hummed along, feeling utterly at home in the city. The song reminded him of the countless times he had biked to and from work along Chang'an Avenue. In Shenzhen, he had never had the same sense of belonging.

Would Lotus like the capital? Or would it overwhelm her, making her feel like a goldfish out of its tank? Bing put down his pen.

The city had grudgingly submitted itself to the night. Merrymakers rented small paddle boats and went out on the lake. Some people hired musicians clad in Chinese dresses to play the pipa, a soft-sounding traditional string instrument. As if by some unspoken rule, everyone placed tiny candles in paper boats on the water. In the darkness, the candles winked as if they were the lake's flirtatious eyes. Would Lotus like to do this with him, or would she worry about wasting the candles?

Bing picked up his camera and looked through his powerful new telephoto lens. He could see clearly the smiling faces of the people on their boats. Soon, he was going to shoot the launching of a satellite with this lens. He could hardly contain his excitement. He thought about his career, about what he had recently achieved and how he could use this as a springboard to launch into greater prospects. He had already sensed how addictive success could be. The glory in the media, the job opportunities, attention from women, and Mei's approval. For the first time in many years, he didn't feel small standing in front of her. In the past, her high expectations and heavy disappointment had crushed him.

Party Secretary Wang's stern warning echoed in his mind. If he did bring Lotus up to Beijing, the question was how to keep her away from the Party's prying eyes.

Was she worth the potential trouble? He'd like to think so. He certainly felt ashamed that he had even suspected that she had some indecent dealings with men behind his back. After his meeting with Pearl that night, the moment he had returned home and seen how she was immersed in her work, his anger had vanished and he believed her. What a possessive and small-minded man you are, he said to himself.

Bing asked a waitress to light the candle on his table and resumed his letter writing.

This afternoon, on Palace Street, I bought you a beautiful white silk dress, a modern version of the traditional cheongsam. You'll look stunning in it. I must take you shopping once we are here together. Not just shopping. There are plenty of things to do.

"Excuse me, may I take away the dishes?" A waitress interrupted Bing's writing.

"Not yet." He picked up a slice of duck and put it into his mouth. It was tender and delicious, like all the dishes he had ordered, yet he hadn't touched much.

On the lake, neon signs from the restaurants and bars competed for attention. He thought of a conversation about romance he had had with Zhang Jianguo during a recent drinking session. The journalist had said that China had become too restless and commercial to allow space for romance.

But an age without romance would be a dark age, Bing thought to himself.

The night has fallen. The moon is hanging in the sky, reminding me of the moonlit night we shared by the embankment. My good Lotus, let me finish the letter with lines from a famous poem about the moon: "Would we live a long life / And together share the moonlight a thousand miles apart!"

I miss you all the time and I love you.

With all my love,
Bing

CHAPTER 27

纸包不住火

You Can't Wrap Fire in Paper

"Lotus, Lotus!"

Mimi burst into the courtyard, her powdered face smeared with sweat.

"What's wrong?" Lotus asked, surprised. She was teaching an after-noon class.

"Your brother," Mimi said breathlessly.

"My brother?" Lotus cried. "What about him?"

"He's come to look for you."

He has come to deliver the good news himself! That was Lotus's first thought. She had just started worrying that she hadn't heard any news from him about his university entrance exams. "Where is he?"

"Waiting outside the house," Mimi said, waving an arm in that direction.

Why would Shadan come all this way and spend so much money just to report the news? Could it be something else? Had Grandma or

Ba fallen ill? No, no. They wouldn't have bothered to tell her unless it was serious, but then if it were serious, surely Shadan would have stayed with them.

Lotus turned to the class. "Children, we are going to finish early today. Gather up your things. For your homework, write down the new characters five times. Neatly, please. Now, I need a quick word with Mimi, but I'll be right back to see you off."

While the students were packing up, Lotus dragged her friend into her room. "Tell me, Mimi, what happened? When did he turn up? How come?"

"I don't know. He just turned up at the parlor, and I usually don't go over so early—"

"Mimi!" Lotus cut her short. Mimi's conversations always led to her talking about herself. "When did he come?"

"About half an hour ago. I thought he was a client. So I—"

Lotus grabbed Mimi's shoulders. "What did he say?"

"He asked: 'Is this 110 East Station Road?' We said, 'Yes, yes,' and 'Come in, come in.'" Mimi paused to push away Lotus's hands and brush back her hair, which looked unnaturally black. She had dyed it again since her new boyfriend had hated the blond bangs. "We don't often see such cute boys. I tried to get him inside for a massage. He asked if the parlor used to be a restaurant before. I said to him: 'If you are hungry, I'll cook just for you.' Xia was all over him. His cheeks turned as red as a monkey's bottom." Mimi touched her own cheeks and let out a brief laugh, but once she noticed that Lotus wasn't smiling at all, she carried on with the story. "All the while, he was dead serious. He then asked if a girl called Luo Xiangzhu worked here. I said no, but then Xia remembered it was your real name. He said he's your brother. Is he?" Mimi looked out the window and began to wipe off her thick lipstick.

"What are you doing?"

"Trying not to look too slutty."

"It's a bit too late for that, isn't it?" Lotus snapped.

Mimi's panda eyes held a hurt expression.

Lotus took her friend's hand. "Sorry, my sister. You go back now. Thank you, Mimi."

"Quite a looker, your brother! Just a bit bony." Mimi winked as she headed out.

Lotus darted a look at Guanyin Buddha before she went to open the door. There she saw her brother, his tall form casting a long shadow on the ground. He was wearing a pale green short-sleeved shirt and a pair of army trousers. His face was tired and his eyes, under his thick eyebrows, were troubled.

Lotus's heart turned to ice. He had found out! He had tracked her down from the mailing address. She had never dreamed that her little brother would have come all the way here to look for her.

"Chouchou," Shadan cried out, his voice cracked.

She rubbed her chest as if trying to warm her heart back to life. "Let me deal with the children first," she said.

Back in the yard, Lotus issued her orders to her students. "Children, line up please. Now off you go."

Squabbles broke out between Big Head and his brother. But all fourteen students managed to line up and started to file out onto the street, like a small regiment.

Standing by the door, Lotus waved at them. "Goodbye. See you tomorrow."

"Bye-bye, Teacher Lotus."

Big Head came out last, carrying his little sister Niuniu on his back. His school bag bounced on his hip as he walked. He stopped and looked sharply at Lotus and then at Shadan. "Who is he? What does he want? You're not happy, Teacher Lotus?"

Laoer took out his slingshot. "If he dares to trouble you, I'll blind his eyes," he threatened, snuffling and wiping snot on the back of his hand.

Lotus cleaned Number Two's nose with her handkerchief. "Thank you, Laoer, but he's my brother. Don't worry, he won't cause any trouble." She flashed a smile at Shadan.

Her brother waved at the children.

Lotus watched the children walking down the road in the bright afternoon sun and disappearing around a corner. A lump rose in her throat. She blinked hard.

She took a deep breath before turning to her brother. Instead of punching him playfully, she silently picked up his simple luggage: a fish-net bag that carried his few belongings.

"Come in, my brother," Lotus said softly.

Once inside, she motioned for him to sit down by the desk, and then made some tea. Several times, she thought her brother was going to say something, but he didn't. She could hear her own heart beating and her brother's heavy breathing. They drank their tea in a tense silence. Sitting in the folding chair, she held the cup in both hands, as if needing the warmth.

"How were the exams? I've been dying to find out," she said, addressing him in their home dialect.

"I don't know. Not too good."

"Why? What was wrong?" Lotus put her tea down so suddenly that some drops splashed onto her dress.

Shadan twisted his mouth. "Well, I haven't gotten the results yet. But it didn't go well."

"Why did you leave home, then? You should have waited for the results." She had never used such a harsh tone with her little brother before—there had never been the need.

He glared at her. "I came to see you. I need to know something."

"What?" Lotus couldn't look him in the eye. She focused on a float-ing tea leaf in her cup.

"Where is your fancy Cantonese restaurant, Sister?"

"Up on East Station Road."

He grunted. "Where did you get that ten thousand yuan? From working as a waitress or as a teacher?"

"I told you in my letter, didn't I? I won a lottery." She realized that her voice sounded too flat for such a big deal. So she raised her voice, trying to inject some joy into it. "Ten thousand yuan in the social wel-fare lottery! I couldn't believe my luck!"

"You've told us so many tales. I don't believe a word of it anymore.

Lottery? Really! Why doesn't Mimi know anything about it? She told me she is your best friend."

"Winning the lottery is best kept a secret," Lotus said sheepishly. She got up and poured more water into her teacup. She was shaking.

"So, you live here with the photographer." Shadan looked around. "As his mistress?"

How had he known so much already? Lotus could see a thin mustache above his upper lip. Her brother was a man now, no longer a boy. "As his fiancée," she replied.

"When is the wedding day?"

"It's not finalized yet. He's away on a trip." Lotus paused for a moment. Bing had said that the Sichuan assignment would take two weeks, but the trip kept getting extended. Then he had sent her a note informing her that he would have to prolong his trip yet again because his daughter was scheduled to have a small operation after his photo assignment. It had made her question whether Bing was deliberately delaying his return. Had he changed his mind? The letter seemed hastily written and lacked his usual intimacy. She thought she might be feeling oversensitive in his absence, of course. She knew she really ought to call him to find out what was going on. But she was afraid. What if he never came back?

"Okay, okay, let me tell you the truth," Lotus said to her brother. "Bing gave me the money. The lottery thing, well, I made it up. I didn't know how to break the news about him to you."

"You'll marry a man old enough to be your father?"

Lotus swallowed a big mouthful of tea. Too hot, it burned her throat. She gasped for air. "He loves and respects me, and he treats me very well." She tugged at the cream-colored cotton dress, a modern design decorated with traditional knotted buttons, one of the few outfits she really liked. "He bought me this dress and lots of other nice things."

But Shadan wasn't interested in her dress. "Why does he want to marry you then? To take advantage of a young girl or to rescue you from your filthy life?"

Lotus put her hand on her mouth. "Do you really think your sister is so low and cheap that no man in the world would like to marry her?"

"No, no, Chouchou!" The boy shook his head violently, biting his lip. Lotus knew he was trying hard to control his tears. "Our mother died early. Big Sister, you're the one who raised me. I thought you were the best woman under the heavens. Then, I discovered, that you, you are . . ." He let out a cry, unable to hold back the tears any longer.

Lotus sat silently for a while, biting her own lip. "Have you told Ba and Nainai?"

"Not yet."

"Please, please don't!"

Shadan didn't respond.

Lotus slumped down in her chair. *Ah,* fate, she thought. You couldn't escape it.

After a while Shadan was able to compose himself, and started to explain that the journalist Zhang Jianguo had gone to the village to interview some farmers. Ba asked Zhang to take a big piece of smoked salty ham to him at the school in Phoenix, to fatten him up before the exam. When they met, Shadan asked about the photographer who had accompanied his sister to their village. The journalist was careful not to give away too much. But Shadan learned Bing's full name and the fact that he contributed to the *Southern Weekend*. He had been curious about the photographer, especially after Bing said his sister worked at a different restaurant than he remembered. At the local library, Shadan searched the back issues of the *Southern Weekend* and found Zhang's profile story on Bing, as well as Bing's photo essay. Shocked, filled with disbelief and rage at his sister, he decided to confront her himself. While his fingers were still aching from scribbling out the answers on the exam papers, he left home for Shenzhen, against Ba's wishes, carrying with him the little bit of cash he had.

"Chouchou, you have to explain everything to me, today," he demanded.

"*Ai,* it's hard to survive in a city. You have no idea." Lotus let out a slow long sigh. "After the shoe factory, I came to Shenzhen and I was raped. After that I couldn't find any work. I don't have any skills. I didn't even have money to go home." Her excuses all sounded feeble. She knew that no matter how hard she tried to explain herself, her brother would never understand. She bent over the table, hid her face in her arms and began to sob.

But Shadan lifted her up, forcing her to face him. "I always wondered how you made so much money. I always had this question in the back of my mind. But I never dreamt it was from selling yourself!"

Her brother's sharp words pierced Lotus's heart like arrows. There was such contempt in his dark eyes where she had only ever seen love and admiration. She couldn't bear it. She broke free of his grip, climbed into bed, pulled the cotton sheet over her head and curled up into a ball.

But there was no hiding. "Why?" her brother bellowed at her. "Because of me?"

"No!"

"For what then? How could you? How are you going to face our ancestors? And how are you ever going to find a decent man to marry now? Was it why you went for an older man?"

Lotus pulled the sheet tighter over her head. "I'm sorry."

"I probably failed the exam! All thanks to you!"

"Sorry, sorry!" Covering her ears, she started to rock from side to side.

When Lotus finally opened her eyes, the storm seemed to have blown over. She sat up and found her brother bent over the desk, his head resting on his arm.

"Shadan," she called, her voice hoarse. She cleared her throat.

He looked up, his eyes red and swollen.

Lotus got up and walked over to him. "My good brother, listen to me. I know my shame and sins are so deep. I couldn't clean myself even if I jumped into the South China Sea. But you are still young. There's a golden path in front of you. Don't waste it."

Shadan was motionless, like a little mountain, his eyes looking ahead blankly. She seated herself next to him. "An acceptance letter is probably waiting for you at home. Which universities did you put down on your application forms? Sichuan University? What are you going to study? Computer science, as we've discussed?"

"I'm not sure I scored well enough to get into a good university. Our family can't afford it anyway."

"I told you not to worry about money, my brother." Lotus stood up in front of Shadan and grabbed his shoulders. "Go to university and then you'll get a good job and become a respectable city man. You must! For your own sake."

Shadan pushed her hands away. "I don't know what I'll do." He looked up at her for a moment and then let his gaze fall. "I'm dying to go to university. But I can't. I can't touch your money. Dirty money," he said, his head turning the other way. "I've already messed up your life. I can't keep doing that."

"Not going to university? What a dog fart! Messing up my life? I'm not a prostitute anymore!"

Shadan twisted his mouth. "A mistress or a prostitute, what's the difference?"

Lotus slapped her brother's handsome face. "You've become so clever, haven't you? If you are really so clever, then do yourself a big favor and go to university! If you are just a stupid egg, then get lost! Go, go, now!" she shouted at him, pushing him toward the door.

Shadan stared at his sister in disbelief.

Lotus instinctively wanted to touch Shadan's reddened cheek, but she controlled herself.

He wiped his nose with the back of his hand and stormed out the door.

Lotus stared at her right hand. She had never hit her brother before. For a while, she seemed to be glued to the ground.

Then hurriedly she put on her sandals and dashed outside. But it was too late; there was no sign of her brother. She ran toward the village square, but she couldn't pick out his tall form among the chaotic crowds. Several ground rat drivers were squatting, playing cards on a piece of newspaper. She asked them if a tall young man had taken a ride, but they said no.

Lotus thought about looking for him outside the village, but how could she find him? Something inside her had died. She felt so heavy that she couldn't run. She couldn't even breathe. She stared at the drivers, with their sleeveless T-shirts rolled up to their chests, faces red and sweaty, spittle flying as they swore and threw their cards around.

Scenes that she had so often imagined flashed through her mind: drums and gongs in the village celebrating Shadan's university acceptance, all the sweet congratulatory words from the neighbors and their admiring looks at her; Shadan strolling across campus, books under his arm; then Shadan working in front of a computer. Slowly, the images faded, leaving a dark, blank screen.

CHAPTER 28

鱼和熊掌不可兼得

You Can't Catch a Fish and a Bear Paw
at the Same Time

"Twelfth floor, please," Bing said to the elevator operator.

Sitting on her stool, the woman in a hand-knitted gray cardigan pressed number 12 with a bamboo knitting needle. "Which room?" she asked as she resumed her knitting.

"Twelve C." As Bing listened to the rattling of the elevator, he prepared himself mentally for his first visit to his ex-wife's home. Upon completing his assignment, he had contacted Mei and requested to see his daughter. She invited him over for dinner.

"To get to Twelve C, you turn right and take the first left," the lift lady instructed him.

"I see. Thanks." Bing wondered why there was a need for an operator. It was just an elevator, he thought, hardly a rocket. But that was state-owned property for you. The building was hidden in Twin Wells, one of Beijing's largest residential compounds, where rows of identical block buildings queued stiffly one after the other. A year after their divorce, Mei had cleverly secured an apartment here, benefiting from a government-funded project to assist poorly paid teachers. She wouldn't have obtained the subsidy if she were still married to a businessman. She was better off without me, he told himself, and we were probably better off without each other.

The elevator lady stabbed at him lightly with her needle. "Are you Little Li's uncle?"

"No. I'm her father."

With a loud clack, the elevator stopped and Bing stepped out, leaving the woman to chew on her newly gained information.

As soon as he touched the doorbell, a distorted electronic chime jangled out. He stuck out his chest in preparation for meeting his ex-wife.

"Daddy!" Through the door he heard his daughter's voice, the scrape of a chair, and running footsteps. The door swung open, and the girl hurled herself at him, nearly knocking him over.

"Oh, Lili, good girl, careful," Bing said, grinning. He had not received such a warm welcome in years.

"I've been waiting for so long," she complained and dragged him into the room. "Come in, Daddy."

"All right. What has your mom been feeding you? You will be as tall as me soon." Perhaps because of her height, she appeared slimmer. Her hair was cut short, with an even line of bangs.

A petite young woman shuffled across a wooden floor shiny enough to serve as a mirror. She handed Bing a pair of slippers. "Sir, please change your shoes," she said humbly in her Sichuan accent.

She must be the family's maid, he presumed. Her full-length cotton apron made her seem even slighter.

Bing took the slippers from the girl. "*Yaodei, yaodei.*"

"Are you from Sichuan, sir?" the girl asked in Sichuan dialect, her eyes gleaming.

"No, but I have a dear Sichuan friend."

Just then, Mei emerged and greeted Bing: "Aha, you've made it."

The maid dashed out of sight.

Mei stood in the middle of the room, poised as ever, smiling brightly as her golden necklace. Even at home, she was elegantly dressed in black silk trousers and a lilac-colored shirt.

Bing smiled politely, rubbing his sweaty hands against his shirt and wondering if a handshake would be too formal.

His ex-wife touched him briefly on the shoulder, as briefly as a dragonfly skimming the surface of the water, guiding him to the cream-colored leather sofa. "Come over, sit down, darling. You must be exhausted from the trip."

"I'm a little tired." Bing sank into the comfortable sofa, which would have been too large to squeeze into their old house. He took in everything in his ex-wife's apartment. Mei had decorated the interior with antique-style furniture, including a red lacquer cupboard painted with butterflies and a table with scrolled edges. What had happened to the old furniture? The only thing he recognized was a Tibetan silk carpet laid out in front of the sofa, a wedding present.

Bing's eyes lit up when he spotted three of his black-and-white photographs on the wall, depicting old men walking their pet birds in cages, youngsters ice-skating in Beihai Park, and a narrow *hutong* coated in snow.

Little Li rushed over to sit beside her father, pulling down a white crocheted blanket draped over the sofa.

Bing reached over and carefully put it back in place.

"Don't worry about it," Mei said amiably. "Have some tea. Dinner will be ready in a few minutes."

The Sichuan girl brought two lidded clay cups—clay was the best container for tea, according to Mei—and left them on the coffee table.

"Thank you," Bing said, putting on as much of a Sichuan accent as he could muster. "I've just been to your province."

"Have you?" the girl asked with a timid smile.

As if suddenly realizing her existence, Mei made the introduction. "By the way, this is Wu Ayi." She used the polite term *ayi* for maid—meaning "auntie." What an abused word, Bing thought. How many urban families would actually shower their maids with the respect due to an auntie?

Wu Ayi nodded at him, and after glancing at her employer, turned away, wiping her wet hands on her apron.

"Daddy, have you got any presents for me?" Little Li demanded.

"Yes, of course, Lili." From his rucksack, Bing took out a large piece of smoked ham, wrapped in red rice paper.

Mei took the ham. "How thoughtful of you!"

He then brought out his daughter's gift bag, which Little Li grabbed and opened. She fished out a square cloth with a circle attached to the middle, decorated with patchwork and colorful embroidery. "What is it?"

"It's a hat used by the Yi women near the satellite launch center in Xichang," Bing explained. "See, the sun is strong there. The Yi women need a big hat to protect their faces."

"You've studied the ethnic minorities in China, right, Little Li?" Mei stepped in. "The Yi are one of them."

"Yes, of course, I know," Little Li replied impatiently, her hands already fumbling inside to search for the remaining items. "What are these?" She pulled out a long black cotton skirt embroidered with brightly colored flowers. and a matching top.

"These are the Yi women's clothing. Look at this embroidery. All handmade. You'll look super cool at school. No one else will have anything quite like it."

Little Li turned her back to him. "Look at my T-shirt, Dad. *That's* cool!" A monkey with a dangling cloth tail was on her back.

"My best friend Peach's mother bought it for me in South Korea." The girl dropped the skirt to the floor disdainfully. "I don't care about this sort of stuff."

Bing looked down at the skirt. He had run from one shop to another in search of just the right size for his girl.

"Hu Li!" Mei yelled, her willow-leaf eyebrows knitting together. "You ungrateful child. You simply don't know how high heaven is."

The young girl rolled her eyes heavenward as if to measure the immensity of it.

"Pick up the skirt. Go to your room. And don't come out until I say so."

The girl picked up the skirt with two fingers as if it were something filthy.

Bing took the skirt and folded it up. He wanted to say something to soften the situation like he used to do, but decided not to interfere.

Little Li headed toward her room, stamping her feet in protest, the monkey's little tail quivering on her back.

"Today's children are all spoiled, aren't they?" Mei commented. "Little emperors. I'm sorry about Little Li."

"It's all right." Where was the girl he knew, the one who was so happy, easygoing, and full of curiosity about the world? Bing wondered. He had done more than his fair share of spoiling her with presents and money. Even if the family hadn't broken up, he imagined that he would still have had a few issues with his willful daughter, as she was growing into her own person.

"It is harder for children in divorced families. I'm sorry that I haven't been a good father." Bing realized that he had entered into potentially dangerous territory. He changed the topic. "She's doing well at school, isn't she?"

"Very well, I must say. She is smart, driven, and competitive, too."

"She's your daughter, I wouldn't expect otherwise."

"Yours, too."

Bing picked up the cup to take a sip of tea.

Mei leaned forward, radiating expensive perfume. "I'm dying to know how your trip went. Did you get some great shots? Does Mr. Liao like them?"

"I think he loves them, very much."

"Well done, darling! So, have you signed a contract with them yet?"

"The Party Secretary did offer me the contract. But . . . "

"But? But what?"

"Nothing. I'm sure it will work out. Come on, let me show you some pictures." He pulled out an envelope.

Mei's face moved closer and studied each picture. "Wow, these are fantastic! Absolutely fantastic! Look at this one." Mei pointed at the

Long March rocket spurting flames from the launch pad. "It must have been such a thrilling experience to witness that."

Bing described how he had waited anxiously with the other photographers, and how he could scarcely breathe during the countdown to liftoff. Then came the moment when the rocket took flight like an angry dragon, breathing fire and leaving the earth trembling. He was overwhelmed, immensely excited, and proud to be Chinese. What a long way China, the so-called "sick man of Asia," had traveled. But he was also struck by the poverty he had witnessed in the desolate villages surrounding the launch center, the same center that boasted the most advanced space technology in Asia. What a paradoxical world modern China had become.

"Where were you? Inside the control center?" Mei asked.

"Of course not." Bing laughed. "The control center is several miles away from the launch pad. And I took this picture at an observation pavilion halfway up a hill some miles beyond the launch center."

Mei slapped his knee. "Don't laugh at me. I haven't been there. How many people could boast of the privilege you've enjoyed?"

"That's very true. I flew down there with a journalist and a photographer from the official Xinhua News agency. And then there was the photographer who works at the center and another one from the Ministry of Aerospace Industry. That was all." Bing made a sweeping gesture with his hand. "My photos will be all over the magazine's next issue."

"I can imagine the text: 'Flying into space; flying into glory. China successfully launches a grand satellite into space, and is one step closer to manned spaceflight.'" Mei mimicked a news anchor.

Bing smiled knowingly, enjoying his ex-wife's company. He told her that he felt very lucky that the launch had been a success. He had heard from the launch center's photographer that several years ago a satellite had exploded on takeoff, and half of the nearby village was destroyed. But there had not been a word about it in the press.

In the middle of dinner with Mei and Little Li, Bing's cell phone rang. The screen showed Zhang Jianguo's name. He jumped up, knocking over his rice bowl as he left the table in a hurry.

"*Wei.*" Bing pressed the phone against his ear as he headed toward the kitchen, a quiet place to talk.

"Sorry to have missed your call, my friend. I was in a meeting."

"Thanks for calling back. Wait a minute." Bing spotted the maid asleep on a low stool by the door, her head lolled to one side. He looked around. Mei pointed at her bedroom with her chopsticks. He went in.

"Sorry. How are you, my friend?" Bing asked as he closed the door.

"Fine. I am stuck in a patriotic education meeting in Shanghai. Anyway, did you see my piece about Lotus's village?" Zhang's voice boomed over the phone.

"Not yet. I've been traveling," Bing said as he paced around Mei's bedroom. "Listen, I'm very concerned about Lotus. I haven't heard from her in a long time. When I returned to Beijing last week, I even sent her a telegram, asking her to call me. I wonder if you could head over to check on her?" Bing regretted that he had forgotten to bring his address book when he left in haste, so he was unable to get in touch with Moon, the only one around Lotus who owned a cell phone.

"I can get Little Wang to go," the journalist said. "He knows where you live."

"How does he know?"

"Don't worry about it. Why have you been away for so long?"

"We had to wait for perfect weather for the launch. And I can't go back to Shenzhen yet, because my daughter is going to have her tonsils taken out next week."

"How's the job situation?" the journalist inquired.

"I need your opinion, my brother." Bing sat down on the chair in front of Mei's dressing table. He explained how the Party Secretary had informed him that the magazine would like to hire him, and, if all went well, would make him a model worker in the near future.

"Sounds interesting!" Zhang chuckled.

But Bing wasn't amused. "I am afraid of being used as a political tool. Also, it will be more difficult for me to move Lotus to Beijing."

"So, a bright future with the magazine, or beautiful Lotus?"

Bing looked in the mirror and saw how the deep folds between his eyebrows made him look old. He took off his glasses.

"I thought you were the last romantic left in China!" Thunderous laughter vibrated from Bing's phone. "If Lotus is the only thing under heaven that makes you happy, then follow your heart. But the sensible option is to compromise, my brother, compromise." Zhang raised his voice as if it wasn't loud enough. "Join the magazine and play along for a while, try to get high-profile assignments, publish your books, and have a few photo exhibitions. Keep your relationship, too, but don't bring her up to Beijing straightaway. Once you establish yourself, there'll be more room to negotiate."

It made sense. And remaining in Shenzhen might be in Lotus's best interest as well. Without her friends and her teaching, she would feel lonely and out of place in the capital. "One thing I really want to do is to publish my book on prostitution," Bing added.

Zhang finished the thought for him. "Well, working for the ministry that controls censorship, you'll likely get a pass."

Bing paused. "'Art is the daughter of freedom.' Who said that? Schiller?"

The other man replied with another burst of laughter.

"But seriously. How can I bring myself to say to Lotus, 'Look, I won't be able to bring you to Beijing'?"

"Say whatever. Realistically, you do need to figure things out first—finding a place to live, buying furniture, and all that."

"'One conversation with you is more beneficial than ten years' reading,'" Bing flattered his advisor. Bing had come to rely on the journalist; he seemed to have a solution for everything. In some ways, Zhang had replaced his university friend Yuejin. Bing always seemed to be drawn to assertive friends.

He put the phone down and his glasses back on. On the dressing table, a golden-capped bottle of lotion called Milk of Youth caught his attention. He picked it up and saw it was a face cream that promised to make one's skin white and young. He wasn't sure if Mei had always used the whitening cream or if this was new.

Bing inspected the room. It was a single woman's space, driven by order and tidiness. He was surprised to find their wedding photo hanging on the wall in a golden frame. He thought she had smashed it. In the photo, Bing, in a borrowed silk suit, was beaming. This photo was the only trace of a man in the room.

He rejoined Mei and Little Li at the table.

"Is everything all right?" Mei asked.

"Yes, fine. That was my journalist friend Zhang Jianguo."

"The one from the *Southern Window*?"

"Yes."

"You rub shoulders with famous people these days," Mei said. "The dishes are getting cold. Shall I ask Wu Ayi to heat them up?"

"No, thank you. The girl is sleeping."

"She is waiting to do the washing up. Poor thing, it takes her over an hour to cycle home from here."

"Let her go home. I'll wash up," Bing volunteered.

"Sure." Mei glided into the kitchen, carrying the now cold chicken soup. "Wu Ayi, you look tired. You go home now, okay?" Bing overheard Mei's words to the maid, her tone both gracious and condescending.

"Daddy." Little Li tapped his arm.

"Yes, Missy Lili?"

"My tonsils haven't bothered me for a long time," his daughter whispered. "Can you ask Mom to cancel the operation, please, Daddy?" she begged, grimacing.

When Mei had informed him that Little Li was scheduled to have her tonsil operation straight after his return from Sichuan, Bing secretly wondered if it was his ex-wife's little trick for delaying his return to Shenzhen, but he didn't dare to ask. "Your mother must have arranged it for a good reason. Be brave, Daddy will be there." He stroked her back. When he realized that he was stroking the monkey, he jerked his hand away.

"Daddy!" She stamped her feet. "I hardly ever ask for anything from you."

"Lili! I . . . " Bing's voice trailed off.

"No bargaining," Mei barked from the kitchen door. A minute later, she returned, carrying a steaming clay pot with the reheated soup and wearing a stern expression. "How many times have I had to take time off work to stay home with you? I can't afford it."

"Not recently," retorted the daughter.

"You are too young to know what's good for you. Come on now, have some soup. Cooked in Atlantic ginseng, full of goodies."

Bing was amused to notice that Mei had grown more like her mother, particular about the nutritious value of food.

"What can I get, then, from this operation being forced on me?" their daughter asked.

"Better health," her mother snapped.

"Tell me, good girl, what do you want? How about a digital camera?"

"No, I want a guitar."

"You've got one already," Mei pointed out.

"But I want an electric one." The girl huffed, puffing air up into her bangs. "Peach's mom has already promised her one for her birthday. If you get me one, we can start our band, called Little Girl Tigers. Do you know the Little Tigers band from Taiwan, Daddy? The boys are so cool."

"Yes, I think so. All right, I'll get you one. Now, have your soup."

Little Li picked up her bowl.

Mei wrinkled her nose. "Naughty girl. She knows you are a soft target. You are naughty, too, for indulging her like this," she complained, but there was no sharp edge in her scolding. "If she wants stars, will you go up to the sky to pick them for her?"

"I'd give it a try."

"I don't doubt it," Mei said.

CHAPTER 29

一叶蔽目，不见泰山

✠━━━━━━━━━━━━━━━━━━━━━━━━━━━━━━━━━━━✠

Can't See the Forest for the Trees

In the lingering sunlight, people in Miaocun were busy as usual. On the mud paths dotted with puddles and litter, several young boys were rolling a discarded rubber tire, running after it and laughing. Those who worked in the city returned, some on their bikes, others on noisy motorbikes. Several girls, all dressed up, were heading to the town center for their big night out.

Everyone was going somewhere, except her, Lotus thought bitterly as she staggered along the path and watched everything with detached interest. When she passed her house, she shivered. Disappointment, bitterness, and confusion all swirled inside her. She couldn't go home; seeking relief, she walked on and dragged herself uphill to the Rooster Crowing Temple. A little out of breath, she rested her head on the front door, its red paint peeling but its wood comfortingly warm. Then she walked into the temple, passed through the forecourt, and came to the main court. There, she sank down on the stone edge of the Giant Buddha

Hall, feeling exhausted, defeated, and utterly alone. She stared blankly at the black mold that ran down the white temple walls like giant tears.

What had just happened? she asked herself. Was she being punished for the sins she had committed as a *ji*? What would she do now?

Lotus leaned her heavy head on her knees and curled herself into a ball. The whole world had turned against her and she felt defenseless. She thought about her friends, Mimi, Xia, and Little Jade, but they couldn't help her—they could barely look after themselves.

She felt a tap on her shoulder. She looked up and saw, in the gathering dusk, a nun bending over her. "Sorry, girl, we are closing now. Come back tomorrow," she said in a pleasant soft voice.

Lotus rubbed her eyes and stared at the nun, a young woman with broad shoulders and a broad face, made larger by her shaved head. She wore a gray robe and a string of brown prayer beads on her right wrist. Lotus looked around and realized she was the only visitor left in the temple. The grounds were silent except for the sound of crickets.

The nun moved away, her robe swishing gently. Another nun was clearing away the melted wax on the metal spikes by the massive incense burner and a third was sweeping the yard. They all looked so peaceful, like the temple itself.

Lotus slowly stood up. Going back home, back to her life and to the world. What was the point?

She ran after the nun. "*Shifu.*" Lotus used the respectful term for a nun. "Please help me. I want to stay here."

"Who are you?" the nun asked, surprised by the request.

"I'm a migrant worker from Sichuan. I, I feel desperate," she stuttered. "I have nowhere to go."

The nun sized her up. "I'll have to ask the head nun. Come with me."

They walked through a side door into the temple's living quarters. The nun went into a room and soon returned, gesturing for Lotus to go in.

"How should I address her?" Lotus asked.

"Call her *shifu*. We are all the same."

Lotus inched into the room, which was permeated with the smell of incense. In the glow of a lamp, she could see a frail woman sitting cross-legged on a hassock on the floor by a small table. She was copying Buddhist sutras with a pen brush.

"Come here, my child, and sit down," the old nun said. She had a surprisingly sonorous voice for such a small woman.

Lotus sat down across the table, on another hassock, trimmed with yellow tassels. She guessed the nun to be in her fifties or sixties, perhaps older. Her hands were wrinkled like those of an old woman, yet her face was smooth and her eyes alive.

"Now, tell me, what's the matter?"

"Well, I . . . " Lotus couldn't summarize what was the matter with her. So she began to tell her story, how she had left her village in Sichuan, dragging her cousin along, only to see her die in a fire.

"What happened after that?" asked the head nun, her eyes brimming with kindness.

" 'A single slip may cause eternal sorrow.' *Ai!*" Lotus sighed. "I ended up working at a massage parlor."

"Massage? That doesn't sound so bad."

"Well, the parlor—" Lotus paused, thinking: I've already come to this pass. Why bother hiding my shame? "Actually, I was a *ji*, a prostitute."

"I see."

Encouraged by the old nun's sympathetic expression, she explained the circumstances of getting in and out of prostitution, her involvement with Photographer Bing and the barriers between them. All these years, the only thing that had kept her going was the idea of getting her brother a university education. However, having discovered her secret, her brother had refused to take her "dirty" money, and all her sacrifices had come to nothing.

The head nun nodded and said: "It's good of you to want to help your brother. What do you want for yourself?"

Lotus pondered this. "I want to live with dignity," she announced solemnly. She had learned the phrase from the waitress-turned-writer Ai Zhi. Lotus hadn't really understood its meaning at first. Having started teaching, she won not only respect from her students and her fellow villagers in Miaocun, but also respect for herself. She knew it must be the dignity that Ai Zhi had talked about. But now she didn't know how to maintain it because of her troubled relationship with the photographer. Bing's repeated delays indicated his lack of genuine commitment, and possibly his change of heart. Even if he was brave enough to marry her, such a move would most likely ruin his career. Could she do that to him? But equally, she wouldn't be content to be his secret mistress: she couldn't allow herself such a degrading existence. Yet, she couldn't really return to her village or even worse, to the factory life. She shared her thoughts with the nun.

"I feel trapped," Lotus concluded.

"So you want to run away from your troubles?" the nun asked.

Lotus cast down her eyes.

"Every so often, a young woman comes to our temple, declaring she wants to become a nun, because she's lost her boyfriend or her job. But our temple isn't a haven that can free you from your troubles. If you don't have the right reason for coming here, you'll be plagued by your problems in this place, just as you would if you lived outside the temple."

"Right now, I feel like my heart is as dead as ash."

"May I show you one character?" The nun picked up her brush, dipped it in an ink slab and wrote a large elegant character composed of a knife above a heart. "You know this word 'ren'? It means 'endure.' Learn from its wisdom. It will give your heart the strength to endure the knife."

Lotus stared at the top half of the character and winced.

"You've suffered, but suffering is simply a part of life. It is called *dukka* in the original Sanskrit, meaning 'unsatisfied.' To ease the suffering, one has to get rid of greed, hatred, and delusion."

Listening to the nun's words, Lotus had a sensation of looking at flowers through mist: all was vague but good. "Is there hope for someone like me? I feel such shame, *shifu*."

A smile blossomed on the nun's ageless face. "In the eyes of Buddha, there are no evil people, only people who don't yet have light in their hearts."

"I feel so confused. May I stay here for a while?"

"*Amitabha!* Mercy is our guiding principle. You are welcome to stay for a while in our guest room." She clasped her hands in front of her. "Huimin will show you the way."

Lotus's room was enclosed by whitewashed walls and sparsely furnished with a bed and a writing desk. Sleeping on the hard bamboo bed for the first time, she had a chilling white dream of her own funeral. Ba, Nai, and Shadan, their heads bowed, stood in front of her grave, next to Little Red's. The white flowers on the tombstone quivered in the wind. But she soon realized that the flowers were made from toilet paper. She woke up in the middle of the night and couldn't get back to sleep again.

Curling up there, Lotus mulled over the head nun's words about suffering and greed. Her thoughts wandered to an experience she had almost succeeded in erasing from her memory. She had told Bing and others a version of how she had gotten into the trade: a story of rape, with herself cast as the unwilling victim, but the truth was something much less palatable and something she couldn't bear to face.

A few weeks after Lotus had discovered Hua's profession, her initial sense of shock had faded. She had been trying to look for jobs outside the hair salon, visiting informal labor markets, reading job advertisements in newspapers, and even pursuing jobs advertised on papers stuck to electricity poles. To her great dismay, she realized that well-paid jobs were like exotic fruit in the supermarket: they did exist, alluringly, but were beyond her reach. Hua told her that companies sometimes hired pretty young girls as salespeople. To pass the interview, the girls would have to package themselves beautifully. Lotus decided to save money to buy a smart outfit.

Sensibly, she didn't quit her hair salon job before securing a new one, but her position there grew increasingly awkward. The other girls would often bring in goodies such as dried squid or biscuits to share around.

Unable to return the favor, Lotus declined to accept their food, and the girls felt she was putting on airs because she wasn't another *ji*. Lotus felt isolated, and her shortage of cash had never pained her as much as it had then. She was horrified by the idea of allowing herself to slip into the polluting pot of prostitution, like all the girls around her, but the thought invaded her mind persistently.

One night, Lotus returned home from her hair salon earlier than usual. Hua was readying herself to go out for dinner with a friendly client. She looked glamorous in her tight black dress and high heels.

"Come along for some good fun and good food," Hua said, in a jolly mood. "My friend will pay. You have to make the best of city life."

Lotus felt some unease with the idea of seeing Hua with a client, but Hua assured her that Lotus wouldn't have a thing to worry about—they could just enjoy the free fancy meal. Why not? So Lotus accepted. Hua lent her a floral dress. It was a little big but made wearable with a belt, and she helped Lotus apply some makeup. When Lotus slipped her feet into Hua's high-heeled sandals, she couldn't help but stick out her chest.

Hua let out one of her whistles. "Look at yourself."

Lotus looked at herself in the mirror and smiled.

They arrived at a restaurant inside an up-market hotel, where Hua's friend was staying. At the entrance, a tall young woman in a red cheong-sam greeted them with a bow and took them inside. Soft music was playing, the lighting was gentle, and every table was covered with white cloth and decorated with a candle and a single red rose in a tiny vase. Lotus had only seen such luxury and sophistication on TV.

They were taken to a corner table where a man of about forty, wearing a stylish woven hat, was sitting. He adjusted his red silk tie as he stood up and beamed, squinting his eyes behind his gold-rimmed glasses to have a better look at the girls. He grabbed Hua and kissed her on the lips. Hua introduced him as Mr. Li. He tipped his hat and bowed deeply. "Gorgeous!" he said to Lotus in a heavy accent. "A fairy lady has descended from heaven!"

"*Nali, nali*—not at all." Lotus muttered the standard polite reply, blushing.

Mr. Li then brought her hand to his lips.

Hua slapped at his hand. "You spare my friend. She is a virgin." Turning to Lotus, she said: "Don't mind him. He's a fake foreign devil."

"A Chinese gentleman." Mr. Li bowed again. He arranged the girls to sit on either side of him.

He ordered fresh-squeezed papaya juice and beer and many dishes: roast duck, drunken prawns, and seafood that she couldn't name. Lotus ate with gusto. Persuaded by both of her companions, she also tried the beer, which turned her face red and made her heart beat fast and her head dizzy. She hadn't felt so good for a long time.

Mr. Li kept picking dishes for both girls. The older girl was all over him, pretending to be displeased one minute and giggling like a silly girl the next. Lotus noticed that when Hua smiled, her nose spread across her face and made it flatter than usual.

Lotus didn't remember what they talked about, except that they laughed a lot. I am having a really good time, she told herself.

Amid their silly laughter, Mr. Li received a phone call. Lotus could make out a man's husky voice, sounding as if he was suffering from a heavy cold. The two men spoke very fast in their dialect, which Lotus couldn't understand. After the call, Mr. Li whispered to Hua, and her friend disagreed and slapped his hand several times to register her displeasure.

"What are you squabbling about?" Lotus asked.

Mr. Li fixed his eyes on her. "My friend just called. He says he is willing to pay five thousand yuan to sleep with a virgin."

"Five thousand!" Lotus's voice came out in a croak. "*Wasai!* That's a lot of money!"

"Sure! My friend is also staying at this very hotel. Room twelve twenty," the man said, pointing a finger toward the ceiling.

"Mr. Li!" Hua barked. "Are you asking my friend to sleep with your friend?"

"Why not?"

Lotus smiled and shook her head. "But I am not a *ji*."

Hua and Mr. Li started to argue. Lotus didn't quite register what they were bickering about. A voice rang in her head: Why not? Five thousand! With a sum like that, she could rent a place of her own and start an independent life, free of the humiliation of living on Hua's charity. And she could get herself a smart dress, which might lead to a good job. She could then make the most out of her life in the city. Lotus stood up, a little unsteadily. "I'll go," she heard herself saying in an unfamiliar voice.

"Have you taken some medicine that messed up your head?" Hua pressed Lotus down onto her seat.

"Let her decide. She's not a child," said Mr. Li.

"I am not a child," Lotus parroted. "I am not a virgin, either. Almost a virgin." She pulled her facial muscles into a smile.

"Haha!" Mr. Li chuckled, but stopped abruptly. "I'll have to ask." He went outside to call his friend.

Hua grabbed Lotus's shoulders. "Have you really done it?"

Lotus grunted an acknowledgment as she chewed a big prawn.

"Think, Chouchou. I don't want you to hate me one day for this."

"Just this one time. I'm fed up with being poor, being your maid and being bossed around by you!" Fueled by the alcohol, Lotus let the unruly words tumble out of her mouth. "I've had enough! I want to rent my own place. You can't wait to get rid of me, can you, Hua?"

The older girl let out a shriek of a whistle. "Who took you on when you were a homeless dog?"

Lotus's tears gushed out. "Sorry, Sister Hua. I hate myself for being so pathetic!" She took another sip of beer.

Just then, Mr. Li returned. "Look, gorgeous, my friend still wants you but will pay only half."

"Three thousand, at least!" Hua countered.

"Okay-la. I'll chip in the five hundred. I can't afford to offend that rich bastard," said Mr. Li, loosening his tie. Then he added, a crooked smile on his lips: "He does treat women well. Don't worry. We'll take you upstairs."

Noticing Lotus was still hesitating, he poured more beer into her glass. "Drink more. Then nothing matters."

Lotus wiped away her tears, picked up the glass and drained it. "Fine." With a struggle, she got on her feet.

Both Mr. Li and Hua rose and held Lotus by the arms and walked her toward the door.

The world felt surreal, Lotus thought as she stepped out of the restaurant and then into the lift. She wasn't sure who she was or what she was doing. In her hazy world, only one thing was clear: three thousand yuan. I am not afraid, she murmured to herself. Not afraid at all.

Lotus had been too drunk to have a clear recollection of that night spent with the husky-voiced man. One thing that stuck out in her memory was that he took a long time studying her private part, poking at it and tasting it. By then she was beyond caring.

She spent most of the following day in bed, nursing a splitting headache. After she got up in the evening, she headed straight to Park'n'Shop and bought ten mangosteens, the most expensive fruit on display. It looked like a plum, but with a hard shell and a green hat. Back at home, she slowly went through the fruit, savoring the heavenly taste of the white, juicy fragments inside.

Lotus bought a smart summer suit and a white silk shirt, but she failed to get a sales job. Some companies required a senior middle school certificate, and others only wanted city girls with local residence permits.

At her hair salon, she began to pick up clients, just like the rest of the girls. She consoled herself with an old saying: "A cracked jar doesn't mind being smashed again."

The temple's bamboo bed protested as Lotus made an abrupt turn in it. How could you throw away your honor and dignity, just like that? she asked herself. She felt bad for lying to others, and to herself, about what had led her to begin that life.

Lotus floated through the next few days. As time went by, she tried to adjust to the rhythm of daily life at the temple. The day began at four a.m., with the sound of a wooden hammer hitting a board—the first wake-up call. She was so used to going to bed late and getting up late; it was a struggle to tear herself away from her bed so early. By four thirty a.m., a dozen nuns would gather in the main hall, dressed in brown *kasaya,* a patchwork vestment worn over their usual robes. Although it was not required of her, Lotus attended the dawn prayers because she found the ritual soothing. Candles flickered in the dark, and the hall was infused with incense. The nuns stood in rows on either side of the large statue of Shakyamuni, facing each other, hands joined in front of them. They were as still as statues themselves throughout the hour-long session. They chanted in unison, their voices powerful in the quiet of the dawn.

At six, a breakfast of porridge and pickles was served. Then it was time for studying and doing chores. All twelve nuns, including the head nun, took part in the day-to-day running of the temple: cooking, sweeping the yard, cleaning up, and receiving visitors.

Lotus wore a gray cotton robe and matching trousers that Huimin had lent to her. She soon felt comfortable in this women-only environment. They moved about their daily routines quietly and efficiently.

In the early hours when she first rose, Lotus often felt waves of nausea, followed by cravings for food. A few times, she kept some of the rice from supper the night before and ate it in the morning before joining the others for chanting while the rest of the world was still asleep. She wasn't ready to reveal her pregnancy yet.

Lotus tried to pray and meditate with the nuns, but her mind often wandered. What had become of Shadan? Had he gone back home or started a job at some construction site? Had she forgotten to lock the door, in her confusion? What about her students? What had happened to Bing? In her vulnerable moments, she was more inclined to believe that he had changed his mind.

She missed her family a thousand miles away. She thought about her Ba's watery eyes and could almost feel the caress of her grandma's gnarled hands on her face. But then she remembered her brother's face, full of contempt.

Lotus's room was bright, with a large window that opened onto a courtyard. In the center of the yard, daisies, azaleas, and roses still bloomed in the flower bed. The peaceful setting wrapped up her wounds like a layer of soft gauze.

Nighttime was harder. Sleeping fitfully on the low bamboo bed, Lotus often dreamed of when she was a little girl and her mother carried her on her back, singing "Little Swallow" and picking mulberries. She remembered her mother's words on her deathbed. "My good girl, take good care of your brother." But without a university education, he would be like another piece of duckweed, floating in the city but never becoming part of it. She had let her mother down. Reviewing her life, she saw failure everywhere.

Each day, Lotus studied the sutras and the book on Buddhism Huimin had loaned her. She learned about the Five Precepts of Avoiding: killing, stealing, engaging in improper sexual acts, lying, and drinking alcohol. How could she even call herself a Buddhist? She was surprised to learn that even Buddha was subject to suffering.

Huimin was always willing to help. "We may be humans, but we're the same as trees that grow in the ground and the rain that falls from the sky. We all have a purpose," Huimin explained.

As one of the few young nuns in the temple, Huimin took special care of Lotus. She came to visit daily, bringing her own cup of bitter tea, which she believed had a cleansing effect. She would sit, cross-legged, on the bamboo bed, as still as a Buddha statue. Lotus found her wise and nonjudgmental, so she readily confided in the nun.

One day, Huimin talked about her previous life. Lotus was amused to learn that Huimin, armed with a university degree, had been a sales manager at a health product company in Shenzhen. But the fatter her purse grew, the emptier her heart felt, she said. She longed for something spiritual. Once when she visited a temple, she bought a book about Buddhism and she was fascinated. To the surprise and displeasure of her parents, she left her job to study Buddhist philosophy before deciding to take vows as a nun. Since becoming a nun, she felt fulfilled.

"Everyone can benefit from Buddha's teaching," Huimin declared. "But my path isn't for everyone." She steadied her gaze at Lotus and said:

"My sister, in your confused state of mind, it may not be a bad idea for you to spend some quiet time here, just to think about who you are and what you want from life."

"Who I am?" Lotus chewed on the phrase. She hadn't really thought about the issue before. What bothered her more was the question of how she could clear away her sins. The young nun told her that, first of all, she must confront and confess all her wrongdoings, then promise never repeat them. "But don't worry," Huimin assured her. She picked up her teacup. "Imagine. If you put a spoonful of salt in this cup, the water tastes very salty. If you put the same salt in a jar, the water is less salty. If you put it in a river, you can't even taste the salt. Your sins are like the salt and your heart the container. In the future, if you perform good deeds and accumulate good karma, the effect of your sins will be diminished."

Lotus felt as if Huimin had lifted a stone that had weighed on her heart for a long time.

"How about fate?" Lotus asked. "Can I determine my own fate, or is it determined by Buddha or some god?"

"You and you alone can determine your fate," the nun said, holding Lotus's hand with her big-boned ones. "You can get rid of suffering, and achieve happiness through your own effort."

Lotus nodded, feeling encouraged, even though she hadn't totally absorbed the nun's words. She stared at Huimin as if seeing her for the first time. The nun's head was rather large but in proportion with her large body. She moved about with an elegance Lotus wouldn't have expected of her. Her gentle crescent-moon-shaped eyes gleamed with wisdom. And she had an aura of contentment. The nun was in fact beautiful, Lotus thought with admiration and a touch of envy.

More than three weeks had passed since Lotus first arrived at the temple. One morning, she was picking green bell peppers in a vegetable garden on a slope beside the monastery. In Mulberry Gully, thin red chili peppers, deliciously spicy, dotted the fields this time of the year. The bell peppers here were much fatter and sweeter. She didn't mind the vegetarian dishes in the temple but found them, free of garlic, scallion, and chili, too bland. She hungered for some spicy food, though she knew it wouldn't be good for the baby. Oh, what would Shadan think when he learned about his unmarried sister's pregnancy?

"Come down, Lotus!" Suddenly Lotus heard Huimin's excited voice. She raised her head and saw the nun dashing out through a side door. "Your brother is here to see you."

"Shadan!" Lotus jumped up so fast she felt dizzy and had to steady herself. She knew that her brother might try to look for her. But now that he was here, she was at a loss as to what to do. Her heart was still aching from the bitter words he had shot at her.

The young nun ran up to the slope, as if her large body was made of feathers.

"Tell my brother I don't want to see him," Lotus said finally, rooted to the spot.

"Are you sure?"

Lotus didn't reply but squatted down and resumed working. Her hands were trembling.

Half an hour later, Huimin returned, her large hand clutching a piece of folded-up paper. "Your brother asked me to give you this letter."

After Huimin left, Lotus sat down on the ridge between two fields. After she was calm enough, she opened the letter. In it, Shadan's handwriting was more slanted than ever, as if blown by a strong wind.

Sister Chouchou,

Good news, my sister, I've been accepted by Sichuan University!

"He's made it, Huimin Shifu!"

But Huimin had gone out of earshot. Nevertheless Lotus shouted with joy: she had dreamed of this moment for so long. "My brother is going to university! Sichuan University!"

Lotus sat back down on the ridge and continued reading.

But first of all, I must apologize, my sister. I am sorry, so very sorry for the shameful way I've treated you. On the day I confronted you, my mind exploded. I just had to run away. By the time I returned, I'd calmed down but you had disappeared. Big Head was there, guarding the house. "If anything bad happens to Teacher Lotus, I'll kill you," he said.

Throughout the night, we looked for you everywhere. The next day, more of your friends joined in the search, asking around about you and reporting to every police station.

In the past weeks, your friends and your students (they all adore you) and their parents have been so kind to me, bringing me food and such. I have to say that I didn't feel comfortable in dealing with the girls, especially in the beginning. In any case, I came to see how I've been unfair to you.

Last week, having heard no news from the police, we put up posters in Miaocun with a picture and description of you. Last night, an old woman hobbled over, saying she thought she saw you at Rooster Crowing Temple.

This morning, I came up here as soon as the temple opened, but you didn't want to see me. I don't blame you. Please come back, dear sister. I'll kneel in front of you to beg for your forgiveness. I need you and your friends need you.

Now, my university. I've never fully realized how much it meant to you until I spoke to your friends. I called up Sichuan University and discovered that they've accepted me!

I'll go to Chengdu to register at the university as soon as possible. But I want to see you first.

Your only brother, Shadan

P.S. We've tried to get in touch with the photographer, but unfortunately, no one seems to know his cell number. If you tell me, I'll inform him what has happened.

Lotus buried her head in her arms and cried quietly for a long while. For what, she wasn't entirely sure.

In the afternoon, when Huimin came to visit, Lotus showed the letter to the nun.

Having read the letter, the nun smiled and asked: "Are you going to celebrate with your brother?"

"I am not sure, Huimin Shifu."

"Are you surprised by his reaction to learning about your past?"

The simple question somehow took Lotus by surprise. "Not exactly."

"Well, I would be more worried if he had no emotional reaction," the nun said in her gentle voice.

"I understand that. But I've pinned all my hopes on him. When he rejected me, I felt the heavens had collapsed."

"I see." Huimin listened attentively. "Are you still angry with your brother?"

"I guess so."

Huimin went silent for a moment. "On the side of the main hall are the words: 'The sea of bitterness has no bounds; repent, and the shore is at hand.'"

Lotus had seen the words but never thought about their meaning.

"It's never too late to mend one's ways, my sister." The nun spoke in her usual calm fashion. "Mercy is the only way to conquer anger, Buddha says. You can't just avoid your brother. You have to face him, look into his eyes and see if he means what he says."

"Then what?"

"Then show him forgiveness and compassion. But first of all, show forgiveness and compassion to yourself and see your own worth."

Lotus spent the evening kowtowing in front of the Buddha statue, praying for the strength to forgive and to endure suffering in life. She prayed for a long time, until a single, star-shattering drumbeat sounded. The signal for the end of the day.

CHAPTER 30

前事不忘，后事之师

Past Experience, If Not Forgotten,

Is a Guide for the Future

Patients and their families crammed into every corner of Peking Union Medical College Hospital and the queues snaked long and winding to the small service window. Little Li's scheduled operation had been delayed for a week, as Mei's doctor friend had gone on a trip and Mei insisted on waiting for her. Standing in line to register, Bing looked around and thought about the similar procedures he had endured when he had come here with his then-expecting wife.

"Are you all right, Miss Lili?" he asked his daughter.

"No, I'm not!" the girl replied with a grimace. But she was apparently delighted with this rare occasion of having both parents around. She leaned on Bing's arm one moment and then rested her head on her mother's shoulder the next.

"I can't believe that it was twelve years ago when you were born here," Mei mused, patting her daughter's cheek. "Look at you, almost a teenager!"

Little Li shrugged her shoulders.

"Because of you, I know this hospital better than the back of my hand," Bing said with a smile. When he had visited his ex-wife's house, he worried that Mei might try to persuade him to stay the night. To his relief, she didn't. He had since visited again and there hadn't really been any awkwardness between them. Maybe it wouldn't be as hard to deal with her as he had anticipated. And together they could still provide a good family for their daughter.

After they registered, Mei's doctor friend soon received them and Little Li was prepped for the operation. Outside the operating room, both parents watched and waved as their daughter, covered by a green hospital sheet, was wheeled in for surgery.

"She'll be all right," Mei said. "You know, all those years ago, when I was wheeled in, I was nervous."

"This is a small deal compared to a cesarean section," Bing reminisced. "I was nervous, too."

"Were you?" she said, turning toward him. "Did you leave the hospital and go to the square so that you wouldn't be so nervous?"

"Well, partly," Bing replied, suddenly feeling defensive. "But I did return before Lili was delivered, didn't I? I wouldn't have missed that for anything in the world."

Mei's thin lips pressed together as if to stem a flow of angry words. "Well, from what I can recall, the baby wasn't enough to keep you in the hospital, was she?"

There was an uncomfortable pause. "Sorry, Mei." Bing's hand went into his pocket. "I'm going out for a cigarette."

He walked toward the inpatient section in the back of the hospital and sat on the bench where he had spent many sleepless hours twelve years ago. The sun was shining without the harsh bite of the summer heat, and the green-glazed tile wall of the main building shimmered. Looking at the familiar surroundings, he lit a cigarette and took a puff. In the swirl of smoke, he immersed himself in memories of the events that had unfolded here.

———

On the twenty-eighth of May in 1989, having watched enough protests in the Beijing streets as mere onlookers, Bing and his best friend, Yue-jin, had decided to organize a demonstration of their own among workers from their soap factory, to voice their support for the democracy movement. Just before he set off, Mei called to say that she had checked herself into Peking Union Medical College Hospital, as she thought she was going into labor. Bing was surprised: the baby wasn't due for another two weeks. *Tamade,* what bad timing! thought Bing as he hastily left the factory. When he arrived at the maternity ward, he found Mei lying placidly in bed thumbing through a baby magazine. Realizing that his wife had not yet started her labor, he pleaded to be allowed to go to the square to join with his protesting colleagues, and he promised to return in a few hours. The movement was reaching a critical point. Bing longed to be part of it. He had promised his friends that he would document this historical movement with his camera. But Mei would have none of that. "Be sensible, Bing!" she said adamantly. "Stay away from the demonstration! Protesting against a powerful government? It's like 'striking an egg against a rock.' You could end up in jail! I need my husband and my child needs a father."

Three days on, there was still no sign of the baby. He became convinced that Mei's early check-in to the hospital was her way of pulling him away from the demonstration.

Bing took meticulous care of his wife, who was increasingly uncomfortable with the large baby inside her. Every few minutes, she would order her husband to prop her up this way or that, or help her visit the toilet. He struggled to please Mei, all the while harboring a growing resentment.

Luckily, Tiananmen Square was only a fifteen-minute walk away. Whenever Mei took her long nap in the afternoon or after she retired early to bed, Bing would sneak out and race to the square, his camera in hand. He needed to be there, to feel the power of the people and the pulse of the nation.

Whenever Mei found out where he had been, she would get angry at him. She ordered him to stay clear of the square.

Running back and forth between the hospital and the square, Bing felt exhausted, torn and guilty.

On June 2, following the doctor's suggestion, Mei gave birth to a girl through a cesarean section, as the baby was too large for a natural birth. Their daughter's arrival greatly reduced the unbearable tension between the couple.

In the early hours of the morning of June 4, Bing was dozing on a chair by his wife's bed when he was awakened by noises from the street. His wife was sleeping soundly and their baby girl was in the nursery with the other newborns. He looked out of the window and saw people running. The rumor of a military crackdown had been circulating for days. Sensing something was wrong, he dashed out of the hospital and raced toward Tiananmen Square, taking the back streets. Before long he heard the gunshots—at first he wasn't sure if they were real. Down a narrow *hutong,* he bumped into a crowd running in the opposite direction. The dimness of the dawn light couldn't hide the panic on their faces. He pressed on against the crush of people until he came to an opening, where he saw tanks charging through the square like mad bulls. He stood motionless as he tried to understand what was happening. The government had opened fire on the protesters! Shooting its own people! He spun around and ran back to the hospital without pausing once. He was breathless when he reached the hospital. He first went to Mei's ward and hugged his sleeping wife. All the petty resentment and conflicted emotions of the last few days had vanished. He was alive. He had a family. Mei was startled. Before she could ask him a question, he had run toward the nursery. He burst into it, demanding to pick up his daughter. He needed to hold the baby in his arms. When a nurse stopped him, he dissolved into tears.

As the day broke, the hospital became pandemonium as people started to bring in the injured and the dead. Bing tried to help, but there wasn't much he could do. He slumped on the bench behind the inpatient ward and sobbed uncontrollably, confused and helpless. So many dreams had been crushed and so many lives lost. Most of all, he feared for his daughter and the kind of country she would grow up in.

A scorching pain on his finger snapped Bing back to reality. He looked down and saw that his cigarette had burned to the end. He dropped the butt to the ground.

Back in 1989, as a patriotic and idealistic youth, Bing had hoped to play a role in breaking the shackles of the authoritarian regime and making China a more democratic and fair society. Nothing could illustrate the point better than his co-organizing of the factory's demonstration. For someone who was naturally inclined to observe rather than take action, it hadn't been easy for him to go that far. He had the bitter taste of regret whenever he thought of how he had not been able to participate fully in the demonstration; he knew he would never have another chance, because there wouldn't be another 1989. China's intellectuals and elites, who had always played the lead roles in mass movements, were now too comfortable to rock the boat. His old classmate Yuejin had become a high-flying official, and several of their friends had become fat bosses who were only interested in power, money, and women.

Nowadays people were enjoying greater business opportunities and expanded personal freedoms, or more precisely, an expanded cage. No one took an interest in politics anymore. And no one talked about Tiananmen and 1989, even privately, as if the whole nation had suffered from collective amnesia.

While in Beijing recently, the old friends had enjoyed a lengthy dinner at Yuejin's private club by Houhai Lake. When Bing mentioned that the movement in 1989 had inspired his passion for photography, his classmate sighed and shook his head. "Nineteen eighty-nine!" He took a big sip of Bordeaux wine. "For me, it was a naïve, hot-blooded young man's impulsive action."

"For me, that was one of the saddest moments in my life," Bing said.

"Of course, it was terribly tragic," Yuejin commented, and then burped. He waved a finger in the air. "Don't get me wrong. I didn't approve of the use of violence. But looking back, I think the government was right in taking control of the situation. China's just too big, and most of its population is poor. It wasn't ready for democracy back then—or even now, for that matter. Our country's priority is economic development, which requires a stable social environment."

Bing sipped his beer and smiled politely. He didn't agree with his classmate, but didn't wish to confront Yuejin, as he feared that a heated argument would ruin the reunion of two old friends. "You sound like a government official!"

"I am!" Yuejin said, patting his "general's belly," which had emerged in recent years. "Believe it or not, I am still patriotic. I want what's best for our country and for myself." After another sip of wine, he added: "Under the current political environment, we have to focus on things that can produce results. Right, photographer?"

Bing nodded, still smiling. Privately he told himself that one could make a difference, even within the authoritarian system. If he indeed took up with *Photography* magazine, he would try his best to make readers aware of injustices in Chinese society, to highlight the plight of migrant workers, prostitutes, and other underprivileged groups.

As a practical matter, the job was the best way to move forward in his career and to really become *chuxi*. Bing would have a stable income, plus extra income from freelance assignments. He was determined to contribute to his daughter's education in the United States. *Photography* now beckoned him. He would have to give up his freewheeling lifestyle and even play along with the Party for a while, and he might have to compromise his morality to some extent, as many working in the media in China had to. Yet there was surely space for him to voice the concerns of ordinary people and express himself artistically.

Would Lotus support his decision? She probably would, Bing thought. It was in her own interest should he take a proper job with a steady income, although she might have some reservations. In that case, he would compensate her by offering financial help to her family. Despite all of her shortcomings, Lotus was a good-natured girl.

Bing wished that his daughter could be as good-natured. He knew that the girl, already a little snob, wouldn't be too fond of Lotus due to her rural background and her lack of education. But so what? They didn't have to share a roof.

He wondered if Little Li's operation was finished yet. He checked his watch, then headed back toward the operating room.

Once she awoke from the general anesthetic, Little Li had the luxury of lying comfortably in a hospital bed; most patients had to go home after such a small surgery. But despite this special treatment, the girl became increasingly demanding as she grew less drowsy. A nurse told the parents that the best thing was to give her some water and perhaps some ice cream.

Bing rushed out and returned with a carton of Häagen-Dazs. After just one spoonful, however, Little Li complained the ice cream was too cold for her throat and shoved away her father's hand, sending the metal spoon flying. The two other female patients and their families all turned their heads but said nothing. He smiled at them apologetically and picked up the spoon.

Later in the evening, Mei went home and Bing stayed at the hospital with their daughter. After a good nap in the afternoon, Little Li was in a better mood, if slightly bored. He fished out a copy of *Harry Potter and the Sorcerer's Stone*, recently published in Chinese. At first the girl plugged her ears. Witches? What kind of silly story was this? But he kept reading, adopting his CCTV broadcaster's deep voice, and the girl was soon drawn into the magic of the tale. Harry Potter reminded Bing of the Monkey King from *Journey to the West*. The magic monkey could jump 108,000 *li* in one somersault, and wielding a golden stick, like Harry's magic wand, he could transform himself into a white-boned demon or an insect.

Between chapters, when Bing took a break to sip his tea, his thoughts would turn to Lotus, remembering how she was captivated by his reading of *The Portrait of a Lady*. How was she? Zhang Jianguo would find out soon.

He read on until his voice was too hoarse to continue. "I'll read more tomorrow, all right?"

"Five more minutes, Daddy?"

Bing read for another ten minutes. "Is your throat still hurting?"

"Not much, only when I swallow. Daddy?"

"Yes, Miss Lili?"

"Why did you suddenly stop playing with me?" Tears welled in her eyes.

Bing wiped her tears with a tissue and stroked her nose. "When you were born, a nurse handed you to me. You were wrapped up in a cloth like a tiny bundle, only your little face exposed. You looked utterly sweet and beautiful. I knew I would love you forever." His voice cracked.

"But why haven't you come to see me?"

He heaved a deep sigh. "The court gave custody rights to your mother. I couldn't just come to see you whenever I wanted to, Lili. I missed you terribly. And I did write to you and send you presents, didn't I?"

The girl went quiet for a while. "Mama and Grandma said they had to protect me from . . ." She paused to look for the right word. "From bad influences."

Bing held her hand. "Listen, Hu Li, Daddy did spend lots of time with some poor migrant girls in Shenzhen. They are forced to do things they don't like to do."

"Do you still see them?"

"I do."

Little Li rolled her eyes—this time, out of confusion. "But why does Mama let you see me now?"

Bing pulled up her blanket and started to tuck her in. "It's time to rest, Lili. You've talked far too much for someone who's just had an operation."

The girl motioned for Bing to come closer. "Bring your ears to me, Daddy. I'll tell you a secret."

Bing bent down. Little Li's hands formed a protective ring. Her speech blew air in his ear.

"Mama cried one night. I woke up in the middle of the night and heard noises, like crying. So I got up and opened my door a little bit. She was crying on the sofa."

Bing sat down. His ex-wife, with a will stronger than the Great Wall, cried to herself? "When was this?"

"Shuuush, quiet." She put a finger on her lips. "A few months ago. I've never seen her cry before. Did you quarrel with her?"

"No. Maybe she was upset by something at work."

The girl pulled Bing over toward her. "I told you a secret. Come on, Daddy, tell me yours." She whispered into his ear. "Do you have a new girlfriend?"

Bing considered for a second. "There is a nice lady I like very much."

Little Li pushed him away. "I'm going to be Cinderella with an evil stepmother!" She blinked rapidly, trying to squeeze out some tears.

"Don't be silly, Little Li. She is a loving person. We are not married yet, anyway."

"Not yet? Are you going to?"

"Maybe," Bing said vaguely. A fat tear rolled down the girl's face.

"I'm not sure," he added.

"Is she one of your, your *ji*?" Little Li clutched Bing's arm, her eyes glaring at him.

Bing stood up. *Ji?* Where did the young girl learn that word?

"No," he replied. He looked around the room, noticing that the older patient in the room was already sleeping and the other was listening to music on her Walkman.

Bing kissed his daughter on her forehead. "It's getting late. Try to get some sleep, my good girl."

He walked out of the room and came to the empty corridor. He took off his glasses and rested his head against the white wall, as if too tired to carry its weight.

He was just about to light a cigarette when his cell phone began to vibrate. Zhang Jianguo's name flashed up.

"*Wei*, any news about Lotus?" Bing's voice echoed in the corridor. He had written another letter to Lotus, urging her to call, but he still hadn't heard from her. When he had first learned that Little Li's operation would be delayed, he had briefly entertained the idea of flying back to Shenzhen first. But Mei said he ought to spend some quality time with his daughter. So Bing complied. He worried about Lotus, but part of him tried to wave off overblown fears that she was somehow in trouble. And part of him felt resigned to the possibility that her silence meant she had decided to run off with Mr. Gao.

"Bad news, I'm afraid," Zhang said.

Bing waited, holding tight to his cell phone.

"You'd better come back, my brother. Lotus has gone missing!"

CHAPTER 31

车到山前必有路

The Cart Will Find Its Way Around the Hill When It Gets There

On the morning after receiving Shadan's letter, Lotus was looking out of her open window onto a sun-speckled yard when she spotted Huimin approaching.

"You have quite a few visitors!" the nun announced.

"Who?" Lotus asked as she walked over to the door.

"You'll see," Huimin replied, gesturing Lotus to follow.

Lotus took a deep breath and walked with Huimin toward the temple entrance. Outside the gate, she saw Mimi, Little Jade, Xia with her son, Baobao, and Big Head with his two siblings, all gathered in the shade of a kapok tree. Standing a short distance away was her brother, Shadan.

"Lotus!" they called out upon seeing her.

She paused on the stone step, one hand holding on to the wooden gate, squinting in the bright morning sunlight. "What are you doing here?" she asked after a long while.

Xia approached, her bony hips swinging. "We came to tell you off," she said, without a trace of a smile. She brought Lotus to the shade. "It was wrong of you to disappear like a plume of smoke. You left behind your students and you let us worry to death about you. What are you doing here, anyway?"

Mimi elbowed Xia. "Shut your big mouth, Xia! How are we going to get her to come back with us if you're being nasty?"

Shadan looked on nervously, shifting his weight from leg to leg.

"Sister Xia, I came here to think about things."

"Thinking about what?" Mimi grabbed Lotus by the arm. "It must be so boring to live in a monastery, with just a few vegetables to eat, Sister Lotus. Come home. Can't you think about things at home?"

Lotus felt a light tug at her robe. She looked down and saw Niuniu trying to get closer through a forest of legs. "Niuniu!" She bent down to fuss with the toddler's pigtails.

"Sister Lotus, I have a gift for you!" Niuniu said, waving a clenched fist.

"What is it?"

Niuniu opened her palm to reveal a half-melted sweet in a dirty wrapper.

"Thank you, Niuniu!" Lotus picked up the little girl and kissed her drum belly. Niuniu giggled with delight.

"Will you come to teach us again, Teacher Lotus?" asked Big Head.

Lotus smiled at her favorite student without replying.

Shadan came up to her and said: "Sister, I came here to beg for your forgiveness and for your return. I wasn't sure whether you'd listen to me, so I brought your friends along."

Lotus fixed her gaze on her brother. In his bright, clear eyes, she thought she saw what she had been looking for. She then took time to look at each of her friends. She realized that she wasn't alone—she hadn't been alone for a long time. And she had been missing them and missing teaching.

But leave the temple just like that? Lotus stood there, unsure what to do.

"Excuse us, just for a few minutes," Huimin said, taking Lotus inside the temple. "Go with them. They need you." She reassuringly held Lotus's shoulder. "Besides, this isn't the true place for you."

"My brother?" Lotus bit her lip. "I am still not entirely sure how to deal with him, after all that has happened."

"Just go on loving him like you've always done. Go back."

"Go back? To do what?"

"To do what you love doing."

"But if Bing . . . " Lotus faltered. "I'm not sure what will become of us and if I'll be able to support myself."

"Buddha will give you the strength you need," Huimin said in her soft, firm voice. "You told me that you felt unworthy. Can't you see your worth from your friends?"

Lotus nodded.

The nun took off the string of beads from her wrist. "Sister, here's my farewell gift for you, made from bodhi seeds."

Lotus took it, as if holding something holy, and bowed deeply toward the nun. She put the string of seeds on her wrist. "How can I ever repay you, Huimin Shifu?"

"Thank Buddha. I am only glad to be of some help to you. It's good for my karma, too," Huimin said, her broad face radiant with a smile. "Now, my sister, you can do things for others, but you must live your life for yourself and believe in yourself."

While the nun went out to tell her friends to wait, Lotus returned to the temple to change out of Huimin's robe and to put on her own cotton dress. She looked around one last time at the sparsely furnished room, her sanctuary for the past few weeks. Being on one's own wasn't as terrifying as she had thought. Then she closed the door gently behind her and went to the head nun's place to say goodbye. The old woman bowed slightly. "May you find your own path and may Buddha stay in your heart."

Her sonorous voice injected Lotus's heart with strength. She marched toward the gate of the temple. A new life was waiting for her.

———

The sun was beaming. Cheered by its glory, Lotus and her friends headed downhill along a shady path. As the leaves danced in the breeze, shadows played hide-and-seek on the ground.

Carrying Niuniu on his back, Shadan ran ahead with the vigor of a kung fu master. Lotus walked among her friends and listened to their updates, taking in the scenery along the way.

Soon they arrived in Miaocun. The pleasant mountain path gave way to a dirt road that wound around the crumbling traditional houses and new white-tiled ones. Everything looked familiar yet somehow more vivid. Lotus used to dislike this place. Now it felt like home.

Big Head's mother was waiting for her by Bing's house, fanning herself with a wide-brimmed bamboo hat.

"Teacher Lotus, I just knew you'd come back," she said. Her face, open and flat like a Ping-Pong paddle, had no hint of her usual fury.

"Why?"

"Why?" she roared with her gruff voice. "I know you can't say no to my children, because you have a heart as soft as bean curd. Lotus, take a rest. Then, come over for lunch at our house, all of you," she said, waving her hat.

"How kind of you. Thank you." Lotus bowed, clasping her hands in front of her.

Shadan opened the door and Lotus was almost carried inside by her friends.

Xia placed her on the desk chair. "You sit. I'll boil some water and make you a nice cup of tea."

The familiar smell of the room comforted Lotus. Every piece of furniture looked dear to her, and the smiling faces of her friends glowed like medals. At length, she got up and announced that she was going to wash up before lunch.

The Beautiful and Clean Bathing Center in the village square was divided into two sections: showers downstairs, for the many Miaocun residents who had no washing facilities at home; and a bath upstairs, where one could indulge in a bath in a private room. Lotus decided to treat herself to an herbal bath.

Soaking in a wooden bathtub, she rubbed her body with a washcloth. Ever since that night with the husky-voiced man, she had hated her body. But the baby inside her had purified her. Some amazing changes were taking place. Her breasts had swelled. She cupped them and smiled to herself. They were growing into Mimi's *boba*, a pair of freshly steamed buns. The skin there had become transparent; she could see thin blue veins. Her nipples had grown larger and the color had darkened. She soaped her stomach, which was starting to expand. A new life— the combined blood and flesh of Bing and herself—was growing inside her. She rested her hands there and felt connected with that little being.

How would Bing react when he heard the news about the baby? Lotus wondered. Now in a positive frame of mind, she was less worried about whether Bing had changed his heart. Instead, she had started to question whether the relationship was a healthy one and whether she could ever become an equal partner in it. She used to be terrified by its possible failure. Now she knew she had the strength to live on her own, if she had to.

Everything would be fine, Lotus told herself, with Buddha in her heart. Her prayers must have been heard. Her brother was going to university! When was the registration date? If necessary, he could fly to Chengdu. She had some extra savings hidden in a sanitary bag.

So many things to do. She got out of the bath, dried herself off, and put on a white dress that she reserved for special occasions.

As she passed the village square, Lotus was surprised to find her brother sound asleep under the banyan tree. She went over and gently tapped his shoulder.

Startled, Shadan opened his bloodshot eyes; then he cracked a smile. "Chouchou." He sat up. The square was empty. Everyone had gone home for lunch. He pointed at the mah-jongg players' stone table. "Sit with me for a bit, Sister," he said.

"*Yaodei.*" Lotus placed her net bag on the table and started brushing her hair.

"You look different."

"Do I?"

After a pause, Shadan said: "I am really sorry."

"You've apologized enough." She cut him short. "Actually, there were also other reasons that drove me to the temple. Let's just forget about it."

There was an awkward silence. Shadan sized her up and down and scratched his head, looking embarrassed. "I found a book about babies under your pillow," he said. "Do you have *xi*?" The boy used the word *xi*, meaning "happiness," the traditional way of referring to a pregnancy.

"Yes," she admitted, smiling. "I'm having double happiness, a new life and a new baby."

"About Hu Laoshi, I'm sorry, Sister. He sounds like a good man. Why not marry him?"

Lotus smiled, amused at hearing his adult tone. "He's a good man. In fact, I don't think I can find a better man as the father of my child." She gazed up at the banyan tree. Long woody tendrils hung down from it, wafting in the wind like a wise old man's beard. "But marrying him? I'm not entirely sure. Not for the moment, anyway."

"Why not?"

"So many reasons. In time, I'll explain them to you, my brother."

"Sister, about the baby, I won't tell Nai or Ba if you'd prefer."

"Maybe not yet." Grandma would have laughed her remaining teeth out with joy over the news, but only if she were properly married, Lotus knew. She would worry about that later, she told herself.

Shadan sat on the edge of a low stool, his long legs awkwardly sticking out from both sides. "Sister, what a stupid egg I've been," he said, his face contorted. "I was so horrible to you. I guess I wanted to vent all my anger and suffering on you." He began talking about his eventful journey to Shenzhen. At Chengdu station, his ticket was stolen, and he didn't have any extra cash to buy another one. After asking around, he learned that the only way to get some quick cash was to sell his own blood. So he did, and with the money he bought a new ticket.

Lotus gasped. "Selling your blood? That can be dangerous. And all that money I sent home—" She abruptly stopped herself and wiped sweat from her forehead.

"Don't worry, Sister, I was careful. Anyway, now I know how every penny you sent home, you earned with blood and sweat."

"We are a family," she said softly. "I haven't congratulated you yet for doing well in the exam."

A grin stretched across his face. "I could have done better." After some hesitation, he said: "Sorry, Chouchou, I've decided to study law. Are you disappointed?"

Lotus did feel a little disappointed. At the same time, she also felt sorry that she had never bothered to ask what he was interested in studying, as if she had the right to map out his future for him. "At the end of the day, it's your choice, my brother," she replied. "But can you make enough money?"

"I can. I'll take rich clients, too. I'll charge them bags of money."

Lotus stared at her brother, her heart swelling with pride and joy.

He scratched his head again, as if it was covered in lice. "Hmm, I'm concerned about the registration. The date is usually on September 1. I may be a few days too late."

"Let's call the university and find out right now." Lotus sprang up and pulled her brother toward Cripple Kong's.

The aroma of pork stew greeted the siblings as they stepped into the front yard of Big Head's house, carrying with them beer and soft drinks. The yard was cluttered with jars, pots, rubber wheels, and a three-wheeled flatbed cart. The vehicle—a wooden plank fitted with wheels—was the tool of their livelihood as vegetable vendors. In one corner, Big Head's mother was stirring a huge pot on a makeshift cooking range.

"*Aiyah, aiyah!*" She straightened up and came over to take the drinks. "No need to bring anything, Teacher Lotus, you give us face just by coming to our pig's hovel."

"We need to celebrate!" Lotus declared. "Shadan has been accepted by Sichuan University. And it's okay if he registers in the next few days."

"*Wasai!* Big joyful news, as big as heaven!" The woman waved her palm-leaf fan toward the sky.

Like a gust of wind, Big Head and his two siblings shot out of the house into the yard. The children, all bare-chested, clapped their hands. They were happy to see their teacher back, excited by the unexpected feast to come.

"A poor peasant boy getting into university—it must have been as hard as climbing up to the sky. Boys," said Big Head's father, "study as hard as Shadan, okay?"

Big Head nodded like a hungry hen pecking grain. He dragged Lotus into the house. "Teacher Lotus, come! I did lots of homework for you."

Lotus followed him into the house, holding chattering Niuniu in her arms. Not wishing to be left out, Laoer grabbed at her white dress with his dirty hands.

Two single beds and more junk filled up the room. Sitting on Big Head's bed, Lotus read his composition. She had to guess some characters, but she understood enough to know that the boy had been worried about his teacher when she disappeared and that he had helped search for her. "I like Teacher Lotus, because she is the only person in the world who ever praised me. Good will be rewarded with good."

"*Wasai.*" Lotus tickled his bare chest. "Writing such flowery sentences already!"

Big Head burst into laughter, heaving a rib cage that resembled his mother's scrubbing board.

A few minutes later, they heard cheerful voices outside. Lotus brought the children out to the yard and saw that Xia and the rest of the gang had arrived. A party was now in full swing. The hostess was busy distributing drinks to the guests while her husband and Shadan were setting up a table in the middle of the yard. And without being prompted, the two boys started to bring bowls and plates to the table.

Big Head's mother asked the adults to take their seats by the table. "Look at my monkey boys, Teacher Lotus," she said in her thick accent, standing beside her guest of honor. "You have no idea how naughty they used to be. I often wanted to kick them to death. But they just become angels in front of you."

Lotus smiled. She knew exactly what the boys had been like before.

"We heard you may go up to Beijing with Hu Laoshi. Is that true?" As the hostess talked she fanned Lotus with her large palm fan.

"I don't know yet. Probably not," Lotus said.

"Speaking of your photographer, I am sorry that we failed to get in touch with him, Lotus," said Xia from the other side of the table, a large beer bottle at hand. "You see, he was always around and there was never the need to call him."

"It's okay," Lotus assured her.

Big Head's mother returned to the teaching issue. "If you stay here, all the families would like to chip in money so that you can rent a small place and teach our children properly. What do you think?" the lioness asked, fanning harder.

"But I have no proper education myself."

"I am an ignorant woman who knows only three and a half characters, Lotus," said the hostess, a tinge of regret on her coarse face. "I thought my boys were hopeless and that education was useless. Then I noticed how they've changed after attending to your class. But it's too late now to send them to a normal school." She hit herself with her fan as a symbolic self-punishment. "But if you can carry on teaching them, I'll kowtow in front of you every day."

"Listen, Lotus. We all like to pay you, too," Xia chipped in. "You know how expensive it is to send migrant children to the local schools. Anyway, Baobao never stops raving about you. Isn't that right?" She pushed her son forward to say something, but the boy hid behind his mother, nodding and peering at Lotus with his sad eyes. He looked small for a thirteen-year-old.

"Let me think about it," Lotus said. She was moved by the way her neighbors had come to this decision. While the others were standing around and chitchatting, a light bulb seemed to click on in her head. Isn't this something I've always dreamed of doing? she asked herself.

There was no better way to turn over a new leaf. She even had the seed fund to get the school going—the money from Mei, something she hadn't been sure what to do with. Thanks to her background, Lotus had habitually regarded herself as being poor. Now that her brother's university costs had more or less been taken care of, she realized that she no longer needed to live for money. The "lottery" money as well as some of her savings would help with the first couple of years, and Shadan figured he would tutor and save money to help with the rest. "Okay, I'll give it a try," she announced at last. "Any idea where we can rent a place?"

"I may just have the perfect spot for you, Teacher Lotus," Big Head's father said as he brought over an enamel washbasin full of steaming pork stew and set it in the middle of the table. "It's right in the village, five minutes' walk from here."

"Are you thinking of that haunted house?" his wife butted in. "People always hear funny noises from there at night."

"Haunted house? Dog shit!" Xia snapped, shaking her legs. "It is most likely that some *ji* and their clients or a pair of wild mandarin ducks have a quickie there now and then." She let out a hearty laugh.

Lotus turned to Big Head's father. "Can you take me to see the place?"

"I will. No hurry. Let's have lunch first."

When the siblings returned to the house after the long lunch, the first thing Lotus did was kneel in front of her little shrine. She prayed for a long time with clasped hands.

When she finally rose, Shadan asked: "Do you really want to run a school, Sister?"

"Yes, I do!"

"I'd love to help you, Sister. That's the least I can do, after all you've done for me."

"Let's talk about it later."

"I really mean it, Big Sister!" he said earnestly. "Teaching will make me more eloquent, something good for my future career."

Lotus smiled.

"I think I'll learn to deal with your friends," he added, almost hero-ically.

His sister let out a brief smile. "You'll find they are just normal women."

Shadan nodded. He picked up the mail that had accumulated on the table while she was gone and handed it to her: a letter, a postcard, and a telegram, all from Bing.

Lotus settled by the desk and picked up the postcard. On the front was a picture of a woman in a colorful embroidered outfit, her rumpled face framed by a large cloth hat made from colorful patchwork.

Next, she took the telegram, which had already been opened. It con-tained a short message from Bing, saying he had returned to Beijing, where he would have to work for a few more days, and asked her to give him a call.

She looked up at her brother, who stood by the desk.

"I opened the telegram because I worried that there might be some-thing urgent," he said defensively. "So you think Hu Laoshi is okay?"

"I'm sure." She then picked up the letter and studied it before open-ing it. She took out the sheet and flattened it on the desk with both hands. With her back turned to her brother, she read the letter. For a few minutes, she covered her face with her hands to calm the emotions that the letter had stirred in her. She wished to have some time to her-self, but her brother was still standing by her side.

"Shadan, go to the supermarket opposite the East Station and buy a blanket there."

He moved reluctantly.

"Take this money. Buy some vegetables for dinner. I'm tired. I'd like to lie down for a while."

After her brother left, Lotus read the letter again. From Bing's description, she imaged the scene at Houhai Lake in Beijing. She took off her white dress and put on his black T-shirt. She went over to the bookshelf and wiped his projector with a cloth. Bing had showed her many of his slides, projected on the wall by this little magic device. Then

Lotus looked through the neatly piled books. She picked up *The Portrait of a Lady* and looked at the lady on the cover with her feathered hat. She remembered how Bing had described it as a story of a girl confronting her destiny. Now she understood it was all about the girl deciding her own life.

Lotus let down the mosquito net and lay down. She rested her head on Bing's pillow, where his smell still lingered. She took out the letter and read it through, then placed it on her heart. She recited the lines from the poem, imitating his standard Mandarin: "May we live a long life / And together share the moonlight a thousand miles apart!"

The details of that full-moon night they had shared at the Long Embankment flooded her mind. She could almost feel his hands touching hers. She hugged the pillow and sniffed deeply into the fine bamboo cover. The smell filled her heart with a sweet peacefulness.

CHAPTER 32

树欲静而风不止

---

*The Tree Craves Calm, but the Wind
Does Not Subside*

After a battle with the safety lock that he had painstakingly installed, Bing pushed open the door and stepped in with his suitcase. He scanned the tidy room: a blanket folded on the bed, the mosquito net tied in a knot, and his mail stacked in a pile. There was even a faint smell of Lotus. As he walked to the center of the room, he noticed the little shrine was gone, as were her clothes from the clothes rack.

Bing's desk chair creaked in protest when he sank down into it. He lit a cigarette, thinking aloud as to where she could possibly be. While in Beijing, he had called and questioned the photographer Little Wang regarding Lotus's whereabouts, but it was like squeezing an empty tube of toothpaste. No one was at home, Little Wang had said and no, he hadn't asked any neighbors about Lotus, either.

Had she decided to go home? Perhaps she had gone off with that rich businessman after all? Last night, he had dreamed that Lotus was locked in jail, curled up in a ball, waiting to be rescued.

The morning after he heard the news about Lotus's disappearance, Bing had bade goodbye to Little Li and Mei. It was hard to tear himself away from his daughter.

Now he was finally home, but the place was depressingly empty. Mimi might have some idea where Lotus had gone. Bing checked his watch. It was nearly five p.m. Mimi ought to be at work by now. He locked up and hurried toward the massage parlor.

Bing was out of breath and soaked in sweat by the time he reached the parlor. He could see the girls leaning against the glass front, chatting, smoking, and cracking melon seeds.

Xia saw him first. Her powdered face froze for a moment. Then she lunged at him like a leopard descending from a mountain, knocking him down and punching him with her brown iron fists, all the while screaming abuse.

He held up his hands to shield his face, but one of Xia's rings cut his cheek. "Stop, Xia! What are you doing?"

"*Pei!* Was your heart eaten up by a dog or what?" Xia's padded bra slipped ridiculously to one side. She turned to her stunned colleagues. "Don't just gawk. Come to give him our special massage. See if he dares to treat our sister like dog shit again."

"Stop it!" Bing held on to Xia's hands.

Little Jade and Mimi came over and fired a shower of spittle and sunflower husks at him.

Then Bing heard the tinkling of bracelets and Moon's hoarse voice. "What's going on here?" The boss reached down to help him to get to his feet. "Are you okay?" she asked.

"I'm fine," Bing muttered. He brushed off his white shirt and touched the cut on his cheek. A crowd was circling him, enjoying the spectacle.

"What's the matter with you?" Moon asked Xia. "Is this your way of attracting business?"

Xia pulled her bra back into its rightful position. "Sorry, boss."

"Xia, what have I done wrong?" said Bing. "And where is Lotus?"

"What's wrong? You know exactly what's wrong!" Xia yelled.

"You two come inside," Moon ordered. Turning to the crowd, she barked: "Get lost. Or I'll charge you for the show."

Xia and Bing followed Moon into the empty parlor, with Mimi and Little Jade trailing behind. The boss turned on the main light. She stood, her arms crossed, with the solemnity and aloofness of a judge.

"My photographer, are you trying to smash my 'rice bowl'?"

"I wouldn't dare," Bing replied. "Lotus seems to have disappeared. I rushed back as soon as I heard about it. I came here, thinking you girls would know where she is. But as soon as I arrived at the door, Xia attacked me. Where is Lotus?"

"I've heard of her troubles," said Moon. "And I am sorry that I misplaced your name card and we couldn't get in touch with you." Then she asked Xia: "What's the latest with Lotus?"

Instead of replying to her boss, Xia pointed an accusing finger at Bing. "He used Lotus and us, and then chucked us. He ate the meat and dumped the bone!"

Bing jumped. "What are you talking about? I love her and I want to marry her. Where is she? What happened?"

Xia raised her plucked eyebrows. "I don't get it. Lotus told us that she wasn't going to Beijing with you and she was going to stay here on her own."

"Look at you, Xia. *Tse, tse!*" Moon shook her long finger in Xia's face. "So, you presumed that Bing left Lotus?"

"Yes, we—all of us—were dead sure of that." Xia glanced at Mimi and Little Jade. "We thought she was just too proud to tell us."

Both young girls mumbled their agreement. "Otherwise, why wouldn't she want to climb up the ladder and fly up to the capital with you?" Mimi said.

Bing grabbed Xia's bony arm. "Did Lotus tell you about her plan? What happened? Where is she?"

Xia took a hard look at him, then told him about Shadan's visit, Lotus's escape to the temple, and their search for her.

Her words weighed on Bing's heart like a rock. He could imagine the shame Lotus felt when her brother had found out the truth.

Xia also told him that Lotus and her brother had decided to open a school.

"A school? You mean her backyard school?" Bing asked.

"No, no!" Xia waved a hand dismissively. "Something more proper than her backyard class. We actually asked her to run the school."

"Really? Where is the school? Will I find her there?" .

"Yes. She and her brother just moved there yesterday," said Xia. "Ask Big Head to take you there. The school is at Big Head's great-uncle's old house."

As he turned to go, Xia held his wrist. "Whatever happens, photographer, you have to be good to Lotus. She is carrying your child."

Bing headed back to Miaocun in a daze. Lotus was pregnant! And she intended to stay here, on her own? And open a school? What had happened over the past seven weeks? A typhoon of events had swept through and changed everything. And yet, he had been kept in the dark.

He found Big Head in his yard, washing vegetables. The boy was only too happy to take Bing to the school.

"Come, come." The boy skipped out of the house and gestured to Bing to follow. "I was just over there, helping out. The school is going to be great, Hu Laoshi," Big Head said excitedly as they walked. "Guess how many students have signed up?"

"How many?"

"Twenty-five already, not just from our Miaocun. Dad said we can get more. I am running around and telling everyone about our school."

"How good of you. Teacher Lotus is lucky to have a helper like you."

"She said I am going to be the monitor of my class." The boy's face beamed with delight. "There will be two classes: mine, for the older kids, and one for the younger kids. Teacher Lotus will teach the kindergartners and Teacher Luo will teach the older kids."

Teacher Luo? It took a minute for Bing to work out that Big Head must be talking about Shadan. "But I thought he was going to university?"

"He is going next year, I think." The boy kicked an empty water bottle on the ground and offered a suggestion. "You can be the headmaster, Hu Laoshi."

"I'll have to ask Teacher Lotus."

"See that huge kapok tree? The school is the house beside it." Big Head kicked the bottle along.

When Bing reached the school, he paused for a moment, brushing invisible lint off his shirt. The rusty iron door was wide open. On it was pasted a handwritten sign: "Rich and Auspicious School."

Big Head pulled his sleeve. "Come in, please."

But Bing didn't move. He was longing to see his Lotus, but afraid at the same time.

"Who thought of the name, 'Rich and Auspicious'?" he asked.

"It is the name of my dad's uncle. This is his house. Hu Laoshi, you know, my dad got this place for Teacher Lotus, all for free," the boy said proudly.

Just then, Bing heard a familiar coughing noise. "There you are," Lotus said, appearing at the door. She wore a cream-colored T-shirt and a pair of black cotton pants. The plainness of the outfit emphasized her youth and natural beauty. Her hair, rather long now, was tied up in a ponytail.

Bing approached her and took both her hands. "Lotus!"

For a long time, Lotus looked into his eyes, without blinking, so much so that he had the urge to look away. Then a smile, as glorious as a golden chrysanthemum in deep autumn, blossomed on her face. "How are you?" Her voice was full of emotion.

"Not bad. Thank you." There was so much to talk about that Bing hardly knew where to start. He leaned forward to embrace her but she pulled away slightly, glancing at Big Head.

"My hands are dirty." She started to wipe them on her pants.

"Are you well, Lotus?" Bing asked.

"I'm fine." She went over to the boy, rubbed his large head, and kissed it.

The boy was surprised by this demonstration of affection but pleased.

"Did you just fly back? How was your trip?" she asked Bing. Her voice was calmer, sweeter, and softer than he had ever heard it.

"I just got back." Bing stared at Lotus. He expected to find a tired flower after what she had gone through. But she radiated a glow often seen in brides. Was it because of her pregnancy? Her stomach was flat, but her breasts had visibly grown fuller and heavier under the T-shirt.

"Come on in," she said. "Sorry, it's all very messy here." She walked with Big Head into the yard, with her arm around the boy's shoulders. "I am going to meet your great-uncle later today, to thank him for lending us his place."

Bing followed them into the yard as Lotus talked about the school. The great-uncle had gone to live in the city center to run his photocopy machine business. When Big Head's father had asked him if they could use the place for free, he agreed, on condition that the school be named after him.

Several people were painting the walls of the house, a traditional one. On top of the roof, Big Head's father was replacing the broken tiles with new ones.

"Dad, Hu Laoshi's back," Big Head called up to his father.

His father lifted his head, pushed back his battered straw hat, and grinned, exposing his crooked teeth and gums. "Hu Laoshi, it's good you are back," he greeted Bing. Then, he spoke to his son in Hakka. "Have you cooked supper yet? Your mom will be mad at you if you haven't."

"You'd better go, then," Lotus said.

"I'll come back tomorrow morning to help you," the boy offered.

"*Yaodei!*"

Big Head shot out of sight.

"He's been so helpful. His whole family, too."

"You have a magic way of bringing out the best in people."

She giggled, covering her mouth with her left hand. The ring still glittered on her third finger. "I haven't heard your flattery for a while."

At her door, she took off her slippers and stepped inside onto the bamboo mat, the same kind he had at his place. He followed suit. The familiar feel under his bare feet immediately put him at ease. He turned to shut the door behind him. But it wouldn't shut properly.

"Don't worry about the door," Lotus said as she started to clear a round table in the middle of the room. Her shining wooden comb was left on it.

The humble room still smelled of paint. The wooden support beam had blackened with age. A camp bed without any bedding stood against the freshly painted wall. On the bed lay a rolled-up paper—that must be her picture of the Guanyin Buddha. Beneath the bed, a corner of her bulging snakeskin sack stuck out, nestled against a plastic basin. The rest of the furniture consisted of two plastic folding chairs and the wooden table, one of the legs resting on a brick to replace a missing piece. Bing bumped into the mended leg as he sat down.

"What happened to your face?" Lotus asked.

Bing touched his cheek. "Oh, I cut it on a branch."

"I just bought some Band Aids."

"I'm fine. Why didn't you call me, my sweet? I've been worried sick about you."

Still standing by the table, she darted an apologetic look at him. "I'm so sorry. I went to stay at the temple." She looked up briefly as if communicating with her deity, a faintly perceptible smile on her lips. "I only got back a few days ago. I kept meaning to call you, but I wanted to figure out some things first."

Bing dragged the other chair closer to him. "Okay, then. You sit down by my side. Let me take a good look at you."

She seated herself. "No need, the same old me," she said with a sweet, genuine smile that made her dimples dance and her striking eyes shine. She suddenly had the fullness and beauty of a mature woman.

Bing thought about the last time they had made love and how playful and ready she had been. He leaned over, intending to cup her face in his hands.

But she raised a hand to stop him. "Please don't," she said in her low voice.

"Why not?"

"I don't want to . . ."

"Don't want to what?" Bing clasped her hands. "Tell me, please, Lotus. What's happened? Xia just attacked me. She claimed that I deserted you."

"Oh, no. So she did this to you, not some branch?" She held his chin in her right hand and examined his cut.

Bing pressed her small hand to his face. "What have I done wrong, Lotus, please?"

She shook her head. "No, no, you've done nothing wrong, Hu Laoshi. It's just . . ."

"Hu Laoshi!" He had never hated the term more than in that instant. It raised a fence between them. Bing let go of her hand.

Lotus sat straight in her chair. "I want to be your friend, but not your girlfriend. For now, anyway."

"You are my love, my future wife. I want to have a family with you and bring up our child together."

Lotus blushed. She lowered her head.

"A lot has happened," she said. She fingered a string of beads he had not seen before.

"Xia has told me some of it. I am sorry that Shadan found out about everything. I take some responsibility for that. But surely, that's not the reason to abandon me."

"No, it's not the reason," she agreed. "I don't really want to go to Beijing. I belong here. I feel useful here." She spoke with deliberate care, as if her fragile words would fall to the ground and smash into pieces.

"Okay, fine, we can stay here. All right? I've always said that we can stay anywhere you wish."

"No, you must go to Beijing," she said firmly. "When you were away, I thought a lot about you, our relationship, and what I want. I know I care about you, but I am not sure that I love you."

As she talked, Bing stared at her rose lips, the sweet lips that he had kissed so many times, and listened to words that he had never imagined she would utter. He felt his face getting hot.

"I don't exactly know what love is," Lotus said with a timid smile. "I need to be on my own to figure it out."

"I need you, Lotus. I love you. Tell me what I can do to change your mind." Bing reached out for her hand resting on the edge of the table and held it. He couldn't bear the thought of losing her. He sank to his knees. "Please, Lotus, I've never knelt in front of anyone before in my life. I am kneeling in front of you now. I beg you to come back to me, because I love you with my whole heart. Will you marry me?"

Lotus stood up, pulling him up with remarkable strength. "Please don't."

He put his arms around her and held her tightly. Please, heaven above, please let me have her, Bing prayed silently. I'd give up anything: my job, Beijing, the book deal. This is my treasure. He embraced her with the desperation of a drowning man. She didn't object. He sniffed the fragrance of her hair.

"Are you doing this for my sake, Lotus?" he asked quietly.

She stirred in his embrace. "No . . . I discovered that I like being on my own. I never dreamed I could live by myself. But now I can, I think."

Lotus sat down and picked up the comb from the table. She undid her hair, pulled together all the loose strands, and combed them into a tighter ponytail.

"You don't regret getting involved with me?" Bing asked.

Lotus looked horrified. "No! Heaven knows. I used to think I was trash. But you gave me love and respect. I can never repay you for that." She stood up and approached him, bending over and pressing her lips to his forehead.

He could feel the warmth of her body. He shut his eyes, willing the moment to last forever. But that kiss was simply a gesture of gratitude, meant for Hu Laoshi.

"Thank you, too, Lotus, for giving me the happiest time in my life. I owe everything to you." The statement sounded strange, as though he were bidding her a final farewell. What about the baby?

He fixed his eyes on her belly. "How are you feeling? When is it due?"

"Early March," she said, her face glowing. "Do I look fat already?"

"You look stunning, Lotus. Xia told me about the baby."

"Oh, Sister Xia, she's got a frog's big mouth! I was hoping I could break the news to you myself. Were you shocked?"

"Surprised. Yes, a little surprised. But I'm overjoyed!"

He gazed at her, only an arm's length away yet he couldn't reach her. His mouth felt as dry as desert. He swallowed. "The three of us can live together like a family, right?"

"We'll always be a family. But that doesn't mean that we have to live together." She smiled abashedly. After a brief cough, she continued: "Actually I was hoping that you'll help with the registry of our child and you could give us some financial help, well, when you can. More important, I'd like you to be a good father and bring the child up to become an educated city person, someone useful to society." As she talked, her eyes shone with hope. She said she had been looking forward to talking about the baby with him. Her pregnancy wasn't public knowledge yet. "I sometimes find myself talking to the baby." Lotus giggled. "Funny, I thought only old people talk to themselves."

Bing smiled.

"There's something I'd like to confess," she said after a pause, and the color deepened on her cheeks.

"Confess? What?"

"I lied to you about something. Er, I wasn't raped."

Lotus cleared her throat and continued with downcast eyes. Once, when a client asked her what had made her start turning tricks, she came up with the story that she had been raped. The girls often made up such stories to win sympathy from clients. Over time, Lotus had developed the story, adding elaborate details. She repeated it so many times that she almost believed it herself. She spoke coherently, as if she had been rehearsing the speech.

"I understand," Bing said gently. He had never doubted her rape story, but this confession didn't impact him much. He just thought her somber tone, her rosy cheeks, and her shining eyes looked touchingly charming.

"You also want to know exactly how I got into the trade, don't you?" Lotus asked.

"Of course."

She told him about the drunken night out with Hua that had transformed her life. When she finished, she looked at him expectantly, as if waiting for a verdict.

"I see," he said simply, lightly touching her hand. "Don't worry. It's all in the past."

Lotus nodded and smiled at him gratefully. "The thing was that by then I had lost my virginity," she added, red-faced. "I did it with Little Qian, a guy from the factory, after the death of my cousin. I never understood why I gave something I used to cherish to a man I didn't even care about."

"I guess you were not quite yourself then," said Bing.

Their conversation was interrupted by the sound of footsteps in the yard. The door swung open and Shadan's tall form towered in the doorway. He was carrying bags full of bedding and blankets.

"Ah, you are back," Bing said as he rose.

"Hu Laoshi!" Shadan said with a slight bow. He walked in and put the bags on the camp bed.

Lotus picked up a face towel from the plastic basin and handed it to him. "Sit down, Brother. You must be tired, running around so much."

Bing sat back and felt a pang of jealousy: he used to get such treatment from Lotus, a face towel and gentle greetings. That seemed like a lifetime ago.

The youngster wiped his face. He glanced at his sister and then at Bing. "I have things to do. You carry on talking,"

"Please, Shadan, do stay," Bing said. "I'd like to hear about your plans."

His sister gave him her chair, then perched herself on the camp bed, next to the pile of shopping.

"Are you going to university soon?" Bing asked.

"I've asked the university to delay my admission for one year."

"Why? Is that wise?" Part of Bing wished the young man would just go to his university. If her brother were not around, he felt Lotus would be more likely to return to his arms.

"For now, I'd like to stay and help my sister to get the school going," Shadan stated. "Besides, it will be a good experience for me."

"Will the village authorities allow it?"

Both men turned to Lotus.

"I am not sure the village authorities would care. Otherwise, Xia said she would sleep with the head of the village." Lotus let out a laugh. "But I'm going to go ahead without fearing there's a wolf before me or a tiger behind me." As she talked, she delicately twirled the beads on her left wrist.

"Good for you, Lotus. But will you be able to make a living?"

"All of the parents are happy to pay. We should be able to get by and even make a tiny bit of profit."

"Your journalist friend said the policy regarding migrant schools has relaxed," Shadan cut in. "We should be okay. He offered to give us his old computer."

"Zhang Jianguo? When did he come?" Bing asked.

"This morning," Lotus said. She added that the journalist did mention that he had tried to call Bing but to no avail.

Someone tapped on the window. Big Head's father's grinning face appeared. "Time to go to see my uncle, Lotus. I'll go home to get my cart. Back in a minute."

Bing slowly stood up. "I'd better go then," he said, feeling unbearably sad and exhausted.

Lotus rose, too.

They came out into a gentle evening. The sun was trying to hide behind the mountains. They stood under the kapok tree. Its leaves rustled in the breeze. A chorus of cicadas sang a slow serenade.

"Have you thought of a name yet?" Bing asked.

Lotus looked up at the tree's straight, tall trunk and its magnificent crown. "Funny you should ask," she said, a smile on her face. "Just the other night, I dreamed about kapok tree blossoms. So I thought if it's a girl, let's call her Red Cotton. If it is a boy, we'll call him Hero. What do you think?"

"Great idea!"

Lotus clapped her hands, smiling brightly.

With the ringing of a bell, Big Head's father reemerged with his three-wheeled cart. He made a U-turn and then put a foot on the front wheel to brake. While waiting, he fanned himself with his battered straw hat.

Shadan hurried out, clutching a plastic bag containing bottles of spirits and a carton of cigarettes. He sat on the edge of the vehicle's wooden plank. "Get on, Sister."

"I have to go," Lotus said to Bing, giving him an apologetic smile. She bowed with clasped hands, turned, and walked away with her light-footed steps.

Bing followed her, intending to help her get onto the flatbed. But Shadan had reached her first. Holding on to her brother's hand, she nimbly jumped up on the plank.

The cart lurched ahead, accompanied by another clanging of the bell.

Lotus waved at Bing, then looked ahead, her full chest bouncing under her T-shirt and her ponytail swaying as the vehicle navigated along the muddy path.

Bing watched until they were out of sight. He thought about an enamel bowl he had cherished as a child. On the bowl was a colorful picture of a red tractor in a golden wheat field. He used it for every meal. It was his favorite toy, too. But one day as he used it to scoop out black tadpoles from the river, the bowl suddenly slipped out of his hands. It floated fleetingly as it drifted toward the center of the river and sank. He stared at the black water, unable to comprehend how he could have lost his treasure, so quickly, without warning.

Standing under the tree, Bing was unable to move. What was he going to do now? Stay in Shenzhen, close to Lotus, or start a new life in Beijing? Maybe he would discuss his situation with Zhang Jianguo tomorrow. He felt a little better when his thoughts turned to the baby. The little being would always serve as an unbreakable link between them.

The cicadas chirped on, as if trying to fill the void inside him.

CHAPTER 33

留得青山在，不怕没柴烧

*While the Mountain Remains, We Shan't
Lack Firewood*

Miaocun was soaking up the last rays of the setting sun. In the gentle
evening air, the warm smell of cooked rice and the scent of many tropi-
cal flowers competed with the stench from the ditch.

Perched on the flatbed of the three-wheeled cart, Lotus was aware of
Bing's gaze as he stood under the kapok tree. Several times, she nearly
turned around but restrained herself. Gratitude filled her heart as she
recalled how they had met, become intimate, and lived together, and the
great changes that he had brought to her life.

She felt sorry to have left him like this. But she had to figure things
out on her own.

After the siblings had found the schoolhouse, Lotus decided to set
up her home there. From there, she would start to build her own independent little world, one brick at a time. And each brick would bring
her closer to her dream. The task would be arduous and the road long,
she knew. But she would relish the challenge.

When the cart ran over a bump, Shadan protectively steadied her with a hand on her shoulder.

Lotus flashed a grateful smile. "I'm okay."

How wonderful to have her brother by her side, she thought with gratitude. Having made sure that Shadan could defer his enrollment for one year, she had accepted his offer to stay. She would have coped with running the school by herself, but she could do with a helping hand in the beginning, and learn things from him. And she looked forward to living under the same roof with her brother again.

When they came to a bend, Lotus turned her head and saw that Bing was still standing under the tree. A tender feeling swept over her body. She comforted herself with the thought that she had set him and herself free. She fingered her string of beads and regained her resolve. She thought about how she had escaped to the temple in a moment of crisis; yet there, her life had taken a new direction. It must have been the divine intention of the Buddha.

The vehicle went over a big bump, which shook the two passengers. Lotus instinctively held her stomach.

"Are you okay?" Shadan asked, his voice thick with concern.

"Sorry, sorry," said Big Head's father. "I'll drive slowly."

She smiled. "No problem. The baby is still tiny. It won't even feel such a small bump."

Nowadays Lotus loved putting her hand on her tummy, her way to communicate with the baby. The very thought of it would elevate her soul to Ninth Heaven. She knew that the little being would demand a fair amount of time and energy from her, but wouldn't interrupt her teaching too much. She remembered how her own mother had returned to the field one week after giving birth to Shadan, wrapping the newborn to her back with a long piece of embroidered cloth.

And her friends would help, too. Xia had already given her a long list of things to do during pregnancy, including sleeping twelve hours a day; eating more lean meat, vegetables, and nuts; and crawling on the bed every day to relax the pelvic floor. She also gave Lotus a longer list of what not to do: no sex, no shifting furniture, no cold water or strong tea, nor using washing-up liquid or taking a very hot bath. There were many folk recipes—as many as hairs on a cow—for pregnant women wishing for a boy. Xia recommended eating six walnuts every night for this purpose, though Lotus thought she could safely ignore this advice because she didn't mind whether the baby was a boy or a girl.

The cart was now clattering along the side road, heading to the city center. The honking of cars rent the evening calm. Lotus was absorbed in her thoughts, oblivious to the noise that used to rattle her nerves. Red Cotton or Hero, what great names! By the time the baby arrived next March, the kapok would be in bloom. She closed her eyes and the image flashed in her mind: the large flowers clustered on the bare branches, bright red, dazzling, and full of life, like dancing flames.

ACKNOWLEDGMENTS

This book took me, on and off, twelve years to complete, and I'm grateful to many people who helped me bring this novel to life over those years.

To start with, I'd like to thank my instructor Lavinia Greenlaw for her encouragement as I gingerly planted the seed for *Lotus* while working for my MA in Creative and Life Writing at Goldsmiths College, University of London.

I am indebted to Professor Pan Suiming, whose groundbreaking work on the underground sex industry in China provided useful information. My thanks also go to Huang Yingying, a colleague of Professor Pan's at Renmin University; Professor Cheng Yu of Sun Yat-sen University; and the young American academics Willa Dong and Shen Tingting from Asia Catalyst, for sharing with me the results of their research on different aspects of prostitution in China.

I am grateful to the late photographer Zhao Tielin, whose experience of living among the working girls in a slum on Hainan Island inspired the creation of the photographer in the book.

I want to express my heartfelt thanks to Lanlan. You not only allowed me to volunteer for your NGO, Tianjin Xingai Home, distributing condoms to female sex workers at massage parlors and hair salons, but you also graciously opened up to me. Without your help, I wouldn't have gained much-needed insight into Lotus's world. Your journey, from a working girl to an NGO worker helping fellow sisters, was truly inspirational. Of course, I want to thank all the girls I met and interviewed in Shenzhen, Dongguan, Beihai, Tianjin, and Beijing. I know it wasn't always easy to talk about your experiences. Thank you for sharing.

The following people (in no particular order) read the manuscript, in part or in full, in many of its different forms: Bridget Whelan, Juno Baker, Tuva Khan, Janice MacLeod, Helen Wing, Karen Ma, Mary Kay Magistad, Ed Jocelyn, Kim Vernon, Sarah Bajc, Alexander Blanco, Jo Michie, Nick Griffin, and Dominique Othenin-Girard. I am grateful for your comments, feedback, and suggestions. I am particularly grateful to Karen, who understands the challenges of writing for an audience of a different culture.

I am indebted to my ex-husband, Calum MacLeod, for polishing the very first draft. I sincerely apologize for having burdened you with the early manuscript. It couldn't have been much fun to hunch over a computer again after your long day at work. Sadly, I didn't quite realize that editing fiction was such a different ballgame from editing nonfiction.

I'm thankful to my old friend Bian Yang, from my rocket factory, who first introduced me to the high plane of literature while I was still slaving down on the factory's greasy floor. Old Bian, thank you for patiently spending hours with me discussing the characters and other details of the novel. With your permission, I also generously incorporated into the novel the details of your transformation from a village boy in a teacher's family to an urban intellectual.

I need to thank my psychotherapist friend Natasha Redina for helping me to understand the mental status of my main characters, especially how they'd cope with trauma.

A big thank-you goes to writer and film director Tara Wilkinson. I immensely enjoyed our brainstorming sessions, from which I learned more about drama, tension, and storytelling than from my creative writing course.

At different stages of writing and rewriting this book, the following friends polished or edited the manuscript, for free: Jenny Quan, Julie Burke, Melanie Ansley, Richard Trombly, Kate Alden, and Gabriel Corsetti. Thank you, you kind people, for your time and effort. I'd like to give special thanks to Richard, who read through the whole lot and offered careful suggestions.

At first, I thought my main obstacle to bringing this book to light was my need to develop my English-language skills. Then it dawned on me that I needed an editor.

My first decent professional help came from Mary Kirley. Though she first declined the job of editing an earlier edition of the manuscript on the grounds that she was a nonfiction editor, I persuaded her to take it up. Thank you, Mary, for the outstanding work and for raising my writing to a new level.

Then I had the good fortune to meet Laura Fitch, the former art and community editor of *City Weekend*. She was not just an editor but also a book doctor. She cleaned up the language, cut out overwritten passages, and pointed out parts that were emotionally untrue. Thank you, Laura. Without you, I couldn't have found a publisher.

Over the years, I shamelessly and constantly pestered Peter Holmes, Heather Steed, and David Moser. Peter, a professor of economics, can always find an economical way to structure a sentence. Heather, a fellow writer I met at Goldsmiths, always kindly described my harassment as a welcome "mental tease." And David, a sinologist who has a demanding job and many interests, always somehow squeezed time between teaching and playing gigs to deal with my requests efficiently and brilliantly. Thank you three for your unflagging support.

Alfy (Alison Birkett), thank you for the time and energy you put into the book, picking up errors that could've easily been missed. And your "abusive comments" did make me think. Lodging with me was no true recompense for all your efforts. In fact, I now declare you a permanent honorable resident in the Zhang household.

As expected, I have to thank my daughters, May and Kirsty. I am sorry that I often had to hassle you to look into some words, sentences, or paragraphs, even when we were on holiday. I trust that my wrong choice of words and my poor pronunciation provided a certain amusement for you. When I started out on this project, I was desperately trying to get you girls to read chapter books. By the time I finished, you were already in a position to help me with my English. You grew much faster than I matured as a writer!

I'd like to thank the distinguished writer John Man for helping me with the proposal and synopsis.

My gratitude goes to Chen Guangcheng for introducing me to Henry Holt and Company.

I am grateful to Nick Griffin for introducing me to Kuhn Projects, a literary agency based in New York. Thank you, David Kuhn, for taking me on, and thank you, Becky Sweren, for fighting so hard on my behalf.

My final thanks are reserved for my editor, Emi Ikkanda. Emi, thank you for your faith in the book, for your enthusiasm, for your fabulous editorial advice, and for your tireless efforts to make the book better. I can't thank you enough!

ABOUT THE AUTHOR

LIJIA ZHANG, a former rocket factory worker, is a writer based in Beijing. Her writing has appeared in *The New York Times* and *Newsweek,* and she has been interviewed on CNN, NPR, and the BBC. Her book *"Socialism Is Great!": A Worker's Memoir of the New China* has been published in eight countries. She earned a master's degree from Goldsmiths College, University of London, and a fellowship in the International Writer's Program at the University of Iowa. *Lotus* is her first novel.